SHADOW OF THE KING

Shadow of the King
Book 1 of the Caretaker Trilogy

Published by Mockingbird Hollow Press

ISBN 979-8-9902130-0-5

Shadow of the King

Book 1 of the Caretaker Trilogy

DARRELL J. PURSIFUL

The Elementals are not spirits, because they have flesh, blood and bones; they live and propagate offspring; they eat and talk, act and sleep, etc., and consequently they cannot be properly called "spirits." They are beings occupying a place between men and spirits, resembling men and spirits, resembling men and women in their organization and form, and resembling spirits in the rapidity of their locomotion.

—Paracelsus, Occult Philosophy (16th century)

1

Rune hefted the satchel that held everything he owned and one thing he didn't. Sweat trickled down the back of his neck.

It wasn't only the early-autumn heat. The stench of grime and rust and smoke combined into a noxious haze. The screeches and bellows of motorized carriages wheedled their way into the back of Rune's brain. His whole head throbbed.

He stopped for a second on the residential sidewalk to settle his breathing. *Settle down*, he told himself. But he couldn't help looking over his shoulder one more time, just in case.

He took a breath, then stopped short in a fit of coughing. This world smelled wrong. Maybe he'd get used to it. Hopefully soon.

Rune forced himself to relax and tried again. His lungs expanded, and he savored every bit of air as it entered his body. And along with revitalizing oxygen came the airy chaos, the elemental engine of creation that was as much a part of Rune as his bones and his blood. It pulsed through him and swirled around him, and with the slightest effort of will, Rune let it clear his mind and expand his senses.

It only took a moment, but everything was suddenly sharper, more coherent. To his relief, his heightened senses brought no sign of pursuit: no skulking shadows, no furtive footsteps, no flash of knives in the falling night.

The sun finally set, and darkness cooled the air. It was a clear night, but where were the stars? The garish lights of every storefront window had driven them away.

He had lost track of time. He was tired, hungry, and cold.

At least he had finally shed the last of his scales.

All he could do was press on. Leaving behind the din of the crowded major road, he passed through block after block of houses so similar they might have come out of a factory. A dog barked in the distance. Its neighbor, maybe a couple streets over, made reply. Partygoers in somebody's back garden played obnoxious music with a pounding beat.

When he couldn't take it any longer, he let go of the airy chaos and dialed back his senses. Details blurred. The cacophony of street sounds abated.

But it was a trade-off. Deadened senses made him even more aware of sounds and sights he could no longer identify. Was that a normal human couple walking toward him, or had Dancer finally caught up with him after all these weeks?

It wasn't Rune's first time in the Fallow. But before, it was always with a plan: a definite objective, a map, an extraction point, and a waymaker standing by in case anything went wrong.

Before, he was never alone.

He tapped his fingers against his satchel. This aimless wandering was getting him nowhere. He stretched out his left arm. The stab wound had almost completely healed, and even the stiffness was mostly gone. It had taken most of his healing salve, though, with no way to replace it.

It was one more thing to cross off his list of assets, starting with the umbersay cloak he had lost at Cruc Máw and half the shot in his cartridge case. All he had left was a little bit of money, some personal items…and a small metal coffer, dwarf-made and nearly indestructible.

If he couldn't find a way to destroy it, this whole ill-fated excursion would end in disaster.

The couple walked past. Rune turned to watch them continue down the sidewalk, deep in conversation. A motorized carriage passed in the other direction.

His skull pounded, but he had to protect himself. So he took a deep breath and reveled in the swirl of the airy chaos passing over him and through him, imbuing him with power. With his eye on his surroundings, he willed the chaos into shape: a gossamer veil descending over him, masking him from sight.

It was darker now. Who could say how long he'd wandered? Time flies when you're running for your life. And still no more than a few dozen stars where there should have been thousands.

He grieved all the things he had lost—everything he had given up. He never realized the stars would be on that list.

Lost in thought, he stepped off the sidewalk.

Angry lights flashed from oncoming headlamps. A horn blared, and Rune lashed out with his left arm, gathering the airy chaos into a buffer of compressed air between himself and the motor carriage.

That was a mistake. The satchel flew off his shoulder and onto the approaching vehicle. Something creaked with the sound of bending metal, followed by the crackle of broken glass. The satchel bounced over the carriage and onto the street behind it.

Dwarf-made coffers were nearly indestructible, after all.

Tires squealed as the carriage screeched to a stop. The driver's quick thinking and Rune's own burst of magic were just enough to weaken the force of impact. Rune slammed his hand against the front of the vehicle, countering much of the blow. But he still fell backward onto the concrete with a thud.

"Ohmygod!" someone shouted as the carriage door clicked open. A young voice, female. Human. In a second, she was kneeling over him in the light of her carriage's headlamps. Behind big, blue spectacles, her eyes widened with panic.

"I'm so sorry! I'm calling 9-1-1!"

She started jabbing her thumbs at the small, rectangular device in her hand. Rune didn't understand what she meant, but he figured she was calling for help.

"No," he said. When she kept jabbing, he reached up for her wrist and held it tight. His first instinct was to glower at her, but that wasn't going to get him anywhere. Instead, he fought through the glare to look her in the eyes the way Whisper had taught him. Just long enough to note their deep brown color, not too long or too intensely to be threatening. She looked about his age, maybe a bit younger. "No. Please."

"Hey, is anybody hurt?" Another voice, older and male, called from the steps of the nearest house. Rune sucked in a breath. This was getting out of hand. He let his right hand brush against the butt of the pistol tucked inside his doublet.

"I'm fine," he told the girl. And he put a whiff of magic behind it.

"He came out of nowhere!" she said. "I swear, he just… appeared!" Her voice squeaked with nerves.

"I've got a first-aid kit!" the newcomer called. A second later, a door opened and shut.

"Really. Just let me sit up and—"

"You're not fine. You need a doctor."

"No doctors," Rune said through gritted teeth. Fallowman doctors meant questions he didn't want to answer. He teased a little more magic out of the air. Pain and disorientation made it a genuine effort, but he kept his composure. His eyes bored into hers.

The uninformed spoke of mind control as if getting someone to do what one wanted was like pulling the strings on a puppet. It was never quite that simple, at least not without the right set of tools. What Rune could do—what Whisper had taught him to do—was convince people that what he wanted was in their interest, too. Show them what they wanted to see. What they needed to see.

It didn't matter that his temples throbbed. It didn't matter that a tender knot was forming on the back of his head. He'd suffered worse and survived.

As Rune pulled himself to a sitting position, he projected an image of a perfectly healthy and perfectly human person: no peaked ears, no high-arching eyebrows, no sharp, foxlike features.

The girl frowned. "Okay," she said. "But the neighbors are looking out their windows. If you'd rather talk to them…"

All he needed was a quiet place to rest. Why did these Fallow folk have to make things so complicated?

"Just. Need to. Rest," he said. He sent out another whisper of magic.

The girl swallowed. She jerked her head up as the neighbor with the medical kit jogged to the curb.

"I'll be fine," Rune said. He arched his eyebrows the way people did reflexively when meeting a friend and relaxed into an easy smile, more glamour than real. Pulling too much air was making him restless, agitated. The headache was easing off, but the dizziness was worse.

"He's…he's fine," she said.

"Are you sure?" The neighbor looked worried.

"You stopped in time," Rune said. "I'm just a little shaken up."

"I…stopped in time," the girl said.

Rune turned to look at the neighbor who was now peering over him.

More confidently, the girl added, "He's just a little shaken up." She looked back at him. Her expression suggested she wasn't convinced.

Rune looked at the scrapes on his hands where he'd caught himself as he first hit the pavement. "Bandages."

"Do you have some bandages?" the girl asked. "Maybe some antiseptic?"

"Sure," the man said. He opened his kit and started pulling out the items the girl requested. "Are the EMTs coming?"

She stared at him, her mouth open. "H-he'll be fine," she said again. "He just needs to rest."

"It looks worse than it is," Rune assured the neighbor. "I'm just…winded." He held out his hand for the bandages and ointment.

The man frowned. "If you're sure…"

"I'm sure." Rune looked at the girl. "Help me up?" He extended his arm. Whisper had taught him that asking for a small favor planted the idea that the one giving it was already on your side. The girl offered him her arm. He stood up, maybe a little too fast. He wobbled a bit, but he turned toward the neighbor and smiled. The man smiled back and went inside.

Rune squeezed the girl's arm appreciatively. "My bag?"

"Oh, was that—" The girl's face fell as she turned into the head-lamps. Only then did the damage to her carriage sink in.

"My car!" she moaned. "What did you do to my car?"

"I'm sorry about that. I'll pay for the repairs, of course." He hoped he could pay for the repairs—somehow. He would have to find a money-changer. Thankfully, Mahwe had provided a list of contacts he could count on.

Or he could simply adjust the girl's memories. It was hard to decide. He could poke around a bit and leave her with a hole in her memory and some mysterious damage to her vehicle. It was just another exercise in not-quite mind control, a simple bit of elven-side. He had plenty of look-eye powder in his satchel.

He sighed. Altering memories took time, and time was one of many things Rune didn't have.

He limped to the back of the carriage to collect his things. An amorphous sense of dread came over him as he stooped to grab the strap of his satchel. This part hadn't gotten any easier. Underneath the dread was the thrill of power, raw and unrestrained. He stared at the bag for the span of three or four breaths before snatching it up with a shudder of triumph.

The satchel hung heavily as he rested the strap on his shoulder. He could be done with these Fallowmen in an instant, and wrack the consequences.

Another carriage came up behind them, its headlamps boring into Rune, jolting him back to the present. He shrugged off his fantasies of power with a shiver of shame and revulsion.

The girl moved her vehicle out of the middle of the street to let the other one pass. As the second driver crept past them, Rune once again forced a smile and a wave.

"Are you sure you're okay?" the girl asked again, jumping back out of her carriage. "You look…different."

"I'm fine."

"Yeah, but when I first saw you in the headlights, you were…I dunno. Different. Whiter—I mean, no offense."

Rune considered the girl's own light brown skin. Maybe the comment related to the distinctions Fallowmen drew between themselves. He found offense, so he let the comment go.

"Listen, I know you said you're okay, but I'm sorry, you need to see a doctor. Just let me make a call." She lifted the calling device again.

"Really, it's all right," Rune said. There was no telling what a Fallow doctor would find with his tests and probes. He'd take his chances with a good night's sleep and a chew of willow bark. He needed to get away, and none of his efforts were working. For a second, he considered simply vanishing into the night. Let the girl think she'd seen a ghost.

Then he eyed her carriage, and a better plan began to hatch. Whisper said the greatest challenge was often the greatest opportunity. Right now, Rune's greatest challenge was to be shed of his would-be rescuer. But what if he could use her instead? In his mind he ran through his checklist for putting a victim at ease. Eye contact. Smile. Mirror body language. Appropriate touch.

"You don't need to call a doctor. Look at me. I'm all right." In truth, he did feel a bit better. His burst of wind blunted almost all of the carriage's impact. Other than the knot on his skull and the scrapes on his hands, he felt nearly normal.

The girl swayed from side to side, her arms in constant motion. Rune adopted the same posture and closed the distance between them.

"I'm more concerned about you," he said, "alone in a neighborhood like this."

He subtly began to alter the illusion he'd put in the girl's head. He kept his human mien but embellished the environment. Furtive footsteps. Whispered conversation. Broken shutters on the windows. An ominous wind in the trees.

The girl shivered. Her eyes darted up and down the sidewalk. "I…I come home this way all the time," she protested.

"Are you sure? It doesn't seem like a safe place." Rune added a scraping sound to the illusion. Metal against stone. Weapons being readied.

"Don't you think it would be better if we both got out of here?" He nodded, priming the girl to agree with him.

She looked left and right. Rune could see her mind churning, working out the dissonance between what her senses were telling her and what she knew.

"I could use a ride," Rune said. He took a tentative step forward. "We should get away from here." He smiled. "What do you think?"

When he read the pity on her face, Rune knew he'd won. He took another step toward the carriage—the "car," she'd called it. Unbidden, she opened the passenger door, and Rune slumped into the seat. The crack in the wind-screen didn't look quite as bad as he'd feared, just a spider-web of fine cracks fanning out from where his bag had hit it.

She hurried around to the other door. "You got a name?" she asked as she got in.

"Rune."

"I'm Zoey."

A subtle grin spread across his face, and this time he meant it. He shivered as his last bit of airy chaos evaporated.

Zoey gasped as she slid into the driver's seat.

"Is something wrong?"

"Your…face. It's different again. Were your ears always that…"

"That what?"

She bit her lip. "Never mind. I guess I'm just I'm a little frazzled." She looked forward, turned some sort of lever, and the vehicle hummed to life. "So where do you live?"

Rune squirted some of the ointment the bystander had given him onto his right hand. "I'm not from here." With any luck, that was all he'd have to say. He threw his head back and closed his eyes.

"Are you in some kind of band?"

"I beg your pardon?"

"I just thought, with that pirate costume and the eyeliner and all…"

"It's not a… Never mind." Rune pushed up the puffy sleeve of his shirt to better apply the bandage. Zoey's own attire was more casual: short pants the color of butternut and a purple, short-sleeved top.

"I just need someplace to rest," he said.

"Okay, there's a motel on Bardstown. That's not too far."

The vehicle lurched forward. At the end of the street, she turned onto a wider thoroughfare.

"It's not that expensive. One of those economy places. Is that okay?"

Rune sighed. "I have no money."

Zoey swerved as she glanced over at him. "Seriously? No plastic? Nothing?"

He had a few quigs and a handful of silver. In his own world, it would have been plenty, but the quigs would be useless here, and the silver would have to be exchanged—another nuisance he didn't have time for.

"Is that a problem?"

Zoey raised an eyebrow. "Mister, I'm sorry I hit you, and I want to make sure you're okay. I'm trying to be the Good Samaritan here, but you've got to work with me!" The girl's increasingly frantic voice was doing nothing for Rune's headache. "I'm taking you to the emergency room. That's what I should have done to begin with."

"No!" Rune summoned the airy chaos once more, but the carriage made it difficult. Too much iron in the thing's hull.

"I don't see any other options," Zoey said with a crack in her voice. "Do you?"

Rune could think of one. He didn't like it. In fact, he hated it. But it might at least contain the damage. They were alone: no other prying eyes or listening ears. He wouldn't violate the Covenant if he had to tip his hand. Anything to keep others from getting involved.

But there was one more thing to try first. "Perhaps you have a spare room?"

Zoey laughed out loud. "Are you flipping serious? Like I'm going to bring a strange man—and definite emphasis on the strange part—home with me and put him up in the guest room? Does that sound like something a sane person would do?"

"I can repay you."

"You don't have any money!"

Rune's headache had reached the limits of tolerability. "I can get some tomorrow. Enough to repair the glass on your carriage— your car—and extra for your trouble." He groaned. "Just tell me how much."

"And why should I believe any of this?"

Rune grumbled to himself. No one had told him Fallow folk could be this uncooperative. He would have to do the unthinkable and hope for the best. "Because it is nearly impossible for me to lie."

The automobile screeched to a halt. Zoey turned warily toward him. "You want to run that past me again?"

Rune sighed deeply. "I am bound by…certain rules."

"Well, I try to be a good person too, but—"

"No," he continued. "I'm not like you."

Zoey's scoff was a dissertation on the evils of stating the obvious.

He exhaled. Even a thimble's worth of airy chaos would be helpful. "I'm…I come from what you might call a different world."

Zoey barely held back a laugh. She pinched the bridge of her nose beneath her spectacles.

Rune pressed on. "Lying…is not healthy for me."

Zoey stared at him. A second passed. Five. Horns blared as other vehicles approached from behind and then swerved around them.

"You're from another world. What, like Mars?"

"Your people sometimes call it the Otherworld. The Dreamtime. Fairy Land."

Zoey's face twisted in a bemused mixture of petulance and incredulity. "You're a fairy."

"That's not a term we use."

"But that's your story?"

"It is the truth."

"And you…just…materialized in front of my car?"

He tilted his head. "More or less."

"So you and reality aren't actually on speaking terms. Good to know."

Another five seconds passed as Zoey stared at Rune. He filled the inside of the carriage with all the magic he could muster, hoping it would make a difference. He looked at his hands, but his mind reached out to hers with calming thoughts. She had to trust him, if only for the next few minutes.

He shrugged. "I don't know what else I can say." He was nearing the end of his magic. The carriage's steel frame leeched it out of him, but he had already planted the seeds. If he could nudge her a little bit more, they would take root. Just a little more…

Zoey stared at him for what seemed a full minute. Finally, she said, "I can't believe I'm doing this."

"I won't hurt you," Rune said. "I only need somewhere to rest. I promise."

Zoey rolled her eyes. "And you always tell the truth." She studied him from top to bottom with her mouth hanging open, caught somewhere between a scream and a giggle.

"That's right."

Her eyes narrowed as she stabbed a finger at his chest. "Do *not* make me regret this."

2

Avice slid off her horse and onto the mud-caked ground. She took a few tentative steps to shake out the stiffness. She'd been too many days in the saddle, but her errand wasn't half done.

A gentle rain had fallen for at least an hour. Beneath her slate-gray umbersay cloak, she was mostly dry but chilled to the bone. Somewhere behind the clouds, the sun would be setting. The board above the tavern's door depicted a horned serpent wrapped around a frothy tankard, its eyes crossed comically. She let a wry smile spread across her face.

A goblin boy appeared, a dusky-faced urchin who came up to Avice's waist. He met her with a bow and a practiced servile grin. "Stable thy hoss then, ma'am?" He spoke in the trade jargon that served as the common tongue in these parts.

Avice nodded. "Look thee her good after," she said in the same cant as she pulled a silver half-kenny from the pocket of her doublet. The boy's eyes lit up when she pressed it into his hand. He smiled and gripped her horse's reins.

She had lost the traitor's trail in Anvelton, but there were only two more stops on the coach road from Llinbach, so she had decided to press northward on the horse she bought a month ago. Eventually she picked up a lead that brought her to Dunswale. Not long ago, her quarry had passed through this jumble of farmsteads at the end of the coach road.

The autumn wind picked up: a good sign. She stepped onto the wooden porch, pulled her cloak's hood down onto her shoulders, and ran a hand through her dark, wavy hair.

The great room of the Drunken Dragon hardly lived up to the name. The smallest taverns in Athelhoew were royal pavilions compared to this cramped, rustic dining hall with its simple wooden tables and benches and a mere handful of patrons. There were a couple of small folk; a dwarf or two, squat and sturdily built; and a single troll, six and a half feet tall, his face a mosaic of geometric tattoos. The rest were goblins in a patchwork of skin tones and body types—and humans, so like elves and yet so different. One, a yellow-haired boy not yet old enough to shave, sat at the bar nursing a glass of whiskey.

A broad-shouldered and silver-haired dwarf poured drinks behind the bar. Avice made her way over to him and leaned in. "I need a private room. And a bath."

"Four unce a night. Another for your horse," the barman offered. "You want a bath, *cóhshema*, that's six kenny extra."

Pretending to be everybody's cousin probably came with the territory for innkeepers, but the dwarf's term of affection didn't register on his face. Avice chose to overlook his forwardness. Instead, she laid two hard, black beans on the counter. "There's two quigs. Plenty for a week."

The dwarf grunted.

"And did I mention I want privacy?"

The dwarf shot a quizzical glance at the boy with the whiskey, who shrugged and took a sip. The dwarf scooped up the quigs and traded them for a large brass key. "Upstairs. Last door on the left."

Avice pocketed the key. "I left my horse with your boy. Have him bring up my saddlebags, if you please."

The folds of her cloak licked about her boots, stirred on a breeze no one else could feel. A couple of goblins looked up from their drinks as she passed. A human woman in too much makeup smiled and batted her eyelashes.

"Which one of these ninnycocks is Mahwe?" Avice asked the woman.

The woman nodded toward a table near the back. Four men played cards while others stood around watching. "Him what gwan win."

The troll sat down beside the woman and wrapped a muscled arm around her. She giggled and whispered something in his ear.

Avice strolled toward the game, her booted feet silent on the bare wooden floor. The men were playing annis. Two of them, an older goblin and a human with curious wide-set eyes, had already folded. It was down to a smallkin, seated on a wooden box as a booster seat, and Mahwe. He was a smirking low elf with clearly more than a few humans in his family tree. He was brown and lanky, with arching eyebrows and subtly pointed ears adorned with silver baubles.

The smallkin called, and Mahwe threw down his hand, grinning. The elf gathered his winnings. Deal passed to the goblin, who shuffled the cards and dealt a new hand. The next few rounds went quickly, and Mahwe won nearly all of them.

One of the onlookers captured Avice's interest, a grizzled human who stood behind the goblin. Every now and then, Mahwe shot him a furtive glance, and the man would either scratch his nose or his chin or fiddle with the ribbons on his trade shirt. It was subtle, impressively so.

Avice grinned.

The next hand ended with the goblin cursing and Mahwe raking in the pot.

Avice eased up to the grizzled human. She raised her eyebrows before relaxing into an easy smile. At the same time, she expressed the slightest whiff of airy chaos to warm the hue of the lamplight and fill the air with the subtle aroma of a perfume she wasn't wearing. "Buy me a drink?" She nodded, anticipating his agreement. He smiled stupidly and lumbered off to the bar.

She returned her gaze to Mahwe. The two held eye contact until Mahwe turned his attention back to his cards.

The deal had passed to the human, who shuffled the deck and dealt four cards to each player. Each looked at their hands and discarded a single card. Mahwe waited until the last minute, trying not to make it obvious that he was looking for his accomplice. But Avice noticed. When the human returned with a tankard of cheech, Avice accepted. The reddish-gold brew was mediocre at best, but she smiled as if it was the best she'd ever tasted.

When the human slid next to her behind the smallkin, she turned him toward her and put a hand on his shoulder. "This game is boring. Find us a seat, hmm?"

His lips spread into a hopeful grin, but he looked toward Mahwe. He might have even thought Avice didn't notice. "In a minute," he said.

Avice smiled once more. She stood on her tiptoes and whispered in his ear. "I'll cut off your ear if you don't leave now," she cooed. "And then I'll move on to the more interesting bits." She stepped back and moved her hand just enough to show the hilt of her sword beneath her cloak, smiling all the while.

The man scooted away with one last forlorn glance at Mahwe. A moment later, the smallkin whooped and raked in the pot.

The elf wasn't nearly as impressive without his accomplice. He won only one of the next five hands while Avice stood at her post, arms crossed. His face darkened with every loss.

Eventually the game broke up. The smallkin hopped down from his chair, scooped up his box, and left with a full bag of silver and a smile on his swarthy face. Avice slid into his empty seat. The human player and the goblin had already left. She stared at Mahwe across the table.

"The way I see it, cohsh," Mahwe said, "you owe me some money."

"The way I see it, *cohsh*, cheating is against the rules."

The low elf smiled.

"I'm looking for Mahwe. They tell me that's you."

He lit a cigarillo and took a leisurely draw. "Should I know you?" He leaned back in his chair.

"You're a waymaker." It was a statement, not a question.

He grinned and bared a gold tooth. "You got someplace you wanna go?"

Avice leaned toward him. The color of her umbersay cloak roiled and shifted as if made of storm clouds.

"You took someone across the Mere a month ago. Goes by the name of Rune. A low elf—"

Mahwe arched an eyebrow.

"Forgive me. A *half-elf*, but he can pass for human."

Mahwe scoffed. "I take lots of folks to lots of places."

"This one was a fugitive. He stole something—something very valuable. I'm taking it back."

"We're all running from something," Mahwe said. He stood up and walked slowly around the table toward Avice. His confidence was pure…and woefully misplaced. "Truth is, he don't sound familiar. But maybe if there was a way you could, ah, jog my memory?"

He chuckled and spread his arms to make himself look bigger, more menacing. His narrowed eyes threatened violence. It was almost cute. Leaning over her, he put a firm hand on her shoulder.

Her cloak moved before she did. The corner whipped out and wrapped Mahwe's leg in an opalescent tentacle of umbersay. His eyes went wide as his foot came out from under him. The move gave Avice half a second to push the waymaker the rest of the way to the ground, draw her pistol, and jam it under his chin. She pulled back the hammer as her cloak moved on its own to tangle his hands.

Chairs scooted backward as patrons gasped, cursed, or simply excused themselves from the room. The dwarven bartender took a step toward Avice, saw the gleam in her eye, and stopped short.

"Perhaps I didn't make myself clear," she said, eyes firmly on the waymaker. "Rune is a criminal. I'm bringing him in, and nothing—*nothing*—is going to stand in my way. Do we understand one another?"

All the swagger had gone out of him. His eyes crossed as he looked down the bronze barrel of Avice's firearm. He nodded, half-flinching, barely holding back a defeated whimper.

"You're going to tell me where you took him. You're going to tell me anything he might have said or done in your presence. And then, once my business here is in order, you're going to take me there as well."

Another frantic nod.

Avice smiled. As she relaxed her stance, her cloak unwrapped itself from Mahwe's wrists. She stood up, and the waymaker scurried out from under her.

"I'm glad we could handle this like adults."

The small, private room was no more impressive than anything else at the Drunken Dragon, but it was clean, the lock on the door was well made, and the bathtub—little more than a big wooden barrel with some decorative brass fittings—was full of warm, soapy water.

Avice sank into it with a sigh. Mahwe had left half an hour ago after telling her everything she needed to know. Rune had indeed passed that way about three weeks before. He'd made contact with the waymaker and paid him for passage across the Mere. He was alone, and he didn't say much, but he held on to his leather satchel as if his life depended on it.

That meant he still had the coffer.

As the water soothed her tired muscles, Avice worked out what to do next. She would need some assistance, someone who could blend in unnoticed across the Mere. Fortunately, she'd made such a contact on her journey northward.

And she'd need to know as much of what lay on the other side as Mahwe could tell her. They had set up a meeting in three days' time. If he didn't show, well, that wouldn't be smart for him.

For now, she just wanted to relax. She poked one foot and then the other out from the water to give her legs a good stretch. Then she rolled her shoulders. The knot in her back loosened.

She slipped deeper into the tub, leaning back until her hair was under the water. Only her face and her knees poked up into the cool air of the room.

Something rapped on her window. She glanced over the lip of the tub. The tiny ceramic lantern she'd lit on the windowsill flickered. A furtive shadow, a patch of darker black against the night, moved outside.

Avice gazed at the ceiling. She should have known she wouldn't be allowed a proper bath. Rising from the tub, she pulled on her umbersay cloak, drawing it closed in front.

She padded to the window. The cloak responded to her hand gestures and opened arm slits at the sides.

As expected, a petite woman peered in from outside: a bright-eyed redhead with an almost childlike face. Avice slid the window open and took up the lantern. "Saffron."

"Dancer. Sorry to barge in on you like this." The woman slipped in through the window. Her own cloak whipped about, a reflection of the unrest Saffron felt but wouldn't let her body reveal.

"It can't be helped. You have something to report?"

She blew out an exasperated breath. "Whisper grilled us forever. Me, Goodfellow, Zodiac. Everybody who was there when

Rune…when it happened. He'll want to talk to you too when you get back."

Avice gritted her teeth. It was only expected, but she didn't relish reliving the disaster at Cruc Máw.

"But he knows where I am?" she asked. "Why I couldn't fall back with the rest of you?"

"Oh, yeah," Saffron said. "He wants Rune caught worse than anybody. I'm supposed to hang around as long as you need me."

One person for backup was fine, but more would be better—and some Knights of the Hand for good measure. Still, this far from home, Dancer could appreciate the need for discretion. Maybe she could reach a compromise.

"No," she said. "Go back to Athelhoew. Fast as you can. Bring the whole team if they can be spared. Then lay low here until I send for you."

"Will do, Dancer. Fast as I can."

"Good. Was there anything else?"

Saffron lowered her eyes.

"What is it?"

Saffron reached inside her cloak for a sealed letter and passed it to Avice. "It's from the Keeper."

Avice's eyes flashed.

"She says there's somebody across the Mere you're supposed to see."

Avice opened the letter and scanned its contents. Didn't her mother understand she had no time for side trips? She skimmed the formalities but stopped short at what came next:

I have been in contact with a certain human arcanist across the Mere from your present location. I have included instructions for a ritual with which you are to assist him.

"Of all the sarding…," Dancer growled. "And Whisper agreed to this?"

"He gave me the letter himself. Trouble?"

"It's nothing." Underneath the letter were a few leaves of parchment. "Thank you for delivering this." *I think.*

"Listen, if it's something I can take care of for you—"

"No, that's fine," Avice said, still reading.

His Majesty is eager to secure this human's allegiance. I have cultivated a relationship with him for several months. In fact, I have taken on your mien in anticipation of your stepping in at this point.

"Sard! She's been borrowing my face?"

Saffron's brow furrowed.

You would have been briefed more fully, but unfortunately the unpleasantness at Cruc Máw has prevented this. I assure you, however, that timely contact with the human is vital to His Majesty's plans.

"Just because she's my mother…" Avice's voice trailed off when her umbersay cloak tightened around her. It didn't like disloyalty.

"So," Saffron said. "Should I be going then?"

"What? Oh. Yes." Avice spun around and stalked to her saddlebags draped over the room's single chair. She set the lantern on the dressing table, pulled out a leather pouch, and counted four black beans into her hand. "This should be enough to rent a room for a couple of weeks."

"Yes, ma'am." Saffron received the beans and slipped them into her own money pouch.

"If any of you want a bath, you can pay for it yourselves."

"Whatever you say."

"Just get back here fast. Rune is slippery, but he's close by. I can feel it." She regarded the tiny elf. "Now hurry. And moonless night to you."

"Moonless night, Dancer."

The night swallowed up Saffron as quickly and quietly as she had appeared.

Avice read her mother's message again. The Keeper of the Mirror wanted her in the Fallow to work with a contact she'd been cultivating. Easy work, most of the time. But she had a fugitive to bring in.

It was barely past nine o'clock. Maybe she could contact Mr. Daws tonight.

Sard!

There was no traffic on the road this late. That suited Avice perfectly. The fewer prying eyes to see what she was up to, the better.

She didn't bother to reclaim her horse from the stable. It was only a few miles south to where she had first bargained with Daws. Beneath her umbersay cloak, she blended perfectly into the shadows. Her booted steps were silent on the dirt path.

She drew the airy chaos into herself to scan her environment. The darkness seemed fleeting, as if it were already nearing dawn.

At the appointed place, somewhere in the farmland between Dunswale and South Hemling, she scanned the skies. Seeing nothing, she closed her eyes and settled her mind, allowing any unbidden thought to pass through her unremarked.

She allowed a single word to take shape. *Daws.* She whispered the name and sent it forth on a gentle breeze. If her contact was close enough, her call would find its way to his ears.

Five minutes later she whispered the name again. *Daws.*

This time, the answer came almost immediately. *Coming.*

Five minutes after that, her contact flitted across the night sky and lit in a maple tree beside the road. Three friends joined him, spreading out to find vantage points all around.

"Well, Mr. Daws?" she said.

The crow said nothing, not even to his lieutenants on the nearby branches.

"I didn't come to Dunswale so you could give me the silent treatment," she griped. She reached into her pocket for the trinket she had brought, a gold watch she'd taken from an enemy's corpse ages ago.

The crow fluttered downward. By the time he hit the ground, he had assumed the form of a stooped figure, four feet tall, halfway between man and bird. The werecrow snatched up the watch in the two-fingered claw on his now-stubby wing.

"Shiny!" he said appreciatively. "And you say it 'Duns'l.'"

"I actually don't care," Avice said.

"We ain't got no word on that…uh…thing you was asking about."

"No. It has moved, unfortunately."

Mr. Daws shook his head as he drew the watch's chain around his neck. "So me and the boys can be on our way then?" There was something twitchy about his movements, not quite birdlike but close.

"The fugitive has taken the coffer to the Fallow. I still require your help to retrieve it."

"Listen," Daws said, swaying back and forth, "if you want us to cross the Mere, it'll cost extra."

"Now, you look here—"

"I'm just tellin' you how it is," the werecrow said. He cocked his head at an odd angle. "It takes work to open a portal, and waymakers don't come cheap."

She frowned because Daws was right. There was no way she could afford passage for the entire flock.

"Hallowfest is coming," she said. "The boundary will be thinner then. No need for a waymaker."

Daws nodded with his whole body. "That might do it. Me and the boys can give it a try—but you're gonna have to make it worth our time."

Avice took a deep breath as she considered her options. "The King of Shadows wants his treasure back. I'm sure you realize he treats those who help him exceptionally well."

"Yeah, when he don't swallow 'em whole!" Daws made a sound somewhere between a laugh and a throaty rattle. His head twitched, and his eyes scanned the near horizon. "Listen, the King o' Shadows ain't here, sister. I'm talking to you. You want us to go looking for your little box on the other side, it's gonna cost you."

She bristled at the creature's presumptuous familiarity, but she could only say, "Fine. I'll take it under consideration."

"S'a pleasure doing business with you."

"And there's nothing more you can tell me about the fugitive? The one called Rune?"

"The Nightwalker?" Daws said. "I mean, the other Nightwalker? We ain't seen him since that one night in South Hemling. Right, boys?"

The other werecrows, still in fully avian form, squawked and bobbed their heads.

"Must be sticking to the Fallow side."

"That doesn't surprise me," Avice said. "And he is *at best* a former Nightwalker, if you please. He is a traitor and a thief, and I mean to bring him to justice." She stroked her side and winced with phantom pain.

"I'll be crossing soon," she added. "I want you and your…boys to follow as quickly as you can."

"You got it, sister."

"And if you love your life," she said, eyes blazing, "stop calling me your sister."

Daws hopped back a step.

"Contact me on the other side to let me know you've made it. I'll give you further instructions then."

"Whatever you say, sis—I mean, boss. You don't have to worry none about us."

"I hope you're right, Mr. Daws," she said. Her scowl could have curdled milk.

3

The city beyond the Mere was big enough to get lost in, and Rune eked by as best he could. With no sign of Avice, he applied himself to Mahwe's list of contacts and worked on building a new life.

Even after a month in the Fallow, every day brought surprises. Today, it was that Fallowmen were so keen on eating breakfast foods at all hours of the night.

Rune sat at the far end of the counter at a diner. With his back to the wall, he could see everything around him. He had chosen not to mask his appearance. People saw him as he was: a slender, youthful man with hair the color of cornsilk neatly combed and pulled back in a braided ponytail. The tops of his ears bent at an obtuse angle, what Fallow folk described as "pointed." If they only knew!

His journal lay open on the counter. The last page recorded the notes and tips the waymaker had given him—names and places and warnings to help him make it on this side of the Mere. He had filled several other pages with his own observations: connections to be made, pitfalls to avoid. Whenever he had a spare minute, he reviewed what he had learned.

He sighed. He'd had too many spare minutes lately, and his rent would soon be due. Which is what brought him to the diner in the first place.

Work had been hard to come by. The skills Rune had learned at the Haw didn't translate easily into a promising career in the Fallow. But armed with information from the waymaker, he'd made some contacts and done some favors. He'd be fine. Someday.

Two men sat at the counter and paid him no attention. A couple, a man and a woman, sat in the corner booth, chatting and eating pancakes. Rune took it all in as he sipped his tea.

Outside, the city was dark and the streets were empty.

Three people were working at the diner: a waitress, a fry cook, and a manager who helped both as needed. Seven Fallow folk in all.

It was the waitress that Rune had come for. Jo Ellen Hollart looked just like his client had described: average build, mid-twenties, mousy brown hair, not a great beauty but pretty enough by this world's standards. She wiped down tables, lost in thought.

Rune wondered what was on her mind. Was she wrapped up in her work? Worrying about bills? She had a small child; was she thinking about her? Was she worried she was being watched? Is that why she seemed so jumpy?

Human emotions were a puzzle. That's what made this job different…and dangerous. How would she react to him? And how much did she know? Even Fallow folk could be dangerous if they understood the Covenant, and the waitress was sure to know something. A bit of iron or a circle of salt could turn even a simple errand into a disaster.

One of the men at the counter paid his bill and left.

Rune scanned the room. There were still six Fallow folk in the diner. Any more than three, and his options were limited. The Covenant was clear when it came to secrecy. He couldn't use any overt magic—not that he intended to—but neither could he openly discuss the details of Mrs. Hollart's situation.

He checked his pocket watch. Forty-five minutes at the diner, and he still wasn't sure of the best way to proceed.

I am a Nightwalker, he reminded himself. *Trained by Whisper himself. I have faced dragons! I will not be thwarted by a lone Fallow woman!*

She smiled at him then, and his stomach stirred with pixy dust.

Alright, the dragon was asleep, and there was a dozen of us. But still…

When the waitress came by to see if he needed anything, he took a deep breath. Ready or not, it was time to act.

"Mrs. Hollart," he said under his breath. He tapped his fingers nervously against the countertop. He didn't make eye contact but watched her body language. She took a half-step back.

"The name's Davis," she said. Her voice had a brittle edge. "Jo Ellen Davis. Can I get you some more hot water for your tea?"

"Thank you."

She practically ran to the hot water pitcher. Rune felt a twinge of guilt for upsetting her. Names were serious business—certainly in his own world but also in this one, he had learned. Knowing someone's name gave you a measure of power over them, especially if they didn't know yours. But the offense couldn't be helped. Rune had a job to do.

When the waitress returned and set the metal pitcher in front of Rune, he lowered his voice again and said, "I mean you no harm, Mrs. Hollart."

"I told you, my name is—"

"Your husband sent me." Rune said. He kept his tone steady—no need to spook her if he could avoid it. He raised his head to look her in the eye. His steely gray stare drained the color from Mrs. Hollart's face. Her mouth dropped open for just a second, and her eyes went wide.

"He'd like to—"

She didn't give him a chance to finish. Faster than he'd have thought possible, Mrs. Hollart grabbed a ketchup bottle and squeezed a stream of it into his face. He slipped off his chair, which swiveled him toward the wall, blinded and sputtering.

Mrs. Hollart bolted. Rune turned back to the counter and snatched a paper napkin.

"Jo Ellen!" the manager shouted, his eyes wide. "What's going on?"

"I gotta go!" she shouted, a quaver in her voice.

"What the hell are you doing attacking a customer?"

"I ain't kidding, Curtis, I gotta go!" She was no longer defensive; the words came out like daggers.

"I'm sorry, sir," Curtis told Rune. He rubbed his forehead, obviously nervous. "Let me get you a towel or something to—"

Without finishing his sentence, the manager whipped around toward Mrs. Hollart, but she had already slammed the door of the back room behind her.

Rune wiped ketchup off his face and tried to regain his bearings. Everyone watched the drama playing out. He bit his lip. His one chance was slipping away.

"You can't just clock out early!" Curtis called. "I gotta write you up as it is. Don't make things worse!"

"Write me up, then," Mrs. Hollart shouted from the back. "Sheila's gonna be here any minute. You and Jake can handle things that long."

"Come on, Jo Ellen," Curtis groaned. "Don't make me do this! Do you *want* to get fired?"

"It's fine," Rune cut in. He raised his hand in what he hoped was a calming gesture, just as Whisper had taught him. "Just…a misunderstanding."

The couple in the corner didn't even try to hide their stares. The eyes of the man at the counter bounced between Rune and the manager.

"I'm sorry," Mrs. Hollart said, reemerging in a blue lightweight jacket and clutching her purse.

"I'm serious, Jo Ellen. One more step and I'm—"

"No, you're not," Rune interrupted, his voice even, unafraid. He leveled his gaze on Curtis and expelled the slightest whiff of glamour—just enough to project an intimidating presence. Curtis swallowed whatever he was going to say next.

"The ketchup was my fault," Rune said. He kept pressing his glamour to keep the manager off balance, but he turned his eyes to the waitress. "I didn't mean to startle you, Mrs. Hollart. It's just that your husband would like to talk this out." He took a tentative step toward her. "I can set up a meeting. You decide when and where."

"I don't want nothing to do with Gimp Hollart," she spat. "Not anymore."

Rune persisted. "I can wait until your shift is over. Or, if you prefer, you can leave with me now and we can discuss this—*with your manager's permission*." He shot Curtis another deadly glare. "Either way, Mrs. Hollart, we need to talk. In private."

"I said no!" she hissed, swinging around the counter and rushing toward the door.

Rune grabbed his brown bomber jacket from the back of his chair and started after her.

By that time, the man from the corner booth had gotten up. He met Rune near the door. "There a problem, buddy?" He was several inches taller than Rune and more heavily muscled. He clenched his fists, and the tattoos on his forearms rippled.

"Hey, hey!" Curtis yelled. The fry cook hissed a curse and ducked under the counter.

Rune gritted his teeth. *Stars above, I haven't got time for this!* "No," he said, glaring. "No problem." He tapped his fingers against his thigh. His throat was suddenly parched.

He gazed around the room. All eyes were on him, all six pairs— no, five. Mrs. Hollart had stormed away. Rune could dispatch the man in any number of ways with a flick of his wrist. He could draw the breath from his lungs, or throw him around the room with a gale-force wind, or overwhelm his mind with visions of unearthly torment. He could strike with literally inhuman speed and bring him down with a single punch.

But he couldn't do any of those things in front of this many witnesses. The Covenant wouldn't let him.

And Mrs. Hollart was getting away. He locked eyes on the man and reached deep inside himself to call forth the airy chaos.

The forces of creation permeated this world, as they did every world. It was rarely difficult for Rune to tap into his elemental essence, draw it forth, and weave it to his whim as he had done to intimidate the manager. He did that again, only more intently. He took a deep breath and, with the slightest effort of will, exhaled a pulse of magic in the man's direction.

The man's expression deadened. His mouth dropped slightly open.

"No need for concern," Rune said.

The man wobbled almost imperceptibly.

Air-weaving could do any number of useful things. But Rune preferred the subtle approach—and right now, it was the only option. He couldn't blow the poor fellow through the doors, but he could get the same result by clouding his mind.

The man stood silently, dumbstruck. When it was obvious Rune wasn't going to start a fight (yet not at all obvious that he had already ended it), the woman ran to her boyfriend. She said nothing, just gazed in fright at Rune.

Another second passed, and the woman coaxed the man to return to his seat. Rune grabbed another wad of napkins. "I'll be on my way," he said. He set some of the worthless slips of paper the Fallow folk used for money on the counter and slipped out the door.

There was no sign of Mrs. Hollart on the street. The air was full of a sweet, tangy smell: the scent of ketchup clung to Rune's face and collar. There was even more on his hands where he had tried unsuccessfully to scrape the stuff off.

Stars above!

He took a deep breath, once more tapping into the airy chaos. This time, instead of pushing the unseen essence of creation outward, he drew it in, allowing it to sharpen his senses, to hone his mental clarity and pierce the clatter of the city.

The scent of ketchup assaulted him, and he took a second to steady himself. His gaze swept up and down the street. Between his weaving and his naturally acute vision, Rune saw the world under the streetlights nearly as well as most Fallow folk could see on a clear day at noon.

He looked first to his right and then to his left, peering down dark alleys. The noise of traffic made it a long shot, but he stopped to listen anyway. He attuned his ears to any sounds that would lead him in the right direction: hurried footsteps or a rustling jacket.

Nothing.

Mrs. Hollart was long gone, and his prospect of getting paid left with her.

He sighed as he scraped the last of the sticky mess off his face and began to walk toward downtown. His ketchup-splattered shirt was probably ruined, and his rent was still due.

But there was nothing he could do about any of that now. Gimp Hollart was waiting for him, and he wasn't going to like what Rune had to say.

4

It was a thirty-minute walk downtown. With every step, Rune replayed the encounter with Mrs. Hollart in his mind, imagining all the things he could have done differently. Should he have tried to establish rapport with her, taken a few days to become a "regular" at the diner before revealing himself? Could he have addled everyone and left with Mrs. Hollart in the confusion? What would have happened if he had waited outside and just followed her home at the end of her shift?

Causing problems was a lot easier than fixing them. Whisper had reveled in that fact. It wasn't nearly as fun to handle the fallout.

Rune eventually arrived at the Brown Hotel, a hundred-year-old landmark at the corner of Fourth and Broadway. Kings and prime ministers had been guests at the Brown over the past century and availed themselves of its many amenities. But Rune wasn't interested in the fitness center or the shoeshine service.

He bypassed the main entrance. Instead, he walked around to a small door in the back of the impressive stone building. He stood under the red canopy, knocked, and waited for someone to answer.

Thankfully, Rune recognized the swarthy figure who appeared.

"How ya doin', cohsh?" Morty said. His bellman's uniform wasn't a perfect fit, with his barrel chest, bowed legs, and too-long arms, but he wore it with pride. He shuffled a stack of boxes from one arm to the other and offered Rune a huge, calloused hand.

Morty raised his eyebrow. "Geez Louise! Is that blood on ya?" He sniffed. "Oh. Just ketchup. Better take care of that before it leaves a stain."

"I know," Rune said, his jaw clenched. He braced himself against Morty's powerful handclasp. He was a tad shorter than Rune but at least twenty pounds heavier and all muscle.

Morty was on the list of names the waymaker had given him. He was an ayleck with an acquisitive nature and a sometimes unpredictable temperament. Rune didn't ever want to face Morty in a fight, but he could be trusted with anything.

"I'm meeting someone upstairs."

Morty ushered Rune inside and headed down the hallway. "Nobody up there but the usuals."

Knowing Morty, he could have told Rune to the minute when each guest had arrived and probably their drink order too. There was a reason aylecks were the best security guards in Rune's world.

"He'll be here," Rune said. "A troll. A pale redhead about your size."

"I'll let him know you're here."

The two walked side by side through empty service corridors. The place was practically dead at this time of night. On the other side of the wall, Rune could hear the clink of silverware and the conversations of a catering crew tearing down after a banquet or wedding reception or some such.

They passed a spot of bare plaster on the wall. Rune arched an eyebrow.

"That's new."

"Yeah, somebody…uh…put his fist through the wall there."

"Somebody meaning?"

"Nothing you need to worry about, cohsh. Know what I mean?"

Rune let the issue pass. At last, the two stopped in front of an elevator.

"Oh, before I forget. Here." Morty reached in his jacket pocket and handed Rune a small plastic rectangle. "It just came in."

Rune recognized his likeness and physical description. "And you say this card is necessary?"

"Folks in this world are always wanting to see your ID. Now you got some."

"I appreciate it."

"Don't worry about it," Morty said. "By the way, what do you know about muryans? There's been an infestation. In Underborough, I mean. I could get you on the cleanup crew."

"I believe I'll pass."

The elevator doors finally slid open. "Well, I better get going," Morty said with a gesture to his packages. "See ya."

Rune nodded and stepped into the elevator. With the index finger of one hand and the thumb and index finger of the other, he pressed the combination of buttons that would take him to his destination.

As far as the staff and guests of the Brown were concerned, the fifteenth floor was a storage area. Local historians told stories about how the whole level was haunted. People on the fourteenth floor reported the sounds of footsteps and moving furniture or the aroma of cigar smoke. And, of course, the elevator often inexplicably stopped at the fifteenth floor.

Ghost hunters theorized it was the hotel's long-dead founder visiting his private suites. The truth was even stranger. There were, in fact, two fifteenth floors, occupying the same space but slightly offset from each other—vibrating, as it were, at two different frequencies.

No mundane human had seen the fifteenth floor where Rune was headed. Jo Ellen Hollart couldn't have found it if she tried.

And in her current state of mind, why would she? Rune wondered what it would be like for a Fallow woman to learn that she had married a creature out of fairy tales. It happened, of course. It always had. The fairy tales themselves admitted the possibility. But people of the Fallow rarely took their legends as seriously as they should.

Rune's own people bore some of the responsibility for that. The Dream Book was their idea, after all. Convince the Fallow folk that the people of Saynim were nothing but harmless fantasies. Most of the time, the masquerade worked well for both sides. Saynim folk could do as they pleased, and Fallow folk could get on with their lives without worrying overmuch about the things that go bump in the night.

Jo Ellen Hollart had learned the truth, though. Her reaction—running away as fast as possible—didn't seem entirely irrational. Rune wondered what he'd have done in her shoes.

Now he simply tapped his feet as the elevator continued its slow, rumbling journey. The doors opened again, and he stepped out into the foyer of Gamaufry Tavern.

Gamaufry was where Saynim folk gathered in Louisville. They went there to unwind, hear the latest news, or do a little business. It was the one place Rune had found that felt like something approximating home. Or at least the parts of home that Rune missed.

The dark wood furnishings, brick columns, and subtle hint of cigar smoke gave the place a welcoming feel. A cook stirred a huge copper cauldron suspended near the fire of the stone hearth. The aroma of herbs and stewed meats made Rune's mouth water.

Goblins played a game of four-card annis at a short-legged table and quaffed mugs of frothy greenbrew. Beside them, huge windows looked out upon a covered porch masked from mundane eyes under powerful glamour.

The bar was straight ahead, where a couple of hulder folk chatted with the bartender as he filled bowls with pretzels and peanuts.

On a raised platform in the corner, beside the fireplace, two dwarves played a fiddle and a lute while a goblin woman accompanied them on a recorder and a huge, green-skinned troll belted out "Livin' la Vida Loca."

Maybe the place wasn't as much like home as Rune had thought. But it was all he had, so he savored it.

He ordered a mug of hot yaupon tea and took his drink to a table in the corner near the card-playing goblins. Everything was as Morty had described—just the usual nighttime crowd. Gamaufry Tavern wasn't busy all the time, but you could always count on somebody being there to have a drink, tell stories, or eat a simple but satisfying meal.

In a few nights, the place would be packed with Hallowfest revelers. Tonight, it was an intimate gathering of nondescript Saynim folk with nowhere better to be.

The elevator chimed again, and Gimp Hollart appeared in the entryway. The pale, stocky troll looked about, clutching his flat cap in his two brawny hands. He noticed Rune, started, and shuffled toward him, slumping into the seat across from him. Reading Rune's expression, he hung his head. The troll's prodigious nose was red and splotchy.

"She's still worked up, ain't she?" He spoke with an earthy twang cultivated in the heart of Appalachia.

Rune shrugged. "I suppose these things take time."

"But I'm the same person I was when we got married!" Mr. Hollart blurted. Tears welled in his eyes.

Rune focused on the table, unsure what to say. He'd been trained to suppress his emotions, and the airy chaos made it easy to disregard those of others. It was a useful skill, though not without drawbacks.

"She must not see it that way." He took a long, slow breath. "She might not ever."

"You're giving up?" Mr. Hollart said with a sniffle, wiping his nose on the sleeve of his flannel shirt. "The Merlady said you could do something."

Rune averted his eyes. Maya Tecumseh was another name on the waymaker's list—as someone to be avoided. He didn't like the idea of the Merlady sending him work, but he wasn't in a position to turn down a job.

And now that he'd taken it, Rune didn't relish the idea of disappointing her. Masking her feelings was *not* one of Maya Tecumseh's strong points.

"I did everything you asked," he finally said. "I found your wife. I told her you wanted to talk."

Mr. Hollart shook his head. "You're still just a youngling. You don't understand. Jo Ellen is everything to me."

"I assure you I'm of age, Mr. Hollart. And I don't see what else I can do." Rune finally looked him in the eye. "I'm sorry. I don't know what to say."

"It's been three months," the troll rumbled. His large, calloused hands curled into fists. "I ain't seen my daughter in three months. You gotta do something!"

That last outburst got the attention of the card players. One of the goblins, with a bald pate and a gap-toothed sneer, looked up from his cards long enough to shoot Rune and Mr. Hollart annoyed glances.

"Please calm down," Rune said. "Are you pulling earth right now? You need to stop."

Mr. Hollart leaned back and hung his head. "Just a little," he said. "This high off the ground…with everything else going on…"

"I understand," Rune lied. The troll weaved earth just as Rune weaved air. That meant he took matters like family and duty more seriously than most. Rune had never heard of an earth-weaver's marriage ending. Ever.

But the earthen chaos made him stubborn, and that wouldn't help anybody right now.

"You told me she's staying with her sister," Rune said.

Mr. Hollart nodded. "Marla. Marla Davis."

Rune bowed his head. He had wanted to keep the sister out of this. That's why he tried the diner first. The fewer people involved, the better. And approaching someone at home could be tricky in any case. Still, it wouldn't be too hard to find Mrs. Hollart's sister.

"Give me another week," he said. "But I make no promises."

"Thank you, Mr. Rune."

Rune grimaced at what had to come next. He tapped his fingers against his thigh. "I'll need a little bit of an advance on my payment."

Mr. Hollart reached into his pocket. "Yeah, I figured you'd work around to that."

"It's just that I have expenses."

"I understand," the troll said. He set two black beans on the table and slid them Rune's way. "Will that do you?"

Rune frowned. "Actually, I need Fallow money. The green pieces of paper?"

"I know what Fallow money is!" Mr. Hollart snapped. "I just ain't got none to give right now. It took all I had to get to Louisville in the first place. And rooms ain't cheap around here, neither. And—"

"It's all right," Rune said, raising his hands defensively. "I can take your quigs." He scooped up the magic beans and put them in his pocket, adding to his crowded to-do list a trip to convert the magic beans into dollars. "Thank you."

"Just tell her…tell her I love her."

"I will."

Gimp Hollart slumped away without another word. His heavy shoes clomped on the hardwood floor. As he passed the card game, the gap-toothed goblin cursed under his breath and shot a withering glare in Rune's direction.

The band started playing "Funkytown."

Another man shouldered past Mr. Hollart: short, pudgy, and shabbily dressed. He flinched when he and Rune made eye contact, but he steeled himself and waddled forward.

"Y-you're the Nightwalker?" he said.

Rune's eyes darted left and right. Some things were no one's business but his own. Gazing up at the man, he nodded.

"I expected somebody older."

"Then come back in fifty years."

"No, I mean…" The fat man took the seat once occupied by Mr. Hollart. "You *are* the one they call Rune, right?"

"Do I know you?"

"Call me Boggs," he said, trembling. "You know you got something on your shirt?"

Rune ignored the question. "I take it you have some business to discuss?"

"Yes—I mean, no." Boggs took a labored breath. "Maybe. I don't know."

"That covers all the options, I think," Rune said. "If you'll excuse me, I was about to get some supper—"

"Mr. Rune," Boggs interrupted. For an instant, at least, he had mastered his nerves. "There's something you need to know. It's about the King of Shadows."

Rune swallowed. Pressure built in his temples. "What about him?"

"He's working with somebody here in town. A sorcerer."

Rune arched his eyebrows. "You mean a Fallowman? Are you sure?"

Boggs nodded. "Someone I work for. Nothing long-term. Actually, my pact is up in a few days."

Rune studied the man's expression. Boggs didn't strike him as especially trustworthy, but there was no denying the fear in his watery eyes. "And you say he has something to do with the King of Shadows?"

"My employer has been talking to somebody on the other side. A black-haired elven woman. Mean as a water panther."

"Avice," Rune hissed, more a curse than a name.

"Whatever her name is, she's working for the King of Shadows. She's been passing on inside information. Sigils and words of power and such. Big-league stuff, and it's all coming from the King of Shadows himself!"

Rune's head swam. *Stars above, I thought I was through with him!*

He looked Boggs in the eye, still not sure he could trust him. "This sorcerer's your master," he said. "You're supposed to do his bidding."

"Only till Hallowfest," Boggs protested. "And he never bound me to silence." He chuckled. "Sarding Fallowman thinks I just hang around all night waiting to get summoned. He don't know I give myself time off when he goes to sleep. But listen." He leaned in. "Whatever the King of Shadows is planning, we're all gonna have to live with it—and for more than just the next few days."

"You fear him more than you fear breaking your pact?"

"Wouldn't *you?*"

Of course he would. The King of Shadows had been a legend since before Rune was born. If he could extend his reach by a single inch, he'd do it. And Rune knew what life was like under his thumb.

"They say you…," Boggs stammered, "I mean…"

"Yes?" Rune clenched his jaw.

"Nothing," Boggs said. "Forget it."

"You want to know if it's true that I once served the King of Shadows. Earlier you called me a Nightwalker."

"Look, Mr. Rune, I don't mean to pry—"

"It's true," Rune said. The words seemed to pierce Boggs's consciousness like a knife. He gazed at Rune, eyes wide. "I've left that life behind."

Boggs said nothing, but he started to shake again.

Rune was just as agitated, but he was better at hiding it. The last thing he wanted was another confrontation with his former lord. It was bad enough that the King of Shadows had designs on large sections of his own world. If he was working with a sorcerer, then he wanted a toehold in the Fallow, too.

There were people who'd want to know about this, people who could do something about it. But they would want assurances that Boggs's story checked out.

"This sorcerer," Rune said. "Who is he?"

"He goes by Jericho," Boggs said with a smirk.

"He uses a byname?" A lot of Saynim folk took up an alias or title. At least, the ones most likely to make enemies did. Some Fallowmen did the same if they had dealings with the other side. You couldn't be too careful about names. Rune couldn't remember the last time anyone had called him by his true name.

"That's right," Boggs said. "His real name's Keenan Phipps. He lives over by the university. Got himself one of them houses the Fallow folk think is old." He pulled a scrap of paper from his pocket and scribbled an address.

Rune took the paper when Boggs slid it toward him. After a glance, he folded it and put it in his shirt pocket. "If I look into this, you'll owe me a favor."

Boggs swallowed hard. Favors were serious business in Saynim, and breaking one's word had consequences. "I understand." He stood and backed away. "Thanks."

Rune stayed in his seat. He thought about getting up and helping himself to some stew but he had lost his appetite.

He could have walked the distance between downtown and home before the buses started their next day's runs. He decided to ride the wind instead.

On the porch of Gamaufry Tavern, looking down over the darkened city, Rune leaned into the wind while pulling as much airy chaos as he could. Soon he was in the center of his own personal whirlwind. His body became light, practically weightless, and the pulse of chaotic energies surged up and down his spine.

When the time was ripe, he allowed himself to fall forward over the railing.

The wind enveloped him and slowed his fall. As it always did.

He jetted south and east. He could only ride the wind for a few minutes at a time, but it was better than pounding the pavement for two hours. Three big jumps from rooftop to rooftop brought him to his neighborhood in about ten minutes.

The airy chaos still hummed through him as he landed a few blocks from home.

He was still distracted by the exchange at the diner. What had Gimp Hollart expected to happen when his Fallow-born wife discovered who—what—he really was? And how had he not come up with a plan for when she did? The troll was clearly an idiot.

Rune took a breath and settled his nerves. That was just the chaos talking.

Every chaos had its own effects. Earth-weavers like Gimp Hollart became lethargic and pessimistic. Water-weavers got overly moody. Fire-weavers, selfishly voracious.

Air-weavers like Rune grew restless and detached. Whisper called it the Blessing. "Nightwalkers can't afford to be sentimental," he would say. "The Blessing lets us reach a state of disinterest. Embrace it. Nothing matters but the errand."

And so, in the back of his mind, Rune played with options for how to get Mrs. Hollart to listen to him. Possibilities. Random chance. But it wasn't about the Hollarts working out their differences. He couldn't care less about that. It was a mental puzzle, a locked door for which he had to find the key.

That, and he needed to be paid.

The usual benefits of air-weaving had left him. His body felt sluggish and heavy. His senses, still superior by human standards, weren't nearly as sharp as they had been. He glanced to and fro, soaking in his environment lest he miss something obvious.

He walked past a row of houses, humble but clean, their lawns littered with fallen leaves. Another block and he'd be home. There was plenty of time to feel something for his client tomorrow. Besides, the Hollarts and their problems hardly mattered next to what Boggs had told him.

The thought of the King of Shadows lurking about worried Rune. He would have to take a look around at the sorcerer's house. That posed its own obstacles, but it couldn't be helped. At this point, what he most needed was information.

He turned at the corner and headed to a modest structure behind a larger house. Swinging open the white picket fence, he entered the yard and strode to the door, key in hand.

Rune's night vision was still uncertain from pulling so much magic, so he flipped on the light. He could see most of his apartment from the front door. At the far end of the sitting room was a small kitchen to the left and a similar sized bedroom and bath to the right. The whole place was sparsely furnished. In the month since he arrived in the Fallow, he had barely earned enough to pay for rent and food. The sofa and chairs, kitchen table, bare walls, and lumpy bed that came with the apartment would do for now.

He shrugged off his jacket and draped it over the arm of the sofa.

A bottle of orange juice sounded good. In the Fallow, you could purchase it in small, single-serve bottles. After skipping supper, Rune needed something to keep his stomach from rumbling.

As he peered into the refrigerator—a fascinating contraption!—he became aware of someone approaching his porch. His head popped up in time to see a shadowy figure standing at the door.

5

Zoey couldn't sleep. Mostly she blamed *Othello*.

She and the Moor of Venice had issues. She read the play and the online study notes. She wrote the paper, or at least most of it. All it needed was a good conclusion.

But English was not her best subject, and Mr. Wilkins was out to get her. The more she worried, the more her stomach tied itself in knots.

She looked at the row of knick-knacks on the shelf above her desk. She'd collected them over the years from different ethnic festivals around town: a little brass incense burner from India, a tiny Chinese doll, an Ethiopian icon of the Virgin Mary. (Her dad had teased her about that one because they were Baptists.) Her most recent acquisition was a small pendant, a wrought-iron heart of Celtic knotwork. She didn't think it came from anywhere interesting; it just caught her fancy at the Saint James Court Art Show a few weeks back.

Those little treasures reminded her of all the places she wanted to go, all the things she longed to see and experience…but first she had to graduate from high school. And that meant she had to conquer *Othello*.

At least she had Caitlin Evans's party to look forward to. Well, it wasn't Caitlin's party, precisely. Just a get-together Caitlin had been invited to. She was a year older than Zoey, a freshman in college. Some of her new college friends were going to hang out, and they said it was fine to bring Zoey along, too.

She sighed. If she could just survive Mr. Wilkins…

Sleep refused to come, so at four in the morning she turned off her alarm clock. She'd been planning to get up early any way and finish her essay. She threw on her school clothes and went to the bathroom to splash some water on her face.

That's when, outside the bathroom window, she saw the light flip on in Rune's apartment.

Her heart beat a little faster.

Maybe she couldn't have exciting adventures abroad just yet, but fate had thrown her something at least as interesting.

Rune had been renting the little mother-in-law apartment behind the Colemans' house for the last month. Zoey's dad had fixed it up not too long before, after her parents decided renting it out could help pay for Zoey's college.

The details of how she met Rune were a little fuzzy. There was an accident, and she drove him home. (Why had she decided to do that?) He needed a place to stay, and her parents needed a tenant.

Getting her dad to agree took a little convincing. Rune had no references and he spoke only vaguely about where he had come from. In short, he raised every possible red flag…but he still needed help. That much was obvious.

Fortunately, Zoey's dad had preached about the Good Samaritan a few weeks before. He really shouldn't do that if he didn't want his parishioners to start helping people they find on the street. The whole idea was right there in the story, for crying out loud!

Being a preacher's kid wasn't always easy, but Zoey had learned how to leverage her situation. She'd gotten pretty good at giving her dad the chance to practice what he preached. Forgiveness: that one came in handy a bunch of times! But also compassion, hospitality, not judging people.

The Colemans were good people. Like everybody else, they just needed a little encouragement every now and then. Eventually she convinced them that they'd be doing Rune a favor by letting him rent the apartment. They'd be helping a "troubled youth" who was trying to get back on his feet. As near as she and her parents could tell, that was the God's honest truth.

So far, Zoey had kept to herself the real question about Rune, the one nobody would have thought to ask in a million years.

Is Rune human?

The best answer Zoey could come up with was, "Technically, maybe." He looked human enough. More so than the drawings of Neanderthals in her old biology textbook, and they counted as human, right?

Zoey adjusted her glasses and gazed out the window toward the light in Rune's apartment. She wondered if he couldn't sleep, either.

Her face warmed as she wondered whether he'd like to go to Caitlin's party.

You barely know this guy, she scolded herself.

It'll be fine, she countered. *He doesn't set off any alarm bells with Mom and Dad.*

That's because they're assuming he's not *a mythological being.*

Whose side are you on? Zoey asked herself.

I thought we'd given up on guys.

We gave up on Jaden, she insisted. *This is different.*

And it *was* different. Rune inspired Zoey's thirst for adventure. He was completely different from the guys at school—he was different from anybody she'd ever met!

And to be honest, he was pretty good looking. Mix equal parts of Legolas and Draco Malfoy, and the result might look something like the mysterious Mr. Rune.

Zoey had to clear her head if she was going to finish writing that stupid paper. She needed a change of scenery, conversation, people. She glanced out the window again. Rune's light was still on.

It was a chilly October morning, so she slipped on her bathrobe and tennis shoes. Her heart pounded as she listened at her parents' door to confirm that they were still sound asleep. Satisfied, she sneaked downstairs, carefully opened the kitchen door, and dashed across the yard.

Rune opened his door before she even had a chance to knock. "Yes?"

Zoey jumped back. He was a bit taller than her, and there was something untamed about the way he carried himself, bold and unafraid. His movements were quick and catlike. His platinum blond hair, usually kept in a tidy braid, framed his face in a wild, silky mane.

She sucked in a breath, startled that he seemed to know she was coming. "It's just me, Zoey." She clutched the lapels of her robe and pulled it tight. "I'm sorry," she said. "I noticed your light was on."

He grunted noncommittally and turned around, striding over to his refrigerator. The fridge door was already open.

Thanks, I'll just let myself in, Zoey thought. Crossing Rune's threshold felt vaguely daring. It was the first time she'd ever visited him at night, without telling her parents. She knew how protective Mom and Dad could be, but it wasn't like she was up to anything. She stepped inside and pulled the door shut behind her.

Rune returned holding a little bottle of orange juice. "You're up early."

Zoey plopped onto the sofa. "This English paper is kicking my butt." She frowned. "I couldn't sleep."

Rune frowned back at her, but Zoey got the impression it was more out of curiosity than sympathy. There was so much about everyday life that seemed alien to him. High school apparently fell into that category.

"Did you go to school? I mean before…?"

"Not the way you're thinking," he said. "My training was more…focused."

He fell silent. Then again, nearly a dozen words in a row might have been a record for him. He looked past Zoey, not at her, distracted by something she knew he would never reveal.

"You should get some sleep," he added.

"I can't," she said. "Too much homework. And if I did fall asleep, I'd probably end up having nightmares about Othello."

At that he finally made eye contact. "Othello? A classmate of yours?"

She snorted. "No, he's a character in a play. I've got a paper due tomorrow—er, today."

"Ah."

Zoey was tired and frustrated, but she managed a smile.

And Rune stood there looking like he'd just stepped off the cover of a romance novel. She'd swear his hair was blowing in the breeze, even indoors.

Whenever Zoey could, she questioned Rune about the world he'd left behind. He usually pretended to be annoyed with her questions, but she figured if she were in his shoes, no one would be able to shut her up about where she'd come from. Now was a perfect time to learn some more. "Okay. I've got another one."

Rune rolled his eyes. "Don't you have to go to school soon?" He tried to look annoyed, but if he really wanted her to stop prying, he could make her. No death glare, no problems. She pressed on.

"The place you're from is called Saynim."

"That's right."

"So if you're a, uh, if you're Saynimese…"

"I'm a sayne."

She nodded. "And all the other things, dwarves and dragons and stuff. They're real, too?"

"We've gone over this before."

Indeed they had, on the day they first met. True, the details were elusive. But how could Zoey ever forget the day she learned that magic was real, that there was a world beyond her own, the world that Rune called home?

She got the impression that Rune was determined to keep her from learning anything more than that. As best as she could figure out, Rune had been on the run, but he was tight-lipped about why or from whom.

He simply said that he couldn't go home. He needed a place to stay. The least Zoey could do was put in a good word for him with her parents. After all, she did nearly run over him with her car.

A solid month later, Zoey was still dying to know more about the world Rune had left behind.

"Come on," she said, "it's almost Halloween." She started counting on her fingers. "I've already asked about dragons, unicorns, sea serpents… What about ghosts? Are they real?"

Rune sighed. "Yes. But not as common as you'd expect."

Zoey's jaw dropped. "Really? I was just throwing that one out there."

Rune shrugged.

"And hippogriffs?"

"Only children believe in hippogriffs."

Hm. That was the first time she'd ever struck out. "Okay, then how about mermaids?"

Rune shuddered—almost imperceptibly, but Zoey noticed. He simply said, "Of course."

"And they breathe underwater?" That would make beach vacations so much more awesome.

Rune said, "They weave the watery chaos," as if that was a straight answer.

"The what?"

Rune gritted his teeth. Zoey could tell he'd soon be done talking, but she gave him a smile and an encouraging nod.

"All Saynim folk are attuned to a chaos, at least a little. Air, earth, water, or fire usually, but there are a few others."

"I see." Zoey didn't see at all, but she tried to put it together. "So if you're an elf—"

"Your kindred has nothing to do with it," Rune said, shaking his head. "Anyone can weave any chaos. The sea nymphs in your Greek mythology? Water-weaving elves. Down south, there are water-weaving small folk."

"Small folk?"

"Tiny people." He indicated a bit above waist height. "And across the sea, there are water-weaving trolls."

"And it's the same for all these…chaoses?"

He shrugged. "More or less."

"Weird." Suddenly, Zoey remembered Caitlin's party.

"So," she began. She bit her lip and then continued. "Some friends and I are getting together tonight. Nothing special, just hanging out."

Rune nodded.

"I was wondering if maybe…you'd like to come along?"

"I have to work," Rune said matter-of-factly.

Zoey's heart sank into her stomach. *Of course*, she thought. *He's got his own life. Why would he want to…*

She sighed. "Okay. That's cool." She got up. "Maybe next time."

"Perhaps."

She gave Rune a small smile and slipped out the door. Rune waited on his stoop until she got safely into her own house.

He shut his door as soon as Zoey shut hers.

Zoey shook her head and trudged upstairs. That essay wasn't going to write itself, after all.

6

Brack woke up to a clockwork canary pecking at his thick skull. He grumbled and sat up on his side of the bed. By the embers of the portable heating stove at the foot of the bed, he glanced at her slumbering form, smiled, and stretched.

The canary perched on his broad shoulder, its whirring gears nudging Brack the rest of the way into wakefulness.

He brushed the automaton away, and it fluttered back to the clock on the wall and crawled into its hole. It peeked its head out to watch as Brack lumbered to the washbasin and splashed cool water against his pale and pitted face.

Through the rock wall, he could hear Duren snoring. Laurin, his eldest, had moved out last year, so Duren inherited his big brother's cavity in the bedrock. Whether he or his sister, Ulfa, was happier no longer to share a room was hard to say.

Laurin was bringing his intended over for supper this weekend, so Duren would have to give up his newfound privacy for a few days. Brack shook his head and chuckled. Soon, he'd be a father-in-law and, before too long, a grandfather. Just as well. Lately he'd noticed a few gray hairs mixed among the black.

The dwarf dressed in the near darkness. He put on thick trousers, work boots, and a cotton shirt with only a few grease stains on it.

"Brack?" Thora called.

"Go back to sleep, sweet," he whispered.

"But you need breakfast."

"Let me work a couple hours first."

Thora grunted contentedly and rolled back over.

Brack stepped into the great room and closed the door behind him. He passed by the stove and the large dining table and then through the door on the other side and into his workshop.

To his right was the bellows engine. Underneath was the firebox, its embers faintly glowing.

"Kettle," he called. "Up and at 'em."

The glow intensified.

"A little light, please?"

"What is matter?" a child's voice in a clipped accent said from the firebox. "Is it morning already?"

"Close enough. We've got a busy day ahead." Brack threaded his way through his workshop in the darkness. He reached a stack of cordwood beside the firebox and laid two quartered logs on the ghost of yesterday's flame. Agitated sparks flew free.

"Come on, old man," Brack chided. "We got work to do."

A jet of orange flame spat out of the firebox. Before it hit the floor, it had expanded and cooled, taking the form of a feathered, bat-winged reptile. It shook its red and gold tail feathers and looked up at Brack the same way Thora did when he asked for something special for supper and she didn't have the ingredients.

"If you please," Brack said.

The firedrake shook itself again and threw off sparks of flame. Once more, its shape changed. It grew until it became a young, golden-haired boy of perhaps ten. His white tunic bore not the slightest smudge of ash. In his hand he held a red flat cap with a golden feather in it. He raised a fair-skinned hand to his mouth and gave a dramatic yawn before gesturing toward the lanterns in brass wall sconces. Their fires leaped to life.

"That's more like it," Brack grumbled.

Brack surveyed his workshop. The cast-iron forge overshadowed half of the brick wall at the back. A steam engine next to it worked the bellows—or would once Kettle got it going—pumping fresh air into a pipe to stoke the flame.

A metalworker's lathe took up the rest of the back wall. A workbench flanked the side of the shop closest to the lathe, and a bank of supply lockers took up the far wall in front of the forge. Front and center stood a great stone anvil.

Brack tugged a leather apron from a peg on the wall. Tying it around himself, he stomped to the front of the shop, unlatched a couple of latches, and turned a crank. A large section of wall rose away, becoming a wooden awning and, in the process, opening a picture window onto the shop, telling the world that Brack was open for business.

Outside, he could just see Goblintown's central square in the distance. High above, glowing fungi overran the wooden planks supporting the cavern's roof. It gave the village a distinctive artificial sky crisscrossed with living patterns of blue-green light.

Kettle had lit the shop's streetlight along with the lights inside. It wouldn't be long before other early risers added their lights as well.

Brack secured the awning in place and went to his workbench. On the wall over his head was a simple hand-lettered sign:

H. Brackwater
Gearsmith, Precision Machinist
Magical Curiosities Made to Order
No Refunds

He fixed his beady black eyes on the mechanism he'd set on the workbench the night before. The calculating clock wasn't Brack's own work. The innkeeper up in Dunswale had bought it in Llinbach a few years ago. If he took better care of the thing, he wouldn't have to keep sending it to Brack for repairs.

But work put food on the table, so there was no point complaining. Brack rolled up his sleeves, exposing his muscular blue-white arms, leathery from long hours beside his forge. His hair, a tangle of black locks, was tied back at the nape of his neck. His beard was full but neatly trimmed.

Kettle set his red cap on the workbench. "Do you want me to start working on light fixtures for Mote Crankshaw?"

Brack kept his eyes on the mechanism in front of him. "No. Why don't you do this instead?" He scooted the calculating clock toward the spot where his assistant usually sat.

Kettle looked startled. "Are you sure? You love working with gears and stuff."

"Exactly," Brack said, and strode to the supply shelves for a big wooden box of parts. "I had a thought about these babies last night. I think I figured out why they ain't working."

From the box, Brack took a huge magnifying glass mounted on a wooden stand and a set of tiny instruments. Then he drew out a metal ball the size of a pea and held it between his thumb and forefinger. A dozen interlocking pieces made up the ball's outer shell. He found the smallest screwdriver in his set and used it to trip the catch. The thing's eight tiny legs opened like a flower in bloom.

Holding the contraption by one leg with a pair of tweezers, he flipped open its inner casing. He gently wrestled the mainspring free and reached for another, slightly larger one. With his tongue in his teeth, he applied just enough force to set the new spring in its place.

He grinned as he folded the whole thing back into its original shape and reset the trigger. Then he turned the tiny gadget over and cranked it up by applying the screwdriver to a hair-thin depression on the top.

"You think it works now?" Kettle said.

Brack smiled. He flicked the ball onto the workbench and it opened on impact. Eight tiny legs deployed. No longer a ball, the clockwork spider righted itself and scampered away. "Not too shabby."

Kettle grinned. "That was radiant, Brack!"

"Go find it, will you? It'll run down in a few seconds."

"Sure thing." Kettle hopped down from his stool at the workbench and scanned the flagstones for hints of movement.

A second later he stopped. "What was that?"

Brack looked up. Something small and black skittered across the street just outside the window. He caught the slightest odor of sewage.

A grumble escaped his throat. A pack of shadelings was the last thing he needed.

"Kettle, bring me Frieda," he said.

Brack's assistant donned his hat as he raced to the other side of the room. Mounted on the wall beside the supply lockers was a musketoon: smaller than a musket but more accurate than a blunderbuss. Perfect for home defense. Brack always kept it loaded, just in case.

Kettle took down the firearm and brought it to Brack. The dwarf ran his fingers along the barrel until they slipped over the trigger of the flintlock firing mechanism, hand-crafted from the finest dwarven gunmetal.

With his assistant at his side, Brack stepped outside and scanned the narrow street that led to the village square.

Shadelings weren't very smart, but they were mean and opportunistic. If they found something to eat, they'd steal it—and wreck the surrounding property out of pure spite. They were also small and quick, and their dark fur gave them natural camouflage.

Fortunately, Brack could see well enough in the dim foxfire. Here on the edge of town, houses and storefronts were carved into the earth. He noted the familiar shapes of the wooden buildings facing his shop and leading toward the square. Anything out of place…

Something darted through an alley across the street. Brack spun toward the movement, his heart racing, his fingers twitching.

Stay cool, he told himself. He took a second to draw the metallic chaos to himself, steeling his courage. As the forces of creation swirled and infused his body, his bones, he became tougher both mentally and physically.

Brack stalked forward across the cobblestones. At the corner, he noted dark shapes huddled around the neighbor's garbage bin. He made out half a dozen hunched forms, maybe half his height if they'd stood upright. Their naked tails twitched eagerly. A seventh, apparently standing in the garbage bin itself, tossed a pumpkin shell to its comrades. Brack could just make out its nimble, black paw before it went back to work in the bin. The shadelings jumped at the stolen treasure with abandon before it hit the ground.

Brack raised Frieda and growled, "Hyaah!"

The shadelings jumped. Two of them darted further down the alley. The one in the bin popped up to take stock of the situation.

The other four backed away from the bin and trained their eyes on Brack. The shadeling in the bin chittered a command as he bounded onto the ground and joined the other four in bolting toward him, the dim light flashing off their oversized incisors.

Brack squeezed the trigger, unleashing a thunderous report and a cloud of acrid smoke. The nearest shadeling fell, howling in pain. The other four scampered off in different directions.

Frieda was a repeater of a design Brack had seen in Llinbach. Along the stock was a slim, brass lever. With the muzzle pointed to the ground, Brack cranked the lever all the way forward, rotating the drum inside the mechanism to load another round and its requisite powder.

As he did this, lights flickered on up and down the narrow street. After barely thirty seconds, Mote Crankshaw appeared in the alley. Mote was a goblin as tall as Brack's youngest child, Ulfa. He was about Brack's age, but he carried his years more heavily. When he spied the scene, his eyes went wide and his face turned as red as his mutton-chop sideburns.

"Scumber!" he sputtered. His flame-red mutton chops danced. "You're gonna kill somebody shooting that thing off! What's going on?"

Brack frowned. "Pack of shadelings in your garbage bin."

"Shadelings!" Mote blurted. "All the way from the swamp?"

"Looks like," Brack said.

Thora dashed up the street, drawing her housecoat across her body. Duren and Ulfa followed close behind.

"Did you say 'shadelings'?" Thora whispered. "Heptifilius, what's going on?" She was worried; Brack could see it on her face. Before he could answer, she turned back to the children. "I told you to stay inside!" she scolded.

"It *is* shadelings!" Duren said, more in awe than fright. "Look!"

The rat-like creature Brack had shot writhed on the cobblestones.

"Did you shoot it, Papa?" The boy's voice cracked on the last word, and he blushed a little. "Is it gonna die?"

"Not on my account," Brack said.

Duren scrunched up his face, trying to remember. "Cause you don't use fell shot that kills, right?"

"Not if I can help it," Brack said. "Ferstitch hurts like fire, but it won't kill nothing."

The shadeling rolled a little too close to Brack's foot, and he kicked it away. "They don't even leave a mark."

"What's all this commotion!" Tiffy Jiggins barged into the gathering. Tiffy was a kindly, gray-haired matron, a smallkin woman at the hub of Goblintown's unofficial news service.

"Shadelings," Mote said. "Brack took care of 'em." He turned to the gearsmith. "How many'd you say there was?"

Brack was busy gesturing for Thora to take the children inside. He answered while keeping his eyes on his family. "Seven. The rest'll be halfway to the river by now—but I wouldn't stop you from setting traps and keeping your own firearms handy."

"By the core!" Tiffy said.

"And we'll need to do something with this one before the ferstich wears off," Brack said.

"Shadelings," Mote griped. "I can't remember the last time shadelings caused any problems in town."

"Been getting worse since Cruc Máw," Tiffy said, wagging her gray head.

Others appeared: Tom and Keeta Burntail from down on the square, with others following behind, mostly goblins like Mote or their close cousins, small folk like Tiffy. By now, more than half a dozen streetlights had been lit.

With the children safely through reluctantly inside, Thora rejoined the crowd.

Mote nodded at Tiffy. "You may have a point about Cruc Máw," he said. "You ask me, we still ain't heard the whole story there."

Tiffy leaned in, as if half the town wasn't within earshot. "I hear the King of Shadows was behind it."

"You got a direct line to the King of Shadows, Tiffy?" Mote said.

She scowled at him. "For your information, Mote Crankshaw"—Mote winced at the use of his full name—"I got a cousin in Cruc Máw. She says a gang of Nightwalkers stormed the Citadel."

"Things ain't been right around here for a while," Tom Burntail added as he and Keeta edged forward.

"What's all this—?" Keeta started, then gasped and grabbed her husband's arm when she saw the downed shadeling.

Mote and Brack explained how their morning began. "And another thing," Mote said in conclusion, "I'd like to know what Hova's got to say about all this."

A rumble of agreement shot through the crowd. The general attitude among Brack's neighbors was that the mayor, based aboveground in Dunswale, acted like he'd forgotten the Goblintown neighborhood even existed.

"He's a fool," Mote said. "That's why I keep saying we need to make nice with the Merlady."

Brack scoffed. "Silver and gold, Mote! You don't trust Hova, so you're just gonna roll over for the Merlady?"

"You got a better idea?"

The shadeling squirmed and pounded the cobblestones. Brack trained Frieda on it, and it inched away.

"Yeah," Brack said. "I'm gonna drag this beast to the tunnels and set it loose. Anybody coming with me?"

"We need somebody like the Merlady, Brack," Mote insisted. "You don't have to like it, but we all gotta face reality." As Brack expected, several of his neighbors murmured in agreement.

"Couldn't be any worse than the mayor," Tom said.

"We could at least find out what she wants," Tiffy added.

"I'll tell you what she wants," Brack said. "She wants to run this place—more than she already does!" He held up his hands to stave off the swelling argument. As he spoke, he allowed the metallic chaos to infuse him, stoking his courage and determination.

"She already controls trade up and down the river. I wouldn't be surprised if she's got her sights on Dunswale itself."

"How do we know she wasn't behind the shadelings in the first place?" Thora said. "They live in the swamp, after all. That's her territory." It was the first time Brack's wife had contributed to the conversation. His heart thumped with pride that she saw things the way he did.

"I heard there's a Nightwalker stalking around over in the Fallow," Tom said. "Anybody know anything about that?"

All eyes turned to Tiffy, who put on an expression of shock and disappointment. "How the rot should I know?"

When nobody else spoke up, Tom said, "Well, maybe he's the one that sent the shadelings."

"I ain't so sure," Mote said. "I hear there was a woman looking for him up in Dunswale, and not too keen on taking no for an answer, either. And we're talking about a woman from out of town, if you get my drift."

"*Another* Nightwalker?" Tiffy said.

Brack had heard from Kettle about the mysterious woman at the Drunken Dragon. Apparently, Mote had heard the same thing.

"I dunno," Mote said. "She's trouble at any rate. Something's brewing, that's for sure. You ask me, the King of Shadows has his fingers all over it—Cruc Máw, Nightwalkers. Why not those shadelings? If he's got people in Dunswale, you can bet he's got his eye on Goblintown, too."

Mote took a step toward Brack. "So who would you rather have running things, Brack? The King of Shadows or the Merlady?"

"He's right," someone murmured.

"Ain't no choice when you put it like that," another whispered. It was obvious which way the crowd was swaying.

These discussions usually ended the same way. Goblintowners would buy Brack's metal gadgets and fixtures but not his ideas.

"I'd rather we run things for ourselves—just as we always have," Brack said, hefting his firearm.

"I've lived here a lot longer than you, Brack," Mote said. "We do things a certain way."

"Maybe," Brack said. He looked at the crowd, a couple dozen strong—nearly every adult resident of Goblintown in an impromptu neighborhood council meeting. And he realized Mote had a point. Brack would fight for his family, his home, without batting an eye. But to fight against somebody like the Merlady— much less the King of Shadows? He knew a losing battle when he saw one.

He sighed and rested Frieda on his shoulder, then cast a glance toward the shadeling at his feet. "For now, who's gonna help me get rid of this pest?"

7

Rune woke up around noon. He took a quick shower and ate a breakfast of dry toast and orange juice. It was going to be a long day: he had quigs to convert, supplies to restock, and a sorcerer to tail. And he still needed to track down Mrs. Hollart and convince her to talk to her husband.

He should have kept running when he crossed the Mere. But Louisville was a big city—not the biggest by this world's standards, but bigger than anything he had ever seen.

It was the perfect haystack to get lost in…until it wasn't.

Boggs knew who he was and what he had been. Rune pushed that thought aside; he just had to get busy. If his past was catching up with him, he could always run farther. Louisville was a lot like Athelhoew: it was only a place, not somewhere he could ever really belong.

He put on his brown bomber jacket. Zoey's church kept coats and jackets to give to the poor, and she'd offered it to him when the weather first turned cool. The leather was cracked and worn nearly yellow at the elbows, but it looked like something a Fallowman would wear, and that, too, was good enough.

Rune had fixed the sheaths of his short, bronze knives behind his back where they'd be hidden underneath his jacket. The sculpted bone handles fit perfectly in his slender hands.

Last of all, he considered his pistol. With its ten-inch-long barrel, it was Rune's most effective weapon, though not the subtlest. Along with a cartridge case for extra powder and shot, it was bound to attract notice. That was the opposite of what Rune wanted.

And, he reminded himself, using it wasn't currently an option. He opened his carriage case, already knowing what he would find:

a handful of spare flints, a single lead ball, and a quig to keep the magic fresh. Back at the Haw, Rune would have been reprovisioned with a dozen balls of fell shot fresh from the alchemists. That was one more thing he'd have to take care of somehow.

Leaving his apartment, he glanced across the backyard to the Colemans' house. He stepped off the stoop and was heading for the picket fence when a woman called his name. He braced himself.

"Yes, Mrs. Coleman?"

"I'm glad I caught you," Zoey's mother said. "Would you come in for a minute?"

Rune took a measured breath. He nodded and crossed the yard, none too quickly.

Mrs. Coleman wasn't especially tall, but she had a force of personality, that Rune had come to respect. He had seen her warm and engaging side, but that wasn't the side she was showing him today.

She stood rigidly on the stoop, holding the door for him. Rune couldn't read her expression. At least it wasn't openly hostile.

As soon as he crossed the Colemans' threshold, he felt a subtle snap. Thresholds held a power that few in this world understood. Magically speaking, a home could be a fortress. Beings like Rune thought twice about crossing them unbidden lest they find themselves stripped of their powers.

As an invited guest, Rune didn't have that to worry about. He just had to find a plausible story about the rent money he owed.

"I got paid last night, Mrs. Coleman," he said. "I just have to—"

"The rent can wait, Rune," Mrs. Coleman interrupted. Rune quirked an eyebrow, suddenly disoriented.

"Have a seat." She took her own seat at the kitchen table. The room was homey in a mundane sort of way: cluttered with jars for salt and flour and other cooking essentials, decorative wall-hangings, and gaudy ceramic knick-knacks. The refrigerator was festooned with family photos.

"You're settling into your job?"

Rune nodded, but his throat went dry. He sat down across from her.

"What is it you're doing again?"

He thought for a second, hopefully not long enough to raise suspicions. "I…fix things."

"I see," she said. "And you work for…?"

"His name's Hollart," Rune said. He had an inspiration and added, "Home repair."

Mrs. Coleman looked him in the eye. She still didn't seem hostile, only serious. "Raymond and I are happy for you to rent our apartment, Rune. We've seen too many young people fall through the cracks. It's not much, but it's something we can do."

"Do not think I'm ungrateful."

"You're how old? Nineteen? Twenty?"

"Twenty," Rune said. At least, that's what his new fake identification card said. And it might have been true. Time worked differently in the Fallow. If Mrs. Coleman thought he looked like a twenty-year-old Fallowman, who was he to argue? At any rate, the twinge of dread and revulsion that passed through his body warned him against repeating his lie any time soon.

"And when will you turn twenty-one?"

"My birthday's in the spring." Mrs. Coleman didn't seem to notice the evasion. Neither, apparently, did the Covenant.

"Zoey isn't quite eighteen, you know," she said, folding her hands together.

"Yes…?"

Mrs. Coleman expelled a breath. "Rune, Raymond and I trust our daughter. At least, we try to."

Another uncomfortable pause. Rune tapped his fingers on his thigh.

"I know she paid you a visit this morning."

"Yes. Something about an English project."

"Rune," Mrs. Coleman said. Her voice went flat.

Rune's pulse pounded at his temples. There was a danger here he couldn't grasp. "I'm…sorry?"

She held up a hand. "I'm not accusing you of anything. I just wanted you to know…that *I* know." She sighed and crossed her arms. "Zoey's got her whole life ahead of her. But she can't always keep her head out of the clouds."

"Yes, ma'am."

She laid her palms flat on the table and leaned forward. "That's all I wanted to say."

"Yes, ma'am."

"Are you on your way to work? I don't want to keep you."

"It's not a problem. Thank you."

Rune got up, bowed curtly, and excused himself.

Soon he was on a city bus, pondering the conversation. Did Mrs. Coleman think he had designs on Zoey? The rules about those sorts of things evaded him, but the message was clear enough: stay clear of my daughter. He shuddered as he thought of his own mother the time when she found him and Jussie Crangle picking strawberries behind the carriage house. At least Mrs. Coleman couldn't turn anybody into anything.

He got off at a stop on Bardstown Road fifteen minutes or so away from home and began to walk. Foot traffic was light. It seemed that most Fallow folk preferred to ride in their automobiles rather than walk or take the bus. He strolled down the tree-lined streets taking in the sights.

Many of the buildings looked old by this world's standards. Some of them might have once been houses. He spied a tattoo parlor, an antique shop, and a vintage clothing shop. The aroma of spices and cooking broths and sauces wafted from high-end restaurants getting ready for the supper crowd. A dozen genres of music called to him from the doorways of a dozen businesses. Many establishments sported colorful awnings, murals, or vibrantly colored window trim. He had visited Bardstown Road many times in the past month, but he still paused to wonder how a Fallow neighborhood could remind him so much of home.

At last, he stood outside a little green shop with a purple awning and a sign above the door that read "Madam Samarra's," the text curling around a drawing of a single, large eye.

The subtle hint of incense greeted him as he stepped into the cramped room. A bell jingled as he swung the door open and again as it closed behind him.

Shelves reached from the floor to the ceiling, with only a little gap for access to Madam Samarra's office in the back. Books took up half of one wall—everything from dusty tomes kept under glass to cheap, photocopied pamphlets with titles like "Palmistry Made Easy" and "Opening Your Third Eye."

Most of the shop was given over to trinkets of every sort. There were crystal pendants, chalices, wands, figurines of clay and wood and stone and metal. Near the cashier's counter were Madam Samarra's dry goods: sticks and cones of incense, herbs both fresh and dried, blocks of beeswax, and glass jars filled with assorted questionable contents. She even had a monkey's paw—obviously fake—high on the shelf over the cash register.

Madam Samarra herself was a slight woman, nearly swallowed up by her green and gold flower-print muumuu. A green silken headscarf barely contained her curly, graying hair, and enormous hoop earrings framed her pink face.

She sat behind the cash register finishing a transaction with a customer, explaining the proper use of the Tibetan meditation bowl the woman had just purchased. When she caught sight of Rune, she registered the slightest expression of surprise. Then she wrapped the bowl in brown paper, taped it secure, and slid it back to the purchaser.

"Thank you, come again," she said.

As soon as the other woman left the shop, Madam Samarra looked toward Rune and turned on the charm. "And what can I do for you, sir?" she asked with a smile. It wasn't sincere, of course, unless the giddy joy of a hawker about to separate a buyer from his money could be sincere.

"I wonder if I could take a look in the back," Rune said.

"You gonna buy something or just look around like the last time?"

Rune glanced around the room, assuring himself no one else had come in. "I'm looking for a bottomless bag if you have one. And some shot, 0.54 caliber. Preferably ferstitch."

She scoffed as she slid off her stool. "I don't carry elf shot. Not enough demand." She held open the drapery separating the showroom from the rest of the building. Just inside and to the right was a narrow door labeled "Storage."

"But I've got a couple of bottomless bags. And maybe some other things you'd like, hmm?"

She turned a big brass key and unlocked the door to the storage closet. When she snapped her fingers, oil lamps sprung to life all around the room. The inside was twice as big as the outer showroom, with shelves on all four walls.

"You want elf shot, go see a guy in Goblintown. A dwarf named Brackwater. Anything metal, he's your guy. This is one of his, see?" She pulled a small box, about as big as Rune's cartridge box, from the nearest shelf. It didn't look to Rune like anything but a mass of tiny brass gears in a lead frame, with a crank on top and a plunger-like lever on one end.

"It's an indifference engine. Wind it up, and people don't pay any attention to you."

"Really?"

"It only works for a few seconds, but it'll get you out of a tight fix. Twenty-eight hundred dollars."

Rune converted dollars to quigs in his head, but he already knew he couldn't afford it. "About those bottomless bags?"

"Over here." Madam Samarra walked briskly to the far end of the storage room, dragging a rolling ladder along behind her. She clambered up to about the limit of Rune's reach and pulled down two leather bags. The smallest was as big as a woman's purse. She set this one in Rune's hand and announced, "That one'll hold up to a hundred sixty pounds, easy."

The other one was twice as large and decorated with ornate beadwork. "That one goes up to about five hundred pounds."

"How much?"

"Seventeen fifty for the little one. I gotta take four thousand for the big one because of the beading. That's quality work, there."

Rune frowned. "Can I look around?"

"If you're buying, take your time." She crossed her arms.

He ran his hands along the shelves. They weren't packed like the ones outside. In fact, there were a lot of empty spaces.

"Have you done any business with a man by the name of Phipps? He sometimes goes by Jericho."

"I don't sell the good stuff to just anybody," Madam Samarra said.

"I don't suppose you could help me find an address in Louisville?"

Madam Samarra chuckled. "You never heard of the Internet? I knew you were fresh, kid, but for crying out loud!"

Rune's face warmed, but he kept his composure.

"I ain't got all day. You gonna buy something or not?"

He saw nothing he wanted, but he wasn't getting anything out of Madam Samarra if he didn't buy something. "What's this?" He pointed to a little tortoise shell box, no bigger than a pack of cards.

"Bottomless snuffbox," she said. "Holds about a year's worth."

It took a slight effort to get the lid off, so at least the seal worked. And it was, in fact, packed full of pungent tobacco. Seal or no seal, the smell was repulsive.

"I'll let you have it for a hundred thirty," Madam Samarra said. "Make it a hundred fifty, and I'll look up that address for you. Cash or credit?"

"Cash," Rune said, holding out a magic bean. "Assuming you take quigs."

Rune jotted notes in his journal on his bus ride downtown. He'd gotten an address for Marla Davis, Jo Ellen Hollart's sister, from Madam Samarra. He promised himself he would check it out first thing in the morning. He also noted the name of the dwarf in Goblintown who might sell him some fell shot.

But he wouldn't need those tonight. Tonight his only plan was to observe. Soon enough, the bus stopped in front of the Brown Hotel. From there, Rune hiked south into Old Louisville.

Despite its name, Old Louisville wasn't the oldest part of the city, but it had maintained its historic charm better than most neighborhoods. It spread out for a few dozen city blocks north of the university: row after row of brick houses in an eclectic, richly ornamented style.

Rune stood beneath a tree at the edge of the sidewalk, studying his surroundings. Nobody noticed him. Under a powerful veil of glamour, he was invisible. He occasionally stepped away from his tree when a group of pedestrians strolled past, overflowing the sidewalk. One time, a beagle, confused by what its nose was telling it, sniffed at him as it passed.

Confounding the minds and perceptions of Fallow folk was no problem for weavers of the airy chaos, but animals had keener senses. Rune could keep a Fallowman from seeing him, but he couldn't always keep a dog or cat from smelling him. Fortunately, the dog's owner had places to be.

The sun had set by the time the first car pulled into Keenan Phipps's narrow driveway across the street. A couple got out, and a man perhaps in his early forties greeted them as soon as they rang the doorbell. Jazz music played on the sorcerer's phono... music-playing thing. Whatever they called it.

Even from across the street, the host's imposing presence was obvious. His bright, intelligent eyes blazed with intensity, and he carried himself with obvious grace. As he exchanged pleasantries on the colonnaded porch, Phipps's body language projected both warmth and restless energy. He smiled as he clapped a vigorous hand on his male guest's shoulder and ushered the couple into his home. As he followed them inside, he glanced across the street, and for a fleeting second Rune feared he had been spotted.

This one could be trouble. His house was probably strongly warded: iron implements, boughs of hawthorn or rowan wood, and possibly other, less obvious tricks. It was a wonder that Boggs, the man's duplicitous servant, could get anything done in there.

And Rune hadn't counted on Phipps having company. Not that he intended to do anything—you don't just barge in on a sorcerer without preparation. But even an ordinary house could pose problems. Unlike Mrs. Coleman, Phipps had never invited Rune in; crossing the threshold unbidden was out of the question.

At most, Rune hoped to investigate the property once the darkness could mask his presence even without glamour. If he was lucky, he'd learn something that could give him an edge. He might even contact Boggs and learn more about what he was up against. All of that would be harder if Phipps was entertaining.

Another car pulled up in front of the house. The woman who got out greeted two men who arrived on foot at the same time—college students walking from campus from the look of them. Five minutes later, two others also walked up. Phipps greeted each visitor at the door and welcomed them in.

Another car, a pale green vehicle with a dent on the passenger door, parked in front of Rune's tree. He stepped out of the way as three more young people got out: a man and two women, trading jokes and gossip.

And then Rune's heart sank.

One of the women was Zoey. She crossed the street with her two friends, heading straight for Phipps's walkway.

This was the party she'd been invited to?

Heart pounding, Rune allowed his glamour to fall. Emerging literally from the shadows, he took off across the street.

"Zoey," he called, urgently if not loudly. She spun at the sound of her name.

"Rune?" she said. She smiled but cocked her head to one side. "How did you…?"

"Is this your friend?" the other woman asked, grinning. "I'm Caitlin. Zoey's told me *all* about you!"

Zoey elbowed Caitlin and gestured toward the young man. "And this is Zack." Zack said nothing, but he raked his fingers through his shock of black hair and nodded. He slipped a long, spindly arm around Caitlin's waist.

"Zoey was really bummed you had to work," Caitlin said, her eyes dancing. Zoey's cheeks betrayed a subtle blush. "Managed to get off early, then?"

"Zoey, I don't think—"

The door opened, and Phipps called, "Caitlin, good to see you! Are these the friends you told me about?"

"Hey, Jericho!" Caitlin called. She dragged Zack toward the porch, though he didn't seem to take much convincing.

Rune glanced watched them go. "Zoey," he tried again. "You really shouldn't—"

"Listen," she interrupted. "I know what you're going to say. But I promise, this is not some wild college party. Caitlin says this guy's on the up and up. Super strict. He probably doesn't even drink. So everything is rated Z for Zoey."

"That's not what I—"

"Come on, you two!" Caitlin called. Zoey pulled away from Rune and headed toward the front door. Rune gritted his teeth and followed. Another ten feet, and she'd be in the sorcerer's lair.

"This is my friend, Zoey," Caitlin said to Phipps. "And *that*," she beamed, "is her...uh..."

"That's Rune," Zoey said, glancing daggers at Caitlin. In the time it had taken to exchange introductions, Zoey had ascended the steps and was standing outside the door. Rune was just a few steps behind.

"Rune, is it?" the sorcerer said. "What an interesting name."

"Pleased to me you, sir."

"You can call me Jericho. Come on in."

The words thrummed like a violin string sharply plucked, snapping Rune to attention.

He'd been invited in. The Covenant was now satisfied, and he could cross Phipps's threshold unhindered.

A look inside might tell him something he needed to know. Was this man Phipps the threat that Boggs made him out to be? Did he have any weaknesses Rune could exploit?

He cast an eye toward Zoey, who was oblivious to his windfall...and her own danger. She was going to go in whether Rune did or not. What kind of trouble was she making for herself? And what could he do about it? He'd have to keep an eye on her, be ready to get her out at a moment's notice. He didn't need the distraction—Phipps called for his undivided attention.

But when was he going to get this chance again?

He eyed the sorcerer's outstretched hand. Time stood still as Rune reflected on the disaster this evening might become.

Wrack it, he thought as he shook Phipps's hand and let himself be shepherded inside.

8

Rune swallowed as he stepped into Keenan Phipps's foyer. Zoey was only a step ahead of him and completely unaware of the danger.

"Everyone is in the sitting room," the sorcerer said, gesturing to the left. To the right was a formal dining room. Straight ahead was both a staircase going up and a hallway to the back of the house.

The dark wood floor and upholstered furniture gave the sitting room a warm, earthy feel. Caitlin, Zack, and Zoey milled about, meeting the sorcerer's other guests. Rune kept an eye on them as he studied the room.

The décor was eclectic. The walls sported prints inspired by life in ancient times: a tree laden with brightly colored birds, sandy pyramids, and fishermen on a river bounded by papyrus reeds. A luxurious rug of intricate pattern marked off an intimate sitting area facing a green tiled fireplace. Bay windows on the opposite wall offered a view of the street. The dimmed electric lights were supplemented by red, green, black, and yellow candles on the fireplace mantel and end tables. The mantel was also home to a collection of photos of a younger Phipps visiting European, Asian, and African landmarks that even Rune had heard of.

Zoey took in everything in wide-eyed awe. She stared at the prints on the walls. With a widening grin, she turned to the bookshelves, running her fingers over every volume. The books were as eclectic as the décor. Judging by the titles, Phipps had wide-ranging interests: not only travel and photography but also history, philosophy, mythology and religion, physics and engineering.

Their host was busy making introductions. "This is Greg and his wife, Ophelia," he said, gesturing to the couple who'd been the first to arrive. Caitlin and Zack nodded and introduced themselves. Zoey pulled herself away from the bookshelves to join them.

A woman Caitlin's age, the one Rune had watched getting out of her car, approached him. Her nose ring twinkled in the dancing lights of the candles. "I'm Cassie," she said with a broad smile. She offered Rune her hand. He took it but avoided eye contact. He was too busy keeping track of Zoey, Phipps, and everybody else in the room. There were too many moving elements, too many variables. If this had been a proper errand, he'd have Saffron or Goodfellow for backup, a second set of eyes to keep tabs on the situation.

"Do you go to U of L, too? I've never seen you on campus." Cassie's eyes sparkled.

"No."

Cassie twirled a lock of purple hair around her finger. "How do you know Jericho?"

It took Rune half a second to remember Phipps's byname. "I don't," he said. "I'm with Zoey." He gestured to his landlord's daughter, who had joined a small circle around the sorcerer and had started peppering him with questions about his travels.

Cassie frowned. "Oh."

Phipps said something about a camel ride in Egypt. Zoey lowered her eyes and held back a giggle. Keenan Phipps was nothing if not a charmer, it seemed—and naturally. Rune perceived no magical intervention: no air to bend the mind, no water to stir the emotions.

Cassie shrugged and said, "Well…nice meeting you." She wandered off, which was fine with Rune. It was time he got to know his host.

He took a second to draw up the airy chaos around him. With a deep, cleansing breath, he allowed its essence to fill him, to clarify his vision and sharpen his wits. If this Fallowman was good enough, he might pick up on the ebb and flow of mystic forces near him. As long as Rune didn't direct his magic outward, though, the sorcerer would never sense it.

He strode toward Jericho, who stood in front of the bay windows. The sorcerer was taller than Rune and broader through the shoulders. His body language bespoke refinement and confidence as he engaged in small talk with Zoey.

"What are your plans after graduation?" he said.

She glanced at Caitlin and then the others around the circle. "I've applied to a few schools," she said. "I guess I'll start hearing back pretty soon. Then it'll all depend on how much financial aid I can get. Maybe I'll hang around here for a while, get some hours somewhere local."

"It's always smart to consider your options," Jericho said.

"That's what my dad says."

"Listen to him." Jericho gave Zoey an approving nod and then leaned in, lowering his voice as if telling a secret. "But don't ever give up on your dreams." He smiled brightly, and it reached all the way up to his eyes.

He noticed Rune standing at Zoey's shoulder and extended his hand. "And what about you…Rune, is it? Where do you go to school?" He looked Rune directly in the eye, and Rune returned the gesture.

"I'm not a student."

"A working man," the sorcerer said with a smile. "Like my father. Good for you."

Rune gave him a neutral shrug.

"Your name is Scandinavian, isn't it? Swedish maybe? It means 'secret.' Mystery. Something like that. How fascinating that your parents would give you such a name."

"I suppose."

"Jericho's middle name is Mystery," Caitlin said, grinning.

He answered her smile with another of his own. "I take it your chemistry test went well?"

"Thanks to you!" Caitlin beamed. Answering Zoey's quizzical expression, she explained, "Jericho gave me a doohickey. What did you call it?"

"A talisman," he explained. "Just something to clear and focus the mind." He waved off an objection that never came. "I assure you, it isn't cheating to go into a test with the proper mental disposition."

Rune kept his mind sharp as a knife, riding the surge of his own airy chaos. If Jericho was doing magical favors for these young people…

"It was like everything clicked into place, you know?" Caitlin continued. "After the test, a lot of folks said it was super hard. I thought I'd done pretty well, but I never expected a 96! That was the highest in the class—and all because of a feather and some cedar chips and a scrap of paper in a little bag!"

That got the attention of the two young men who'd arrived before Zoey and her friends. They stepped out of the corner and drifted to the edge of Jericho's little circle.

"The tools are only there to give shape to what's already inside you," the sorcerer explained. "They connect your own deepest self with the powers of creation. Master those powers and you can master anything."

Everyone else gathered around. Jericho's eyes gleamed. He was in his element, delivering an impromptu lecture with people hanging on his every word. The two men crowded Rune and Zoey closer to Jericho, giving them a front-row view of what came next.

"Are you a magician?" Cassie asked in hushed tones.

Jericho smiled broadly. Unlike Saynim folk, mages in the Fallow weren't bound by the Covenant. Nothing kept them from revealing their true nature—though doing so had become unfashionable since the so-called Age of Enlightenment. Another byproduct of the Dream Book, Rune supposed.

Apparently Jericho was had no qualms about the subject. "Magic is simply the application of knowledge," he said. It wasn't an open admission that he possessed supernatural powers, but it was close. "It's mastering the powers of creation, knowing how the world really works so you can make it work for *you*."

"The powers of creation," Caitlin said reverently, though probably not understanding half of what the sorcerer meant. Zoey grasped Rune's arm. Her eyes twinkled when she looked up at him, but he silenced her with a disapproving glare.

Jericho nodded. "Take the classical elements of Greek philosophy. The element of air, for instance, is connected to the mind. The feather and the cedar chips I gave you—as well as a few other things that went into your talisman—helped make the connection personal."

"The classical elements," one of the college guys said. "I remember them: air, earth, water, and fire, right?"

"Indeed, Mike," Jericho said. "Or, if you prefer the Chinese model, it's wood, water, earth, metal, and fire."

Mike scrunched his face. "But which one is right?"

"That's the wrong question," Jericho said. "If it works, it's right. The elements are simply signposts to the many ways the spiritual and the material impinge upon each other."

"He forgot the element of surprise," Mike's friend muttered, holding back a chuckle.

"Davanté, is it?" Jericho said. His eyes flashed, though he never dropped his affable smile. "I've found that a limited worldview is a terrible impediment to true learning." He looked the second young man in the eye, and now Rune did sense a surge of magic—a subtle impulse of something circling Davanté's body.

"Don't be the victim of your own ignorance," the sorcerer continued. The magic dove into Davanté's heart. He started to sweat, and his eyes grew wide with sudden fright. The others gasped or frowned in confusion.

"Open your mind. Take control. Be the master of your own destiny."

Davanté took a step backwards and nearly tripped over an end table. Rune glanced between the sorcerer and the youngling, hoping he wouldn't have to intervene.

"You don't look well," Jericho said. "Mike, there are glasses set out in the kitchen. Bring your friend some water, will you?"

Mike excused himself, smirking. Rune wondered if he'd seen Jericho pull tricks like this before.

Davanté took a deep breath and stood up straight.

"And I should check on dinner," Jericho said. "It should nearly be done. If you'll excuse me." He slid past his guests and into the foyer.

Zoey pulled Rune aside, her eyes as wide as Davanté's, though more with wonder than panic. "You never told me normal people could do magic!" she hissed.

"You never asked."

"I never—" Zoey grumbled something and turned away.

"Zoey, we need to get out of here."

But she had already left him to talk with Caitlin and Zack. Seconds later, Mike appeared with a glass of ice water for Davanté.

There were no other sounds in the house: just the shuffling of serving trays in the kitchen and hushed conversations in the sitting room.

But what was Jericho up to? His talk about taking control, commanding the powers of creation, made Rune nervous. It sounded like something the King of Shadows might promise a Fallow sorcerer whom he found useful.

"Ooh!" Zoey whispered, shaking Rune from his thoughts. She had drifted out of the sitting room and down the hall. Rune dodged past Greg and Ophelia to catch up to her.

She had found the library. Floor-to-ceiling bookshelves lined two walls, with a writing desk in one corner and two smallish windows opposite the door. The shelves were full not only with books but also more souvenirs from Jericho's travels. A comfortable chair and floor lamp rested opposite the desk in front of a wall of books. Near the floor lamp was a huge ceramic pot decorated around the lip with intricate Celtic knot designs.

Rune entered the room with a start. He couldn't see anything alarming, but his augmented senses told him there was trouble afoot—a presence in the room that he had felt before.

Zoey had found the library, but she hadn't yet discovered its unseen occupant, hidden behind a veil of glamour.

Rune drew his daggers.

"Zoey, leave now," he said, never taking his eyes off the reading chair.

"What are you talking about?" Zoey said.

"Now. Get out."

The woman allowed her glamour to slip as she rose from the chair. She was nearly as tall as Rune and just as fair-skinned, but with brown eyes rather than steely gray. Atop her head was an unruly shock of wavy, jet-black hair, and on her mouth was a cruel, thin line of a smile.

Her umbersay cloak roiled like a storm cloud. She threw it back to reveal black trousers, boots, and doublet over a white cotton shirt. A leather baldric crossed her chest right to left, with a scabbard fastened where it crossed above her left hip.

She took a step forward, drawing a sword of dwarven bronze and leveling it at Rune.

Zoey gasped and stepped backwards.

Rune gritted his teeth. "Avice."

"Dancer, if you please," the woman answered with a haughty smirk. "I'm on an errand, after all. It's been a while."

"Not long enough." He took a step forward. "You seem well."

"Your shot only grazed me," she said, patting her side.

"You moved too fast," Rune said. With a sideways glance, he added, "Now, Zoey. Go!"

Before Zoey could move, Avice gestured with her left hand. A fierce wind churned up and whistled through the room. The door slammed shut, and the ceramic pot shook as if it might topple over.

The air pressure spiked.

"You have no claim on the girl," Rune said.

"You're concerned about her, eh? Good to know."

Rune took a swipe at her with his dagger, but the woman's longer sword held him back.

"R-rune?" Zoey whimpered. She fought with the doorknob, but it wouldn't give.

"Let her go," Rune said.

"Hey!" Zoey shouted, pounding on the door. "Let us out!"

"You're wasting your breath, child," Avice said. "No one can hear you; I've seen to that."

It was true. Rune could sense the swirl of airy chaos enveloping the room, sealing it off from any Fallowman's perception.

"Avice, we can settle this between us."

"It's too late for that, cousin," Avice said. "You know what I want. Turn it over, and I'll think about letting your little pet go."

Zoey gasped. "You two are *cousins*?"

"It's a long story"

"One that has reached its end." In a single, fluid motion, Avice shifted her sword to her left hand and drew a pistol from her belt.

Rune glanced toward Zoey, who was pounding on the door again. He knew she would be next.

Avice aimed for the center of Rune's chest and pulled the trigger.

9

The pistol's report thundered through the room. For a second, Zoey couldn't hear anything. She screamed and fell to her knees. What else could she do? She threw her arms over her head, choking on the acrid smoke.

Her whole body shaking, she forced herself to look up between her elbows. Rune had fallen beside her. He groaned as he twisted and flailed on the floor. Her heart leaped into her throat as it dawned on her that the woman called Avice would come for her next.

Please God, no!

"Now, are you ready to cooperate?" Rune's cousin said. She was reloading her weapon, an old-fashioned dueling pistol like something out of a movie. She moved with easy grace, unhurried, no stranger to violence. She was in control and she knew it.

"R-Rune," Zoey whispered. He thrashed about, gulping labored breaths.

"Claeus is busy right now," Avice taunted. It took Zoey half a second to realize she was talking about Rune. Avice slid her pistol's ramrod into its sleeve and tucked the weapon back into her belt. Sometime during the commotion, she had sheathed her sword as well.

Zoey struggled to steady her breathing. Why wasn't anybody coming? Caitlin and the others must have heard the gunshot!

She had to do something—but what? "He didn't do anything to you!" she shouted, her voice quavering.

Avice laughed. "He's done more than you know, youngling. You'd do well to stay clear of him."

Rune gasped.

"We'll be on our way now," she continued. "Come along, cousin." She kicked Rune's knives away and stooped to grab him by the collar of his jacket.

That was it? She was just going to haul Rune away—but then what?

"He needs a doctor," Zoey said, rising to her feet. "He's been shot."

"Yes, I shot him. Weren't you paying attention?"

That's when something snapped. Zoey didn't know who this woman was, but she had hurt Rune. This had gone far enough.

Still shaking, she sprung forward.

Rune's cousin lifted her right hand, made a fist, and brought it down again with a jerk as if pulling something out of the air. A chill breeze passed invisibly through Zoey.

The ceramic pot beside the reading lamp rattled as Zoey collided with the woman.

Avice's eyes widened as she pushed Zoey onto her backside. "That should have…" she muttered. Zoey could see the realization dawn. "You've got the smell of iron."

"What are you talking about?" Zoey scrambled to her feet. What's that supposed to mean: the smell of iron? She instinctively reached for the pendant around her neck, the wrought iron heart pendant from the art fair.

"Avice!" Rune groaned. Both women turned toward him. He was standing unsteadily, balancing himself with a trembling hand on the nearest bookshelf. There wasn't a drop of blood on him— which only added to Zoey's panic and confusion.

Avice drew her pistol once more and leveled it. Rune flinched, anticipating another shot.

"No!" Zoey yelled.

"Stop right there!" another voice hollered, startling everyone.

A tiny figure stood balanced on the lip of the ceramic pot, and Zoey couldn't imagine where he had come from: a greasy, shabbily dressed man who looked like he'd taken a few extra trips to the buffet line. One second, he was barely two feet tall, but as he hopped onto the carpet and his feet hit the ground, he grew to a little over five feet.

He raised a shaking finger toward Rune's cousin. She trained the pistol on him.

The newcomer squeaked, "That's enough of that."

"Stay out of things that don't concern you, Boggs."

Zoey could see the fear in his watery eyes and the sweat on his sallow skin, but he stood his ground.

"S-sacred hospitality concerns me p-plenty," he said. "This man is Jericho's guest."

"As am I," Avice said.

"Then y-you ought to know better." He gestured toward Zoey. "You think I didn't see how your glamour didn't work on the girl?"

"She bears iron!"

Zoey clutched her pendant.

"Th-that may be, Miss Dancer, but that ain't the whole story. The Covenant's the Covenant. You're all guests in this house."

"Then I'll have to cut my visit short." She swung her pistol toward Zoey.

The room spun as Zoey stared down the barrel.

Everything shifted into slow motion. The new guy—Boggs—gestured as if shoving something big and heavy into the woman's torso. Her eyes flashed with sudden terror. It only lasted for a heartbeat, but it gave Boggs a chance to grab Rune in one hand and Zoey in the other.

Moving faster than he had any right to, Boggs yanked them both toward the ceramic pot.

"Drop the necklace!"

"What?"

"Now, if you want to get out of here!"

Zoey pulled the leather cord over her head and flung it to the floor.

Boggs gave her a second tug, and now they didn't simply move toward the pot; they moved *into* it. Zoey felt her whole body shrink in upon itself. It didn't hurt, but it wasn't fun, either. Her vision went black. Her ears popped. She felt a little nauseated.

And then it was over. She opened her eyes and saw Boggs guiding Rune ahead of her down a spiral staircase.

"This way!" he called.

She looked up and saw the ceiling of the library a hundred feet above them. A gigantic Avice—Dancer, whatever her name was—loomed overhead.

Zoey had no choice but to follow Boggs. At the bottom of the stairs, she saw an old-fashioned sitting room: wooden chairs, an upholstered sofa, and a kerosene lamp on an elegant end table.

"Boggs!" Avice called from above. Her voice echoed through the room. Boggs let out a frantic squeak.

"You're gonna be alright, Mr. Rune," Boggs said. He led him into the room, pulling off the bomber jacket and easing him down onto the sofa.

"BOGGS!" Avice shouted. Her voice made the lamp rattle.

Zoey whimpered. Her sanity must be slipping away. What had she gotten herself into? She'd listened to Caitlin's stories about this "cool guy" she'd seen around campus, how he took an interest in some college students and really seemed to care about them. "He *knows* things," Caitlin had said.

"Don't pay her no mind." Boggs's words pulled Zoey back to the present. Despite what he'd said, the look in his eyes betrayed terror. "She can't get in without my permission—and that ain't gonna happen."

"B-but…" Zoey stammered. "But where are we?"

"My living room. You wanna bring me some cold water from the kitchen?" He gestured toward a doorway tucked behind the staircase. Then he went back to unlacing Rune's shirt.

"Your living room?" Zoey was frantic. "Where's Jericho's library? Avice? The pot?"

"We're inside the pot," Boggs said. "Come on, Mr. Rune, slow and easy breaths. That's right." He looked at Zoey. "Time and space don't always work the same for us folks," he said. "Some water please?"

"Boggs," Avice thundered, "I command you to hand over my prisoner!"

"She'll give up soon enough." Boggs swallowed. "I think."

Zoey headed for the kitchen, her heart pounding.

"And there's a stack of dishrags by the pitchers," Boggs called. "I'll need a couple of those, too."

The kitchen was small and plain but functional. Zoey found two water pitchers and the dishcloths on a small side table. She grabbed the nearest pitcher and a stack of cloths and rushed back to the living room on wobbly legs.

"Cold water!" Boggs said when he saw her. "The blue one!"

Zoey stopped in her tracks. Only then did she feel the warmth of the pitcher. It was decorated with red stripes; the one still on the table was blue. She switched pitchers and hurried back.

Boggs took the pitcher, doused a dishcloth in cold water, and held it to Rune's bare chest.

"Hold that," he said, pushing the pitcher back into Zoey's hands. It started to refill itself as soon as she took it.

"That's…you can't…. Where…?"

Boggs kept his hands pressed to Rune's chest. He began to hum an eerie, ancient tune, something not of this earth. The room felt suddenly cooler, and Rune seemed to relax.

The stranger continued to hum, or maybe it was a chant. Several minutes passed before he said, "How's that?"

"Better," Rune whispered. "Avice—" He tried to stand up but winced in pain. Boggs pushed him back against the sofa.

"He got shot," Zoey muttered. "How…? There isn't even any blood!"

"Fell shot don't leave a mark," Boggs said. "That don't mean it can't make your life miserable. But she didn't mean to kill him or he'd be dead by now."

"That's…great?"

"Let me have some more water."

Zoey offered him the pitcher. "I mean, I'm all for not dying. But that woman…she's…" Her voice trailed off. She had no words.

Boggs poured water over another dishcloth. When he pulled the old one away, Zoey confirmed that there wasn't, in fact, any mark on Rune's chest.

Boggs placed the fresh cloth where the wound should have been. He handed back the pitcher.

"I've got to sit down," Zoey said. She missed the edge of the nearest chair and ended up on the floor. The pitcher sloshed in her arms as it slowly refilled itself. She held it tight.

Rune groaned.

"Is he going to be all right?"

"Depends on what kind of shot it was. It's acting like a plain, ordinary ferstitch. All that does is cause muscle spasms. Worst you've ever had, but that's the extent of it."

"So it could have been worse?"

Boggs nodded. "You can put just about any kind of curse you can think of in fell shot: heart attack, tumors, black leg…. He'll be a little stiff for a while, but the water'll do him good. I put a little mojo on it, just to be sure."

Seated on the floor, Zoey considered the pitcher in her hands. She had so many questions but couldn't decide where to start. She went with the obvious.

"Who the heck are you, anyway?"

"Call me Boggs," he said. He stood up stretched as if his back was stiff. "Who are you?"

"Zoey," she said. "Do you live here? I mean, Jericho keeps a fairy—a *sayne*, I mean—in a pot…in his library?"

"It's only temporary," Boggs said. "What about you? What's Mr. Rune doing with a girl who bears iron?"

"Iron?" She remembered her pendant, now somewhere out there in the real world. "Hey, you owe me a necklace!"

"Couldn't be helped. The magic to bring you here wouldn't work if you were bearing iron."

She replayed the scene in her head. "That woman, Avice, tried to do something to me, but she couldn't."

"That's right," Boggs said. He started pacing back and forth. "Part of that was the Covenant—you don't want to offend sacred hospitality. The hufter had no cause starting something in Jericho's house. But part of it was that little iron trinket you was wearing. She wasn't wrong about that."

"That's freaky." Zoey touched the area below her collarbone where her pendant used to hang. She glanced at the staircase. "Who was that woman, anyway? Is she really Rune's cousin?"

"I'm afraid so," Rune said. With some effort, he pulled himself upright on the sofa and begin to re-lace his shirt.

"I wasn't sure about that," Boggs said. He took a step back from Rune on the sofa and turned toward Zoey. "All I know is, she works for the—well, she works for somebody Jericho's wanting to do business with." He wobbled a bit and wrung his hands. "Crashing waves, I just pissed off a Nightwalker." He steadied himself on the back of the sofa. "I'm dead!"

"What's a Nightwalker?" Zoey asked. She faced Rune. "And why is your cousin out to get you? And why does she have two names? Why do *you* have two names?" She looked past Rune to Boggs. "And how do you two know each other?"

Rune opened his mouth, but before he could say anything, a man's voice reverberated through the living room.

"Boggs?"

It was Jericho. He sounded confused, though not particularly angry.

"Boggs, I bid thee, come."

"I gotta go," Boggs said. He bit his lip. His eyes darted back and forth. "Okay, here's the deal—" He hunched over as if telling Zoey a secret.

"Boggs!" Jericho called.

"You got the kitchen back there and two other doors behind the sofa. As soon as I go, you take Rune and you go through one of them—any one you want! Just don't tell me, got it?"

"What?"

"Just do it!" He spun around and huffed toward the stairs. At the bottom, he turned to them again. "Do it!"

Rune was already on his feet. "We need to do as he says."

He looked paler than usual, but at least he wasn't as shaky as before. Just in case, Zoey slipped underneath his arm and led him to the door on the right behind the sofa.

"I don't understand—"

"It's the Covenant," Rune said.

They stumbled into what turned out to be a modest bedroom. "Okay, I need a dictionary, 'cause y'all keep using words I know, but they don't make any sense."

"The Covenant is the set of rules that governs our magic," Rune said. "It…depletes us…to speak an untruth."

"I still don't get it."

Rune sat on the edge of the bed, obviously exhausted. "We'll have to wait here for a while."

Zoey cast her eyes toward the staircase and understanding began to dawn. "He's getting the third degree from his boss, isn't he?"

Rune nodded. "He's being questioned, if that's what you mean."

"Will he tell Jericho where we are?"

"He'll try to avoid it, I think," Rune said.

That wasn't good enough. Zoey stole one last glance at Rune, then padded across the living room as fast as she could and crept up the spiral staircase. If Boggs was going to sell them out, she darn well wanted to know about it.

10

Zoey tried to keep her breathing steady. It wasn't easy, given the circumstances. She felt as if she were outside herself, an observer, half-crouching and inching her way up the stairs.

I'm inside a pot. She couldn't decide what that meant in practical terms. Had she shrunk to the size of a mouse? Or was it like that TV show where the police box is bigger on the inside?

She suppressed a fit of giggles, a manic defense against the creeping fear that she had lost her mind. A couple of deep breaths kept those feelings at bay.

She edged a little higher. Above her was the open lid of Boggs's pot…and the ceiling of Jericho's library, higher than any cathedral's.

"And the Dancer was here?" Jericho asked.

Zoey could just make out where he was standing from his shadow on the library ceiling. She didn't dare creep up any farther. Somebody might see her if they wandered too close.

"Y-yes, Master," Boggs answered. Before, he'd spoken with authority, even though he was frightened. Now he had adopted the tone of a cringing lackey. Zoey wondered which was the truth.

One of the shadows traversed the ceiling, then returned to its original position. "I wasn't expecting her until later."

"She may not have known you had company," Boggs offered.

The pacing shadow stopped to consider this. "That could be," Jericho said. "Was she angry?"

"She…seemed upset when she left."

"And kicked up a stink, apparently. I thought I heard shouting."

"Miss Dancer was kind enough to glamour the library before… expressing her displeasure."

"It's a good thing she did," Jericho said. He returned to pacing. "I'm making progress—one or two of my guests may have the spark, but I'll do more harm than good trying to awaken them before they're ready."

"As you say."

Zoey's heart pounded. Spark? Awaken? Were she and the others just guinea pigs in some kind of magical experiment?

"But why was she angry? She's the one who came unannounced."

"We spirits of the Otherworld can be flighty at times."

"But I need the information she was bringing. And soon. It takes time to master words of power."

"As you say, M-Master."

"She didn't tell you why she was upset?"

Boggs paused. "Nothing to do with you, I'm sure, Master," he said. "I expect she'll be back."

Way to deflect the question! Zoey thought. If she could do that, her parents would never let her out of their sight.

"She'd better be!" Jericho said sharply.

Zoey flinched at the outburst. Before, Jericho had been cool and collected, but now she saw he had a temper.

Jericho's shadow swayed back and forth. "It's almost Halloween. I need those words soon, or I might as well cancel the ritual entirely!"

A shadow passed above her head. Jericho was gesturing with his arm. His clenched fist looked as big as a sofa. She gasped and ducked down the stairs.

"What was that?" Jericho said.

"I beg your pardon?"

"Just then. I thought I heard something."

Zoey crouched midway down the stairwell and held her breath. The stairs seemed to tilt, and she braced herself against the wall.

Jericho had heard her. Had Boggs? From what Rune said, he'd have to tell Jericho the truth if he had.

And Jericho was up to something: some kind of ritual on Halloween that had something to do with the people at his party. He was looking for people with "the spark," whatever that meant.

"What did it sound like?" Boggs said.

"I'm…not sure." Jericho paused. "Probably nothing."

Zoey expelled a slow, measured breath. She didn't dare make any noise.

"I should return to the dining room," Jericho said.

Yes, you should!

What was happening up there? Zoey steeled herself and crept back upward. Two more steps. Three. Her head was nearly level with the rim of the pot. That was as far as she dared go, but if she rested her head just below the rim, she could peer across the lid on the far side. She still couldn't see the whole room, but she could see Boggs, or at least his top half, swaying and wringing his hands.

Jericho stood by the door. He carried himself with easy grace, unhurried, unflustered, just as he had in the sitting room. "The other details are in progress?"

"Yes, Master," Boggs said. "I've secured most of the implements Miss Dancer has called for. Everything will be in order."

"Good. Carry on, Boggs. My guests will be waiting." He turned toward the door, then stopped and looked back. "I do seem to be missing a couple. A girl and a young man with a ponytail. You haven't seen them, have you?"

Zoey squeaked in spite of herself. She slapped a hand over her mouth and ducked her head.

There was a pause.

Boggs, if you say one word…

"They're not here." Boggs spread his arms.

"Obviously."

Boggs wet his lips. "I imagine they've left your domain, M-Master. Perhaps they found your talk of magic off-putting."

"Maybe," Jericho said. "But I'd have sworn I saw something in that Rune. If any of these people have the spark, it's him. And you're sure you don't know where they are?"

"They're not here now," Boggs repeated. "I didn't see which way they went."

Zoey grinned. So that's why he told them to get out of his living room! Rune's people might have to tell the truth because of that Covenant of theirs, but that didn't mean they couldn't twist things around and lead people to draw the wrong conclusions.

But what if Boggs was doing the same thing to her and Rune? Zoey's stomach churned. She started to replay everything he had said. Was there hidden meaning in his words—anything she needed to know?

"This is important, Boggs. I can't afford any slip-ups."

"No, M-Master."

"I don't like the idea of them wandering off without telling me," Jericho said. "They couldn't possibly know anything, but still…"

"What c-could they know?"

"You're right. My little trick with Davanté must have spooked them, and they left."

"That…sounds reasonable, Master."

"Not everybody has a taste for magic."

"As you say."

"But I can't be too careful—not now, not this close to the ritual." He lifted his hand, palm toward his lackey. "I charge thee, Boggs, to let me know at once if you see either of those two again."

There was a definite pause before Boggs answered, "Of course, Master."

Zoey sucked in deep breaths.

Boggs would sell them out, she knew it! She didn't understand, but it was obvious that Jericho had some kind of power over him.

The next time Boggs saw her and Rune, he'd have no choice but to report them.

"You'd best be going, Boggs," Jericho said. "My guests don't need to hear you lurking around in here."

If Boggs came back to his pot, Zoey and Rune were sunk. She bit back a curse. As far as she knew, the only way in or out was the opening above her head.

"As soon as I straighten out these papers on your desk, Master," Boggs said. "It shouldn't take more than a couple of minutes." He spoke clearly, deliberately. Did he know Zoey was listening in? Was he sending her a message?

Whatever the case, she had to get moving. She had to find Rune—and fast! She scurried down the stairs and sprinted across Boggs's living room.

Rune was still in the bedroom, but at least he was standing. He faced the door, stretching his limbs. He seemed more himself. Whatever magic his cousin had shot him with was wearing off.

"We've got to get out of here!" Zoey hissed.

Rune's expression turned serious—or at least more serious than it usually was.

"Boggs just promised Jericho he'd tell him if he saw us again. And he's coming this way!"

Rune's eyes widened. "Come on," he said, brushing past Zoey. He grabbed his bomber jacket from where it lay on the floor and shrugged it on.

They had the same three options Boggs had given them when he left: the kitchen, the door to the bedroom, and the third door next to the bedroom.

"This way," Rune said, and strode toward the third door.

It opened into a small workshop. Rough wooden shelving on one wall was empty except for some boxes and a few glass bottles. A small table was equally bare.

At the far end of the room was another door.

"Is that a way out?" Zoey asked.

"Could be." Rune sprinted across the room and stood in front of the door.

"But…how is it a way out? We're inside a stinking pot!"

Rune said nothing.

Footsteps clomped on the hardwood floor of the living room. Boggs had come back.

Rune lay his hands against the wood and closed his eyes. He seemed to be listening for something, but Zoey couldn't imagine what.

Zoey set her own hand on the doorframe. It felt cool. A breeze blew through the cracks around the edges. As she steadied her breathing, she picked up the subtle whiff of mildew.

Plates rattled outside the workshop. Boggs was in the kitchen.

"We've got to hurry!" Zoey whispered.

"Yes," Rune said.

"So why are we still just standing here?"

Rune turned the latch and opened the door. The cool breeze blew through Zoey's hair. "Because I don't like setting off alarms. Come on."

Zoey followed Rune into a dark corridor. He pulled the door closed behind them and plunged them into darkness.

Zoey shivered.

"Keep your hand on the wall," Rune said. He guided Zoey's hand until it touched something hard, cold, and damp. "Follow me."

"I don't suppose you brought a flashlight?"

"I can't see in the dark with a light in my face."

"I can't see in the dark at all!" Zoey had never been afraid of the dark before, but she couldn't remember it ever being this dark. Of course, she had never run away from a wizard's magical assistant either.

"Come on," Rune said. Zoey jumped when he grasped her other hand and pulled her along.

"Where to?" Zoey asked. "What if this is just the way to the basement or something?"

"It's not."

"And you know this because…?"

"Domains like this almost always have a back door."

"Almost?"

Rune pulled her onward. "You overheard Boggs and Jericho?" he asked as they went.

Zoey filled him in on everything she could remember. Jericho mentioned Dancer, the other name of that Avice woman, and something about words of power he needed to master. Preparations Boggs was supposed to be making. Something about Halloween.

"Halloween?" Rune asked, cutting her off.

"Yeah, is that important?"

Rune sighed. "The boundary between worlds is thinnest on that day. If Jericho's going to go through with this…"

"With what?"

There was a pause. "Never mind. A little further."

Zoey tiptoed over broad, stone steps leading down into…she didn't know where but couldn't imagine she was going to like it. Rune's pace was maddeningly casual. Zoey refused to believe that anyone could see in so well dark. Even with her hand in his, she stumbled trying to keep up.

"I don't see how this is an improvement over Boggs's apartment."

When Rune came to a halt, Zoey's face brushed against his leather jacket. She took her hand away from the wall and wrapped her fingers around his arm.

"This is quite good," Rune said.

Zoey wasn't sure he was talking to her, but she took the bait anyway. "What's good?"

"I assumed there would be an obvious portal. This is far more subtle—more than I'd have given Boggs credit for."

"Uh. We're not lost, are we?"

"How can we be lost when we don't know where we're going?"

"Rune, sweetie, that wasn't the answer I was hoping for."

"We're almost to the end of the passage," Rune said. "The pressure has equalized."

Only then did Zoey realize the cold breeze had died. The air was cool but deathly still. Her eyes were adjusting to the darkness. Rune's tall, slender frame stood out as a black shadow against dark gray walls. But there was something more: specks of dull, bluish-green light tracing spiderwebs across the walls and ceiling.

The corridor twisted to the right—the first time it had veered in any direction.

"We're close," Rune said. "As soon as—" He stopped again.

Zoey held her breath. Something skittered in the distance. Her heart leaped up into her throat.

They had come to a T in the corridor. Black shadows darted from one side to the other. Rune pulled his right arm free from Zoey's grasp while holding her back with his left against her waist.

"W-What…?"

"Probably nothing," Rune said. "Stay back."

He took a step forward.

Something in the darkness uttered a raspy squeak. More shadows scurried about. Zoey spun around, certain she heard something behind her.

"Stars above," Rune groaned.

"What?"

"My knives. I dropped them back in the library."

"We're doomed, aren't we? We're going to be eaten by monsters and—"

"Stay at my back," Rune said, pulling Zoey's left hand to his shoulder. He began to circle about. "We can get out of this. Let me think…"

"Think fast."

Rune started to breathe slow, deep breaths as if he was meditating. The hair on Zoey's arms pricked up.

Something brushed her thigh. She yelped and jumped back and nearly tumbled over Rune. She shuddered and wiped her hands against her hip and thigh as if she'd rubbed against something foul.

And then an idea came to her. "I might have a plan," she whispered.

"Zoey, there's no time for—"

"No, listen! Whatever these things are, they live in the dark, right? So a bright light would hurt them."

"I'm not a fire-weaver. I can't just summon light to my fingertips."

"Well, I can!" Zoey said. She spun around, pulled her phone from her hip pocket, and hit the flashlight icon as quickly as she could. The corridor erupted with harsh white light, and she squinted as her eyes protested.

At her back, Rune gasped.

In front of her, creatures of nightmare ducked and scurried away. There were three of them. They looked like huge bipedal rats, the size of small children but hunched over and covered with coarse black fur. As soon as the light blazed they scrambled away, their hairless tails lashing from side to side.

Zoey let out the scream she'd been holding back for the past thirty minutes: half triumph, half wild panic.

"Heck, yeah!" she hollered. "And there's more where that came from, you little…you little—"

"They're called shadelings," Rune said. He was holding his hand over his eyes, and he winced as he turned toward Zoey.

"Oh, sorry," she said. "Let me turn this light off."

"No, leave it on," Rune said. "Come this way."

He led her toward the place where the corridor split off. On the far wall someone had etched a symbol into the rock.

"Shine your light here."

She did, but she couldn't make heads or tails out of what she saw. A vertical line ran through the middle of the design. On the left was a circle inscribed with a plus sign. On the right was a circle with rays coming out of it.

"We need to go left," Rune announced.

Zoey knitted her brow.

"This is a waymark," he explained. "It's a kind of travelers' code. This way to the Fallow." He started off with Zoey close behind.

Another dozen yards, and a light fog began to blanket the floor. In the distance, a pinprick of light floated aimlessly on a breeze that Zoey couldn't feel.

"This is it," Rune said.

"This is what?"

"The way out. We're close to the edge of the Mere."

"The what?"

"The Mere." Rune scrunched his face. "How can I explain this? There's the Fallow and there's Saynim. Your world and mine. The boundary between the two is called the Mere." He reached into his pocket. "Sometimes the two worlds overlap. That's where the Mere is thinnest. People have crossed over by accident when they weren't careful."

Zoey clenched her teeth, bracing for bad news.

Rune ran his fingers along the wall. "That's rare, though. Most of the time you need a waymaker to open the door. But this time of year, sometimes you get lucky."

He went to the opposite wall, where he finally found what he was looking for: a small depression in the stone, barely big enough to fit Zoey's thumb.

Rune reached into his pocket and pulled out what looked for all the world like a dried bean. As Zoey watched, he inserted it into the depression.

"We just need a little extra magic. That's what the quig is for."

"You mean the bean?"

Rune nodded. "Quigs store magical energy. Not much, but enough for something like this. Stand back."

He stood in front of the fog-shrouded passageway, staring at the far end with all his attention. After a few seconds, he steepled his hands above him, then brought them both down and outward with a sweeping motion, Moses parting an imaginary Red Sea.

The fog parted, as if inviting Zoey and Rune further down the corridor. The way got wider, and the bare stone gave way to brickwork. Soon, bits of debris appeared in the corners and recesses—broken crates, empty bottles.

Another pinprick of light wafted in front of them, like a glowing ember.

"What's that?"

"Wanderlight," Rune said. "They're drawn to the Mere. They're mostly harmless."

"You've got to quit using words like probably and mostly."

The wanderlight floated out of their way as they passed. Lanterns hung unlit at intervals along the walls. More wander-lights appeared, two or three at a time. Zoey turned off the flashlight on her phone.

They passed a musty, discarded sign, propped against the wall and nearly falling over. It was draped with cobwebs and fine dust, but she could just make out the words "Bourbon Stockyards."

"I think I know this place," she said with a start. "There's this legend about tunnels under Butchertown. They say people used them to drive livestock in from the river. Then later, bootleggers used them during Prohibition."

"Interesting."

"But… But we're nowhere near Butchertown. It would take half the night to walk there from Old Louisville!"

Rune shrugged. "Time and space don't always work the same for our kind." He gestured to a wooden staircase up ahead. On the wall beside it was another plus-sign-in-a-circle waymark.

At the top of the stairs was an old wooden door that opened when Rune put his shoulder to it.

They stepped out into an alley—nothing more than a narrow passage between two tall brick buildings, but it was a good, old-fashioned Louisville alley, with litter and rusty nails and the smell of cigarette smoke.

Zoey took a deep breath of musty air tinged with auto emissions and spicy food. There was a restaurant nearby, and she had missed dinner.

"Stand still," Rune said. He put his hands on her shoulders to square her stance and gazed into her eyes. Zoey's face warmed as his glance moved down her body.

"Uh, excuse me?" she snapped.

He took his hands away and stepped back. "Turn around."

Zoey's pulse pounded with fear and humiliation. "Now wait a minute. I'm not—"

"You've passed through the Mere," Rune said. "I need to see if you've brought any of it with you."

She gulped. "Run that by me again?"

Rune gestured for her to turn around. As she complied, he said, "It's a Fallow thing. People like you tend to stir up magical turbulence. You can turn back around now."

"What do you mean, 'turbulence'?"

He frowned. "I don't see anything. You shouldn't have any troubles."

"I don't like that word 'shouldn't.'"

"Fallow folk and magic," Rune said with a shrug. "Too many variables to be sure. Let me know if you experience anything… odd in the next day or so."

Because that didn't worry Zoey in the least.

They walked out onto the main road. The sun had set since she'd first entered Jericho's house, but only just. The street was still full of traffic.

"I assume we can take the bus home?" Rune asked.

"Huh? Sure, let me see." Zoey dug in her purse for her bus schedule. "See if you can find a street sign, will you?"

Rune nodded and took a few steps away to locate a sign. He pointed down the block. "That way is East Main Street."

"Great." Zoey checked her map. "We should head that way, then." She fell into step behind Rune. "It sounds like Jericho is going to try something on Halloween."

"Yes."

"Something stupid, I take it?"

"He doesn't know how stupid it is."

This night just kept getting better. "You're not going to try to stop him, are you?"

Rune said nothing. He kept his eyes straight ahead.

"Rune?"

"How long until we can catch our bus?"

11

Zoey got on the bus first and paid for both of them. At the top of the steps, Rune stopped and looked down the aisle. His expression was all business. She'd seen him act like that before in crowds of strangers, like he was walking into a lion's den. She imagined him noting possible threats, people who might pose a problem.

In the last couple hours, she'd added another category of threat: people who weren't people at all.

The bus was mostly empty. Folks who worked downtown would have already headed home. She edged toward the back while Rune lagged behind her, apparently in awe of Louisville's public transportation.

Halfway down, a guy looked up at her—maybe in his forties, unshaven and in need of a shower. He stretched his leg into the aisle.

"Excuse me," Zoey said.

He leered at her and made a kissy face. She gasped and stormed past, feeling his hot gaze following her until she plopped into a seat on the back row. Her heart pounded. She took a deep breath and gritted her teeth.

The jerk grinned and winked at her. She made a point not to meet his gaze. *Don't engage*, she told herself. That was the first rule. That was always the first rule.

The bus was suddenly way too warm. She clenched her jaw tight. She wanted to say something so badly, but her brain reminded her of how much she'd regret it.

Don't egg him on. Don't give him the satisfaction.

Rune took his seat beside her, now tense, his brow furrowed. He stayed poised on the edge of his seat even as the bus pulled away from the stop. "That man accosted you," he hissed, genuinely perplexed. It was like he'd never considered the possibility of something like that happening. His expression had turned angry, dangerous.

"It's okay," Zoey said. "Well, it's not okay. It's just…not worth it."

"He must be taught a lesson." Rune clenched his fists. His eyes flashed like a predatory animal's.

"No!" Zoey insisted. "Listen to me. It's over, okay? You don't have to get all…whatever. The creep's not worth the effort, so just chill."

Rune quirked an eyebrow. "You don't think it's warm in here?"

"No." She shook her head. "I mean…don't make a scene."

He leaned back and crossed his arms, but his eyes never left Skeezy Guy. "I will keep silent."

"Thank you." Her fire of indignation dimmed as the bus chugged along.

"But let him say a single word, and he'll learn I am silent but deadly."

That's when Zoey lost it. She tried to swallow her laugh, but it came out as an indelicate snort.

"Are you all right?" Rune asked.

Her whole body shook as she blew out a breath and pulled herself together. She was *not* going to explain to Rune what "silent but deadly" meant! "I'm fine." Her heart raced, but not as fiercely. She was safe. Uncomfortable and insulted. Objectified. But safe.

Rune sat with his trained on Skeezy Guy as if they could bore holes into him. Skeezy Guy got the hint soon enough and looked away. He got off at the next stop. Whether he had intended to beforehand was another question.

With his flaxen hair almost imperceptibly wafted by an unseen breeze, Rune always looked…well, good. But that wasn't who he was, it was just what he looked like—and Zoey was learning that appearances didn't mean much.

Who Rune was, though, she hadn't quite figured out. He was naïve to the point of helplessness. His sheer innocence of her world was endearing, but that was only one side of him. She'd seen another side at Jericho's. If his cousin Avice was any indication, there were sides of Rune that Zoey hadn't yet seen and maybe didn't want to.

And now with the creep on the bus, he showed he was also a gentleman, or at least he wanted to be. He was weird and scary, but in his own way terribly, distractingly charming.

A little farther down Bardstown Road, Zoey signaled for the bus to stop. "We have to change buses here," she explained. They stepped off in front of a fast-food restaurant.

"We should eat," Rune said as he gestured toward the golden arches. It was like he was reading her mind. "An errand can sap your energy quicker than anything."

"An errand?"

Rune's face darkened. "Sorry. Old ways of thinking. What I mean is, this must have been a difficult night for you. You should replenish your strength. I'm a bit hungry myself."

Sure, Rune, I'd love to go get a burger with you.

"Uh…okay. I mean, the next bus doesn't get here for another half hour or so." She suppressed a slight giggle. "Plenty of time."

She led Rune to the counter and fished for her wallet as she placed her order.

"Allow me." Rune reached inside his jacket.

"What? Oh, no. I've got it."

"No, please. It's my fault you missed supper." He pulled out his own wallet and leafed through a thin stack of bills.

"You really don't have to."

"I insist." He turned to the cashier. "The same for me, please."

Zoey carried their tray to the drink station and showed Rune how to fill his cup from the dispensers. After some puzzled expressions and an interminable debate between iced tea and lemonade (lemonade won by a narrow margin), he was finally ready to move on.

They picked a table near the window where they could see the bus stop under a streetlight. Rune pulled out Zoey's chair with an obliging gesture.

She smiled. Jaden, her ex-boyfriend, had never held a chair for her. Her face warmed.

Rune smiled back. The dangerous Rune on the bus who wanted to go medieval—possibly literally—on the guy who'd harassed her was now an affable gentleman with old-world manners. She wasn't scared at all anymore.

Rune sat down and followed her lead in unwrapping his cheeseburger. He took a deep breath, eyes closed, and gestured as if to draw the aroma to his nostrils.

Oh, he's praying…or something. Zoey quickly bowed her head. *Thank you, Lord, for this food…*

That stupid, sexy, unseen breeze tickled the back of her neck and filled her nostrils with the fragrance of fallen rain.

She took a breath. *And if it be your will.…*

Rune finished his ritual, whatever it was. Zoey raised her head and pushed back her glasses. "I never thanked you."

He studied his meal as if unsure what to do with it. "We all have to eat."

"I mean, yeah, thanks for supper. But I was thinking about earlier. On the bus."

"I still wish you'd have let me destroy him."

"Well, I didn't." Her words came out a little harsh, but so be it. She was safe and she was grateful, but Rune still had to learn how things worked in her world. And 'destroy him'? Zoey shuddered.

"All you had to do was be there. Sure, buttholes like that could do with a beating every now and then, but that's not what I needed."

He arched an eyebrow.

"Next time just…just listen to me, all right?"

"Of course," Rune said. He'd tensed his muscles as if preparing for an attack. "Zoey, if I've offended you, please accept my—"

"Don't worry about it," she said. "Women…people…people just need to be listened to."

"I understand." His expression suggested he didn't understand. But he was trying.

"Look, there are things you still don't know about this world." Or about women. "You've got to follow somebody else's lead every now and then. Deal?"

"Deal," Rune said. "From now on, no sporting with menseless hufters without your say-so."

"Yeah," Zoey said, puzzled. "Easy on those darn hufters."

Rune took a bite of a french fry and gave an approving nod.

"You like the fries? I know this isn't exactly fine dining."

"It's good," Rune said. "Different."

Zoey took a bite of her cheeseburger. Rune imitated her, as if he wasn't sure he was doing it right.

"You don't have burgers in Saynim?"

"I don't believe so."

Zoey took another nibble.

"It's a big place, though," Rune admitted. "I can't be sure."

"No, probably not." Zoey sighed. Here she was with the most gorgeous man she'd ever met, and all they could talk about was cheeseburgers. This was getting lamer by the minute.

"It's just that I don't know anyplace in town that serves, like, dragon steaks or anything."

"I should hope not," Rune said. "Their meat is poisonous."

Zoey tensed. "Don't tease!"

"I'm serious. If it's not properly prepared…." He shrugged. "I prefer simple food, myself. Pork. Venison. Pilly fowl."

"What's pilly fowl?"

Rune arched an eyebrow. "Surely you've got them here. Big birds? With a little flappy thing under the beak? They make a sort of gobbling sound."

Zoey grinned. "Turkeys. We call them turkeys."

"Ah."

"I guess some things in your world are pretty much like here."

"Except for the shadelings and the elves and whatnot."

"Well, since you mention it." Zoey chuckled. The shadelings she would gladly forget. But the elves? Well, one elf in particular had her undivided attention. She couldn't keep her eyes off him. It was embarrassing—or would be if he wasn't so distracting. Only then did it dawn on her that his ears looked different. Rounder at the top. More magic, apparently, to help him blend in.

He worked so hard to blend in.

She bit her lip. "Is there anything you miss?"

He studied the ceiling for a second or two. "A few things," he said. He leaned forward, resting his arms on the table. "You can't see as many stars here. I think it's all the city lights."

"Yeah, stars are nice." *Stars are nice?* she thought. *What kind of response is "stars are nice"?*

At least we're not still talking about food! she answered herself.

And talking about astronomy is an improvement? You've got to break the ice. Ask him something personal!

"What about people?" she said, her face flushing. "Is there any*one* you miss?"

"Like my family?" Rune frowned. "That's a complicated story."

"Yeah, I met your cousin, remember?" Zoey swirled her french fry in ketchup while she gathered her nerve. "I mean like…a girlfriend maybe?"

Rune looked down. "Girlfriend?" He flashed a self-conscious grin. "You mean a lover? A paramour?"

"I'm sorry! That was personal. I shouldn't have—" The heat was rising, and not in a good way.

"No, it's all right," Rune said. "And no. I wasn't involved in that way."

The dam broke, and a torrent of emotion flooded Zoey's heart: giddiness, excitement…and then suddenly dread.

She tried to keep her tone light, disinterested. "So I guess that means no…boyfriend, either?" As soon as the words left her mouth, she regretted them. "I am so sorry. I'm getting all up in your business, and we were having such a nice time eating these cheeseburgers, and, and—"

"It's all right, Zoey."

"Not that it's any of my business, I mean *at all*."

"Zoey. Breathe." Rune gave her a disarming smile. The words finally sunk in, and she took a breath.

"Better?"

She nodded. "Thanks." She took another bite of her cheeseburger. "So…I mean, since we're on the subject…?"

"You seem rather curious about such things. Is this a normal line of conversation for your people?"

"No. Not really." She wiped sweat from her forehead with her napkin. "I'm sorry. And mortified. I'll just shrivel up now and… uh…"

Rune placed his hand over hers. Something electric pulsed through her body. "I'm grateful for all you've done to help me fit in," he said. "I suppose you've earned the right to ask questions."

She squeaked something that she hoped sounded like "Thanks."

Rune chuckled. "You are a strange people, you Fallow folk. So direct. Where I come from, there's always more to a conversation than the words that are said. There are nuances. Hidden traps if you say the wrong thing. But not here. Not with you." The warmth of his smile was almost more than she could take.

"Nope." She studied what was left of her burger with renewed intensity. "No subtext at all. Not even a little."

Rune smiled. "The truth is, options where I grew up for what you call 'girlfriends' were…limited."

"Oh," Zoey said, her heart a-flutter. *Girlfriends. He said girlfriends.*

"I just don't see what the big fuss is."

The room tilted. Her heart ceased fluttering. "I beg your pardon?"

Rune stretched out his hand. "Someone else to get in the way of an errand seems inconvenient."

Zoey sighed like a deflated balloon. "Inconvenient."

"It's not for me." He smiled again. Why did he always have to smile like that? "Too many complications."

"Yeah."

"You're better off not having a boyfriend."

"Yeah." The burger suddenly tasted like sand in her mouth. "Lucky me."

This was what the philosophers called a big, fat, hairy mistake. All Zoey could think about was how to get out of it before she made an even bigger idiot of herself.

Fortunately, she recognized someone outside at the bus stop. It was Vanessa, a cheerleader from her school. She and Zoey weren't super close, but they were friends. If she was waiting for a bus too, maybe Zoey could make an escape. She peered through the window and made out the shapes of two or three other friends.

"Listen," Zoey said. "I just remembered there's something I need to do."

"Should we be going? Is the bus here?"

"Not quite. But"—she forced herself to smile—"would you mind if I went on ahead? Some of my friends are out there and…well…"

"Of course," Rune said, puzzled.

Zoey stood, and Rune stood with her. *Of course* he stood up with her! Even with the bewildered expression on his face, he was a perfect gentleman.

The jerk.

"You're sure it's okay?"

"Actually," Rune said, "if you can get home safely, there's something I should do. I should have thought to do it while we were still in the tunnels, but…shadelings."

"Of course. Don't let me keep you from exploring some dark, creepy tunnels when you could…." She trailed off. It didn't really matter. She waved half-heartedly and made for the door.

Vanessa and the others perked up when they saw her. She joined in their conversation, barely noticing when Rune left the restaurant a moment after she did and turned the corner. She looked back for him, but he had vanished into the night.

12

Three days.

In three days, the Mere would be at its thinnest, and Jericho would make a pact with the King of Shadows. He was going to open a doorway between his world and Saynim, and there was no telling who or what might come through it.

Rune would need to defend himself. That meant a trip to Goblintown.

He once more drew on his magic to enhance his vision and other senses. And now he used it to speed his pace as well. Running like the wind wasn't just a metaphor for those who wove the airy chaos. He only stopped to read the occasional waymark so he didn't take a wrong turn.

The tunnels beneath Butchertown slowly took on a homier atmosphere as red bricks gave way to carved stone. There were places where one could cross the Mere freely, mostly deep forests or underground caverns. An ancient ruin or graveyard might work in a pinch.

For most Saynim folk, such portals were never a major challenge if you knew where to find one. Nightwalkers mapped and recorded them whenever their errands took them to the Fallow—you never knew when they might come in handy.

Things were more complicated for powerful Gentry like the King of Shadows. They carried so much magical potency that they were liable to bring a portal down around them if they tried to cross it.

But on Hallowfest Eve, with the right ritual…

Rune shook the thought from his mind. First things first.

He soon came to the portal he'd crossed with Zoey. It hadn't yet closed back, and the fog had lifted. *Thank the wind.*

He pressed on.

The side passage to Boggs's pot was no longer where it had been when they passed that way earlier. In its place was a perfectly ordinary stone wall—maybe real, maybe just a sophisticated glamour.

But he wasn't going to Boggs. He needed to see the man in Goblintown that Madam Samarra had told him about, the one who could supply him with shot.

Rune was bound to run into Avice again before all this was over. With his knives gone, he needed a weapon.

He should have known he hadn't seen the last of his cousin. She had made his life miserable for decades, ever since he'd arrived at the Haw, the Nightwalkers' training grounds and headquarters.

Rune's mother was from a high-born elven family: Redcloaks who crossed the Sea a thousand years before and founded one of the first Easterling kingdoms in Westernesse. Herdis of the House of Claea was a stickler for the old ways. Any son of hers was bound—or doomed—to receive a traditional upbringing, leaving home as a youngling to be fostered by his mother's eldest brother. Leander was meant to make a man out of Rune, teach him how to fight, how to woo, how to keep his head attached to his neck at court.

It just so happened that Leander of the House of Claea was also Whisper, the Warden of the King's Nightwalkers.

The King's Nightwalkers were rogues, saboteurs, and assassins. They did everything from assaulting rival strongholds to blighting crops, driving their enemies mad, and stealing mortal infants to serve in the King's retinue.

Rune learned everything Whisper taught him, and with each passing year, he hated it more. Every crop he destroyed filled him with dreams of his starving victims. Every mind he crushed tore away at his own sanity. Every mewling baby he shoved into a sack, and every bereaved mother he left wailing into the darkness ground away at him.

Whatever he did, it was never enough for Whisper. "You've got advantages," his uncle would tell him, firmly but with admiration. "You must learn to use them."

Whisper's daughter thought differently. To Avice, Rune was just the freak her father took in as a favor for his disgraceful sister.

Avice always bested Rune in combat training. Standing over him, she would flourish her sword and ask him, "Had enough, auph?"

Whisper would chide her—gently—if he heard the slur. More often, his attention was on the other young attendants of the King of Shadows.

As the years wore on, the word burned into Rune's heart.

Auph.

Elf-bastard. Half-breed.

He never knew why his mother had taken up with a Fallowman. Rune suspected it was a matter of obligation. The Redcloak nobility was a dying breed, after all. Natural-born children weren't exactly rare, but they weren't common, either. Avice was one of only a handful of fey nobles Rune's age that he had ever met.

Knowing his mother, she may have thought it an honor to give the King of Shadows a wily half-elven errand-boy. What Rune's elven stepfather thought of the situation remained a mystery.

Humans bore a certain mystique in Saynim. People said they were adaptable, versatile, and unpredictable. The theory went that these qualities made them capable officers…and appealing paramours. The King of Shadows kept a cohort of human warriors brought over from the Fallow as infants and trained to serve as his elite guard, the Knights of the Hand.

People like Rune were supposed to enjoy the best of both worlds—blessed with both a human's versatility and an elf's raw magical talent. In most corners of Saynim, they were admired, albeit from a distance.

At the Haw, though, Avice seemed determined to quash any such admiration of Rune.

Maybe she didn't like anyone competing for her dear daddy's attention. Maybe the circumstances of Rune's birth repulsed her. Whatever her reasons, Avice took it as her sworn duty to make Rune's life miserable for the duration of his fosterage.

Shooting her at Cruc Máw had been a deeply satisfying experience.

It wasn't long until the tunnel opened into a cavern with a ceiling thirty or more feet high. It was at least partly natural, though massive wooden beams supported parts of the roof. Stonework reinforced the entryway and the walls around it. Luminescent fungi had taken root all over the wood and cast a soft blue-green light over the cavern and the little hamlet at its center.

The place wasn't much. Just a handful of drab buildings around a single cobblestone square. On the edge of town a ramp sloped upward, a broad thoroughfare for foot traffic and a rail track for hoisting and lowering heavy burdens. That way led to Dunswale, the little village where Rune had first made contact with the waymaker. Goblintown was a neighborhood of Dunswale that appealed to the subterranean crowd.

The smithy wasn't hard to find on the opposite side of town, dug into the wall of the cave. And just as Rune had hoped, the dwarf was still at work.

It wasn't so late that the streets were deserted, so others noted his arrival. They were mostly goblins and small folk who barely came up to Rune's navel: shopkeepers closing up for the night, parents calling their children home for supper. They cast furtive glances in his direction and moved out of his way as he passed.

Rune slowed his pace, settled his mind, and dismissed the better part of his magic. He made a point of keeping his hands in clear view at his sides. Best not to present a threat. People could be jumpy around strangers. It wouldn't do to rile them.

He stepped into the smithy and gritted his teeth when he saw the cast-iron forge that overshadowed most of the brick wall at the back. The last of his magic dwindled away in the breeze.

It was nearly impossible to work magic around iron. Earth-weavers could do better. Those like this Mr. Brackwater who no doubt wove the metallic chaos weren't affected at all. For air-weavers like Rune, though, even standing in a room with so much iron was distracting. Most Saynim folk preferred to keep metal-weavers at arm's length. Entering the dwarf's shop filled Rune with a shiver of foreboding, as if he was in the presence of something unnatural.

Just superstition, he told himself. And at any rate, the metal-weaver had what he needed. Rune tore his eyes from the forge and took stock of the rest of the room. A copper steam engine next to the forge worked the bellows, pumping fresh air into a pipe to stoke the flame. In one corner was a metalworker's lathe—more iron! Directly in front was a great stone anvil. Workbenches and supply lockers flanked either side.

The dwarf hadn't yet noticed Rune's arrival—or if he had, he didn't let on. He was shorter than Rune, broad-shouldered and well muscled. His skin was blued from years of weaving the metallic chaos and leathery from long hours at the forge. His hair was a tangle of black tied back at the nape of his neck. His neatly trimmed beard didn't quite reach his sternum. His leather apron was stained with oil and grime.

He sat on a stool at his bench, hunched over a magnifying glass, his beady eyes fixed on some kind of tiny ball bearing.

"I beg your pardon," Rune ventured.

The gearsmith grunted and dropped his metal pea into a small wooden box. He set his hands on his thighs but made no effort to stand. Nor did he speak. He stared at Rune, his expression impossible to read. The engine driving the bellows released controlled bursts of steam like a tea kettle that couldn't quite get the job done. Chit chit chit.

"Are you Mr. Brackwater?"

The dwarf jabbed his thumb at a sign over the workbench and grunted again. Rune read the sign. Apparently this dwarf was, indeed, Mr. Brackwater.

"Be nice, Brack," a young boy said. Rune only then noticed him sitting at the far end of the workbench and working at a spinning wheel. Before him was a collection of ceramic bottles, all apparently empty, with labels like "fish breath" and "cat's footsteps." As the flyers spun, he gingerly fed a great wad of what looked like gray fuzz into the orifice and watched as the spun silver thread, finer than silk, collected on the bobbin. His pristine white tunic and blond hair formed a stark contrast to the dim, gray workshop.

Brackwater sniffed. "Never said I wouldn't be nice," he grumbled. "What do you want?"

"I'd like to purchase some shot. Fifty-four caliber, if you please."

For the first time, the dwarf looked Rune directly in the eye. "That so?"

"Madam Samarra gave me your name."

The dwarf merely grunted.

"I have money," Rune assured him.

"Uh-huh." The dwarf crossed his arms.

The engine driving the bellows kept spitting steam. Chit chit chit chit.

"I'd be in your debt," Rune offered.

"Maybe I don't want any favors from…outsiders."

Ah. Rune's reputation had preceded him. "Listen, Mr. Brackwater, I don't know what you've heard about me, but—"

A young dwarf girl appeared from the back room. "Papa, Mama says come to supper. She's…" She stopped in mid-sentence when she caught sight of Rune.

"Run along, Ulfa," Mr. Brackwater said.

The girl kept staring. She got her manners from her father, it seemed.

Rune affected a smile. "Hello, there," he said, as brightly as he could manage.

"Hi," she squeaked.

"Ulfa," Mr. Brackwater grumbled, "I told you to run along."

"Are you the Nightwalker?" the child asked.

A stone plopped into the pit of Rune's stomach.

"Ulfa!" Mr. Brackwater barked. "Where'd you hear that word?"

"I heard Mrs. Jiggins and Mr. Crankshaw talking in the square, remember? They said there's a Nightwalker lurking around."

With wonder in her eyes, she looked up into Rune's face. "What's a Nightwalker?"

"Ulfa, we'd better get to supper," the blond boy said. "Let your papa talk to man." He set his hand on her shoulder and ushered her away. As he pulled the door behind him, he shot the dwarf a wary glance.

Mr. Brackwater glared at Rune.

Chit chit.

"Well?" the dwarf said. "You *are* the Nightwalker, right? I know most everybody in Dunswale, but I never seen you before."

Rune swallowed. "Mr. Brackwater, I'm afraid you've been misinformed."

"You saying you're not the Nightwalker, then?" He got up from his stool and ambled over to the steam engine. He turned a crank, and the mechanism wound down.

Chit, chit…chit….

"I don't know what your neighbors have heard," Rune said, "but I am not a threat to you or your family."

"I don't see how that answers the question." The dwarf pulled a rag from his back pocket and wiped off the table where he'd been working.

Rune expelled a slow, measured breath. "I *was* a Nightwalker, but not anymore. I'm…no longer in the service of the King of Shadows."

Mr. Brackwater arched an eyebrow.

"We didn't part on the best of terms."

"And now you're in the market for shot?" the dwarf scoffed. "Yeah, that don't make me nervous at all!"

"Listen, Mr. Brackwater—"

"No, *you* listen. We ain't got much in Goblintown, but we cherish what we have, you understand? So whatever you're trying to do, I'd appreciate it if you kept it on the other side."

"I'm sorry, but I don't think that's possible."

The dwarf clenched his fists. "That a threat?"

"It's the way it is," Rune said. "The King of Shadows wants this territory."

"You think we don't know that?"

"I'm sure you do. What you might not know is that I'm not the only Nightwalker 'lurking about,' as you say."

The dwarf's eyes, black as coal, bored into Rune. His expression was indecipherable. He scratched his beard.

"The other one *does* serve the King of Shadows." Rune lowered his eyes and shook his head. "And she's better than me. More skilled. More ruthless."

"Silver and gold!" Brack cursed.

"I've escaped from her. Twice," Rune said. "If you'd sell me a box of shot, I might do it again."

"This other one's looking for you, then?"

"That's right." Rune tapped his fingers against his thigh. "To her, I'm a traitor."

"To the King of Shadows?" Mr. Brackwater tromped to a storage cabinet on the back wall.

Rune followed him. "I already said that."

"Uh-huh. Twice now. Say it again, and let's see if I believe you."

Rune stepped back. "You're invoking the Covenant on me?"

The dwarf nodded. "Tell me you're not the King of Shadows's stooge. Then, if the laws of magic don't turn you into anything interesting, I'll know it's the truth."

Saynim folk might get away with a little lie here and there, but invoking the rule of three escalated matters. Tell the same lie three times, and it could tie a knot in the weave of the universe. Telling a lie with the King of Shadows's name in it would be even worse.

Whisper had drilled into his charges never to tell the same lie twice.

"Fine," Rune said. He appreciated the dwarf's caution but felt insulted anyway. "I'm no longer in the service of the King of Shadows. I swear it by my breath."

Mr. Brackwater gazed up at him as if waiting for something to happen, but Rune didn't sprout horns or lose his mind or even double over in pain. After five or ten seconds of intense staring, the dwarf pulled a key from his pocket and fiddled with the lock on the cabinet.

"This other Nightwalker, the one that's gunning for you…"

"Stay clear of her if she comes this way. She's after me, but she's also serving the King of Shadows on another matter. As I said, he has designs on this territory."

"The mayor'll want to know about that," Mr. Brackwater said. "It might even get him off his backside and doing something."

"If you could get word to him, I'd be grateful."

"I got business in Dunswale tomorrow morning. I'll see what I can do," Mr. Brackwater said as he opened the cabinet.

Rune recognized a few boxes as ammunition, most with a red label but a couple with bright blue. "Is that thunderstone?" he asked, indicating the blue labels. A couple rounds of thunderstone might give him the edge he needed.

"That ain't for you," Mr. Brackwater said.

"If it's a matter of price—"

"It ain't." The dwarf pulled down a box with a red label. "Don't know why I even made it. The mayor ordered it for his garrison. Then he changed his mind, and I can't say I blame him."

"But if you're not selling it to the mayor…"

"I ain't selling it to nobody," the dwarf said. There was cold, hard iron in his voice.

"You don't understand," Rune said. "Avice—the other Night-walker—wants something from me. And as soon as she gets it, she's going to kill me."

"Then I hope you're a good shot." He nodded at the red box he was holding. "You said fifty-fours, right?"

"Yes. But I'd really prefer—"

"I ain't selling you no thunderstone," the dwarf said. "It's nasty stuff. I should have gotten rid of them weeks ago. Here." He stretched the red box toward Rune. "Ferstitch'll do."

I suppose it will have to, Rune thought. "All right," he sighed. "How much?"

13

Brack shut and locked the door behind the stranger as soon as he left. He stood with his hand on the latch and watched through the window as the Nightwalker—the *former* Nightwalker—disappeared into the darkness.

"By the Seven," he muttered. Nightwalkers, fell shot, the King of Shadows…. All at once Goblintown seemed very small, very vulnerable.

And he was in the middle of it, like it or not. He found himself drawing the metallic chaos into him to strengthen his resolve.

He turned to the crank that raised and lowered the awning above the shop's window. It slipped into place and the window was secure.

Normally, Brack appreciated this part of his daily routine. The day's work was done, and supper was on the table. Today, his hands were clammy with sweat as he untied his apron and hung it on the nail in the wall.

Had he done the right thing? Brack had his doubts. He'd handed over the box of fell shot, taken the stranger's quig, and counted out his change. At every step, he had questioned whether he was making the biggest mistake of his life.

He sighed. The King of Shadows was flexing his muscles, and half of Goblintown was ready to give the Merlady the key to the city. At least with her they knew what they were getting. But either way, Brack, his family, and his whole town were facing the fight of their lives.

He snuffed out the lamps and clomped through the dark to the door in back of the shop.

"By the Seven," he muttered again.

He knew a losing battle when he saw one.

Everyone was already seated at the table when Brack entered the main room. Apart from the privy, some storage cellars, and three bedrooms dug into the side of the cave, the living quarters behind Brack's workshop consisted of this large, single room that served as kitchen, dining room, and sitting area. A large wooden table dominated the middle of the room.

All eyes were on Brack as he took his seat at the head, opposite his wife, Thora. The children, Duren and Ulfa, sat to Brack's left, with Kettle on his right.

"Was that man really a Nightwalker, Papa?" Duren asked, wide-eyed.

"Duren!" Thora scolded. She shot Brack a flash of petulant anger, a wordless warning: *Don't encourage him!*

Brack took his time spooning turnips and mushrooms onto his plate. Duren was nearly grown, and pretty handy with a firearm. If things kept going the way they were…

"He was, wasn't he?" Duren persisted. "Did you kick him out? Did you run him out of town?"

"He ain't…what you said," Brack said. "Just another customer."

"What'd he want?" Ulfa said.

Brack waited until his mouth was full before he muttered, "Fell shot."

"I beg your pardon?" Thora said. Her eyes bored into him.

Brack swallowed. "Just let it go, all right? Somebody pass the sausages."

Ulfa handed him the platter. He stabbed a sausage with his fork and laid it on his plate.

"But you'd a' kicked him out if he was a Nightwalker, right, Papa?" Duren said.

"I still don't know what a Nightwalker even is!" Ulfa protested.

"It's not for you to know," Thora said curtly, and gave her husband another pointed glare.

"It's an assassin, right?" Duren said. "Or else a spy. Somebody who does the dirty work for the King of Shadows."

"Duren Brackwater!" Brack thundered. "You know better than to throw names like that around."

Duren flinched and bowed his head. Ulfa's mouth dropped open.

"I told you, he was just a customer." Brack cut off a bite of sausage with his fork and wolfed it down.

"Can we change the subject?" Thora said.

"Good idea," Brack said. "When's Laurin coming tomorrow with…what's-her-name?"

"Hilly," Thora said. "The weather's clear. They should be here for supper tomorrow."

Brack grunted and took another bite of sausage.

"Papa," Duren said, "can I have a musketoon for my birthday?"

Thora gasped. Brack gritted his teeth and counted to ten.

"If Duren gets a gun, what do I get?" Ulfa chirped.

"Your birthday ain't till summer," Duren grouched.

"Well, *yours* ain't for another month!"

"I'm just thinking ahead, Ulfa. Don't start an earthquake." Duren turned to his father. "Well, can I?" He pantomimed taking aim and shooting into the sky.

"Duren!" Thora scolded.

Brack looked at his son, at his half-hearted adolescent attempt at facial hair. "We'll see," he said. He pushed his plate away.

"Brack, no!" Thora said. "It's not like we live in the swamp. The boy doesn't need a firearm."

"But Mama!"

"Don't talk back to your mother!" Brack growled. "We'll see," he repeated.

"We most assuredly will not!" Thora snapped. She got up from the table and stormed into the workshop.

Brack expelled a breath. "Finish your supper," he told the children as he scooted backwards in his chair. The scraping sound of the wooden chair legs against the hardwood floor made everyone flinch. "And wash the dishes. Kettle, give 'em a hand?"

"Sure thing, Brack."

Brack followed his wife into the workshop. She had lit a single lantern and was pacing around the anvil. She rounded on him as soon as he shut the door behind him.

"Duren is too young to own a gun." Her voice trembled with barely controlled rage.

"Thora, listen…."

"There's too much mischief afoot around here as it is! I won't have my son be a part of it." She stomped her foot. The whole workshop trembled for a second. "Or my husband!"

"I'm just trying to—"

"*Fell shot*, Brack? You're selling fell shot to a total stranger?"

"That's right!" He took a breath, waiting for the earthquake to hit. When it didn't, he said, "The town's in three kinds of trouble, Thora. You know it as well as I do." He stepped toward her. "Those shadelings, the Nightwalker… Half the town is ready to give in and let the Merlady take over. Is that what you want?"

"Of course not, but—"

"The stranger… I talked to him. He knows things. And maybe now he owes me a favor."

"What kind of favor?" Thora scoffed.

Brack shook his head. "I just know we need all the allies we can get. I can't hold off a Nightwalker by myself."

"You aren't holding off a Nightwalker at all!"

"I may have to."

"You don't have to be a hero, Heptifilius." Thora's voice broke. The sound of his name sent a subtle shock wave through his consciousness. "You're a father. A husband. The best gearsmith in a hundred miles. That's what you're meant to do."

He slumped his shoulders. "Fat lot of good that'll do when somebody's goons start setting up shop on the square."

Thora put her arms on his shoulders. "You work hard, Brack. People respect you—yes, they do! Even if they don't always show it. And you take care of me and the children." Her eyes filled with tears. "That's hero enough for me."

He bit his lip. Hero enough for Thora might not be hero enough for what lay ahead. A storm was coming; he just didn't know when or how bad.

But she was right about one thing: Duren had no business being a part of it.

"I'll talk to Duren," Brack promised. "Maybe he'd like a tool set for his birthday."

Thora came close and held him tight. "That's a fine idea."

He pushed her away just enough to look at her beautiful brown eyes. "The next few days…if anything happens…"

"You'll be right here at home," Thora said. "Where you belong."

He waited several heartbeats before saying, "Yeah."

14

Zoey's heart still raced as she swayed back and forth beneath a bus stop sign on Bardstown Road. She checked the time on her phone. The next bus, due to arrive in a few minutes, would get her home well before her curfew.

It was a cool night, but not yet cold. The stop was well lit, and Vanessa and the others were still right there. Her head told her there was nothing to worry about, but could she trust in reason at this point?

This was the weirdest night of her life. She'd tangled with an elf, escaped from a…whatever Boggs was, fended off rat-monsters, and made a fool of herself with Rune.

All her thoughts led back to him. She'd never met anyone like him—and not just his looks, thank you very much. Zoey had seen plenty of good-looking guys who were total jerks. Rune seemed as nice as they come. He was smart, respectful, and polite. Even chivalrous.

And he had absolutely no interest in her.

He doesn't see the point. Zoey took in a deep breath and let it out slowly. She checked the time again.

He says I'm better off not having a boyfriend. She pulled off her glasses and rubbed her eyes. If she'd been alone in her room, she might have cried a little.

What am I supposed to do, throw myself at him? No, that would probably go over the big idiot's head, too. And at any rate, she'd never thrown herself at anybody before, so she'd probably do it wrong.

He's not interested.

Really not interested. At all. Was that even possible for guys? Zoey wasn't what anyone would call experienced in these matters.

Jaden had been her first and only boyfriend. He was your average goofy teenage boy, but he always respected her boundaries, even if he didn't mind helping her map them out a time or two.

Despite all the red flags from Rune, she'd accepted his story about where he'd come from because nobody appears out of nowhere, bounces off a car, and then gets up and brushes his pointy-eared self off. But if his closed-off personality was typical of his kind, she had to wonder where little baby elves came from.

"Ridiculous," she muttered.

"What's that, Zoey?" Kenya said. She suffered alongside Zoey in Mr. Watkins's English class.

"Nothing. Just…thinking."

"Is anything wrong? I mean, why are you out here by yourself at the bus stop? I thought you had a car."

"I do. It's back at home. I…" Zoey let the rest of the sentence hang in the air. She didn't want to say anything else. She had humiliated herself in front of Rune and wasn't ready for an encore performance.

"Okay," Kenya said. "But if something is wrong—"

"Nothing's wrong."

Everything was wrong. And not just because Rune had slammed the door on any hope she may have had of them getting together. Tonight was something else. Her gut rumbled and churned with the memory of dank tunnels and lurking monsters—and Rune's cryptic warning to be on the lookout for "anything odd."

People existed who could bend reality to their will, and the world was bigger and wilder than she knew. Any other time, that thought would have filled her with giddy joy. But that wasn't the whole story. Apparently the world was also more dangerous than she could have ever imagined. She was lucky to be alive.

Magic was real. Monsters were real. And somewhere in Old Louisville was a sorcerer Rune thought was playing with fire.

What do you do when your eyes have been opened to the capital-t Truth? Zoey checked the time again. The bus was late. Surely it would be here in another minute or two. As soon as she got home, she was going to run and collapse in her mom's arms, just like she did when she was little and scared and lonely.

"Tell Momma all about it," her mother would say.

But how? How could she explain any of this to her parents? Zoey longed to see the world, and her parents encouraged her to follow her dreams. But they weren't the adventurous type. Getting them to try Chinese food was a major accomplishment.

"They aren't ready for this," she whispered. Then she chuckled. *She* wasn't ready for this! She still didn't understand anything that had happened.

Telling Momma all about it was not a good plan, she decided. She would have to keep it to herself until she understood it better… and hope the world didn't end before she got a handle on things.

What was taking the stupid bus so long?

A car pulled up to the bus stop, a bright green two-door with a thumping subwoofer. Zoey recognized it at once.

The young driver rolled down the passenger window. He was tall, dark…okay looking. "Hey, Zoey!" he called. "Need a ride?"

Zoey bit her lip and looked up the street. Still no bus in sight.

"Hi, Jaden," she said. "Do you mind driving me home?"

The other girls were about to tease Zoey about catching a ride with Jaden; she could see it in their eyes. She shot them down with a pointed glare.

"See you Monday!" Vanessa called.

Zoey nodded. Whatever.

She walked up to the car and slid into the passenger seat. Jaden pulled into traffic as she clicked her seatbelt.

"Problems with your car?"

"No," Zoey said. "I was… No."

"You sure? You weren't in another accident, were you?" Jaden's dad ran the glass and body shop that had taken care of her windshield back in September, so Jaden knew all about her "accident" with Rune.

Well, not *all* about it, obviously.

She took a breath. "I was out with Caitlin Evans and her new boyfriend. I…left the party early."

Jaden raised his eyebrows suggestively. "I hear ya," he said as he braked for a red light.

Zoey wanted to smack him. Caitlin was her best friend, and Zack seemed all right. Not a creep or anything. But there was no way she was going into greater detail about why she got separated from her ride.

Nobody said anything as Jaden weaved through traffic.

This was awkward. She and Jaden had only broken up a few months ago. They saw each other in school every day, and both of them tried to be friendly. Jaden had his faults, but at least he gave her space.

Still awkward.

Zoey pushed her glasses back up to the bridge of her nose. Her mind was swirling—so much had happened! Normally, she'd be on the phone with Caitlin, saying her thoughts out loud so she could hear them. But Caitlin wasn't there—Zoey prayed she was okay—and she was about to burst.

"Jaden, do you…?" Nope. It was a bad idea to tell him anything. "Never mind."

"No, what is it?" He pulled off the main road and into Zoey's neighborhood. They'd be at her house in a couple of minutes.

She looked him in the eye. For all his faults, Jaden's heart was in the right place. She would never—ever—go to him for romantic advice, but all the other things she'd been through were stuck in her brain, too. She had to get them out or she'd burst!

Say something, she told herself.

He'll think I fell off the deep end, she retorted.

Only if I'm too obvious.

Fine, have it your way.

She took a breath. "Do you remember when we read *A Midsummer Night's Dream* for Mr. Watkins?"

"Say what?" Jaden clearly wasn't expecting that as a conversation starter. "Yeah?"

"Do you ever wonder if all that stuff...I mean, people don't know everything, right? What if...what if there's something true in those old stories?"

"You mean like fairies and magic?" Jaden's mouth spread into an incredulous grin.

"Well, when you say it like that—"

Jaden laughed, which made Zoey draw back and hang her head.

"Wait, you're serious?" Jaden said. "I didn't know you went in for that stuff. Aliens and psychics and all that? That's Caitlin's department."

Zoey blushed at the scorn in his voice. "Just asking."

"Zo, is something up?" At any rate, she had his attention. "Why were you waiting at the bus stop so late?"

"Nothing's up," she lied. "It's just...we're seniors. Next year is college. The real world."

"I've got an older sister, Zo. College is *definitely* not the real wor—WHAT THE—?" Jaden slammed on the brakes.

Zoey's eyes shot forward, and the seatbelt locked up on her. Three or four white blurs shot across the street in front of the car, each a few feet tall and walking on four legs. Goats?

What were goats doing in the road?

The first two bounded to the curb and scurried toward the nearest backyard. Then came two more, then five or six at once. In all, a full dozen prancing goats barged across the street. The last one stopped right in front of Jaden's car and stared at him as if he'd done something offensive. Its pure white fur gleamed in the headlights.

"Are you seeing this?" Jaden sputtered. His eyes flashed panic.

"That's…odd," she said, nonplussed.

The goat continued to look at them. Its stare, with its weird, slit pupils, sent a shudder through Zoey's soul. Then the creature stuck out its tongue, baaed, and moved on.

Jaden kept his foot on the brake for another few seconds before creeping forward. "That was freaky," he finally said. "One of your neighbors keeps goats?"

"Yeah," Zoey said. "That must be it." That definitely wasn't it.

At last, Jaden pulled into the Colemans' driveway.

"I'm glad I ran into you, Zo," Jaden said. He turned to face her. "We still cool, right?"

"Yeah," Zoey said. It was nice to have a familiar face and a listening ear. "Good night. Stay safe." She smiled and got out of the car. The porch light was on, just as she'd expected.

Now, what to tell Mom and Dad?

Obviously, as little as possible. No sorcerers. No elven assassins. No renegade goats. Just a get-together that broke up early.

Jaden waited in the driveway until she got to the porch. Zoey waved, opened the front door, and stepped inside.

15

Avice spent the evening fuming as she wandered the streets of Old Louisville.

After a full month of checking every rumor, following every lead in her search for her traitorous cousin, he was nowhere to be found. He'd been smart to cross the Mere. On the backwater coach road north toward Dunswale, he would stand out. People talked. It was only a matter of time before informants pointed Avice toward the waymaker and ultimately to Claeus himself.

Humans gave her a wide berth as she walked by. They didn't even realize they were doing it: she projected an aura of glamour that nudged them out of her way. She wasn't invisible—anyone could see her—but she clouded their minds to make them disinterested. People saw her pass and simply didn't care, not about her and certainly not about the sword and pistol strapped to her side beneath her umbersay cloak.

She left Phipps's neighborhood behind and headed north. Now, instead of quaint houses, colorful storefront windows were decorated with spiderwebs and ghosts and bats—absurd tokens of the darkness Fallow folk liked to dabble in at Hallowfest. If they only knew what real darkness was, they would beg for her protection.

But that would have to wait. She had a traitor to find before she could indulge in anything fun like terrorizing the Fallow folk—not to mention helping the sarding sorcerer the Keeper had sent her to babysit.

She stopped herself. It wasn't wise to question orders. Leave that for Whisper to contend with. She could only imagine her father bristling at the idea of attempting two errands at once. It could only lead to confusion. Which took priority: helping the sorcerer or capturing Claeus?

It wasn't her place to question the King of Shadows' plans. Whatever Whisper thought of the plan, he agreed to it. His Majesty wanted a toehold in the Fallow, and that meant Phipps got whatever help he needed—even if Avice would have preferred searching for her cousin.

She never expected to see him at the sorcerer's house. There was no time to prepare, and she hated being unprepared. Almost as much as she hated disappointing her father.

It wouldn't happen again, she vowed. Avice could imagine her father's disapproval. "You should have been paying attention."

"I had no way to know he would be there," she protested, as if her father could hear her.

"You should have expected it," his voice scolded in her mind. "Claeus is no fool. He knew you would find him eventually. And he has the coffer. He was sure to know His Majesty's agents would be at work."

Avice gritted her teeth. The coffer.

In her zeal to find Claeus—she refused to honor his byname, Rune—she had nearly forgotten *why* she was looking for him. The coffer was a powerful artifact, though she wasn't clear on what it was supposed to do. Regardless, the thought of the auph using its powers against her made her shudder.

Then she scoffed. He'd more likely destroy himself if he tried. That would solve part of her problem, but it wouldn't return the coffer to its rightful owner.

She came to an intersection. Fallow automobiles clogged the streets with their noise and their unbearable stink of steel, smoke, and gasoline. Claeus's sanity had been up for debate before he escaped to this wind-wracked place. What might weeks of all this roiling chaos have done to him?

If he became completely unhinged, he'd be more unpredictable and dangerous than ever. And if the coffer was truly as powerful as people said… Avice didn't relish the thought of an artifact like that in his hands.

It didn't matter how formidable her cousin had become. He was still a fugitive from the King's justice. She would find what he had stolen and bring him in, dead or alive.

The more she thought about it, the more she felt the sorcerer might be of some use in that regard. It was a stroke of luck that Claeus had gotten wind of Phipps, but it wasn't entirely unpredictable. Claeus was apparently intent on causing as much mischief for His Majesty as he could. Hiding out in the same city as Phipps, he was bound to show up at some point.

All the more reason that she should have anticipated his eventual arrival.

Next time, she'd be on her guard. But for now, she had work to do. With her head cleared and her limbs stretched, it was time she got busy.

Before long she arrived at the corner of Fourth and Broadway. Avice studied the huge brick building across the street. Mahwe, the waymaker, had told her there was a tavern hidden on the fifteenth floor where Saynim folk liked to gather.

Two or three humans trickled toward the building, third-shift workers reporting for duty. A few minutes later, second-shifters started filing out.

Avice scanned every face as she channeled the airy chaos to heighten her senses. Mahwe had given her a name: Morty Grindle. Soon Avice spotted him, a squat, muscular ayleck with a bulbous nose.

According to the waymaker, Morty knew all there was to know about the Saynim folk of Louisville. If a stranger had come to town, the ayleck had heard about it.

He headed east for a block and then turned north. Avice shadowed at a discreet distance. She followed the ayleck almost to the river until he stood before a brick wall with a seam that marked the division between two tightly packed buildings.

He looked around. At this hour of the night, the streets were nearly deserted. He had no clue Avice was drawing near beneath her glamour. Confident no one was looking, he stepped forward and vanished into the seam.

She stepped through behind him as soon as she caught up. As her booted foot touched the wall, it rippled like a pebble dropped in a pond and spread open in front of her.

On the other side was a narrow corridor lit by a bare electric lightbulb. She stalked forward and then down a flight of brick steps. Flitting shadows told Avice that Morty was only a little ahead of her. She hurried her pace.

At the bottom of the stairs, an archway opened into a vast open space, a warehouse converted to a wild, colorful marketplace, now mostly quiet. Beneath a spiderweb of metal girders, a motley collection of goblins, trolls, and humans hawked their wares from carts, kiosks, and permanent structures of brick or wood. Their clothing was a jumble of Fallow and Saynim styles: beribboned cotton trade shirts over coarse, blue denim trousers; breezy smock dresses and white canvas tennis shoes.

The waymaker had called the place Underborough. It was the largest neighborhood of Saynim folk in all of Louisville. Avice slowly closed the distance between herself and Morty. He didn't seem to notice at all.

Many stores were closed for the night. Others still bustled with activity. It was never truly "night" where Saynim folk dwelled.

The ayleck passed a laundry stall, and the detergent fumes made Avice catch her breath. Soon, the shops gave way to houses—tiny hovels, really—either free-standing at the edges of the bazaar or accessed from the network of corridors that spread out from it. Morty strolled down a dingy side tunnel.

Avice didn't want to confront the ayleck in his own home. Not even she was that self-assured. Aylecks were famously territorial. If she threatened him in his domain, he'd never listen to her.

But aylecks were also famously hoarders. It was a matter of catching his attention in the open, where he still felt he was in control.

She tossed a handful of silver coins onto the ground.

He stopped in his tracks at the sound of metal against concrete. He spun around and looked her in the eye.

Avice smiled and gestured to the silver. "They're yours."

The ayleck's eyes flitted to the coins before rising back to Avice. "And you are…?"

"Call me Dancer." She gestured again toward the coins. "I'm looking for information. I'm willing to pay—and much more than a handful of sickles. Is there a place where we can talk?"

He arched his eyebrows. "What d'you want to talk about?" He scooped up the silver and strode toward her, opposite the way he had been going. She expected as much from an ayleck. He might be willing to bargain—he might be willing to do any number of unsavory things—but he wasn't going to take her home with him.

"I'm new in town," Avice said. "I'm looking for an acquaintance. Someone I used to work with."

The ayleck gave her the once-over. Her umbersay cloak rippled and twitched despite the absence of any wind. "What kind of work would that be?"

"This and that," she said. "This fellow goes by the name of Rune."

In front of the laundry, a gap-toothed goblin swept the stoop while his assistant closed the shutters. They gave the pair a wary look but continued with their chores.

"I know him," the ayleck said. "Pretty sure he ain't interested in seeing friends from his old job."

Avice pulled her money pouch from her vest pocket and loosened the drawstring. With a subtle smile, she pressed a quig into the ayleck's meaty hand. She released a breath and willed the airy chaos to touch the ayleck's mind. "Are you sure?"

The ayleck took a half step back and looked at the magic bean in his palm.

"I would be very grateful for your help." Avice nodded toward him, welcoming his agreement.

His face betrayed no emotion as he turned the bean between his thumb and forefinger and then pushed it to Avice's sternum. He looked her in the eye. Where before there was openness and curiosity, now there was only cold hardness.

"I'm sure you would." He let the sickles she'd dropped slide out of his other hand, and the coins landed at her feet.

Her eyes flashed. Her cloak whipped away from her side and she rested her hand on the hilt of her sword.

The ayleck stepped forward and scowled up into her face. "Are we through here?"

Avice sighed. She'd touched a nerve, and that limited her options. He wasn't interested in her money. She couldn't sway him with glamour. Escalating to threats wouldn't get her anywhere.

She cursed under her breath. "I see." She stepped back. "If you change your mind—"

"I won't," he growled.

"As you wish." She turned her back on him and strolled away. She had hoped the ayleck would prove more cooperative, but surely somebody else knew where the auph was holed up.

A voice spoke up behind her. "You ain't gonna get anything out of Morty. Anybody coulda told you that."

Avice whipped around. The street was nearly empty. Even the ayleck had vanished down the corridor toward his house.

"He don't care much for money. Never did."

She homed in on the sound of the voice. It was the goblin at the laundry stall. He leaned on his broom in front of his door.

"I hear you're looking for Rune. The name's Nooch," the goblin said. His assistant, a youngling goblin girl, hung around in the doorway. It seemed she was looking for other things to do.

Avice approached. Her cloak twitched with excitement.

Nooch flashed her a gap-toothed smile. "Nice cloak," he said. "Umbersay, ain't it? Hard to get stains out of umbersay. The usual detergents just eat through the magic."

"Is that so?"

He bowed obligingly. When he stood up straight, he came up to Avice's ribcage. He wiped a spindly hand across his balding pate. "Ah. See? You got a little stain up there." He brushed his own shoulder and pointed at Avice's. "I could take care of it for you cheap."

"I really don't have the time. You mentioned Rune."

"So I did, so I did." He bowed again. Without taking his eyes off Avice, he said, "Lottie, that's enough for tonight. I'll see you tomorrow."

"Yes, Uncle Nooch." The goblin's assistant smiled and skipped away.

"My love to your mother"

He continued to stare at Avice.

Once the girl had turned the corner, Avice said, "What do you know?"

"That you was wasting your time with Morty."

"He's not interested in treasure?"

Nooch chuckled. "He's plenty interested. But he ain't got much use for silver."

Avice arched an eyebrow.

"Every ayleck hoards something different. Some love money, sure. But others hoard knowledge or books or something else that catches their fancy." He chuckled. "I once knew an ayleck that memorized baseball statistics. You ever wonder why aylecks make such good accountants?"

"And Morty?"

"Morty's thing is contacts. He trades in favors, relationships. He'd sooner chew his arm off than betray one of his people."

"And Rune is one of his people." Avice bit back the taste of bile in her throat. She'd been sure the ayleck was her pathway to her cousin.

"I, on the other hand, am a businessman."

She gave the goblin her full attention. "What's that supposed to mean?"

He shrugged. "I'm a realist. Having somebody like the Nightwalker walking around in my city? No offense, lady, but that don't strike me as the smartest thing in the world. I hear his boss is a poxy son of a—"

Avice had her hands around the goblin's throat in a heartbeat. "Mind your tongue, manikin."

He gagged.

She let go. "Is there something useful you'd like to tell me?"

"No need to get rough," he said, sweat beading on his forehead.

"I'm listening. What do you know about Rune?"

He caught his breath but still looked her in the eye. "You want to know about the Nightwalker? Then tell me what it's worth."

16

Aside from the subtle traces of bioluminescent fungus that spider-webbed across the rafters, the tunnels between Goblintown and the mundane realm were totally dark. But the dim foxfire was enough for Rune to see by even without magic.

As he left the gearsmith behind, a deeper darkness commanded Rune's attention. Avice had finally caught up to him. He would see her again, and no doubt soon. She was nothing if not persistent. The box of ferstitch rested cold and leaden in the pocket of his bomber jacket.

But she wasn't the only one he had to worry about. Jericho was in league with the King of Shadows. Did he even understand what that meant? Whether he did or not, it was still true. His Majesty had two weapons in play. One of them was bound to strike.

Rune reached the point where rough-hewn stone gave way to more elaborate masonry, but he was still at least half a mile from the brickwork of the Butchertown tunnels. He stopped to study a waymark etched into the side of an arch.

Even drawing air, he had to lean in and squint to read the faint etching by the dim glow of an errant wanderlight. He assured himself he was still on the right path and pressed on.

It was hard not to get distracted. What did the King of Shadows need with a portal to the Fallow? Surely it wasn't for Rune's sake! He shivered at the thought. And yet his former lord had made it plain that he would stop at nothing to retrieve the artifact Rune had taken when he decided to seek other career opportunities.

He shook his head. No. The King of Shadows would settle things with Rune if given the chance, but he had bigger plans on his mind.

Of course, Jericho was the weakest link. The simplest thing to do would be to take him out of the equation, and he wouldn't even need a ferstitch ball to do it.

Rune sighed. Drawing this much air was taking its toll, deadening Rune's empathy and making him restless. Intellectually, he knew that was happening. And intellectually, he also knew two other things: one, that he was right, and two, that handling Jericho was well within his abilities.

He wouldn't even have to kill him. Just torment him with nightmares and strip away his sanity—even for a few days. Once Hallowfest passed, the King of Shadows would have to find a new stooge, and there couldn't be that many sorcerers in Louisville.

Removing Jericho would buy Rune some time, at least until the next cross-quarter day, when the Mere was thin again. By then, he could be miles away. He could find a bigger Fallow city to hide in. Or maybe a cabin on some remote mountaintop.

Rune stopped at a crossways he didn't remember from his first trip through the tunnels with Zoey. He looked right, left, and straight ahead. Nothing was familiar.

He scratched the back of his head.

He clicked his tongue and listened as the sound echoed back to him. It didn't help; no direction seemed preferable to the others. He was lost.

"Bound to be a waymark around here somewhere," he muttered to himself as he crept toward the rightmost passageway.

Rune ran his hand over the stonework at eye level, but there were no telltale scratches or imperfections. He started to sweat. There was nothing he could do but backtrack and figure out where he'd taken the wrong turn.

He hadn't gone three paces when he heard something in the dark—something big and rumbly.

Rune reached for his pistol, forgetting for a second that it was still packed away in the Colemans' guest house. His knives were who knows where.

The rumble grew louder.

Rune pulled even more heavily on the airy chaos. He gazed into the dimness, scanning the walls, the floors, the ceiling for any clue to where the danger was coming from. A cool wisp of fog tickled his nostrils.

His focus landed on an expanse of wall to his left. To a cursory glance, it seemed solid enough. Now, with his senses pushed to their limit, he could just spot the imperfections in the glamour. Something big and dark moved on the other side. He clicked his tongue once more and listened as echoes passed through the wall as if it wasn't there. His suspicion was confirmed.

The wall evaporated into nothingness, revealing a great chamber beyond.

There were three figures within: a woman seated on a stool carved of a single mass of mother-of-pearl; a seven-foot-tall troll at her side; and a water panther, as big as a bear, stalking in front of them.

Somewhere between the great cat's torso and its hindquarters, its tawny fur gave way to glistening, coppery scales, and a ridge of spines adorned its back as far as its serpentine tail.

The cat rumbled with a deep, full-bodied growl and gazed at Rune with malevolent green eyes. The troll stood silent in his trousers, blue vest, and linen shirt, arms crossed and face expressionless. But it was the woman that frightened Rune the most. He'd never met her, but he'd heard the stories—and he'd met the troll before. There was no doubt who his mistress was.

"Good evening, Mr. Rune," Maya Tecumseh said.

The steady flow of magic he'd been drawing on crowded out everything but restless energy. The Blessing provided a mantle of cool detachment. It was the only thing that kept Rune from kneeling before the Merlady in abject submission. She was resplendent in every way. She sat on her opalescent stool like a queen, straight-shouldered, her long-limbed swimmer's body a study in effortless grace.

She was barefoot, and her brown skin contrasted with a white linen shift that left her right shoulder bare. Her only jewelry was a necklace of turquoise beads, polished but unshaped. Her jet-black hair fell behind her ears and down her back like an inky waterfall.

The water panther rumbled again and flicked its snaky tail. Rune took a step back.

"Don't mind Mr. Whiskers," the Merlady said. "He's only being friendly."

The troll grinned, making the angular tattoos on the side of his head twitch. The water panther glided forward, casting fluid shadows on the stone walls of the chamber. Glowing green rocks had been strewn on the floor, bathing the room in gentle light. The creature's whiskers flared. They were thick and stiff near the roots, more like a catfish's barbels than anything that belonged on a feline.

Rune's emotions had gone numb, but his rational mind was in overdrive. He was vividly aware of the danger. Maya Tecumseh was no ordinary foe; she was a Gentrywoman—a master of the watery chaos. She might be the most powerful being in a hundred miles, maybe a match for the King of Shadows himself.

And she wanted something from Rune.

His mind raced as he considered his options, and they all boiled down to "Run away!" But where to? Behind the Merlady was a stone-rimmed pool seven feet across. A light source at the bottom created undulating ripples of green light on the ceiling above. That way was suicide, and there were no other obvious exits except the archway he'd just passed through. He wondered how far Mr. Whiskers could leap in a single pounce.

"My lady," Rune said with a stiff bow, grateful to have remembered his manners before Maya took offense. "I didn't expect to see you here."

"Indeed," she said. She made a clicking noise with her tongue, and the water panther glided to her side.

Rune swallowed and bowed slightly to the troll. "The answer I gave your associate hasn't changed, I'm afraid."

"Still not willing to work for me?" She uncrossed her legs and leaned forward with a gleam in her eyes. "You're doing all right on your own, then?"

Rune tapped his fingers against his thigh. His inside jacket pocket was still heavy with the cash he owed the Colemans for his rent. "Well enough."

The Merlady frowned in mock offense. At least, Rune hoped it was a put-on. "But think of how well you could be doing. I could use a man like you on the other side. Especially one with your particular skills."

"I'm…honored, my lady," Rune said. "I prefer my freedom."

Maya smiled. Her teeth were as bright and white as her garment. "Far be it from me to impinge upon a man's freedom," she said.

Mr. Whiskers yawned, baring pearly fangs as long as butcher knives. As he stretched, he spread equally impressive claws from his webbed paws.

"So tell me. How are things coming with the Hollarts? Any progress?"

Rune sucked in a breath. In all the dust-up over Jericho, he'd forgotten about Gimp Hollart and his estranged wife. As soon as Maya said the name, his mind flashed back to his conversation with the troll at Gamaufry Tavern. It was Maya Tecumseh who'd referred Mr. Hollart to Rune in the first place.

The Blessing gave Rune a near-perfect poker face, however. He looked the Merlady in the eye and simply said, "These things take time."

She narrowed her eyes. "I had Vex here pass your name to Mr. Hollart as a favor, Mr. Rune. I assured him you could get results."

"As I said, my lady—"

"Your inaction is liable to reflect badly on me. You wouldn't want that, would you, Mr. Rune?"

His temples pounded, but thankfully the Blessing had stripped him of fear. "Not at all, my lady."

"Good."

"Though, you should know…"

"Yes?" Her eyes flashed. A woman like Maya Tecumseh wasn't used to being corrected.

Rune swallowed. "The King of Shadows is also interested in a toehold on the other side."

"Is that so?"

Rune couldn't tell if this was news to Maya or not. She certainly didn't seem worried about it. "I've had dealings with some of his pawns. A human sorcerer and his servant."

Maya's eyes sparkled. "Mr. Rune, do you honestly believe you could do the slightest thing to oppose the King of Shadows?"

His face warmed.

"You're too young to remember when the Peacebringer fell. The King of Shadows was determined to fill the power vacuum. He might have held sway over this entire region…if it weren't for me."

"You defeated him all by yourself, did you?" Rune didn't know why he said it, other than a lifetime's weariness with posturing, self-important lords and nobles.

Maya's expression turned suddenly sharp. Mr. Whiskers rumbled by her side. The troll's arms dropped to his side and his eyes flashed fury. But Rune held his ground.

"As I recall, the First of Swords offered some minor assistance," the Merlady conceded. "And the Amber Queen, of course."

"Of course."

"Speaking of whom, rumor has it that something belonging to the Amber Queen has lately gone missing."

Rune's mouth went dry. "Is that so?"

"My sources wonder if it had anything to do with the recent unpleasantness at Cruc Máw."

"That seems…reasonable, my lady."

"What seems *reasonable*, Mr. Rune, is that whoever is in possession of that coffer holds a fair bit of leverage. I can think of several Gentry folk who would love to get their hands on it."

"Is that what's missing, then? A coffer?"

Maya Tecumseh flashed a wry smile. "Then again, the thief might be too stupid to realize he's swimming in deep water. He's liable to drown if he's not careful."

"I imagine whoever stole this coffer is aware of the dangers, my lady."

She rested her hands in her lap. "Are you perspiring, Mr. Rune?"

"It has been a long day, my lady."

"In my service, you could have weekends off." She glanced at the troll. "Vex?" The troll stooped to pick up one of the small glowing rocks on the floor. He lumbered toward Rune, who found himself making a deferential nod.

The Merlady smiled, though not quite warmly. "I believe in hiring the best people and then giving them the freedom to excel, Mr. Rune."

"You are a consummate professional, I'm sure," he said as the troll offered him the rock.

"And I pay well," she continued. "I'm not without connections in the Fallow. You could live in luxury. You could enjoy my protection from anyone who would wish you harm."

"As I said, my lady, I prefer my freedom."

"Have it your way." The Merlady gestured, and Vex grasped Rune's hand and pressed the glowing rock into his palm.

"Should you change your mind, use this to contact me."

The rock was cool to the touch, oval shaped, flat on one side, and no bigger than a musket ball. It seemed heavier than it should have been. Rune looked at it, then back at Maya.

"You need merely repeat my name: Mayatakaamhshi."

Rune started. Names had power. For Maya to speak her own full name in his hearing made her vulnerable.

After another second's reflection, though, the truth sank in. The Merlady's name was safe on his lips because there was no way he could ever use it to harm her. She was too far out of his league.

"Do look out for Mr. Hollart," Maya said. "I would consider it a great favor."

One you'll hold over me for the rest of my days, Rune thought. What he said, though, was, "Mr. Hollart has paid for my services, my lady." He tried to affect a casual tone. "If you have an interest in his affairs, that's your concern, not mine."

Maya smirked as she stood up and stepped into the pool. Her shift dissolved into her body as her long legs transformed into an even longer serpentine tail. The rest of her body changed as well. Her skin darkened to greenish black as her eyes grew and her ears shrunk to slits on the sides of her head. Her whole face grew sleek, reptilian. Her long, black hair dissolved to be replaced by a ridge of fibrous spines.

She summoned Mr. Whiskers with another clicking sound. The water panther disappeared beneath the water with hardly a ripple.

"A man of your talents shouldn't have to live in a shed, Mr. Rune." This time, when the Merlady spoke, her teeth were needle-sharp.

She dove into the water. The troll snapped his fingers, and the lights in the chamber went out.

Rune's legs went wobbly, and he spent several minutes leaning against the wall of the chamber, taking deep, measured breaths.

17

Avice whispered into the wind and waited among the tombs for Daws to receive her telepathic summons.

A cemetery—for humans! Why couldn't they all be cremated? That's how it was in the King of Shadows's domain. The row after row of marble gravestones only underlined how backward and uncivilized the Fallow could be.

Elves, dwarves, and every other kind of Saynim folk had a simple essence. Some might call it a soul. By whatever name, it was an uncomplicated thing. It never got in the way. It served its purpose, and when one died, it died too. Human souls were different. Complicated. Too many moving parts. When a human died, sometimes a piece split off. Sometimes that piece didn't want to leave its body.

At least, that's the story Avice had always heard. She couldn't say she'd ever known of a human to rise from the dead, but why take chances?

Daws was late. She whispered again and projected her thoughts into the night.

She went back to pondering things while she waited. What would happen when the auph died? Was his soul elven or human? She'd have to remember to incinerate his body just to be on the safe side.

At any rate, the ley line ran directly through this cemetery. It was perfect for the kind of power the King of Shadows needed. And thanks to Nooch, she knew where to find the last thing needed for the ritual. If she was lucky, it would smoke out Claeus himself.

In the still of night, the hairs on her arms and neck stood up with the ebb and flow of magical energy. The Mere was thin here and getting thinner every hour. In three more days, the conditions would be perfect.

Black wings fluttered overhead. Avice pushed away from the gravestone she'd been leaning on as Daws landed atop it in the form of an ordinary crow.

"Well?"

"No sign of your fugitive," the werecrow said in his gurgling croak. He bowed and averted his eyes as if expecting her censure. "And no luck with the other thing, either."

Avice gritted her teeth. "The other thing" kept her from focusing on her cousin. But thanks to Nooch, maybe not for long. "No worries," she said.

Daws dared an upward glance at her. "You've found something?"

She held out a slip of paper, a laundry ticket with a name and an address scribbled on the back. Daws grasped it in his beak and set it down on top of the gravestone to read in the moonlight. "The, er, other thing."

She nodded. "That's where you'll find it. And keep your eyes open for Rune."

"As you say."

"I'm counting on you, Mr. Daws. I can't be everywhere." She looked him in the eye and smiled. "Moonless night."

Daws cocked his avian head. "But the moon is waxing."

"It's just something we say. It means 'good luck.'"

"Ah. Yes," the werecrow said. "We'll take care of it, Miss Dancer."

"I'm sure you will," she said. "And I'll take care of Claeus."

With the last of her arrangements made, Avice returned to the sorcerer's house, riding the wind. It was a few minutes before midnight. The crowd from earlier had dispersed. Good. Avice and Phipps had work to do.

She pulled her umbersay cloak tight around her. Expelling a sharp breath, she relaxed control and allowed the cloak to evaporate her into smoke so she could slip under the crack of the back door. The effect only lasted a second. As soon as her body re-formed she sped to the basement. Phipps did his ritual work there; that's where she would find him.

It's where she should have found him before. What was he doing having dinner guests when he was supposed to be preparing a ritual? Not for the first time, she questioned her mother's wisdom in approaching the man in the first place.

The thought had barely crossed her mind when her umbersay cloak tightened around her neck, revolting at the slightest whiff of disloyalty to the King of Shadows. She stopped to settle herself. This was His Majesty's errand, no less than capturing Rune. Her lot was to obey.

The cloak eased off.

Still, what would this Phipps do when the veil was pulled back? She didn't trust humans, no matter what side of the Mere they lived on.

The room was cool but not cold. The far end of the bare cement floor was clear of furniture and marked with an elaborate casting circle inscribed with polygons and bounded by glyphs at the four cardinal directions. Just inside the door, Phipps's long, wooden worktable strained under the weight of numerous candles and a collection of ritual implements—chalice, bell, mortar and pestle, mirror, several wands, a ceremonial dagger.

There was also an electric lamp, already lit, stacks of storage boxes, and a neat row of musty, leather-bound notebooks. All the trappings of an arcane sorcerer who had to lean on such crutches to wield power. It was easy to imagine the attraction of what the King of Shadows offered for one such as Phipps.

Tucked in among the tools and implements was a faded photograph: a young human couple sitting together at a park bench. Avice could find hints and echoes of Phipps in both of their faces. The woman was dressed in a floral pattern dress. The man wore coarse blue denim and a plain shirt, a bit dingy, with a name embroidered above the pocket.

Opposite the worktable was a coat tree bearing a crimson robe and stole. Beside that was a bookcase for all the volumes Phipps apparently didn't want out in the open in his sitting room or library.

Avice looked back at the worktable. Tucked underneath it was a simple three-legged stool. A large toad sat upon it, looking up at her with big, watery eyes.

She had seen those eyes before. Drawing her sword, she said, "Is there anything else you'd care to mess up for me?"

The toad croaked. It hopped from the stool to the floor, transforming in midair into the sorcerer's loathsome servant. "Hospitality is important around here," Boggs said, a tremor in his voice. "If you th-think otherwise, then…well…"

Avice took a step toward him, and he backed toward the casting circle.

"You let a wanted man escape."

Boggs sidestepped the circle and edged along the wall.

"S-seems to me the Covenant saw things different," he said. His eyes darted from Avice's glare to her dwarven bronze sword. "I reckon it'll do the same thing again if you get much closer."

She gritted her teeth in frustration. The buffoon was sabotaging the King of Shadows and using the Law of Hospitality to do it. The worst part was that he was probably right.

"You shouldn't have let him escape."

"I'm only doing my job, ma'am. I'm sworn to serve Jericho."

"Is that what you think you're doing?" She took another step. Boggs backed away toward the coat tree. "Your master is but a small part of the King of Shadows's plans. He will have satisfaction on the traitor—and on any who would stand in the way."

Boggs licked his lips. "I may have to ask you to leave."

"You wouldn't dare."

Phipps cut the argument off when he swung open the door. "Boggs, have you—?" He gasped at the sight in front of him. Avice sheathed her sword but let her senses heighten with an onrush of airy chaos. Let the sorcerer make even a hint of a move against her, and she'd draw her weapon again, faster than anything he had ever seen.

"What's going on?" he said. He reached for one of his wands on the worktable.

Avice took a step back. *Quick reflexes,* she noted. But she didn't draw. No need to escalate the conflict…yet. The dark wood in the sorcerer's hand pulsed with ready energy, fierce and hot. A blasting rod, then. Perfect for disabling a magical foe.

"Master—" Boggs began.

"You need to keep a tighter leash on your toad," Avice interrupted.

Phipps's eyes flitted between them. "Is there something you'd like to tell me, Boggs?"

"A…minor disagreement, M-Master. Easily set aside." He gazed at Avice, daring her to say otherwise.

For an instant she considered it. Should she tell Phipps about Claeus, about how Boggs helped him escape? Laying that revelation on the table would be deeply gratifying.

But not, perhaps, productive. The situation was complicated enough as it was. The King of Shadows wanted Phipps to succeed.

To do that, he needed Boggs. Avice didn't have to like it; she only had to submit.

At any rate, she'd find her renegade cousin soon enough now—there were only so many places he could run.

"Nothing to concern you, Magister Jericho," she said with a curt bow. The words tasted like sawdust. "Boggs is your servant to command, not mine."

"That's right," Phipps said, straightening his shoulders. "He's proven a more than capable assistant. Do remember that."

"Of course, Magister," Avice said. She would extend Boggs whatever honor he was due. But if Phipps thought she trusted him any further than pistol range…

Phipps matched her own icy glare. "Boggs tells me you were here earlier."

"I was in the neighborhood," she said. "I hoped to catch you then. My apologies if I disturbed your entertaining." She gazed at Boggs, willing him not to say a word. Thankfully, he didn't.

"Not a problem," Phipps said, slowly.

Avice could almost see the gears turning in his mind. He was no fool, after all. He knew he was walking a tightrope; he'd be on his guard, no matter what. Avice appreciated his circumspection.

And he still had his blasting rod in his hand.

"I can't help but think you've seemed distracted lately," he said. "It's like your heart isn't really in this."

"Not at all," Avice assured him.

"When you first appeared to me in a vision, you seemed more…enthusiastic."

That was my mother, borrowing my face. "Visions are always subjective, Magister Jericho. One's voice and mannerisms don't always come through accurately."

"Is that so?" Phipps glanced at Boggs, who simply shrugged. The sorcerer strolled to the back of the room. Avice followed, hands loosely at her side, ready to reach for a weapon. Her cloak twitched with anticipation. "Because at this point," Phipps added, "I can't afford for anything to go wrong."

"Magister Jericho—"

He held up a hand to silence her. "I know, I know. You serve your unseen lord, and—you say—he desires to strike a pact with someone of my talents."

Her cheeks flamed. Through gritted teeth she said, "I am not a liar."

He smiled and spread his arms, but then his eyes turned cold as he pointed the blasting rod at her and hissed, "*Shari!*"

An electric pulse shot through Avice's body from head to foot. She tried to reach for her pistol but couldn't move her arms. Behind her, Boggs gasped out a curse.

"I command you, Dancer, or by whatever other name you are called, to appear before me." From the center of his conjuring circle, he pointed to a triangle carved in the floor just beyond its perimeter.

Avice's eyes flashed. She leaped to the spot.

Inside his circle, Jericho shifted his weight from one foot to the other. "I adjure you, Dancer, to stay your hand from any harm or mischief that you would work against me—noxious clouds, wasting sickness, fire, water, madness, or any other weapon in your arsenal."

Avice moaned and tried to look away. Electricity coursed over her.

"I charge you, Dancer, to answer truly, honestly, and with a clear voice whatsoever questions I put before you."

"Magister, this is entirely unnecessary—"

"*Shari!*"

Avice doubled over. Sparks rippled across her body. Her cloak fluttered and roiled with the shifting colors of a storm cloud.

"Master," Boggs whimpered.

The sorcerer wasn't listening. "I am not some pushover," he said. He balled his hands into fists.

"Of course not," Avice said. She took a half-step back, careful to remain within the confines of the triangle etched in the floor. "I never said you were." She lowered herself into a ready crouch, willing her cloak to twist and flinch with anxiety, not fury.

"Just so we're clear. I *can* trust you to help me perform your lord's ritual?"

"Implicitly," she spat.

"Explicitly is better." He tapped the blasting rod against his open palm. "Right, Boggs?"

Avice heard Boggs's sigh. "Our kind are sticklers for the letter of the law, Master."

"I serve my lord in all things," Avice said through gritted teeth. "He chose you, not the other way around. He wishes your success, and his wish is my command."

"Good."

"Even if you are a miserable plague sore."

"Watch yourself!" Jericho leveled the blasting rod at her but didn't use it again.

She made a show of holding up her hands defensively. "You wanted truthful answers."

"Heh. Touché."

She bowed her head and clenched her fists.

"Not that it's any of your business, Dancer, but I've been burned before. You'll forgive me if I prefer to cover my bases." Phipps kept rocking from side to side.

Avice remembered. Her mother's letter had explained a little of what she had unearthed about the sorcerer's history. Perhaps it was time to tell him what she knew and see how he reacted. "The King of Shadows is nothing like Torralva."

The sorcerer's eyes flashed and he took a step back inside his conjuring circle. "That's a dangerous name to speak in my presence."

Avice shrugged. "We all outgrow our teachers eventually. I find that most of the time, they're proud of us when we do."

Jericho's face darkened.

"But to your point: my lord keeps his word."

"Everyone says that, don't they? No one announces that they're going to stab you in the back. They just do it."

She wagged a finger at him. "Are you speaking of the past or the present, Magister Jericho? The fact that you and your teacher parted ways—"

"I will not discuss Torralva with a minion," Jericho said. "He left me, not the other way around."

Avice ignored the insult. She was getting under his skin, and the feeling was intoxicating. "You frightened him."

Jericho tightened his jaw. Avice barely concealed a wry smile.

He trained the blasting rod on her again. "None. Of your. Business."

She folded her arms. Her cloak billowed lazily about her calves.

"Now I will have answers," Phipps said.

"Let me guess. You want to clarify the terms of my lord's patronage."

"For starters."

"Power. That's what you want, isn't it? Power to leave behind these clumsy, inefficient tools and command the forces of creation with a word." She swept her hand toward his workbench with its implements and ingredients. "Predictable, I must say. But understandable."

"You know nothing about me. Power is meaningless without a goal."

"And what is your goal, sorcerer?"

He sneered and raised his blasting rod. "A sorcerer works magic only for himself," he said.

Avice grinned. "And you expect me to believe that you actually care about the younglings you surround yourself with?"

"The world is a cruel place," he said. He tightened his lips. "They need an edge, before somebody swallows them whole. I can give it to them." He flexed his fingers around the grip of the blasting rod. "But I refuse to justify my actions to you, Dancer, or anyone else. Talk to me about power—and the responsibilities it entails—after you've walked in my shoes awhile. Right now I'm not in the mood to be psychoanalyzed."

"As you wish. The power will be yours, more than you could imagine. You will be my lord's right hand in this world. You will wield his power. You will be his eyes and his voice."

"And in return?"

"Did I stutter? You will be his right hand. His eyes. His voice." She jutted her toe onto the edge of the triangle in which she stood. Nothing happened. "Anything beyond that, you may negotiate in person when the King of Shadows arrives."

"I demand—"

"Isn't that how this works? The sorcerer—forgive me, the magician—summons an unspeakable power and the two strike a mutually satisfying bargain? You can't put the cart before the horse."

"And the King of Shadows will listen?" Jericho wet his lips. "There are lines I won't cross, not even for the kind of power he offers."

Avice remembered the photograph on the worktable. "Something your parents taught you?"

Jericho glowered. "The most important lesson my parents taught was never—ever—be anyone's floor mat. Would you like to put that lesson to the test?"

"Not today, I think." She paused. "And you were the one who wanted answers from me."

"How good of you to remember."

"Then let me educate you." She breathed deep and drew to herself the airy chaos. "Lesson one. The King of Shadows has offered you the greatness you have always sought. Your only job is to receive his gift and be grateful."

"Now just a minute—"

"Lesson two. I couldn't care less about your faithless mentor or your pathetic parents or anything else. So either help people or enslave them. It doesn't matter to me. I'm here to do a job, and I have sworn to my lord that I will do it to the best of my ability. My people keep their promises."

"I will not have you addressing me in that—"

"*Lesson three.*" Avice's face warmed and her heart pounded. "Never try to bind someone without knowing their true name." She lunged for Phipps's throat, ignoring the confines of the triangle where she'd been standing. With her hand tight on his throat, her cloak rippled around her, and she locked her eyes on him. A malevolent grin crossed her face. "And my name. Isn't. Dancer."

Jericho returned her hateful glare. Fine. She didn't have to like the man to discharge her duties.

"You are…in my house," he croaked.

"You attacked me, remember? The constraints of Hospitality no longer apply." She squeezed his throat tighter. "I have come to deliver the last portion of the ritual. The pronunciation is fairly straightforward, but my lord bids me coach you until you are satisfied. Shall we?"

He nodded, eyes bulging.

"Good." She let go, and Jericho took a deep, rasping breath. She produced a leaf of parchment from inside her doublet.

The magician glared at her, but he took the parchment and scanned the first page. Avice basked in his newfound respect.

He read for a moment in silence. "This bit about a sacrifice?"

"Taken care of. Or soon will be. All will be in order at the appointed time."

He grunted. The fire was still blazing in his eyes when he said, "It seems you've thought of everything."

Avice bowed with a flourish. "As you say, Magister."

18

Maya Tecumseh spoiled Rune's appetite. He forced himself to eat a bowl of stew at Gamaufry Tavern anyway.

It wasn't enough to have Avice and Jericho to deal with. Now he had to check in on the Gimp Hollart situation too. Keeping one step ahead of the King of Shadows was already a full-time job; he couldn't afford yet another powerful member of the Gentry breathing down his neck. And why did the Merlady even care about some troll from the backwoods?

Hollart had been staying in a room in the sub-basement of the Brown Hotel that the tavern-keeper kept for guests who preferred to sleep closer to the earth. Rune sent him word suggesting they meet the next afternoon and pay Mrs. Hollart a visit. Maybe she'd had time to cool off after her run-in with Rune at the diner. Maybe she'd be willing to hear her husband out. Then at least Mr. Hollart would be satisfied that Rune had done what he could.

He hoped it would satisfy the Merlady, too.

Rune pinched the bridge of his nose. This was getting complicated, but he would have to see it through. He finished his supper, left his payment on the table, and took his leave.

Hurrying through the tunnels, navigating in near-total darkness, and keeping his wits about him in Maya's presence had left him magically exhausted. His mind was numb from too much sensory input, and all he wanted was to close his eyes, dismiss the airy chaos, and sleep. Thankfully, the buses were still running, so he went home the Fallow way.

Rune slept until after noon, then bathed and put on the same clothes he'd taken off the night before. It was still a few hours until Mr. Hollart was expecting him, which was fine. He didn't relish confronting the troll's wife. At least he'd slept off the last effects of the Blessing. On a good day, interpersonal contact was a challenge. He preferred to keep to himself, which he chose to believe was more a defense mechanism than a personality quirk. Empathy was a trait rarely rewarded at the Haw. A good night's sleep replenished whatever empathy the Blessing had stolen from him.

There was still one thing he needed to do. With his envelope of rent money in hand, he strode across the yard and knocked on the Colemans' back door.

Zoey's father answered. He wasn't an especially tall man, a little heavy around the middle, but full of energy as he swung the screen door open and stepped onto the stoop. His salt-and-pepper hair was neatly trimmed, and he carried himself with the confidence of a natural leader. He wore what Rune had come to think of as the man's Saturday-morning uniform: faded blue jeans and a University of Kentucky tee shirt. Any other day, he'd have been in a suit and tie.

"Rune," he said with a respectful nod.

"Reverend Coleman," Rune said, offering him the envelope. "I'm sorry this is late, but it's all there."

"I'm sure it is," Rev. Coleman said.

Rune listened for other voices inside. The only ones he heard were on the television. Now that he'd regained possession of his emotions, his thoughts turned to Zoey. How was she feeling after last night's mischief?

"Is…Zoey here?"

Rev. Coleman frowned.

"I mean…she's all right, isn't she?"

He quirked an eyebrow. "Why wouldn't she be?"

"No reason," Rune said. He drew in a breath and, with it, a bit of airy chaos to settle his mind.

Rev. Coleman peered down at Rune from the stoop. "You wouldn't know anything about what Zoey was doing last night, would you?"

Even without the Blessing, Rune had been trained to keep his thoughts and feelings to himself. That skill served him well as he looked Zoey's father in the eye and considered how to answer.

"Wasn't she planning to go to some kind of party?" Rune said, putting on his most innocent expression.

"That's what she told us," Rev. Coleman said. "She left here last night with her friend Caitlin, but she came home with Jaden McNeal. Do you know him?"

"No, sir."

Rev. Coleman sized Rune up and decided he was telling the truth. "Her mother and I would rather she didn't revisit that particular mistake."

"Dad, where's—" Zoey appeared at the door and stopped abruptly when she saw Rune. "Where's the toolbox? It's not in the laundry room." She hesitated for a second, then added, "The hook on the bathroom door is loose."

"I had it in the basement yesterday," Rev. Coleman said. "I'll go get it." He glanced from his daughter to Rune and nodded. "Bye now."

When Zoey's father left, Rune whispered, "Is everything all right? This Jaden fellow—"

"Listen," she hissed. "You've got to do something. Last night…I think something happened."

Rune was suddenly alert. "Tell me."

"I saw goats. About a block from here, just crossing the street like it was nothing."

"Do any of your neighbors own goats?"

"Duh. No, that's what I'm talking about. You said to watch out for anything weird. Is that weird enough for you?"

Rune opened his magical senses and looked Zoey over from top to bottom. There was definitely some kind of aura now, something he'd missed the night before, snaking across her shoulders like a wisp of early morning fog.

"You're frowning," Zoey said.

"It looks like you brought something back with you."

"What!" she squeaked. She looked over her shoulder to see if her parents were listening, then stepped onto the stoop and closed the door behind her. "Last night you said everything was okay."

"I'm sorry," Rune said. He considered all the possible side effects of Fallow folk passing through the Mere. There was only a little time skip, and anything really dangerous would have happened almost immediately. Still. "Sometimes it takes a while to manifest," he said.

"Oh, Lord. I'm turning into a f… I'm turning into one of you, aren't I?"

"Of course not. These things are almost always temporary. And besides, it shouldn't be anything serious. We weren't in the Mere any longer than an hour."

Zoey put her hands on her hips. "Almost. Shouldn't. These words are not encouraging, Rune."

"I'm only telling you what I know," he said. He reached into his pocket for a quig and offered it to Zoey. "Take this. Keep it in your pocket."

"Is that a bean?"

Rune nodded. "It will siphon off the residue."

Her eyes brightened. "You used one of these last night on that passageway."

"That's right. Quigs are like tiny nodules of magic. Whatever you brought over will be drawn to it."

Zoey took the bean and slipped it into her jeans pocket. "Now what?"

"Now I have to go to work."

"But you can't just—"

"You'll be fine, and there's something I have to do. Something urgent."

"Something to do with Jericho."

Rune sighed. "No, actually. Something else." He'd have to deal with Jericho later. Though there was something Zoey could help him with now. "Before I go, might I make a telephone call?"

Zoey's mouth opened even wider. "You want to call someone?"

"If you'll show me how."

"I mean, sure," she said. "I've just never seen you using technology before."

"The victor adapts to his surroundings," he said, sounding a bit too much like Whisper.

Zoey quirked an eyebrow. "Anybody ever tell you it's okay to tone down the warrior talk every now and then?" She pulled her device from her hip pocket and used it to find the number Rune needed. He called the diner where Mrs. Hollart worked, found out what he needed to know, and passed the phone back to Zoey.

She grasped his hand. "I'm scared, Rune."

He expelled a slow breath before saying, "No doubt this is difficult for you."

"That's what we mere mortals call an understatement."

"Just keep that quig with you. If you like, I'll come by later to see how you're doing."

"Yes, please."

"Good." He turned to leave.

"What are you going to do now?" Zoey asked. "About Jericho, I mean. And that woman. Your cousin."

Rune bit his lip and remembered the lessons Whisper had taught him. "Observe the situation," he said. "Gather resources. Be ready to act."

"Why does that sound dangerous?"

He ignored her question. "This errand shouldn't take more than a few hours. I'll meet with you after supper. I promise."

"I'll be here."

He crossed the yard back to his apartment, feeling her eyes on him the whole way.

Preparing to act wasn't any easier today. Rune still had to figure out how to carry a firearm in a Fallow city. And this time, he didn't have his knives as a backup. If he were better at glamours, he'd just make people indifferent to his weapons. That's what Avice would do.

But he didn't have time to practice glamours. Instead, he loaded his pistol and transferred the rest of the shot he'd bought from the dwarf into his cartridge case. The case went into his empty satchel along with the pistol itself and a few basic magical tools: some string, a pocketknife, a tin of healing salve, and the bottomless snuff box Madam Samarra had extorted him into buying.

Last, he added the stone Maya Tecumseh had given him. How bad would things have to get before he'd be willing to use it? For weeks, he'd succeeded in staying out of local politics, but the Merlady seemed determined to bring him in on her side. The thought gave him the shivers.

He had one quig left to his name. He put it in the pocket of his bomber jacket, just in case.

The bus ride downtown gave him time to ponder how he was going to approach Mrs. Hollart. It all came down to convincing her that her husband had good reasons not to reveal his true nature— her reaction when discovering the truth was proof enough of that—and that he loved her even so.

Beyond that…well, Rune's experience with matters of the heart was limited. There was much he didn't understand, things he was sure he couldn't learn in an afternoon.

Just get them together, he thought, *and make sure Hollart gets to speak his piece.* The troll couldn't ask for more than that. For that matter, neither could the Merlady.

He didn't go to the Brown Hotel but to a parking garage a few blocks away. As per Mr. Hollart's instructions, Rune found him waiting on the second floor beside an old pickup truck. It might once have been solid green, but now bits of it were flecked with rust, and the tailgate and passenger door were blue. The truck bed sported a tool kit, a dingy ice chest, and something Rune didn't expect.

"Is that a bata?" He eyed the knobbed fighting stick with curiosity.

"We got coyotes back home," Mr. Hollart said. "You don't want to meet one walking in the woods." He opened the door on the driver's side. "Anyways, thanks for coming. You ready?"

"Not especially."

Rune paused at the passenger door, dreading the shock of cold iron. But he'd come prepared. He pulled a calfskin glove out of a side pocket on his satchel. He slipped it on and, shielded against the disorienting touch of the latch, he braced himself, opened the door, and took his seat. The glove worked like a charm; he didn't feel a thing.

He wouldn't have much magic available until he could get out of Mr. Hollart's rolling metal coffin, but as long as he kept his hands to himself, he would be fine.

The troll seemed unbothered by the large quantity of iron, which didn't surprise Rune. First, people like Hollart who wove the earthen chaos weren't as strongly affected by the foul metal. Second, Rune judged that Hollart's magical abilities were fairly limited. Less power meant he used it less often, and so he endured its departure with less anxiety. Third—and Rune hoped this was true—Hollart had lived in the Fallow for so long that he'd probably grown used to the touch of iron. Rune wondered how long it would take for him to build up his own resistance.

"Where's we going?" Hollart said.

Rune handed him the paper with Marla Davis's address written on it. "That's where she's living with her sister," he explained. He pulled a city map from inside his jacket. "Let's go."

Mrs. Hollart's sister lived in South Louisville, between the University and Churchill Downs. Rune was not familiar with that part of town, and Mr. Hollart was even less so. It took them a good hour to find the address Rune had gotten from Madam Samarra. The sun was close to setting when Mr. Hollart pulled to a stop two doors down from the Davis house.

It was a cloudy day. A light drizzle of rain had started to fall.

"Are you sure about this?" Mr. Hollart said. His voice was tired and tinged with desperation. Rune wondered how much sleep he'd been getting.

A truthful answer might discourage his client, so instead Rune said, "She's bound to be here."

"She might be at work," Mr. Hollart said.

Rune bowed his head. "I called the diner. Your wife doesn't work there anymore."

There was an uncomfortable silence before Mr. Hollart said, "I shoulda never pulled the truck outta the mud."

Rune shot him a puzzling glance.

"We live on a dirt road," he explained. "One day it came a rain, and the truck got stuck in a rut halfway up the drive. I wasn't even thinking."

"Your wife saw you use magic?"

Mr. Hollart choked back a sob. "I just…hauled the thing out."

"Impressive." Rune hoped Gimp Hollart didn't have a bad temper.

"So what could I do?" he continued. "I crossed the Mere thirty years ago. It was either that or declare for one of the clans, and they been feuding since before the Dream Book." He scoffed. "I figured things could only be better in the Fallow—and they were."

"But?"

"A fellow gets lonely after a while." Tears trickled down his wind-burnt cheek. "And I ain't never met nobody like Jo Ellen." He swallowed. "The look on her face when she saw me down there in the mud…. Well, what would you have done? I figured all I could do was tell her everything."

"She didn't take it well."

Mr. Hollart sniffed. "We's here, ain't we?" He sighed. "Shoulda used both hands hauling the dang truck."

"I doubt that would have made a difference," Rune said.

"Maybe not," Mr. Hollart said. After a pause, he added, "Mr. Rune, I ain't sure this is gonna work."

Rune agreed, but he knew better than to admit it. "Let me go on ahead," he said. "I'll motion for you."

He got out of the car and drew in a welcome breath, glad to be free from the troll's pickup. The airy chaos sprung back to life around him, inviting him back into its full embrace.

Rune stood up straight and began to walk. The houses in this neighborhood were modest but comfortable. They weren't too different from the Colemans' home in that regard. Many of them had pumpkins on their porches. A few—and mercifully, only a few—were decked out in ridiculous panoramas: foam rubber gravestones, plastic cauldrons, and whatnot. Phony plastic bats and spiders hung from branches. The people in the house across the street had taken the trouble to affix a whole flock of almost lifelike crows in their tree.

The Davis house bore no such decoration. By the porch light, Rune made out the address on the little plaque beside the door.

He tapped his fingers against his thigh, looking this way and that, wondering what to do.

He took a breath and approached the stoop. After ringing the doorbell, he retreated several paces to give the woman some space.

No one answered. For a second, Rune was almost relieved. Maybe she wasn't home after all. Then he could say he tried and get back to more pressing matters like Phipps.

He looked back. Two doors down, Mr. Hollart was out of his truck, leaning against the tailgate, looking like he wasn't sure what to do with his hands.

Rune sighed and rang the doorbell again.

This time, the door swung open. From behind the glass storm door, Jo Ellen Hollart glared at him. She had a child on her hip that might have been a year old.

"Listen, mister," she started, "I don't know who you are, but—"

"Mrs. Hollart," Rune interrupted, his voice steady.

"I ain't Mrs. Hollart no more!"

"It doesn't matter to me what you call yourself," Rune said. He motioned toward Mr. Hollart. "Tell *him*."

Mrs. Hollart's mouth fell open. Rune wished he were better at judging expressions. Was she surprised to see her husband? Angered? Maybe both; human souls could be complicated like that.

She pushed open the storm door and stepped onto the stoop, adjusting her daughter to the other hip. The youngest Hollart had bright blue eyes and curly red hair. Her face was round and full. And cute, Rune judged. She would probably favor her mother when she was grown, but from the way she wiggled in Mrs. Hollart's arms, she was every bit as strong and restless as any half-troll child. Mrs. Hollart held her tight and gently shushed her.

"We're through, Gimp Hollart!" she grumbled. Rune could hear the stress in her voice. She brushed past him faster than he could get out of her way. She stepped onto the lawn. "You just get in your truck and go back—" Her voice caught, and she had had to force her words out. "Go back to wherever the hell you came from!"

Something rustled in the trees. Apparently some of those crows next door were the real thing.

The little girl wiggled and squirmed.

Mr. Hollart took a tentative step forward onto the neighbor's yard. "Sweetie, you don't mean that!"

This, it turned out, was a mistake. At the sound of her father's voice, the youngest Hollart twisted around to see him.

"Dah!" she squealed.

The wind picked up. A crow flitted from one branch to the next to get a better look.

Mrs. Hollart shushed the baby, but the little one wasn't having it. "Dah!" she yelled, more forcefully this time, and with a surge of trollish strength she broke free from her mother's embrace, slid down her leg, and landed—with only the slightest wobble—on the grass.

"Stay with me, Tara," Mrs. Hollart said.

Mr. Hollart fell to his knees and opened his arms, inviting Tara to come to him.

"I said stay with Momma, sweetheart," Mrs. Hollart said, reaching for her daughter.

But Tara had already taken a couple of tentative steps away. When her mother grabbed for her hand, she pulled it back and started to run, or at least stumble forward with reckless enthusiasm. Trolls developed fast, after all. Half-trolls too, it seemed.

Mr. Hollart waddled forward on his knees.

"Gimp!" Mrs. Hollart threatened as she darted for her daughter.

But she wasn't fast enough. A surge of wind blew across the lawn, and by the time she'd spoken her husband's name, something big and black had knocked her to her knees. At the same time, something else bowled into Rune. The impact knocked him off balance, but he kept his footing.

They were diving out of the trees: black and feathered and only approximately crow-shaped. As they took flight, their bodies grew and contorted into an almost human form—the crows from before weren't Hallowfest decorations after all. But they weren't ordinary crows either.

Time slowed down as Rune drew the airy chaos to himself.

"Stay down!" he ordered the Hollarts as he dove for Tara with supernatural speed.

The largest of the flyers had already grabbed the little girl by the arm in its talons. It was soaring into the air, buoyed by a blast of eldritch wind. Rune felt the child's heartrending scream in his bones.

"Tara!" Mr. and Mrs. Hollart yelled at the same time.

There were at least a dozen of the werecrows. Most had kept their fully avian form, but four had shifted. Those led the way, flying north into the cloudy night.

A second flyer grabbed the toddler by an ankle. They soon cleared the rooftops, jerking and bouncing in midair as Tara fought to break free.

Something cold and heavy fell into the pit of Rune's stomach.

As strong as she was, Tara would eventually break loose.

And she was climbing higher every second.

19

Rune's senses sharpened.

Little Tara Hollart tugged and twisted and screamed, but her captors still bounced along in the air, shooting up ten feet for every five the child's struggles forced them to give up.

Rune's options were limited, and none of them were good. He'd never fought werecrows before, but everybody knew their reputation: sneaky, ruthless, and stronger than they looked. He weighed the benefits of doing nothing at all.

"Mr. Rune!" Gimp Hollart called, his voice breaking.

Mrs. Hollart sat on her knees on the grass, groaning and gazing up into the sky.

"Mr. Rune!" Mr. Hollart shouted again. "You gotta do something! That's my little girl up there!"

Visions of children torn from their parents assailed Rune's senses—lured into the woods or stolen from their cribs. He bit his lip. It wasn't so long ago that he was the one fleeing into the night with a kidnapped child under his arm.

Two nights ago, he'd assured Boggs that he had left that life behind. Now it was time to prove it.

"Satchel!" he called as he broke into a run.

Mr. Hollart barely beat him to the passenger door of his truck. The troll swung it open, and Rune snatched his bag and threw the strap over his head so his tools rested by his hip. He looked up. The werecrows were nearly out of sight.

The rain picked up along with the wind—though the wind was Rune's doing.

He slipped his hand inside the satchel. His pistol was on top where he'd left it, but he'd never be able to use it without endangering the child. He needed another weapon, something he could use with precision.

"Bata!" he said.

Mr. Hollart understood immediately. He grabbed his fighting stick from the truck bed and slapped it into Rune's waiting hand.

"Please, Mr. Rune…"

Rune simply nodded as the torrent of wind gathered around him, whipping the fallen leaves into a frenzy.

Mr. Hollart ran to his wife and helped her stand.

Rune flung himself into the sky. He landed on a neighbor's rooftop and then took to flight with a second bound, aiming for the fading patch of black snaking northward against the darkening clouds.

He had just cleared the utility lines when he sensed a neighbor down below, rushing out to see what was wrong.

Rune held the fighting stick close to his body and willed the wind to propel him forward faster and faster.

At last, he smashed into the werecrow that had taken the rear position. He swung at it with all his might, driving the creature from the sky. The swing altered his trajectory, and he too plunged toward the earth. He touched down on another rooftop. A second later, he threw himself upward once more.

This time they were ready for him. Three or four creatures still in crow form broke away to drive him off. These were the more agile flyers, relying entirely on their wings rather than on the airy chaos to keep them aloft. They swooped down, cawing madly, forcing Rune to break his pursuit.

He swung at them frantically as they pecked his arms and legs and tore at him with their talons.

With another pulse of magic, he fell into a barrel roll, flinging them off in every direction. In another second, he caught up to

Tara, still suspended between two humanoid werecrows, still screaming and fighting to detach herself.

Rune's heart sank. If she got herself free, he might be able to catch her, but the closer he got, the harder it would be to change course. He could weave the airy chaos for lift and thrust, but maneuverability was another matter.

So he soared higher, blinking the rain out of his eyes and readying his bata for another swing.

He stretched out his hand. Tara's free leg kicked at the air. If he could only reach it…

Another werecrow slammed into him from above, tearing at his back. Only his leather jacket kept its razor-sharp talons from shredding his clothes and skin. Rune gasped, disoriented by the attack. The whole swarm of werecrows circled closer.

They enveloped him like a dark, demonic blanket. Above the constant cawing, he heard a savage, half-human voice shout, "Get him!"

Rune spun in the air and lashed out blindly with the fighting stick. The werecrows chattered and cawed and drove him from the sky. He slammed shoulder first into the flat roof of a multistory office building.

The fighting stick slipped out of Rune's hand as the werecrow swooped around him.

He leaped to his feet.

The humanoid werecrow plowed into his gut with a flying kick. This time, the talon ripped through his shirt and into his abdomen. Rune gasped as white-hot pain surged through him. The creature grabbed the fallen bata in its wing claw and swung it with a flourish, daring him to try something.

"You can't have her!" the creature shrieked.

Thunder rumbled. The rain fell even harder.

Tara was still screaming somewhere close. As Rune and his attacker circled one another, he spied her, still restrained by her two captors as they perched on a church's bell tower a stone's throw away.

So they'd stopped to enjoy the show.

Well, then Rune was obliged to give them one. He sucked in a breath, and with it as much chaos as he could bear.

The werecrow swung the bata, but Rune was ready. He lashed out, grabbed the shaft, and used his attacker's momentum to fling him over the side of the building.

With a running jump, Rune took to the air in a beeline across a parking lot toward Tara.

The other werecrows converged on him, scratching and biting. One nipped at his ear. Another latched onto his leg. He yelped and shrugged them off. Then he surged forward on the wind until he lit upon the bell tower roof.

That's when the last pulse of magic pushed him past the intangible psychic boundary, and the Blessing took over. A subtle calm washed over him. All that was extraneous to the errand fell away like autumn leaves: emotion, empathy, caution. Rune had a job to do, and he couldn't afford to be sentimental.

Werecrows circled around him.

The tower was square, with a steep tiled roof and a cross at the top. On each side of the tower were two tall window slits with rounded arches. Inside, Tara screamed.

Rune dropped onto a window's ledge, and the child's abductors took flight.

He groaned and wiped a trickle of blood from his forehead with his sleeve. Individually, the werecrows weren't much of a threat, but there were a dozen of them, and they were faster and more agile than Rune in the air. At this range, he could most likely hit one of the creatures that wasn't holding Tara, but reloading a muzzle-loader took time, and one target made little difference among so many. Rune's heart pounded. His back and limbs throbbed with the punishment they'd taken.

He leaped into the air again, only for the werecrows to swarm against him before they dove back into the belfry, the child howling in fear.

Rune landed on the church's tiled roof. His grip gave way, and he slid down to the eave.

Above him, the werecrows hooted with derision. They were playing with him.

Rune cursed under his breath. His senses were fully opened, but he had forgotten his training.

Why would the abductors hang around with Tara? They might have easily gotten away while he was fighting on the rooftop, but they didn't.

There could only be one answer: they were stalling for time. But why?

They weren't expecting me. Rune peered up at them. One of them looked off into the clouds, and his face—as best as Rune could decipher birdlike expressions—was lost in thought.

Telepathy, he guessed. *They're getting new instructions.*

Tara screamed again inside the belfry.

But that, Rune realized, was a trap. Get him confined inside the belfry and block the exits until someone…or something… arrived. Rune didn't care to find out what the werecrows were waiting for.

After another second, he came to the only reasonable conclusion.

They're working with Avice!

It was fully dark now, but not so dark that he couldn't make out the shape of an old pickup truck in the distance. Gimp Hollart must have been following him the whole time. That at least gave Rune a glimmer of hope.

He could still save the Hollarts' daughter, but it was time to fight smart for a change. That meant using something besides a borrowed fighting stick.

Clinging to the church's rain-slicked roof, Rune concocted a plan.

The easiest way to weave the airy chaos was to manipulate the phenomena of wind and sky. But that was only the most obvious approach. With effort and concentration, Rune could also bend thoughts and perceptions—to pass invisibly, to heighten his own senses to supernatural levels, or even to befuddle the minds of others.

This was the skill he began to ply. He reached deep into his mind and latched on to an image. He took several long, slow breaths, focusing all his attention.

Thunder boomed. Rune paid it no attention.

When he was ready, he channeled the image he'd devised through the airy chaos and into the minds of Tara's abductors.

Rune's form appeared above them, leaping over the side of the building.

The werecrows screeched and cawed, taking flight as he plummeted toward them, firing his pistol.

As they took off, Rune—the real Rune—timed his own launch so that the child's abductors were flying overhead just as he shot up from the rooftop. He grabbed Tara around the waist as he smashed the bata into the beak of the werecrow that had hold of her arm, then swung her around, dragging the second creature with them. Rune spun in the air until it flew off and into the church's brick front wall.

He landed on his feet on the sidewalk and clamped his hand over the mouth of the still screaming child. She chomped on the flesh between his thumb and forefinger, but Rune held back his yelp and cradled her even closer.

The illusionary Rune would vanish soon. It probably already had without his constant attention. But it had served its purpose.

He took off at a run toward his client's truck, waving him onto a side road while veiling himself with glamour to hide from any pursuers.

They were bound to find him, though. He had a minute at most, so he started to work as he ran and struggled to keep the toddler from fighting free, gnawing through his hand, or crying out and giving them away.

Fortunately, she had started to settle down.

He took his hand away from her mouth long enough to find the quig in his jacket pocket. Rather than screaming, the little girl whimpered in fear as she gazed up into Rune's steely eyes. She was no longer actively fighting him, but she still trembled in his arm.

Good. This part would be easier with a free hand.

Rune rubbed the magic bean over the child's face, her hands, her chest. All the while, he expelled slow, even breaths—or as close as he could manage while running. He summoned the airy chaos and focused it on the quig itself and on every contour and hue that the quig was collecting.

He touched it to the one foot he could reach without letting go of her. He slid it behind her ears. He placed it to her lips—and pulled it away as she tried to eat it.

"Tara!" Mrs. Hollart called from a dozen yards away. She had left the truck's passenger door open and was sprinting up the street.

Rune finished his weaving just as Tara's mother snatched her from his arm. She backed away, glaring at Rune as if he was the one who'd kidnapped her.

His client was two steps behind.

"You've got to leave," Rune said. "They'll find you again."

As he spoke, he willed the quig to give up its magic, to unfold itself into the form that Rune had mentally constructed for it.

"Now listen here, you—" the wife started. Her husband held her back. She stopped herself, bewildered at what she saw.

The tiny bean in Rune's hand blew up like a balloon. It sprouted pudgy little limbs and a head of curly red hair. It covered itself with pinkish skin and a tiny yellow tee shirt and blue jeans: the very things the Hollart child was wearing.

"Is that a fetch?" Hollart asked.

Rune shook his head. "Just a shadow." And a rush job at that, but maybe it would be enough. "A trick I learned from a water cannibal." Whisper's training was thorough and eclectic. Rune had to give him that.

The sound of cawing rose again in the distance.

"They're coming," Rune said. "I'll head north, lead them away."

"But—" Hollart began.

Before he could finish, Rune summoned a whirlwind and jetted upward.

The werecrows were on his tail in an instant, but Rune barreled on, leaping from rooftop to rooftop over the city. He made sure to turn his body toward them to give them a good look at the false Hollart child he had concocted.

He set down in the middle of the University's football field, then took off again in a different direction, forcing his pursuers to keep up. Daring them.

There were still nine of them by Rune's count. More than enough to finish him off if he let them get within striking distance.

He would just have to wear them down…and hope Avice didn't show up.

Rune hurtled into the rain.

Nothing mattered but the errand.

20

The shadow construct that Rune had cobbled together wouldn't fool anybody up close. Its movements were jerky and unnatural, its face lopsided, and it only had one leg. But if the werecrows got that close, the game was over anyway. Rune just had to buy enough time for the Hollarts to get away. Once he was sure the werecrows had seen a redheaded child in his arms, he sped northward as fast as he could.

They were on him just as quickly, with all the murderous fury they'd shown before.

Rune dropped to a rooftop and then surged back into the sky in a different direction. He did the same thing again, and then again. The tactic kept his pursuers off balance. It kept them from closing the distance, but he couldn't shake them.

And he was getting winded. In theory, Saynim folk could sling as much magic as they wanted as long as they were willing to pay for it, and Rune was well past counting the psychic costs.

But eventually, weaving the forces of creation would take a physical toll as well. Like a starving man, his body would begin to consume itself to power his magical feats. The running battle over the rooftops was wearing him down. He'd been clawed or bitten more than once. His shoulders ached, and his hand throbbed where the real Tara Hollart had bitten him.

In theory, he could keep fighting indefinitely. In reality, the airy chaos would eventually claim him.

And somewhere out there, Avice was coming. Or maybe the werecrows were steering him to her.

Either way, this game of chase wasn't going to last forever.

They flew over the University campus. City streets had given way to paved walkways between stately buildings.

And above it all, Rune dodged, weaved, and leaped from rooftop to rooftop.

The rain was falling hard now. That slowed his pursuers, but it slowed him, too. Maybe, though, the reduced visibility could work in his favor. If he could keep going until he was sure the Hollarts had a good head start…

A werecrow clamped down on his ankle with its beak. Rune kicked it off, but the attack slowed him enough for two more to swoop down on him.

He hoped the Hollarts were safe. He couldn't do much more.

Rune let go of his shadow construct and willed himself to drop to the roof below.

The werecrows snapped at what they thought was their quarry, but it broke apart in a puff of dust almost as soon as Rune turned it loose.

He slammed into the roof at an angle, rolling to his feet and, in the same movement, pulling his pistol from his satchel. The first werecrow to take humanoid form and rush him got a chest full of ferstitch, which dropped it writhing onto the gravel.

The flash and the noise of his shot gave Rune the only chance he was likely to get. In the heartbeat of confusion, he dropped off the side of the roof to the ground below, pistol still in hand. He rounded the corner of the building and found himself in a criss-cross of paved footpaths.

A couple of students hurried past under umbrellas. They stared upward, looking for the source of the gunshot. A stone's throw away, a group of maybe half a dozen stood underneath the covered entrance to a building. If they'd heard the shot at all, it didn't seem to concern them. If Rune was lucky, they assumed it was thunder.

Rune tucked his pistol into his pack and walked away from the building as the werecrows, now in pure avian form, took up position. Three of them pecked at a fast-food bag that had just missed a wastebasket, though they kept their eyes on Rune.

Another circled overhead. The rest were gone. Seeing the shadow construct vanish, they must have flown off in pursuit of the Hollarts.

One of the werecrows leaped onto the wastebasket and glared at Rune.

Another college student hurried past. The rain was letting up, but only a little. It trickled down the collar of Rune's jacket.

But he was safe—for now. The Rule of Secrecy kept him from using magic in the presence of this many Fallow folk. But the werecrows couldn't attack him, either. They could look as menacing as they wanted, they could caw and scratch the ground, but they couldn't change shape, couldn't threaten him, couldn't drop the masquerade that they were anything but ordinary crows.

Rune began to walk away.

The werecrows followed him, of course. The one in the air found a tree to perch in. The one on the wastebasket took flight while its partner hopped along on the ground.

Rune's legs were sore, especially where an attacker had taken that last bite. He limped, using Hollart's bata as a walking stick. He wished he'd thought to pack bandages. That drop kick back at the church had slashed his stomach. He'd recovered from worse injuries, but the front of his shirt was torn and splattered with blood. His right hand throbbed. It looked a little swollen. And even with his supernatural senses cranked up, his vision was blurry.

He reached for the healing salve in his satchel, which set the werecrows to squawking and flapping their wings. He glared at them and made a show of moving slowly. He twisted off the top and scooped out a finger's worth of salve, applying most of it to his stomach and wiping the rest on his ear, his forehead, and, with a little bit of juggling, his right hand. His wounds itched as they slowly began to close.

He zipped up his jacket lest anybody notice the rip or the blood on his shirt. Then, with slow, deliberate movements, he returned the salve to his satchel.

Avice was coming. She was bound to be.

He'd never been able to best her in a fair fight. Now, at the end of his endurance, he didn't relish another family reunion.

With his hand still in his satchel, he rummaged about for the trinket Madam Samarra had forced on him. He only took it so she would make change for him, but maybe he could find a use for it after all.

He palmed the tortoise shell box and slipped it into his jacket pocket.

Rune studied his surroundings: tall buildings on every side, with lawns and trees between them. No real cover to hide behind when the fighting resumed—which it most certainly would. Worst of all, he didn't dare reload his pistol with Fallow folk around. They'd just report him to the campus police.

Whisper would find a way out, he told himself. *He would latch on to something that gave him an advantage.*

But what could that possibly be?

He turned a corner. His feathered escort followed.

Avice was waiting beneath a porch. As soon as their eyes met, she stepped out onto the path.

She wore the hood up on her umbersay cloak, which swished this way and that in anticipation of violence. She made no effort to hide the sword and pistol underneath. The cloak billowed in angry waves of gray and blue and black.

"Good evening, Claeus."

"Have you been demoted?" Rune took a wary step forward, his breathing heavy. "Collecting His Majesty's changelings seems beneath your station."

"She's not a changeling," Avice snapped. "As if you deserved an explanation."

The two circled each other, only stopping to let a student walk past.

Two more werecrows joined the three that had followed Rune from the roof. They, at least, had given up on chasing the Hollarts.

"At any rate," Avice said, "you're the greater prize."

Rune and Avice continued to circle.

"The child was bait?"

"Of course not," Avice said, a wry grin spreading across her face. "She was meant to be a sacrifice." She rested her hand on the hilt of her sword.

Rune's blood chilled. "For Jericho," he guessed, shifting the bata to his right hand.

"We'll make do. There's plenty of time to find a fitting substitute." Her eyes bored into him.

The fact that the King of Shadows—or at least his agent—knew about the Hollart child was disconcerting. What other surprises did they have in store?

"You won't get her back," Rune said.

Avice shrugged. "Your blood will do just as well, *auph*."

Ah. She needed the blood of a half-human, then. Fitting if the King of Shadows meant to bridge the gap between two worlds. And it was probably what Avice had hoped for all along. Rune clenched his teeth. "I'm flattered."

Avice scoffed and leaned in to whisper, "You may feel differently once we've found a private place to chat."

Rune backed away. "I prefer the open air, if you don't mind."

"Fair enough," Avice said. "Let's chat here." She stopped circling and poked a finger in Rune's chest. "What did you do with the coffer?"

Another werecrow arrived and found a ringside seat in a tree branch.

"Did you lose something, cousin?" Rune said. The pause in the fighting helped, but he was still at the end of his strength. His every muscle ached. His temples throbbed.

Avice, however, was fresh and ready.

"We can't discuss missing property if I'm dead," Rune said.

Avice smiled. "Haven't you been listening? The King of Shadows doesn't need your life. Just a bit of your tainted blood."

She took a step forward. Rune sidestepped her, and they went back to circling one another, pausing every few seconds to await the other's move.

"Though, once you've divulged your secrets," she said, "I'm sure His Majesty will have his own ideas about how to reward your betrayal."

The rain had nearly stopped. Rune glanced around. There were four Fallowmen in sight. More than three observers would tie a knot in the weave. There'd be backlash if either Rune or Avice tried any magic.

Two of those Fallowmen were headed toward a dormitory, though, and the Rule of Secrecy would no longer apply. In a few more seconds, it would be back to fighting, and there was no way Rune could win.

He would just have to cheat.

"I'll wipe that smirk off your face," Avice said.

Rune kept his eyes on her hands, but he followed the two students with his peripheral vision. He began to draw his chaos to him.

Just one more second…

"Are you listening to me? I should—"

Rune leaped into the air without warning, coming down on the nearest rooftop. He filled his lungs and took a low, defensive stance.

Below, a college student let out a curse. He'd have a story to tell—as if anyone would believe it.

Avice had her sword in her hand when she landed facing Rune. He parried her slash left-handed with the bata then shouldered into her. He grabbed the wrist of her sword arm and flipped her onto the roof. But she used his momentum against him. Tugging at his jacket, she threw him down on his back. He rolled away, but Avice was already on her feet and charging toward him.

Werecrows circled overhead, ready to join in. A quick count revealed that their number was back up to seven. More had given up the search for the Hollarts.

With a substantial effort of will, Rune expelled the magic he'd been hoarding.

The airy chaos governed movement. With enough skill, an air-weaver could use it to ride the wind or run and fight with the speed of thought. For Rune, time itself came to a crawl. When his magic was done, he would be too. But he had bought himself an advantage—if only for a second.

Avice lunged, and it seemed to Rune like the half-speed practice blows Whisper had drilled him with long ago. He side-stepped her sword thrust and spun about.

Two werecrows converged on him, flitting lazily like butterflies to Rune's eyes. He swatted them away.

"Gaaaah!" Avice screamed, hurtling toward him, gaining speed of her own.

Rune's advantage had expired. It was time to go. He took a deep breath, as deep as his aching lungs could bear.

He pulled the snuff box from his pocket and ripped off the lid. Reaching to the depths of his magical reserves, he willed the bottomless container to empty itself. Coarse, pungent flakes of snuff exploded across the roof just as Avice reached him. Stunned, she tripped, but not before her blade kissed Rune's thigh.

Fiery pain shot through his leg. It took all he had left to stay on his feet.

Avice stumbled past. She started to sneeze, and so did the werecrows.

She took a wild swing as she fought back tears, blinded by the cloud of tobacco in the air. The werecrows had fallen to the roof, unable to fly as they hacked and gagged.

Rune had little magic left, but it would have to do. Emptying his lungs and sucking in a cold, ragged breath, he stumbled to the edge of the roof. He wrapped himself in a whirlwind and soared into the night.

He stayed aloft for no more than half a minute before landing hard on a grassy embankment. His legs almost buckled under his weight. His lungs were raw. His body ached in ways he had never imagined.

He was in a narrow, fenced enclosure. At the bottom, rainwater flowed in a cement causeway, rushing toward a storm drain a few yards away that looked about his size. At least it would give him some cover.

He limped until he couldn't stand, and then he crawled the rest of the way, wincing with every movement.

In the distance he saw the lights of a Ferris wheel. He was somewhere near the fairgrounds. Miles from home.

The Blessing was the only thing that kept him going. Without it, he'd have been terrified that Avice and her cronies would catch up to him. He'd be afraid his wounds were too severe. He'd probably be in shock.

As it was, his actions were practical, methodical.

Though his limbs trembled, he crawled into the drain and wrestled his satchel off his shoulder. The sword wound in his leg oozed blood. It needed proper attention—and soon. The other wounds would have to wait.

Mostly, he just needed a place to hide. Let Avice give up on finding him.

He'd have plenty of time to panic then.

His clammy hands shook as he fought with his tin of healing salve. At last he fumbled it open and began to rub the last of it on his leg. His pulse was fast but weak.

Rune shivered. Why was it so cold all of a sudden?

Everything went dark.

21

Avice reached behind her back for one of Claeus's knives, which she had taken after he dropped them at Jericho's house. She used it to scrape the blood from the edge of her sword into a small vial, careful not to touch anything with her fingers.

She paced on the rooftop, spying the horizon. There was still no sign of Daws and his cohorts.

Or Claeus.

He was wounded, she told herself. *He can't have gotten far.*

That he got away at all filled her with rage and shame. He'd done it again!

She fought back a sneeze. The odor of snuff clung to her clothing, her hair. The gentle evening rain wasn't nearly enough to wash it all away.

She sheathed the sword and the knife and turned her attention to the vial. A magical fixative would keep the blood from drying until she could put it to use. Fortunately, she'd come prepared. She squirted a dropper of the greasy unguent into Claeus's blood and shook it. After stoppering the vial, she slipped it into a pocket of her doublet.

The blood would anchor an excellent tracking spell. She was no expert in ritual magic, but it wouldn't be hard to forge a bond between the captured blood and the body it came from.

Unfortunately, without the half-troll whelp, she had a more pressing need for the auph's blood, and the little bit she had wasn't nearly enough.

"Tempest," she muttered. Why couldn't she have taken him in Jericho's study? Then everything would have proceeded as planned, and she could interrogate Claeus at her leisure.

She strode to the edge of the roof and peered to the east, the direction Claeus had fled.

A single black shape sped toward her, soon followed by another and then another.

Daws lit a few yards away.

"Anything?" Avice said.

"We looked everywhere." The werecrow held open his wings in an almost human shrug of resignation.

"Obviously not, or you'd have found him."

"We do what we can do," Daws squawked. "If you don't like it—"

"I *don't* like it!" Avice took a step toward him, and he flinched. She breathed deeply and then released the air. "I don't like it, Mr. Daws…but you and your cohorts aren't entirely to blame. The auph was always better at running and hiding than anything else."

Daws responded with a throaty rattle.

"He'll show up again," she said. "Likely when it's most inconvenient."

The werecrow hopped tentatively forward. "He might be dead, you know."

"I'm not that lucky," Avice said.

Daws rattled again as three more werecrows joined him on the rooftop.

"So you want me and the boys to hang around here?"

"Secure the gathering place. And keep your eyes open."

"What if we see the Nightwalker?"

"If you see the *traitor*, report to me immediately." Avice raised her voice so all could hear. "I'll give ten quigs to the one who leads me to him. Deal?"

"Deal," Daws said. If he'd had a proper mouth, Avice might have imagined his lips curling into a greedy grin.

Claeus would turn up soon enough. For the moment, though, she needed to clear her head. She drew in the airy chaos, and the werecrows took flight as the wind around her picked up. She strode to the edge of the roof and hurled herself into the sky.

Avice entered Gamaufry Tavern by the double doors leading in from the porch. There were nearly twenty people inside, including a musical group on the stage in the near right corner. All of them stopped what they were doing when she appeared. She returned their furtive gazes, shaming them into minding their own business.

The room was large enough to accommodate seven tables. Two were on a raised platform in the left corner, built for smallkin patrons. She headed for a table at the far right, past the stage, the great fireplace, and the elevator entrance.

Three patrons, dwarves by the look of them, sat at the bar, chatting with the bartender. A billiards game was underway: two low elves, each with a small cheering section.

Avice sensed the unease her presence inspired. So be it. Gamaufry Tavern was neutral territory, and she wasn't there to make trouble. She just wanted a place to relax and maybe learn something useful.

The dwarf on the fiddle tore into a raucous tune, and a smallkin woman started to belt out the words to "Bad Reputation."

Avice kept an eye on the porch and the elevator entrance. Beside the fireplace, a smallkin woman, a tiny blonde, stood on a wooden stool and stirred a copper cauldron that was bigger than she was. The aroma of stewed meats, vegetables, and spices mixed with the subtle whiff of cigar smoke.

Avice was about to get up for a bowl of stew when the elevator dinged. The doors slid open, and out came a troll she had expected would show up eventually.

He was over seven feet tall and easily 450 pounds. He sloughed off his leather longcoat to reveal simple but well-made clothing underneath—trousers, royal blue vest, and linen shirt. His head was shaven but for a black topknot, and dark, angular tattoos graced the left side of his brow.

The crowd sucked in a collective breath as he lumbered into the great room, but quickly returned to their business. They clearly wanted nothing to do with the newcomer.

Avice let her arms fall to her lap. Her pistol was in easy reach, and she tensed her muscles, ready to move fast if she had to.

The troll called himself Vex. She'd never met him, but she knew things about Maya Tecumseh's associates. He was well placed in the Merlady's organization.

She considered the possibility that it was pure coincidence he'd shown up. She'd visited Gamaufry Tavern a couple of times since crossing the Mere without a peep from the Merlady or any of her people. Had her luck run out?

In any case, the troll towered over Avice's table. She made no hostile moves, but she did start to gather her magic, sharpening her senses.

The click-clack of billiard balls had stopped. Players and onlookers circled around the table, heads down, willing themselves to pass beneath notice.

"Buy you a drink?" the troll said. His voice was nasal and wheezy. He pulled out the chair across from Avice and signaled to the bartender. "A bottle of Old Serpent!" he called. "And two glasses, if you please."

Avice sniffed.

The troll sat down. The chair creaked under his weight, but it held.

"I don't recall inviting you to join me," Avice said.

"And I don't recall the Merlady permitting the King of Shadows to operate in her territory," Vex said, his voice now cold. He folded his hands on the table and leaned in. His big black eyes bored into her.

The woman who'd been tending the stew skirted around the edge of the room toward the bar and disappeared into the kitchen. The elves at the billiard table huddled closer together. The people here knew who Vex was, who he worked for. They clearly didn't like the idea of the confrontation that was brewing.

Avice didn't move.

Nothing changed the fact that the next forty-eight hours were critical for His Majesty's plan. It looked like she would have to slap this troll's hand to warn him off.

"The Merlady claims the river," she said. "That's where she should stay."

The troll glowered. "The Merlady goes where she pleases. And she does as she pleases. It's as simple as that."

"Not anymore."

Avice sometimes wondered how Fallow women managed without magic. They seemed so vulnerable to violent men. The average man was taller and stronger—physically if not mentally. True, a trained combatant in good physical condition could hold her own and even come out on top in a fight. But what if the man were equally proficient?

Of course, Vex was far from the average man. Picking a fight with someone nearly two feet taller and three times heavier would be suicidal.

Magic changed that calculus. It didn't ultimately matter if Vex could bench-press five Avices at once if one Avice could confound his mind or suck the breath from his lungs.

She glared across the table at an equal. He might well be a formidable opponent, but she didn't fear him. Not in the least.

Her heart thumped with anticipation. Just let him try something…

"The King of Shadows will possess this territory," she said. "What the Merlady thinks of that is irrelevant."

"Milady," a voice interrupted. "Milord." Avice recognized the approaching tavern keeper, a swarthy goblin with bright blue eyes, a shaven head, and a few extra pounds around his middle. Dressed in a bright green tunic with interlacing patterns embroidered at the collar and sleeves, and with his ears festooned with multiple earrings, he gave the impression of someone who loved to make a show of his wealth. He might have proven to be a gregarious host, though at the moment he wasn't smiling. In his trembling hands were a bottle of whiskey and two shot glasses.

He set the glasses in front of them and filled each with smoky, golden liquid from the bottle.

"Master Gamaufry," Vex said with a nod. Avice nodded as well.

"My establishment has always prided itself on its…neutrality," the tavern keeper said, voice quavering.

"For which I am grateful." Vex shot Avice a sidewise glance. "Far be it from me to violate your hospitality." He poured himself a drink.

"Perhaps you'd like a conference room? Somewhere…less conspicuous?"

"You're very kind," Avice said. "But please don't trouble yourself." She glared at the troll. "We have nothing more to say."

Master Gamaufry waited until Vex nodded, then shuffled back to the bar.

Avice leaned in. "The Merlady can't win. The King of Shadows is too strong."

"Is that so?" Vex's nasal voice was getting on Avice's nerves, and she wondered if it was a put-on. He leaned back in his chair and smiled broadly. Trolls could be insufferable.

"It is indeed," she said. "Though His Majesty is a reasonable man. I'm sure there could be a place for the Merlady—and you, of course—in the new order of things."

Vex threw back his head and laughed. The tattoos on the side of his head practically danced. "Oh, you kill me," he said.

Don't tempt me!

He looked Avice in the eye, and his jaw dropped. "Crashing waves! You're serious?"

All eyes turned toward their table. The band stopped playing. A few of the patrons around the billiard table scampered to the elevator.

Avice faced warmed. Sweat tickled her neck, and her hands curled into fists.

How dare he!

"Listen, I get it, lady. You're just doing your job. I know what that's like."

"You know nothing about—"

"But take my advice." Vex leaned forward. There was a twinkle in his eye. "Just go home while you can. Find yourself a nice elvish husband and, I don't know, bake him some cookies or something."

Her hand was on her pistol before she knew it. She swung it up into the troll's chest and drew back the hammer.

Everyone in the tavern hit the deck with a flurry of overturned chairs, spilled drinks, and profanity.

But it was nothing compared to what Avice told herself as realization dawned.

The troll had been weaving water the whole time, needling his way into her mind, provoking her emotions. Then, just as she was about to give vent to her offended rage, he pulled back and let her mind clear.

Vex sat there and grinned. "You're just not cut out for this."

He pushed back from the table and stood up. He waggled his finger in front of her pistol and affected an expression of disappointment. "Neutral territory." He raised his voice to the tavern keeper, who popped his bald head out from beneath the bar. "Has been ever since you opened the place, hasn't it?" Vex sighed. "I just don't know what this world is coming to." He lumbered to the elevator, but turned back at the alcove to flash Avice one last infuriating smile.

She ground her teeth. The whole conversation had only taken a few minutes, but it was enough. She could hear her father's disapproving voice. Keep your cool no matter what, he would say. Never let your emotions guide you. Ever!

"Tempest," she muttered. She couldn't have cast the King of Shadows in a worse light if she had tried.

Suddenly it was even more important for Jericho's ritual to work. It might be the only opening His Majesty was going to get.

And somewhere out there, Claeus was lurking in the shadows—yet another wrench in the works.

Avice would have to find him, and she thought she knew a way.

22

Zoey struggled more than usual to stay focused during church. She zoned out halfway through her dad's sermon on the Three Hebrew Children, only coming to herself when Kim Hamilton passed her a note scrawled on the back of a worship bulletin: "Plans for Halloween?"

Of course, she had plans. She was going to stay home in her room and hope that nothing else weird happened. She'd been on edge ever since the impromptu goat stampede Friday night. Rune's comments yesterday afternoon still weighed on her.

It did indeed look like she had "brought something back."

Kim poked her in the side, and she jumped.

Mother Simmons shushed them from the pew behind. Zoey didn't turn to look at the stern matriarch, but she could imagine her disapproving expression beneath her big, floppy hat. Instead, she glared at Kim.

She took a pen from the pew rack and dashed off her own note. "Staying home. Not feeling well."

"You look fine," Kim mouthed.

Maybe, but inside she was a mess. Last night during the storm, she had jumped every time the lightning flashed. Was it just a regular storm or something else? Even after she went to bed, she peered out her window, looking for any signs of weirdness. There were no more goats—no livestock of any kind, thankfully— though she couldn't shake the feeling that the birds outside her window were tweeting out the tune to "The Way You Make Me Feel."

Another missive came in from Kim: "Not even Trunk-or-Treat?"

Faith Tabernacle hosted the event for the neighborhood kids every year. The youth group always volunteered and then went off to somebody's house for a party of their own. Any other year, Zoey would have been in the middle of it all.

She shook her head at Kim and whispered, "Sorry."

Mother Simmons tapped her on the shoulder. Zoey sat up straight.

Dad had gotten to the part where Shadrach, Meshach, and Abednego defied the king even though he was about to throw them into the fiery furnace. From her place in the choir, Mom kept her eye on Zoey. Zoey pretended to be interested in the sermon.

What she was really interested in was what had happened to Rune. He had said he would come by after dinner to do something about how she'd suddenly become a great big weirdness magnet. But he never came home. In the short time she'd known him, he'd always been careful to keep his promises. If he was tied up somewhere…

The magic bean Rune had given her felt warm in her pocket. Was it doing something—anything? Siphoning off whatever she brought back from wherever it was she'd been? Warding off rampaging goats and feathered Michael Jackson impersonators?

She scoffed. *I've got a magic bean in my pocket. I got it from my friend, the elf who rents from my parents.* She fought back a manic giggle.

Mother Simmons shushed even harder. She sounded like she'd sprung a leak.

None of this made sense. Zoey focused on the candles on the Communion table, anything to get her mind off her troubles.

Her dad continued to preach. "Be strong." "You're not alone in your troubles." "Greater is he that is in you than he that is in the world."

The words barely registered. She kept her eyes on the candles.

As she watched the flickering flames, they turned blue.

Zoey gasped. She glanced toward Kim. She hadn't noticed—she was busy writing another note. Nobody else seemed to notice either. Was she seeing things?

She wasn't. Mother Simmons sucked in a breath and prayed, "O my Lord!" Zoey turned to see the matriarch's eyes glued to the front of the sanctuary.

Dad hadn't seen the candles yet. He was assuring the congregation that "God will be with you even in the flames."

Zoey felt as if she were outside her body, watching the whole thing like a scene from a TV show. Her vision narrowed to the table and the candles, not entirely sure that what was happening was real.

Mr. Lingard, who sat in an aisle seat on the second row, jumped up with a shout. For a fleeting second, Zoey wondered if he was just worked up over the sermon. Of course, it couldn't be that simple. When Mr. Lingard jumped, so did a spark of blue flame. It sputtered up from the candle and came down on the Communion table's floral arrangement. A single orange marigold began to smolder, then burst into flames with an audible *poof.*

Thankfully, Mr. Lingard kept his cool. He bounded for the flowers, flung them to the ground, and stamped out the flames before they could spread.

Only then did most of the congregation clue in to what was going on. Zoey's dad watched in bewilderment as the crisis played out. He gave Mr. Lingard a puzzled look, and the older gentlemen motioned for him to proceed.

Sometime in the excitement, the candle flames had returned to yellow.

"What happened?" Kim asked, looking up from her note.

Mother Simmons glared daggers at her.

Dad cut the sermon short, and three people came forward to get right with God.

Rune wasn't coming back. Not anytime soon, at any rate. And the weirdness was getting out of hand.

Maybe the magic bean was defective. Or maybe its battery was running out. It wasn't helping, at least not that Zoey could tell.

A quick Internet search turned up at least a dozen ways to break a spell, some of which contradicted each other and most of which involved ingredients her mom didn't have in the kitchen. Magical types on the Internet either didn't know what they were talking about or were looking to sell overpriced mixtures and trinkets. For all she knew, they were legit, but it wasn't like she could call their customer service number for personalized support. She needed something now! Today, before things got even further out of hand.

But maybe…

She knew of a place. She'd driven past it a hundred times on her way to get cookies at Kizito's on Bardstown Road. Caitlin had even mentioned it once or twice back in the tenth grade during her crystals and astrology phase.

Fifteen minutes later, Zoey was pulling her old Toyota Corolla into a parking spot half a block down from Madam Samarra's.

A little bell rang when she opened the door and stepped inside. Every wall of the small showroom was covered in dark wooden shelves burdened with books, pamphlets, curios, and boxes full of herbs, incense cones, and little trinkets of every kind. Behind a glass counter near the back wall sat a tiny woman in a vibrant, orange and black muumuu and matching head wrap. Her enormous hoop earrings swayed as she nodded and smiled.

"Good afternoon, miss. What can I do for you? Dreamcatcher? Maybe a nice incense bowl? I got a new shipment all the way from India."

"Hi. Uh." Zoey was still taking it all in. The subtle smell of incense didn't quite match the plastic pumpkins, cardboard black cats, and fabric ghosts scattered about the room. She ran her fingers along the edge of a wooden table in the middle of the shop. Like the shelves, it was weighed down with baubles and trinkets: wands, chalices, crystal balls, and a bunch of things Zoey couldn't put a name to.

"Just browsing, then?" Madam Samarra said. Her voice remained light, but her smile vanished.

"Actually, uh…" How to explain this?

She's going to think I've lost it!

You fought Bardstown Road traffic to get here, you doof! And besides, she looks like she lost it years ago.

Zoey braced herself. "Do you have anything for…curses, I guess?"

Madam Samarra arched an eyebrow. "You're under a curse?"

"Maybe. I don't know how to describe it." She bit her lip. "Things are just…weird."

Madam Samarra's face brightened. "On your left. Bottom shelf."

Zoey stooped to look.

"Halfway over."

She found a cardboard box filled with silver pendants, each in its own clear plastic packet. They had barely any weight to them. There was no way they were real silver. She scowled. "What's this?"

"Good luck charm. Navajo. Seven ninety-nine."

Zoey doubted the little pendant in her hand had ever set foot in Navajo country. And she was quickly losing faith in Madam Samarra.

"Look," she said, "this is very nice and all, but I really need something a little more"—*magical? real?*—"effective."

"Those things are plenty effective," Madam Samarra said. "They're good for all your basic hexes, entropy curses, hotfoot spells. You name it."

Zoey frowned. "I don't know. Are you sure you don't have something—"

"Have a look in that box one shelf up. The one marked 'Periapts.' Thirty bucks apiece, but they're worth it. I mean, I could whip you up a little charm myself, but it'll cost you, and—I'm not trying to be judgmental here—I'm not sure you could afford it. What are you, sixteen? Seventeen?"

Zoey had a few hundred dollars in her bank account, money she'd been saving for college. Rune said her problem was temporary. Maybe she could just wait it out.

She strode to the counter and set the pendant in front of Madam Samarra. "I'm just not sure…"

Madam Samarra's face had turned white. Zoey gazed down at the plastic packet.

The pendant had melted into a glob of silvery goo.

Madam Samarra slowly lifted her eyes to Zoey. "You're paying for that."

Zoey gulped. "Yeah. That's fair." She pulled her wallet out of her purse.

"And you're for real about that curse thing, aren't you?" Madam Samarra's demeanor had changed. She was suddenly all business.

"That's what I was telling you!"

The shopkeeper left the counter and started to gather things from her shelves: some herbs and whole seeds. She pulled a mortar and pestle from behind the glass counter. "How long has this been going on?"

"Just a couple of days."

"Do you know who did it to you?"

"Nobody. Or…I kind of…"

Madam Samarra started crushing the seeds in the mortar.

"I kind of went somewhere I maybe shouldn't."

The shopkeeper's eyes flashed. "You crossed the Mere?"

"It was only for an hour or so!"

"Doesn't matter. Looks like you brought something back." She pulled a leaf of parchment from a packet behind her and started to write while muttering an incantation.

Zoey watched, spellbound by the old woman's strange words. They weren't French. They might have been Latin. As she spoke, her movements were precise and methodical. As if every last detail was important.

When she finished, she sliced the parchment into strips and set them in the mortar along with the herbs and the crushed seeds.

Finally, she turned her attention back to Zoey. "When?"

"When what? Oh, Friday night."

"You've probably got a few days left then. This will help." She nodded toward the mortar. Again she left the counter, this time to fetch a small velvet pouch from the table in the middle of the shop.

"Also…somebody gave me this." Zoey showed Madam Samarra the magic bean she'd been keeping in her pocket.

The shopkeeper's eyes went wide again. "Where'd you get a stinking quig?"

"A friend."

The woman rolled the bean between her thumb and index finger. "Might be out of juice." Madam Samarra laid it on the counter and placed all her ingredients in the velvet pouch. "Yeah, you need a proper charm, all right."

"And these things will work?"

"Listen," the shopkeeper said. Her eyes were hard and cold as steel. "I've been down this road you're on. I'm telling you: get out while you can."

"Right. I'm out."

"You're not listening." She clambered up onto her stool and still came only to Zoey's eye level. "I wasn't always Madam Samarra, you know."

"You weren't?"

"You think people are gonna buy their New Age junk from Edna Liptak from Terre Haute? Besides, the name was already on the sign when I bought the place." She scoffed. "Do you know how much sign painters charge?"

"Not really."

"Take it from me, you don't want to get messed up in…well, this." She gestured vaguely at everything her shop. She dropped the filled pouch into a small brown paper bag and set it on the counter.

"But…." Zoey scrunched her face in concentration. "But you're…what, like a wizard or something?"

"I just know a few things," Madam Samarra said. "And I'm telling you, there are better ways you could be going. Ways that don't come with such a high price tag."

"I don't understand."

"Of course you don't. You and ninety-nine out of every hundred people who come in this place. You're dabblers. You're why my invoices say 'For entertainment purposes only.' Even if you know it's real, you're clueless. If it's up to me, you'll stay that way." She leaned forward and lowered her voice. "The things over there on the other side…they'll mess with you, understand? You make a deal with them—no, scratch that. *Do not* make a deal with anyone or anything you meet from the other side."

Zoey swallowed hard. She didn't have a clue what she was getting into, but at this point, how could she ever get out of it? She'd fought rat-monsters. She'd spied on a sorcerer. Her dad was renting an apartment to a freaking elf!

"Take this home," Madam Samarra said, pushing the paper sack toward her. "Spit on it three times. If you want to say a prayer or whatever, go for it. Can't hurt."

Zoey picked up the bag. "Spit on it."

"Then keep it somewhere on your body. It's got to touch your skin."

"And this will work? I can't thank you enough."

"Darn right," Madam Samarra said. "That's why I charge." She looked at Zoey. "Cash or credit?"

"What?" Zoey's heart raced. "You never said—how much money are we talking about, anyway?"

Madam Samarra sized her up. Her expression was part disappointment, part pity. "Don't worry about it. We can work something out."

Zoey exhaled. "That would be…" Something outside caught her attention before she could finish. She turned toward the window. Heading toward the shop door was a tall, good-looking man, sharply dressed.

Jericho.

She gasped as she swung back to Madam Samarra. "Restroom!"

"Through there," the shopkeeper said, raising an eyebrow.

Zoey darted in just as the bell over the door rang and Jericho stepped inside.

"Good afternoon," Madam Samarra called.

From behind the restroom door, Zoey heard Jericho offer a curt reply, followed by, "I'm looking for some calamus oil. The best quality you have."

"Of course. On your right, all the way at the end," Madam Samarra said. A few seconds later, she added, "Third shelf down."

Zoey cracked open the door. Jericho had his back to her, examining the shelves and their contents. When he brought a vial of yellowish-brown liquid to the counter, she stepped back a bit. He didn't notice her, and his face betrayed no emotion.

"Forty bucks."

"Seriously?" Jericho said. "For this little?"

"It's good quality. The best," Madam Samarra said. Zoey could hear the steel in her voice. She was definitely not going to budge. "If you can find a better price, take it."

Jericho gestured with the hand that held the vial. At the same time, he bored into the shopkeeper with his eyes. It reminded Zoey of what he'd done to Davanté Friday night, working some kind of unspoken spell. He didn't say anything out loud, but his lips moved subtly.

"I've given you a lot of business the last few years," he said aloud.

If Madam Samarra hesitated, it was only for a heartbeat. "I appreciate it," she said and then paused, staring at him. "You gonna buy that or what?"

Zoey might have guessed the spell wouldn't work. Most people would have looked at this woman and seen Madam Samarra, the eccentric but well-meaning New Ager with a little boutique in the Highlands. Now that Zoey knew the truth, she grinned as she watched the encounter play out.

Eventually, Jericho's shoulders slumped. He broke his gaze, glancing instead to the shelves beside him to study the jumble of vials, boxes, and zip-top bags they displayed. "Add a couple of mandrake roots and it's a deal."

"I'll give you a good price on the mandrake," Madam Samarra said. "But my price is firm on the calamus." Her face was leaden. She wasn't going to give in. Not even an inch.

Jericho's face darkened as he pulled out his wallet. "Fine. I'll take the calamus oil, the mandrakes, the frankincense…and a dozen sheets of parchment, the kind you sold me last time."

Madam Samarra was suddenly all smiles. "I know the ones you mean." She climbed on a step stool to reach something out of Zoey's view on the wall behind her. When she returned, she laid the parchment next to the vial and the two zip-top bags.

"You can't go wrong with the calamus," she said. "It's got a million and one uses: healing, inspiration, fire magic—"

"Strong ritual energy," Jericho offered.

"Exactly! I knew you were a man of distinction. You know what they used to call it, don't you?"

He nodded. "Dragon's blood."

"Dragon's blood!" She grinned.

A wry smile crossed the sorcerer's face. "But it's not quite as good as *real* dragon's blood, is it?"

Madam Samarra's expression turned from jovial to confused. Zoey might have expected as much. She didn't say a word about real magic earlier until Zoey melted her good luck charm. If she was being tight-lipped with Jericho, then she didn't know who he really was. That was strangely comforting.

The shopkeeper gave a fair approximation of somebody who didn't get the joke but was still enjoying the conversation. "It's just a name, Mister"—she checked his credit card—"Phipps."

"Names have power, Madam Samarra, as I'm sure you're aware." Jericho put away his card, and Madam Samarra handed him his items in the same kind of paper bag she'd given Zoey.

"Have a nice evening." The smile came back, her composure regained.

"You too," Jericho said. He strode toward the door, then turned back. "And if you ever come into a supply of actual dragon's blood, I'd be eager to buy some at any price."

Madam Samarra rolled her eyes. "Dragons are from fairy tales, Mr. Phipps."

He simply smiled, bowed, and walked away. The bell on the door chimed happily as he stepped outside.

Zoey shook her head. "Get out while you can," Madam Samarra had said. But she didn't know about Jericho. She didn't know about Caitlin. Zoey's best friend thought Jericho was the coolest man ever.

Zoey couldn't get out. Not now, anyway.

Her eyes fell on the paper bag in her hand. She was in way over her head.

And Rune was still missing.

23

Rune's mind was a fog.

Everything was dark, muddled.

He remembered a city. A tall building. A fight.

Avice.

He couldn't move his limbs. Where was he? Was he dreaming? An image flitted across his mind, a bustling city with a castle on a central hill.

Cruc Máw. That's where all of this began, in the city of the Amber Queen.

When Whisper had explained the nature of their errand, he told Rune how, many years before, Corcc the Peacebringer ruled from the Shawnahay Mountains to the Mother of Rivers. Then the King of Shadows forged an alliance to unseat him. The war was savage, brutal. It ended with the fall of the Peacebringer…and, soon after, the collapse of the winning alliance.

All because of the Amber Queen. She had turned on the King of Shadows at the first opportunity. Whisper insisted she had gone back on her word, but it had always seemed more likely to Rune that she had interpreted the terms of the alliance differently from the start. Such was the nature of politics in Saynim.

Whatever the true story, Rune had been born into a land divided among half a dozen petty kingdoms, each led by Gentry folk determined to extend their reach as far as possible.

The King of Shadows claimed everything for himself, of course, and vowed to reclaim what was rightfully his.

All of that was mere prologue before the heart of Whisper's briefing. The King of Shadows had overthrown the Peacebringer by means of a powerful artifact, Whisper explained, a coffer of finest dwarven craft. It had a single purpose: to trap the Peacebringer's essence.

The King of Shadows had used it in the final battle. Corcc vanished with a blood-curdling shriek, his forces scattered, and an era of peace came to an end in a single morning.

But the coffer went missing. Had there been a spy in the King's court? A thief from outside? Rune had never learned that part of the story, and Whisper offered no explanation. He simply announced to his Nightwalkers that His Majesty's spies had at last located the artifact. The Amber Queen had hidden it away, they said, in her citadel at Cruc Máw.

Whisper had spent the spring and half the summer devising a plan to retrieve the coffer—and thus cement his lord's authority once and for all. With the blessing of his wife, the Keeper of the Mirror, he commandeered the best scryers at court to bypass the Amber Queen's magics and probe the layout of her keep. He stockpiled weapons and equipment. He bribed informants and tricked guards into divulging the Amber Queen's movements.

And at Ingathering, the festival of the fall harvest, the Nightwalkers struck.

Whisper had sent earth-weavers into the surrounding city all that day, small bands posing as travelers in town for the holiday. The Amber Queen herself was on a state visit to the nearby principality of Akuliota; storming the citadel with her still there would have been suicide for even a thousand Nightwalkers.

At sunset, the earth-weavers transformed into mice and snakes and scurried into the citadel through vents and drainage pipes. Once inside, half of them took up positions throughout the citadel while the other half, a team of the best burglars in the King's service, made for the Amber Queen's treasury.

At the same time, a lone water-weaver sat at the bottom of the well on the town square and silently began to roil the emotions of the crowd: a twinge of fear here, a fleeting pique of anger or jealousy there. Nothing flashy—water-weavers could be subtle. She seized whatever opportunities she could find, doing nothing to raise suspicion that magic was afoot.

It wasn't long before fists started to fly. As expected, the citadel garrison moved in to restore order, leaving the citadel itself distracted and understaffed.

That's when a fire-weaver, watching safely from a distance, shot a jet of flame into the sky.

At that signal, the Nightwalkers came, riding the wind with the setting sun at their backs. They were six in number: Rune, Goodfellow, Zodiac, Saffron, and Sparrow, with Dancer in command. Their job was to penetrate the upper levels, take the coffer from the burglar who'd stolen it, and escape in the confusion.

Rune landed on the ledge of a tall, narrow window. He wanted to call on his umbersay cloak to let him pass through the cracks in the glass, but he'd been warned about the Amber Queen's magical wards. Instead, he waited on the ledge until a smallkin, now back in his two-legged form, threw the window open from the inside. Rune dashed in and came skidding to a stop in a long stone hallway, his musketoon at the ready.

Goodfellow flew in behind him. "Which way?" he whispered.

His brawny partner's eyes were wide, and Rune wondered if he himself looked twice as nervous. Neither of them had ever been on an errand like this. It was miles beyond the simple child-stealing and crop-blighting runs they usually made.

"Pull more air," Rune hissed. "Focus."

Goodfellow nodded, and the two of them sprinted down the hallway toward the stairs.

No one knew which of the three stairwells the burglars would use to bring the coffer up. It all depended on what kind of resistance they faced and what they had to do to get around it. The shortest route might not be the safest. They might have to evade guards, or double back, or crawl through the vents. They might even have to fight their way up.

Rune and Goodfellow took the stairwell closest to the throne room. Once in position, they pulled on the hoods of their cloaks and crouched in the shadows under a veil of glamour as powerful as they could muster.

Rune, report! Avice's voice echoed in Rune's mind.

In position, Rune thought toward her. He trusted that Avice and the others had taken up their own positions and were waiting, just like him.

It was five minutes before a goblin woman in a simple black tunic appeared from below. She moved so quietly that they didn't hear her coming, even with the airy chaos swirling around them to heighten their senses.

Rune dropped his glamour and threw back his hood. Goodfellow followed suit. The goblin looked up with eyes like saucers.

"It ain't there!" she hissed.

"What do you mean?" Rune demanded.

"We got in, looked everywhere…I tell ya, the sarding thing ain't there!"

"Tempest!" Goodfellow moaned.

Rune's mind reeled. Had they been set up? Was this some kind of trap?

"Where are the others?" he asked.

Before she could answer, a door below slammed open below.

"This way!" someone shouted. Footfalls echoed up the stair-well.

"We've got to get out!" Goodfellow said, and bolted upward.

"Goodfellow!" Rune called. But he was already gone. Rune turned to the goblin. "He's right. We've got to retreat."

"Hopin' you'd say that," she agreed. A second later, she was a tiny brown mouse darting through a crack in the stonework.

Rune grasped his weapon and turned to follow his partner. At the top of the stairs, he found himself alone.

Below, sounds of gunfire shook the stairwell.

He exhaled. The Blessing hadn't yet come. Between riding the wind, enhancing his focus, and remaining invisible for so long, it would overtake him soon. He was on the verge of slipping into a mental tunnel of unfeelingness. There was no time for frustration or fear.

Maybe the coming Blessing was what brought him the mental clarity to see the situation from a different perspective. Or maybe it was his supposed half-human creativity—if that was even a real thing. But as he bolted toward the window where he'd come in, he began wondering where *he* would keep a magical artifact of unspeakable power.

Not in the treasury, he told himself. *That's the first place somebody would look.*

He reached the window, leaped onto the sill, and hesitated.

The sounds of fighting drew closer: the report of musketoons, the clang of swords.

You hide something like that in plain sight. Someplace just a little too obvious—*where nobody would believe it's that easy.*

In a flash of inspiration, he jumped back down and sped toward the throne room. He burst through a side door and took stock of the hall in an air-magnified instant. He was in an expansive apse adorned with rich tapestries. In the main part of the hall, the same high, narrow windows from the hallway opened to the moonlit night. Lanterns in brass wall sconces burned with amber light.

A single figure stood near the middle of the room, a maid who had been dusting.

Rune raised his weapon to his shoulder and, willing the airy chaos to guide his shot, pulled the trigger. The maid crumpled to the floor in agony as the fell shot tore into her belly. Her feather duster spun across the marble floor.

Just as quickly, she was no longer Rune's concern. As she thrashed about, whimpering and crying, he strode to the throne itself and studied its exquisite workmanship. It was all gold and ivory, carved with depictions of nymphs and satyrs cavorting around bound human prisoners.

Rune, Goodfellow, where are you? Avice projected.

Rune ignored her. He was getting impatient, restless. He'd spent too much time in this room already. He stooped to get a better look at the throne's construction. Beneath the seat was a compartment of sturdy wood, painted white and adorned with gold filigree. It matched the style of the throne perfectly, but to Rune's mind it didn't look quite as old.

With a mirthless grin, he reloaded his weapon, this time not with ferstitch but with a thunderstone. His next shot blasted the throne to splinters with a crack of lightning.

In the debris, he spied a glint of bronze.

The box was squat and cylindrical, not quite half a gallon in size. On each end and along its length were dials and levers—some kind of locking mechanism. To Rune's magical senses, it radiated power and vitality. Whoever possessed this coffer could do anything, face any foe. His heart surged as he considered the possibilities.

He took a breath. His stomach churned.

There was shouting outside and more clanging of swords.

He lifted the coffer. It was heavier than it looked, and it throbbed with energy. Something welled up within him—a feeling of victory and freedom.

With this, I could be a king.

As soon as he formed the thought, his umbersay cloak tightened at his throat. Rune flinched. Where did that thought even come from? He looked at the coffer with growing dread.

This was what his lord, the King of Shadows, had used to bring down the Peacebringer. This was what the King had been searching for since before Rune was born.

And in that instant, Rune imagined what the King of Shadows could do if he ever got it back.

How many more would Rune be called on to destroy when they displeased the King of Shadows? How many more innocent Fallow children would he have to collect to serve as His Majesty's knights?

What would the world look like with the King of Shadows at the helm? His cloak clung to his thighs and back, another subtle warning to mind his thoughts.

In that moment, seeing clearly was more a curse than a blessing.

"You've found it!" Avice's voice snapped Rune back to the present. He spun around, shifting the coffer from his right hand to his left.

He couldn't see how she'd gotten in. Probably from a different side passage. She jogged toward him with a grin, skipping over the still-writhing maid. She held out her hand. "Now give it here, and let's be gone. The guards are coming."

Rune felt his grip on the coffer tighten. He couldn't let it go—not to her.

"I…"

"Give it here!" she repeated. "We don't have all night."

Rune took a step back.

Her eyes met his, and recognition dawned. "Don't even think it. Give me the coffer, or by my breath I'll put you down where you stand."

She drew her musketoon and leveled it on him.

Rune's cloak twitched and constricted. He undid the clasp and sloughed the garment off. "We can't let him have this."

"You're a King's Nightwalker!" Avice hissed. "You swore an oath!"

Rune shrugged. "I don't care." As soon as the words left his mouth, he started to itch. Something dry and spidery crept over his skin. By breaking his oath, he'd broken the Covenant. His body was already feeling the knot he had tied.

He would have to worry about that later. He lunged to the right just as Avice fired. He fell onto his stomach as her shot zoomed over his head, but the force of his landing bounced the coffer out of his hand.

Avice darted for it, but Rune slammed into her just as fast. Her cloak wrapped around him, catching his knife-thrust. She twisted her body to turn his momentum against him. He landed on the floor with his arm bent almost to breaking. His hand was now covered with blotchy leprous scales.

Outside, guards pounded on the doors. The timbers started to crack. Avice glanced toward the door, then to the closest window. She kicked him in the face and drew her sword. With a savage scream, she brought it down toward his raised left arm.

She didn't notice the pistol in his right hand.

Rune pulled the trigger, but an explosion of pain in his scaly hand ruined his aim. The shot only grazed her, but her expression of pure agony as she crumpled to the ground said it was enough. She gasped and spat curses. Rune scrambled for the coffer, shoved it into his pack, and made for the window.

"You'll pay for this, Claeus son of Herdis of the House of... ungh!"

She pounded the floor as another wave of agony shot through her, stopping her from pronouncing Rune's full name. Even so, he felt a twinge as Avice's magic brushed against him. He had to go now, before she could try again. He shouldered open the window and mounted the sill.

The doors flung open, and a dozen of the Amber Queen's guards burst into the room.

But Rune didn't care. He was through with Avice, with Whisper, with the fighting and the posturing. He was through with the King of sarding Shadows.

He turned away and flung himself into the starry night.

The memory of that moment of exhilaration finally shook Rune awake in the present, and he remembered everything—the Hollarts, the aerial fight in the rain, barely escaping from Avice, wounded and spent.

Now his whole body hurt, and it took him a minute to focus his eyes in the dim light. To his surprise, he was warm and dry.

His itchy skin had returned to normal—yes, a month ago. It was all coming back to him.

He lurched up, then hissed as the wounds on his leg and abdomen flared.

A little dwarf girl gasped and backed away.

"Momma!"

Rune was in a house, in a bed. As his senses came to him, he recognized the girl. She was the gearsmith's child. Brackwater. But how…?

He reached out a hand. "It's okay," he croaked. "I won't—"

A dwarf woman shouldered her way past the child and leveled a musketoon at Rune. "Just lay back down," she said through clenched teeth. "And don't even think about touching my daughter."

24

Rune froze in place. He raised a hand in defense—but too fast. He gasped, and his gut erupted in a flash of pain. The brass barrel of the dwarf woman's firearm demanded his full attention. Instead of grasping his side or curling up or lashing out, he lowered his hand with a wince. "I won't harm you," he said.

Mrs. Brackwater scoffed. "I don't reckon you will, …elf." The floor trembled almost imperceptibly.

He propped himself up with his left arm. The blanket slid off his bare torso. Rune and his captor stared at each other.

"You start mucking around in my brain…" Mrs. Brackwater gestured with her weapon. "Just don't go mucking around in anybody's brain."

"Of course not." Rune's head swam. He took in a long breath, calling the airy chaos to himself. The magic barely rustled in his consciousness, but the aroma of cooking vegetables in the next room made his stomach rumble. It might have been a pleasant sensation; it was too soon to tell.

Mrs. Brackwater brought the firearm to her cheek and stared at him down the barrel.

"Please," Rune said, lifting his right hand again, as if that would do anything if she decided to pull the trigger.

"Momma, he's bleeding!" the girl said. Between his throbbing head and his battered body, with a firearm trained on him, Rune had forgotten she was there.

Once more, he lowered his hand, letting it brush his stomach. He'd been bandaged. His fingertips came away damp with blood.

"Ulfa, run and get me some fresh bandages."

The girl stared wide-eyed at Rune.

"Now," her mother said.

Ulfa backed away, then turned and scampered off.

They were in a modest bedroom. On the far wall, over Mrs. Brackwater's back, an ornate clock hung above a chest of drawers. In the corner stood a dressing table with a mirror and washbasin. There were two doors, one to Rune's left by which the girl left and another next to the dressing table, probably a closet.

He finished his scan and met Mrs. Brackwater's deep brown eyes. Her expression was passionless, her lips pursed.

"You bound my wounds," he said. It wasn't a question, though the fact of it raised plenty of others.

"That was my husband." The musketoon never dropped from the woman's shoulder. "I did a little work your ribs is all."

"I'm in your debt."

"Just say thank you," Mrs. Brackwater said. "I ain't holding no debt from a…"

Ulfa returned with a roll of bandages and a lidless wooden box.

"…from you," the woman finished.

"Can I help?" Ulfa asked.

Mrs. Brackwater's eyes tracked between her daughter and Rune.

Rune coughed, which made him groan. "I assure you I won't try anything."

"You'll forgive me if I keep Frieda handy just in case." The woman cocked her head toward her weapon, then lowered it while still keeping it aimed at Rune. "Feet on the floor," she said. "Ulfa, cut away the old bandages. Let's see what he looks like."

Rune complied, though his muscles protested. His bare feet brushed across the thick pile of a braided rug. He puzzled at his woolen trousers, too short and too baggy.

Mrs. Brackwater must have noticed his confusion. "Your clothes are drying by the stove," she said. "Ulfa?"

At her mother's signal, the girl crept forward and snipped Rune's bandages with a pair of brass scissors. At last they came loose, and she shied away as her mother exposed the wound.

Streaks of half-dried blood traced lines across Rune's belly where the werecrow had torn into him. He'd been stitched up, but not exactly professionally. He was in one piece, though he'd probably have a scar. His thigh ached as well, and now that he was fully awake, he could feel bandages rubbing underneath his borrowed trousers. He brushed his hand over his leg.

"The cut on your leg was long but shallow," Mrs. Brackwater said. "It was a bloody mess is all. Don't get in no footraces for a while and you'll be fine. It's your gut that's the real problem. Whatever it was that ripped into you wasn't what you'd call clean." She tsked. "You were on your way to a nasty infection."

She leaned her weapon against the foot of the bed, out of Rune's reach. She never took her eyes off of him as she pulled up a stool, sat on it, and unscrewed a tin from the box Ulfa had brought her. The woman dipped in two fingers and smeared his stomach with a foul unguent, all the while grumbling under her breath. At last, she slapped a meaty hand against his ribs—and none too gently.

Rune hissed in pain.

"Hold still." Mrs. Brackwater's bedside manner left much to be desired, but as soon as she pulled her hand away, his chest felt looser. Whatever she had done must have worked. The salve had started to work, too, bathing his body in a cool, refreshing energy.

"Ulfa, go find one of your papa's old shirts. There ought to be one or two in the basket of fabric I put aside for Laurin and Hilly's quilt."

The girl started for the door.

"And then go check on supper," Mrs. Brackwater said. "The hash is about ready. Can you make the cornbread?"

"Yes, Momma."

The woman turned back to Rune, shaking her head.

"I'm sorry to have inconvenienced you, Mrs. Brackwater."

Unspeaking, she motioned for Rune to raise his arms as she wrapped fresh cotton bandages around his belly.

"I'm truly sorry."

"We'll give you hospitality," she said. "Don't let nobody say the Brackwaters shirk their duties. But don't get your hopes up for anything more than that."

A door creaked open somewhere over Rune's shoulder, on the other side of the wall. A young man's voice called, "We're home!"

"Laurin!" Ulfa called back, no doubt from the kitchen.

"Just a minute," Mrs. Brackwater said. She got up and left Rune, leaving the door open. Another door swung open, and Ulfa squealed with delight. From the sounds of footsteps, several people had filed into the room behind Rune's head. They brought greetings and laughter and pats on the back, and finally the clomping of heavy boots drew near.

Mr. Brackwater peered into the bedroom. His wife followed close behind. The gearsmith's brow shot up as he noticed the firearm still at the foot of the bed. He leaned in to give his wife a side-to-side hug. "Any trouble?" he whispered.

She shook her head but glared at her husband.

Someone else approached. Rune could lean forward just enough to see a young, dark-haired dwarf outside the doorway. From his build and facial features, he had to be another Brackwater. Ulfa had said his name: Laurin. A woman stood at his side. She was redheaded and solidly built. Rune noted her captivating eyes, one blue and one amber, and the arched eyebrows on her sloping forehead. Something about her seemed untamed, full of energy.

She moved into the room and came close enough to address Rune. "How are you feeling?"

"I've been better."

"You've been worse," the gearsmith said. "You're lucky we found you."

"From a distance, Papa thought you were a dead shadeling," Laurin said. "He'd come to meet us at the Drunken Dragon up in Dunswale. Something about a calculating clock for Mr. Barley—he's the fella that owns the place."

"You found me in Dunswale?" Rune asked.

Brack pulled up the chair from the dressing table and leaned the musketoon against the wall where he could reach it. His wife stood behind him with her hands on her husband's shoulders. "No," he said, shaking his head. "Here in Goblintown on the way home. There you were, sprawled out and sopping wet next to the well in the town square. Thought we'd pushed you over the edge ourselves when we loaded you into my son's cart."

"By the well, you say?"

Brack nodded.

Rune's head swam. He'd passed out in a sewer drain. Somebody had taken him and left him beside the Goblintown well. Somebody, apparently, who was at home in the water. Maya Tecumseh—or more likely one of her cronies.

If the Merlady had saved his life, that made him nervous. It was yet another thing he owed her for. Rune shivered when he wondered what she would demand when she came to collect.

"Hey," Brack said, snapping his fingers in front of Rune's face. "You still with us?"

Rune shook off his troubling thoughts. "I'm fine," he said. "I'm in your debt."

The gearsmith waved off the statement. "I don't need your debt. Just get well." He raised a bushy eyebrow. "And then get on your way. Understand?"

"Of course, Mr. Brackwater."

"Brack," he said. "Everybody calls me Brack. Thora's my wife." He chuckled. "I suppose you got to know her pretty well. She and I see eye to eye on most things…especially our children's safety."

Rune nodded.

"Ulfa you met. This is Laurin, my oldest." The black-haired dwarf bowed. "And Hilly, his intended." The redhead smiled, exposing canines only slightly larger than Rune might have expected.

Brack looked around. "Where's Duren?"

"Reckon he's off getting into trouble," Laurin said with a laugh.

Brack rolled his eyes. "Better not be goofin' around with those Crankshaw boys. They nearly broke their necks last Hallowfest with their foolishness."

"It'll be fine, Papa," Laurin said. "There's nothing wrong with a little foolishness on Hallowfest."

"Hallowfest ain't till tomorrow night," Brack said. "And in the meantime, we've got things to do: cook the food, mix the wassail, put up the decorations—"

"The food will get cooked," Thora said. "It always does. You're just agitated because you get a day off tomorrow."

Brack grumbled.

She looked at Rune. "My husband never does know what to do with himself when he gets a day off from work."

"Is that where Laurin gets it?" Hilly chimed in. She sidled around to where her intended stood and wrapped an arm around his waist.

"Dwarves like to work," Brack said with a shrug. "Might as well get used to it."

"Well, trolls like to let their hair down," Hilly said, grinning. "And *he's* gonna have to get used to *that*." She squeezed Laurin so tight he yelped. His cheeks reddened, but he didn't back away.

"Your future father-in-law is a little more dwarfish than most," Thora said to her. "But he grows on you."

"And what about you, Mr. …Rune, was it?" Hilly continued. "I imagine there aren't that many elves in Goblintown."

Rune met her gaze. "I suppose not," he offered. He should have known it would only be a matter of time before somebody started asking questions he'd just as soon not answer.

"Are you from Dunswale, then?" Hilly pressed.

Rune shut his eyes and bowed his head. "No."

"Mr. Rune is a Nightwalker!" Ulfa announced from the door.

Hilly gasped. Brack and Thora gritted their teeth.

Rune's pulse raced, but he willed himself to reveal no emotion. "Actually, I'm…it's complicated."

Hilly sidestepped Laurin to get closer to Rune. She gestured at his body, his bandaged belly and his many bruises. Her eyes widened. "Did *they* do this to you?"

Rune found Thora in the little group and locked his eyes on her. "I'm no longer in the King's service," he said. "We didn't see eye to eye on the terms of my severance."

Thora harrumphed.

"But he's our guest for now," Brack said with a note of finality. He looked up and back to where his wife still stood behind him. "Right?"

"Of course," Thora said. "Until he's well enough to go."

"I won't overstay my welcome, Mrs. Brackwater," Rune said. As soon as he could move, he would leave—and not for Louisville, either. He was no longer safe there. It was only a matter of time before Avice tracked down where he'd been staying in the Fallow.

No, it was time to move on. Avice would leave the Colemans alone if they couldn't point her to Rune. He would just retrieve the King's coffer from where he'd stashed it and go somewhere else, some forgotten corner of the Fallow where nobody would think to look. Somewhere the King of Shadows could never find him.

"Momma! Papa!" a boy called, his voice cracking. Before Rune could take another breath, the last of the Brackwater children burst into the outer room. Soon he appeared at the bedroom door, a youngling who moved with the gawky bearing of a young man not finished growing.

"Duren!" his mother shouted. "What do you mean, barging in like this? We didn't raise you to—"

Wide-eyed, he looked around until locking eyes on his mother. "I'm sorry, Momma, but…but…"

"What is it?" Brack said.

"Well, I was hanging out with Dob and Jemmy Crankshaw, and Mr. Crankshaw overheard me talking about the Nightwalker, and—"

"What?" Mrs. Brackwater gasped.

"By the Seven, Duren! How'd you get it in your head to start blabbin' about that? Your momma and I told you that was private."

"I know, Papa. I'm sorry, I just…" He shrugged. "I guess it slipped out, but he's coming!"

"Mote Crankshaw? Coming here?" Brack said.

Duren nodded. "He started cussing up a storm. He says you're gonna get everybody in Goblintown killed keeping a Nightwalker under our roof. And he means to do something about it."

"Silver and gold," Brack grumbled. He glared at Rune with his beady eyes.

There was nothing Rune could say. He'd never asked them to take him in, but he'd be dead if they hadn't. And he was in no condition to travel. His presence was ruining everything. "Mr. Brackwater," he started.

"Can't be helped now," Brack said. He rose from his chair as someone rapped on his workshop door.

"Heptifilius Brackwater!" a voice threatened.

Brack took a step toward the door. Laurin moved to follow, but Brack held up a hand to motion him back.

"Help your momma set the table." The gearsmith gestured toward Rune. "Set one more place if he's up to eating anything."

He cracked his knuckles and stomped away.

25

Brack and Mote Crankshaw sat across from each other at Brack's workbench. The steam engine that worked the bellows was silent. It was just the two of them, the dwarf and the goblin, but the gleam of embers in the firebox signaled that Kettle was near and no doubt listening.

"What are you trying to pull?" Mote said, his voice hard and cold as stone. His flame-red mutton chops highlighted his scowl.

"Mote…"

"You knew he was a Nightwalker. You know there's another one prowling around Dunswale."

"He nearly died."

"And?" Mote shifted on his stool. He didn't shout; he was in perfect control…but for how long? The goblin's feet dangled inches above the floor. "What do you know about him? What do you know about the woman who's looking for him? He could be the bad guy, you know!"

Brack studied Mote's stony face. The goblin could be stubborn when he wanted, and he had a fair bit of clout with the neighbors to boot. He and his family had lived in Goblintown for generations. Brack wasn't just rocking the boat by bringing Rune into his home; he was rocking Mote Crankshaw's boat.

But he had talked with the elf, looked him in the eye. Was he happy Rune was holed up in his house? Not even a little. The whole situation dropped an ice-cold lump of lead in his belly. Even so, the elf said he'd cut his ties to the King of Shadows, and by the Seven, Brack believed him—at least about that.

"Then what happens if he dies in Goblintown and his people find out?" Brack said. "You don't think that might ruffle somebody's feathers too?"

Mote's eyes flashed. "I'm saying we'd all be better off if you'd just minded your own business. Suppose that woman's still lurking about? She's still working for the King of Shadows. Probably a Nightwalker herself. And after Cruc Máw—"

"After Cruc Máw, what?" Brack slammed his fist on the bench. "We just forget about common decency? About sacred hospitality?"

"You brought this on yourself, Brack." Mote furrowed his brow. "You shoulda left him where you found him. As it is, we're all in trouble. Everybody in Goblintown: you, me, your family. You understand that, right?"

Brack studied Mote's face, and he realized what was going on. He'd seen that gleam in the goblin's eyes before. It wasn't anger—not entirely. It was the wheels turning inside Mote's head.

"But we can still salvage the situation," Mote said. He leaned forward, bracing his feet on the footrest of his stool.

Here it comes. Brack grinned in spite of himself. It wasn't like Mote to let a perfectly good crisis go to waste. "You've got a plan," he said. "Why does that make me nervous?"

Mote licked his lips. "Say we let the Nightwalker hang around for a while—"

"*We?*"

"Just hear me out," Mote said. "He can stay till he can move on his own. If somebody don't like that idea, I can smooth things out with 'em."

Brack had no doubt about that, but there was clearly something more. "Then what?"

"Look, you gotta admit, we're in a fix here even without the Nightwalker," Mote continued. "Who's gonna stand up for us? The mayor? He ain't smart enough to know what a fix we're in." The goblin looked ready to pounce, but he held back, waiting for Brack to respond.

Brack chose not to give him the satisfaction. He sat silently, arms crossed, for a full ten seconds. The firebox subtly brightened.

"Don't you see?" Mote said at last. "The Nightwalker gives us leverage. Somebody wants him for something. If you ask me, it's probably more than one somebody."

"You want to turn him over? To the King of Shadows?" Brack clenched his fists as he drew the metallic chaos to himself.

"My first choice would be the Merlady," Mote said with a shrug. "It don't really matter, does it? The point is, we can use him, Brack! He can buy us some breathing room. Lay him at the Merlady's feet, and she'll have to take us seriously."

Now Brack laughed out loud. "You think you can bargain with the Merlady as equals?"

"Of course not," Mote said. "But if we put her in our debt, she'd have to admit it, wouldn't she? Even Gentry folk like her have to pay their debts…"

"By the Seven, you're serious."

"And if she thought, for example, that we might give him up to the King of Shadows instead—"

Brack slammed his hand on the workbench again. "That's enough. The elf is a guest in my house." His pulse pounded in his temples, and his throat went dry.

"But for how long, Brack? The way I see it, as soon as he walks out that door, you've done everything expected of you."

"And you'll just arrange for somebody to be around to, uh, *meet* him when he leaves?"

"All I'm asking is you give me a heads-up when he's ready to leave. I'll take care of the rest."

"Get out of my house."

"You're making a mistake, Brack. That Nightwalker's gonna get us all killed."

Brack pursed his lips. "Maybe, maybe not. But at least I'll still have my name."

Mote hopped down from his stool, tipping it over with a crash.

A flash of light signaled Kettle's arrival. He appeared beside the bellows in the form of a young boy. His eyes gleamed as he stepped forward, glancing first at Brack and then at Mote. Every lamp in the workshop brightened.

Brack motioned for his assistant to stay put.

Mote glared at the boy. After a second's distraction, he turned on Brack and growled, "You wanna say something, just say it!"

Brack slid off his seat. "All this time I thought you were a man of honor, but you're not. You're three times a coward, and you can't see anything past saving your own skin."

Mote's face reddened, but to his credit, he didn't rush Brack then and there. Then again, Brack was a foot taller and about sixty pounds heavier. "You say coward," Mote said. "I say practical. The Nightwalker is gonna bring us trouble, more trouble than you and I can handle. Do you deny it?"

Brack's eyes narrowed to slits beneath his heavy brow. "I told you to get out."

"You're gonna regret this." The goblin stormed away and slammed the door behind him.

Brack sighed as Kettle hurried to set Mote's overturned stool upright.

"Damn fool," Brack grumbled. "You want to know who's gonna make trouble in Goblintown?" He raised his bearded chin toward the door.

"Uh-huh," Kettle said.

Brack met his assistant's gleaming eyes. In all his years, he'd never been able to read what was going on in Kettle's head. "You don't sound convinced."

"I'm plenty convinced," the firedrake said in his clipped accent. "But…"

"But what?" Tension built at the nape of Brack's neck. He kneaded the flesh while Kettle lowered his head and kicked at the flagstones.

"It is not like he has no point," Kettle said. "About Nightwalker, I mean."

Brack sighed. "I know." What had he been thinking, taking Rune in? Somebody was looking for him; Mote was right about that. And from the look of things, they'd damn near caught him!

"Then why you brought him home?" Kettle said.

If Brack could have answered that, he'd be a wise dwarf indeed. He shrugged at Kettle. The firedrake's youthful, innocent face hadn't changed a bit since he was Brack's father's assistant.

Why did he bring Rune home? It didn't seem enough to say that it felt like the right thing to do. Was it an act of defiance, an up-yours to the mayor, the Merlady, and anybody else who had their sights on Goblintown? Was it simple bravado, the delusion that one person really could take a stand?

Kettle stood there in his pristine white tunic.

"Dunno," Brack said.

In the back, wooden chairs scraped against the stone floor. Hilly's muffled laughter cut through the tension in the workshop.

"It's time for supper," Brack said. "You coming?"

"If it is same to you, I figure I head up to Drunken Dragon for while."

The dwarf sat with his head down. What had he gotten himself into the middle of?

"Brack?"

"Help yourself," he sighed. "Have a drink for me."

"Have good night, Brack."

The dwarf grumbled and turned toward the door.

Rune slouched at the table, now wearing an oversized shirt of homespun cotton to match his short-but-oversized trousers. When Brack entered the room, he tried to sit up straight, even though his stomach would have preferred he didn't.

Brack silently strode to his seat at the head of the table. He didn't say a word, but Rune had heard everything. In fact, he had expended the slightest bit of magic to hone his senses, just in case. He was sitting down for supper, but that didn't mean he was safe.

The dwarf sat with Thora to his right and Rune to his left. Laurin sat opposite his father, with Hilly on his left and his younger siblings on his right.

Rune tried to read the gearsmith's expression. Brack had admitted that the goblin, Crankshaw, had a point, that Rune was bound to bring trouble. What would a man like Brack do if he thought his family were in danger?

Rune braced himself. He had learned at Whisper's table that dinner could be a battlefield. The world revolved around honor: one's standing among peers—and one's ability to assert one's place in the pecking order.

Rune's presence upset the status quo. It had sullied Brack's reputation with Crankshaw. Now the dwarf would want to assert his dominance at home. At least, that's what Whisper would do.

Thora would probably make the first move. Take the lead. Probe peoples' weaknesses while Brack sat back and observed, waiting to strike. That's what Rune's aunt Maug would do.

There was nothing for it but to give in—but not too much. Rune couldn't afford to lose face, and with it whatever goodwill his reluctant host was willing to extend him. He would have to tread a fine line.

Thora dished a heaping spoonful of food onto Rune's plate. It was some kind of hash made with sausage and potatoes. He lifted his hands to waft some of the aroma to his nostrils, preparing to breathe it slowly out as an offering to the airy chaos.

Then he thought better of it. No sense drawing attention to yet another way he was different from these people. Earth- and metal-weavers no doubt had their own rituals, their own ways of connecting with something greater than themselves. He waited to see what would happen next.

A platter of fried hoecakes passed his way. He slid one onto his plate.

"Smells good," Hilly said.

Everything did, in fact, smell wonderful. Rune tried to remember the last time he'd eaten anything. Hilly forked a bit of hash into her mouth. Apparently, earth-weavers didn't have a mealtime ritual. Or maybe they did but Rune had missed it.

"It's just leftovers," Thora said.

Rune tentatively took a bite and waited to see how the others would respond.

"Tomorrow's Hallowfest Eve," the troll woman said. "We'll all have enough cooking to do then."

Smart, Rune thought. She didn't take Thora's bait. Instead of commenting on the food, she turned the conversation to tomorrow's duties. Earth-weavers loved nothing more than working together on a project.

"Do you like your hash, Mr. Rune?" Hilly said.

Rune gulped down a bite. His pulse raced. He reached for his cider to buy some time.

Don't bring me into this!

It was bad enough that his own presence caused friction in the Brackwater house. He didn't need to get into a contest of honor between a woman and her future mother-in-law. He tried to think. Ulfa made the cornbread, but who made the hash? Thora or Hilly? What was the right answer?

"You probably ate better in Athelhoew," Thora said. She was sitting directly across from him. Her brown eyes bore into him, but her expression was cryptic. "That's where you're from, ain't it?"

He started to sweat. There was no way out; he'd have to say something. He only hoped it was the right thing.

"Not at all, Mrs. Brackwater. This is very good." And it was. He took another bite. It was warm and hearty and just a little bit spicy. The stew at Gamaufry Tavern was nothing but warmed-over gruel in comparison.

Thora regarded him without comment. In fact, the entire room drifted into silence. Rune had never been able to read a room like Avice could, and courtly machinations had blindsided him more than once. Duren and Ulfa gobbled up their supper. Hilly and Laurin whispered to themselves—about wedding plans of all things. There were none of the subtle nods and gestures of allies in a dining room power play.

Thora sat stone-faced. More troubling, Brack hadn't said a word since he sat down. But the other shoe was bound to drop eventually.

Rune expelled a sigh. He couldn't figure out elves at court. How could he hope to understand what was going through the minds of dwarves and trolls?

"I heard Athelhoew has walls of glass," Duren said.

Thora shushed her son with a sharp hiss.

"I don't see how that's any of your business," Brack said.

Rune glanced furtively toward his host, immediately to his right. The dwarf's body language told him nothing.

"Well, does it?" Duren persisted.

Rune tapped his fingers against his thigh. By persisting with his question, the child had challenged his father—and in front of a houseguest, no less! Things were going downhill fast, and

Rune had a ringside seat. He rehearsed the layout of the room, calculating the quickest way out.

"You shouldn't bother our guest, Duren," Laurin said. But there was no threat in his voice, no shift in his posture to warn the younger boy to listen to his father. Then he looked at Rune… and smiled.

Rune sucked in a breath. Something was happening, but he didn't know what. He wasn't lightheaded anymore, but the room still spun.

"I'm sorry, Mr. Rune," Duren said, deflated. "I didn't mean nothing."

All eyes turned to Rune. What were they expecting him to do? Accept the boy's apology? Defer to the father? He took another sip of cider.

"It's not true," he muttered, shocked to hear the words leave his mouth.

More stares. His face warmed. Once more, the room fell silent.

Stars above, get me out of here!

"I'd heard that, too," Hilly said, also smiling.

Why were these people smiling?

"It's obsidian," Rune said. It took him a few seconds to realize the room was not going to explode. "Volcanic glass. Here and there. Decorations, you know?"

"Is that so?" Hilly said.

Rune nodded. "Imported from the south. It's very pretty." And very brittle.

"Simple folk ain't got no use for such frippery," Brack scoffed.

"But you make such pretty things, Mr. Brackwater," Hilly said. "I've seen them in your workshop."

Rune's mind reeled. Now the troll woman was going after Brack himself!

"That's different," the gearsmith grumbled. "Those things serve a purpose." He locked eyes with Rune.

Rune noted the gearsmith's clenched fists, his steely glare. The message was clear enough: What purpose do *you* serve?

But still the storm refused to break.

"Pass the cornbread," Ulfa said.

And everyone suddenly remembered that there was a young child present.

"Mr. Rune, would you like more cornbread?" Ulfa held the platter, ready to pass it across the table to her guest. The innocence in her expression brought Rune up short.

"Yes, thank you," he said. He forked another hoecake from the outstretched platter.

"I made it."

"I heard." He took a bite. "It's delicious."

Ulfa beamed.

Whisper always said that war is deceit. He had trained Rune to always be on guard, to look for the unexpected angle, to leverage knowledge to buy whatever advantage he could find. That's what being a Nightwalker was all about: lurk in the shadows, misdirect, lead people to the wrong assumptions. Don't let anyone know what you're really up to.

It was an attitude ingrained in high-born elves. Their courts were exactly as they were: bright, beautiful…and deadly. Every social interaction—even something as simple as dinner—was a contest, a battle to see who would gain the upper hand.

But this wasn't war. Rune wasn't sure what it was.

Duren and Ulfa didn't know they were supposed to be guarded, tense. They expressed themselves, even when their parents objected. But they weren't being disrespectful.

They were just being…children.

It was almost too much for Rune to take in.

"I…I'm afraid I…"

"Yes?" Thora said.

Rune bowed his head, took a breath, and started again. "I just want to say…thank you—all of you—for your hospitality. I know my presence is a challenge. I won't overstay my welcome."

"I know," Brack said. The gearsmith leaned back in his chair.

Rune dared to look him square in the eye. "Tell me to leave, Mr. Brackwater, and I'll be on my way."

"You don't have to do that, Mr. Rune," Ulfa said. Rune winced. Surely this was too much even for Brack to permit!

But the storm still refused to come. Brack stared at Rune as if he could read the depths of his heart through his eyes.

"I'm a guest in your house," Rune said. "It's up to you."

Brack dabbed his napkin against the corners of his mouth. "You'll stay till you're fit to travel," he said.

Ulfa and Duren smiled at each other.

"You said it yourself," the dwarf continued. "You're a guest here. Until I say otherwise, that's the way it's going to be."

Six pairs of eyes fixed on Rune, but strangely he felt no threat.

"Besides," Brack said, "nobody should be alone for Hallowfest."

With that, whatever tension was in the room evaporated. The bowl of hash went around again. Thora refilled everyone's drink. At one point, Laurin actually told a joke.

It was like nothing Rune had experienced before.

The night wore on, as best as Rune could tell. Underground, there weren't any obvious cues to the passage of time. But the clock on the wall told him they had sat and eaten and talked and laughed for an hour or more.

Thora brought out dessert: bread pudding with brandygreen sauce and sprinkles of cinnamon. It melted in Rune's mouth and warmed him from head to toe. As he savored every bite, he realized his stomach wasn't tight anymore.

"Mr. Rune," Duren said, "how many people live in Athelhoew anyway?"

"I don't know," Rune admitted. He had only rarely left the Haw to visit the city itself. "Ten thousand, more or less."

Duren gasped.

Ulfa was just as impressed. She leaned forward and asked, "Do you miss it?"

Eyes turned his way again, not accusingly but with genuine interest.

Rune felt a tightness in his chest that had nothing to do with his wounds. He was going to miss Goodfellow. Maybe some of the others from the Haw. But he couldn't think about that. He had made his decision. He'd left Athelhoew for good. And now, it seemed, he would soon be leaving Goblintown…to say nothing of the Fallow city beyond.

"No," Rune finally said, lips pursed. He took a breath. "I don't."

26

After supper, Brack and Laurin set up the board for a game of king's table. The strategy game brought Rune memories of Athelhoew and all the games he'd won against Goodfellow—and all the humiliating defeats he'd suffered at Whisper's hands.

Laurin beat his father in both rounds, a rarity by the way the others reacted. Brack accepted everyone's good-natured ribbing and joked—joked!—about not getting enough respect in his own house.

The dwarf caught Rune's startled reaction. He gestured toward the game board. "Do you play?"

"Some," Rune said. "I'm not really in the mood," he added when Brack started to set up for another game. "I'm…just sore from sitting."

"Then let's get your bed ready," Brack said. "A good stretch will make you feel better. Then we'll play."

Standing up and stretching took a bit of effort, but it was worth it. Rune perked up as his blood began to circulate. Brack led him to the workshop and only had to steady him once. Rune leaned against the stone anvil and watched as the Brackwaters put his bed together.

Thora and the younger children gathered bedding and set up a folding cot in a corner as far from the iron foundry and machinist's lathe as possible. The cot was old but sturdy, and Thora dutifully made it up for him. Hardly necessary, Rune thought, as he planned to be in it before long.

Meanwhile, Brack set up the game board on his workbench. "Attack or defend?" he asked.

Rune shuffled over and studied the board with its eleven-by-eleven squares and the carved wooden game pieces Brack was arranging. "Attack," he said, almost apologetically. "I'm a little rusty."

"Doesn't matter to me," Brack mumbled.

Rune slid onto a stool. Brack didn't make eye contact. He just counted out the game pieces, twenty-four for the attacker and twelve, plus the king, for the defender.

But this meeting had nothing to do with king's table. The Brackwaters were different from any family Rune had ever experienced, but some things were universal. Whisper used a multitude of strategies to learn what he could about anyone visiting the Haw, from spies and informants to careful observation of the way visitors carried themselves in social situations. Rune could imagine what might be going through Brack's mind. *Is this stranger telling the truth? How big a threat is he, really?*

And there was no denying Rune was a threat—to Brack, his family, and everyone in Goblintown. Not intentionally, but just as surely. Avice was still looking for him, and she would stop at nothing to drag him back to the King of Shadows. The goblin, Crankshaw, wanted to use him as a bargaining chip. He didn't seem like the type who'd let a trivial matter like Brack's friendship get in the way of the windfall he assumed Rune represented. And who knew what Maya Tecumseh had in mind for him—and what she might do to Goblintown to get him?

Brack finished setting up the board and straightened on his stool. He still didn't meet Rune's gaze.

Rune wondered if he should say something. Not for the first time, he wished he were better at reading people's feelings. It was obvious his presence had made things rough for Brack and his family. And yet the dwarf seemed willing to let him stay…for now.

He seemed to be a man of honor, but more often than not honor was a matter of personal interpretation. What might set him off? What might make him decide Rune had crossed some invisible line?

Rune picked up one of his black game pieces. The features of a dog-headed warrior with spear and fur-trimmed jacket were carved into the wood with obvious skill. "This is a fine set."

"A customer paid for an astronomical clock with it years ago." The dwarf still hadn't looked up.

"Ah. My uncle has one of those. Very impressive."

"Just something to keep my hands busy."

The attackers in a game of king's table were divided into four customary tribes. As Rune studied the rest of his pieces, he saw that each had its own distinctive design. This was no ordinary game set. He held one up and admired it. "This is the finest set I think I've ever seen."

Brack grinned. "It was a pretty big clock."

"It must have been," Rune mused. He set the piece back in front of him. He glanced around the board at the other designs. "You've got giants in the northern quarter," he said, eyeing the pieces to his right, "dogheads in the east, blemmyes in the south." He scanned the edge of the board closest to Brack and added, "And nimerigars in the west."

Brack grunted.

"By the way," Rune said, "thank you for not handing me over to Maya Tecumseh." It was only fair for him to say thank you. It was the subtlest way he could think of to signal that he knew about the conversation with Crankshaw. If the dwarf tried anything, Rune would be ready.

Brack's expression went sour, but he didn't say anything for several heartbeats. When he finally spoke, he said, "You gonna make a move?"

Rune moved one of his giants next to Brack's soldiers, clustered in the center of the board.

Brack countered. Two moves later, he captured one of Rune's dogheads.

After another well-considered move, Brack said, "What do you know about her, anyway?"

Whisper never talked while he played. It was unsettling, but Rune got used to it. And he suspected Brack wanted to talk. There were things he needed to know.

Rune continued to press with his giants. Brack had moved his king halfway to the castle square in the southeast corner of the board.

"The Merlady? She has designs on this part of the river," Rune said. "She's looking for allies. She may have one in your neighbor Crankshaw."

Brack scoffed. "A pack of shadelings would make a better ally than him." He moved a piece and captured one of Rune's blemmyes. "No, Mote Crankshaw is only interested in Mote Crankshaw. That's what makes him weak. Undependable."

"I see." Rune moved another blemmye. Brack was a good player but quick and direct. He had no patience, it seemed, for the schemes within schemes that Whisper preferred. Rune moved a giant so that it trapped one of Brack's soldiers between it and a doghead. He snatched up the white piece and set it to the side.

"She's gonna be the death of us all if we ain't careful," Brack said. He advanced his king. "Play footsie with her, you're tickling a dragon with a mighty short stick. But if it comes down to her or the King of Shadows?" He waved helplessly.

"I can't say you're wrong," Rune said. At least on that front, he and the dwarf saw eye to eye. Neither of them would last long if the King of Shadows got his way. He studied Brack's furrowed brow, his clenched jaw.

"What if there were a way to hold him off?"

Brack's eyebrows jumped. "What are you talking about?"

Rune took a long breath. "Not to defeat him, mind you. I'm not sure anyone can do that. But what if there were a way to make him keep his distance?"

Brack straightened up and peered directly at Rune. "Yeah?"

"You may know parts of this story better than I do. You were around when the Peacebringer fell."

The dwarf cursed. "Yeah, Thora and I remember those days. Still gives me the shivers." Corcc had called himself the Peacebringer, but everyone knew the kind of peace he brought. He *pacified* the lands he claimed by any means necessary. The Peacebringer was a ruler to be feared, not loved.

"Do you know how he was defeated?"

"Don't everybody? A bunch of the other Gentry decided it was time for him to go. They wanted to do their own thing without answering to him."

"But how did they do it? Do you know?"

Brack furrowed his brow.

Rune bit his lip and then pressed on. "They used…an artifact, I suppose you'd call it, that trapped his power."

"I figured some three-times powerful magic was involved."

Rune chose his words carefully. "That's what I thought, too. Then a few months ago I learned it was true."

Brack's bluish face went pale. "What are you getting at?"

"Suppose there was a container. A coffer of dwarven make. Something with multiple locking mechanisms. Powerful wards."

"Silver and gold," Brack hissed. Rune could practically see the gears turning in his mind. "A few months ago…at Cruc Máw?" His black eyes flashed. "That's what the mischief at Cruc Máw was all about?"

"If there was such an artifact, do you think…do you think you could destroy it?"

Brack's mouth fell open. "By the Seven! That's why they're after you," he guessed. "You were there. You got your hands on this…thing, and now the King of Shadow wants it. Is that it?"

Rune nodded. "Rather badly, I'm afraid. Between you and me, I'd prefer he didn't get it. And I expect you'd like that, too."

Brack sucked in a breath. "Silver and gold, son. I hope you put the damn thing in a good hiding place."

"It's safe," Rune said. "But he's coming for it."

The dwarf gripped the lip of the workbench. "What's that supposed to mean?"

"Maya isn't the only one looking for allies," Rune said. "The King of Shadows has someone across the Mere. He's planning something."

The dwarf groaned and rested his head in his hands. "So how bad is it?"

"Best I can tell, the King is set to pay a visit to the Fallow." Rune studied the game board, not because he was ready to make a move but because it helped him focus.

"And soon," Brack guessed.

"Whatever he's planning will take time. At least, I hope it will." Rune couldn't say he believed that with great conviction, but it let him sleep at night. "I'm sorry." What else could he say? "I didn't mean to bring all this upon you. I just…"

Brack waved off the apology, but he was visibly shaken. "Yeah. I…I've got to take a walk. Figure this out." He slid off his bench with the game half-finished. He stalked to the front door. "The cleaners'll be in later, but they won't make no noise," he said. "You better get some rest. You still don't look too good."

Rune sighed with his head down.

The dwarf was right. He was still shaky, and he'd been up too long. He limped over to the cot and sat down.

He shouldn't feel so attached to the Brackwaters. He'd only known them for a few hours. But there he was, a guest in their house…and likely to be their downfall.

Whatever happened in the next couple of days, he would be in the middle of it. He was the lightning rod, the target that everyone was shooting at: Avice, Maya, and even Mote Crankshaw.

And he was tired. His thoughts turned to the coffer, to the way he felt bold, even invincible, when he held it. A little invincibility would come in handy about now.

But no. There had to be a way to get rid of the thing without turning it over to the King of Shadows or Maya. And he didn't dare use it himself. That much power didn't belong in anybody's hands.

But right now, all he wanted was to sleep. He lay back and rested his head on the pillow.

27

Zoey spent Sunday night alone in her room. She had French homework plus some reading for English. It shouldn't have taken her more than an hour to knock it all out, but she milked it until bedtime. Church that morning and the near encounter with Jericho that afternoon was all the excitement she could handle in one day, and if anything else weird was going to happen, she'd rather it not be in front of her parents.

When she got ready for bed, Rune still hadn't shown up. That worried her. A lot.

He's got superpowers, she told herself. *Whatever's wrong, he can handle it.*

But the bad guys have superpowers, too!

She rested her head in her hands and stared at her collection of trinkets and souvenirs. She imagined the Ethiopian Virgin Mary gazing down at her with pity.

"If you've got any advice," she told the icon, "I'm all ears."

Apparently, she didn't. And when Zoey woke up early the next morning, nothing had changed.

She peered out her window. Rune's apartment was dark.

She got dressed and used a safety pin to attach the pouch she'd gotten from Madam Samarra inside the waistband of her jeans. "This is ridiculous," she muttered. And yet nothing odd had happened since she melted the silver good luck charm at the magic shop, so maybe she'd gotten some protection after all.

She toyed with the idea of pretending she was sick and staying home, but that trick stopped working around fifth grade. What if something spooky happened, though? What then?

All she could do was go to school and hope for the best. Ten minutes before the first bell, she pulled her car into her designated parking spot: one of the perks of being a senior. She sat with her hands clutching the steering wheel, eyes closed, praying for guidance.

Fortunately, it was Halloween, and nobody seemed interested in either teaching or learning. Half her teachers handed out candy. Zoey kept to herself. Between periods, she went from one classroom to the next with her eyes straight ahead.

She walked on eggshells all day, jumping at every little thing that seemed the least bit unusual. Jaden almost made an A-minus on a history project. That might have counted as a minor miracle, but she didn't see how her situation had anything to do with her ex-boyfriend's grades. No farm animals suddenly burst onto the scene. No birds broke into pop tunes. Nothing melted.

Everything went fine until fourth period. Madame Johnson was going over the French homework from the night before. She turned away from the class to write a practice sentence on the board for everyone to translate together. That's when Jaden said something to his buddies, and the whole back corner of the room started snickering.

Zoey whipped around, ready to look at him disapprovingly. It had taken her several weeks to perfect her "Jaden, you're making an ass of yourself" scowl. She didn't see why she couldn't still use it even though they weren't dating anymore. When she turned around, though, the room began to tilt. She grabbed the edges of her desk to keep from falling.

Everybody else sensed it, too. Something about the room was suddenly off-kilter, like gravity had shifted about thirty degrees off the perpendicular.

"Nope. Nope. Nope. Nope," she whispered. She put her hand against her belt, feeling for the velvet bag underneath, and as soon as she did the room straightened itself. Students looked at each other, open-mouthed.

Madame Johnson was the only one who hadn't noticed. She finished writing her sentence and turned back to the class. The whole thing lasted less than five seconds.

Zoey certainly wasn't going to bring up what had happened, and apparently her classmates all felt the same.

After school, she drove straight home.

Rune still wasn't back.

Now she was even more worried. It was getting harder for Zoey to convince herself that something hadn't gone terribly wrong with whatever errand he left to do on Saturday. Was he hurt? Had he been kidnapped?

Was he dead?

And she worried for herself. Charm or no charm, until Rune returned and put some more of his elfish mojo on her, she was afraid weird things were going to keep happening.

It was best to stay in her room where there weren't any witnesses or innocent bystanders.

She went upstairs and dove straight into her homework. She'd barely gotten started, though, when a text came from Caitlin. "Going out. Want to come?"

Zoey didn't, really. Not until she knew that things were back to normal. Not until she knew Rune was alive and safe.

"Busy," she texted back, which was a lot easier to type than, "Sorry, I might set the house on fire."

"Too bad," Caitlin answered. "Jericho has something special planned."

A weight dropped into Zoey's stomach. Caitlin was going back to Jericho's? Rune had said that whatever Jericho was planning had to do with Halloween.

You've got to be kidding me!

"Hold on," Zoey texted frantically. She had to think. Caitlin might be walking into danger. Scratch that: she was definitely walking into danger. Zoey couldn't let that happen.

She texted a flurry of responses.

"Why don't we just hang out here?"

"Help me give out candy?"

"Or Trunk-or-Treat at my church?"

"Or watch a scary movie?"

Zoey waited for the answer to come back. She imagined Zack looking over Caitlin's shoulder at the messages and the two of them talking things over. She prayed they would agree to at least one of her plans.

A minute passed. Another.

Finally, Zoey's phone buzzed. She read the screen. "Sorry you can't make it. See you tomorrow."

"Augh!" Zoey growled. Why did Caitlin have to make this so hard? She found her friend's number in her contacts and tapped "Call."

Caitlin picked up on the second ring. "What's up?"

Zoey took a breath and willed herself not to sound panicked. "Are you sure you don't want to come over?"

"It's Halloween. Zack and I want to go do something."

Zoey's throat went dry. "We could watch a movie in the basement."

"I thought you were busy."

Dang it, Caitlin, when did you start paying attention to what I tell you?

She took a breath. "Not *that* busy," she admitted.

"So why not just come with us?" Caitlin said. "It'll be fun. You left the other night with Rune before you could spend any time with Jericho. He's great!"

Zoey's pulse pounded in her temples. *Sure, I bet he's the coolest evil sorcerer you've ever met!*

"I just…"

"He *knows* things, Zoey. And he's really interested in college students. The other night he said he was the first in his family to even go to college. He wished somebody had been around to give him a hand up every now and then. Zack and I think he's a good person to get to know."

You. Are. Not. Cooperating!

But Caitlin was one of Zoey's closest friends.

She took another steadying breath. "Yeah, maybe," she lied. "I…guess I could come along."

"Great! We're all supposed to meet at his house at eight and go from there."

"Go? Where?"

"He says it's a surprise."

Zoey could almost hear the giddy smile on Caitlin's face. "Fine, that's…fine."

"See you then," Caitlin said. "Bye."

"Bye," Zoey said. She stared at her phone, terrified of what she'd just gotten herself into.

Come on, Rune. Hurry home!

28

Thora was standing over Rune when he woke up, disoriented but not hurting. The dwarf set a stack of clothes at the foot of his cot. He breathed in deeply. As his mind cleared, he remembered where he was.

"There's your clothes," Thora said. "Couldn't do nothing about your shirt. Even if I could get the bloodstains out, it was too torn up. I patched up your trousers, though. They'll do until you can get home and put on a proper pair."

Rune tried to sit up but winced at the tightness in his stomach. The wound was still too tender for him to move quickly. Better to lie back down.

"I found you another one of Brack's shirts. It's a couple years old, and he's gained some weight since then."

"Thank you."

"Brack was out late last night, walking. He does that when he needs to clear his head. You wouldn't know anything about that, would you?"

"We…talked over some things," Rune said.

She frowned. "I bet." She set Gimp Hollart's fighting stick at the foot of the cot beside the pile of clothes. "You might need a walking stick."

Now fully awake, Rune heard the bustle of activity in the house. Along with the clatter of pots and pans came pleasant aromas of food cooking.

He never heard the cleaners Brack mentioned, but the workshop was tidier than it was last night. He must have slept like a stone.

"What time is it?" He tried again to sit up, more slowly this time. With one arm propped behind him, he eased his body around and slid his bare feet onto the floor.

"You missed breakfast," Thora said. "And lunch. I put you back a plate."

"You didn't have to do that." He stretched his arms, careful not to pull too much at his side. "The stew at Gamaufry Tavern isn't too bad."

Thora scoffed. "Like you're ready to go anywhere."

Rune shook his head. "I said I wasn't going to inconvenience you any longer than I have to. I—"

He stopped when he heard movement over his shoulder. Duren and Ulfa crowded by the cracked workshop door.

Thora hissed and shooed them away. She turned a stern eye to Rune. "You're the most interesting thing they've seen in a while."

She may not have meant it as an accusation, but Rune wondered if one was implied: *don't give them any ideas.* All the more reason to leave as soon as possible. He slumped his shoulders.

"You might as well come in," Thora called. The two children nearly knocked each other over as they spilled into the workshop.

They stood and watched as their mother lifted up Rune's shirt and examined his bandages. He hadn't bled through, but she changed them anyway.

While she worked, Ulfa crept closer. Leaning around her mother's elbow, she whispered, "Momma, can Duren and me go guising for Hallowfest?"

Mrs. Brackwater sighed. "Don't know why not." It was clear she had other things on her mind. But mothers had a way of tending to everyone's needs at once.

Or so Rune had been told.

She probed his side with her fingers. "I don't feel nothing moving around in there. Do you?"

He shook his head.

"I mean across the Mere," Ulfa said. "In the Fallow. Last year Papa said if I was good—"

"Not on your life!" Mrs. Brackwater spat. "Not with all the foolishness that's going on." She gave Rune a venomous glare.

"But Momma…"

"You heard me," Mrs. Brackwater said without looking away from Rune.

But Ulfa wasn't finished. "Jemmy Crankshaw's papa lets *him*—"

"If Jemmy Crankshaw tried to ride a water panther, would you jump on behind him?"

"But—"

"I ain't arguing with you," Mrs. Brackwater said, "so you might as well give up now."

"I just want to see what it's like! Those Fallowmen won't even notice us. And the Dream Book—"

"Ulfa, hush!" Thora's eyes bored into Rune like a ferstitch ball, and the ground rumbled in earnest. "Dream Book," she muttered.

"Jemmy says it's a real book and it keeps us folk like us safe in the Fallow."

"I'm gonna make you quit hanging out with that boy."

"But Hotha Bivins says it's something else and they just call it a book."

Thora stared up at the ceiling. "If I tell you about the Dream Book, will you forget about going guising?"

Ulfa's face fell, but she nodded. Thora started packing up her medical supplies. "The way I heard it, it's some kind of spell. A trick some elf played on the Fallow folk a few hundred years ago to keep folks safe."

Duren furrowed his brow and finally spoke. "*All* the Fallow folk? Nobody can do that!"

"Of course they can," Rune said—and immediately regretted butting in. His eyes darted to Thora.

"But how?" Ulfa said.

Thora arched an eyebrow. "You want to take it from here, Mr. Rune?"

Not now, he thought. But Thora gestured for him to get on with it. "Well, er," he stuttered. "Your mother is right." He bowed to her slightly and eased back on his cot in case she decided to swat him.

"Back then, things were getting a bit dicey. You see, we Saynim folk always had the advantage because we had magic and the Fallowmen didn't. At least, most of them didn't. But then their technology and science began to grow—and fast."

"The Fallowmen can't reach us across the Mere," Duren protested.

"No, not usually," Rune said. "But sometimes, at the right time and the right place, they can. And sometimes our kind visited the Fallow. Even now, a lot of them spend their whole lives there. So, you see, something had to be done."

"So an elf made the Dream Book?"

Rune shook his head. "A Gentryman across the ocean commissioned a Fallowman to write it."

Duren frowned. "You're making that up!"

"It's true," Thora said. "At least, that's the way my momma explained it to me."

"You heard right, Mrs. Brackwater," Rune said. "The Gentryman blessed this Fallowman with the gift of storytelling. Fallow folk still say he's one of the greats. And the Dream Book… well, it must have had some kind of powerful enchantment, because it really did change the whole world. Before it, Fallowmen were afraid of us." Rune didn't add, *with good reason*. "But they were also armed against us. They knew about entrances to the Mere. They knew about our strengths and weaknesses—and how to beat us."

"How's your leg feel?" Thora said. She had a jar of healing salve in her hand, the last of the supplies to go in her box.

Rune took a second to decide. His gut was so torn up, he'd almost forgotten the slash across his thigh. "Better," he said. "Still sore, but better."

Thora grunted and slipped the jar into her box.

Ulfa said, "Then what happened?"

Rune stretched his legs. "Right. Then this fellow wrote the Dream Book, and in about a hundred years, everybody thought of us as tiny, mischievous creatures: more of a joke than an actual threat. And before long that no one believed we existed at all."

Wonder spread across Ulfa's face. "All because of a book?"

Rune nodded. "My uncle made me study it when I was about Duren's age. There are parts I still remember by heart."

The girl's eyes lit up. "Tell me!"

"Well, let's see." Rune looked at Thora. The weight of his presence, upsetting her life and that of her family, rumbled in his gut. He took a second to settle himself and recited:

If we shadows have offended,
Think but this, and all is mended,
That you have but slumber'd here
While these visions did appear.

"What's that mean?" Ulfa asked.

"Well, the Dream Book is a play. At the end, one of the characters—a goblin, in fact—is telling the audience, 'Don't worry, we're all just a dream. You'll forget all about us when the morning comes.'"

"Wow."

He turned from Ulfa to look Thora in the eye once more. She still didn't trust him. Not really. "But he's also saying he's sorry if his presence was upsetting. He meant no harm." He bit his lip and recited the closing lines of the speech:

Give me your hands, if we be friends,
And Robin shall restore amends.

"I'm not a monster, Mrs. Brackwater." He gazed up at her from the cot, looking for any hint of emotion. "I won't disrupt your family."

"You already done that," Thora said. She bit her lip. "I'm sorry, I didn't mean to—"

"It's all right," Rune said.

"It ain't just you," Thora said. "You just showed up at the wrong time. Duren's already talking about a gun for his birthday."

"I know what I'm doing," Duren protested. "Let me prove it."

Thora gritted her teeth. "Don't you have chores to do?"

"I can be responsible, Momma. I promise I can."

"No boy your age needs a firearm."

"But what if the shadelings come back?" Duren turned from his mother to Rune. "There was a pack of 'em in town last week, but Papa took care of 'em." He stuck out his chest. "A man's got to stand up for himself."

Ulfa snickered. "What about a boy?"

Duren turned red.

"You don't need no gun to stand up for yourself," Thora said. "Just a backbone."

Rune thought about Brack standing up to Mote Crankshaw the night before. That goblin was trouble, he feared. Rune had never been in the same room with him, and he didn't care to be. But Brack stood his ground against Crankshaw's threats. The dwarf seemed like the type who took responsibility for his actions, even when it cost him.

He hung his head. "I should leave now. I'm only upsetting life for your family."

"You'll leave when I say you're ready," Thora said.

"But—"

"You heard what I said. You'd think a soldier would be better at following orders."

"I'm no soldier, Mrs. Brackwater."

"The name's Thora. And if you don't mind my pointing out the obvious, you used to be."

Rune frowned. "Not exactly. The King of Shadows has plenty of warriors, but I was never one of them."

Thora furrowed her brow. Duren and Ulfa crept closer.

How to explain? Rune drew himself up on his cot. "The King's elite troops are the Knights of the Hand. Humans, for the most part. They're called that because they serve as the King's right hand. They uphold his will, establish order, and defend his realm."

"Then what are Nightwalkers?" Duren asked.

Thora shot him a fiery glance but didn't scold him.

Rune sighed. "I suppose you could say we're the King's left hand."

Duren's face twisted into a befuddled frown.

The look on Thora's face said she took Rune's meaning, but Duren? Rune pondered what to say next.

"It's complicated," he said at last, deflated. "Sometimes the King needs things done…subtly. Quietly."

"Underhandedly," Thora added.

Rune couldn't disagree. "Can we settle on 'creatively'?"

Thora scoffed.

"But that's behind me now, whether or not you believe me. Or at least it will be if I can ever convince my dear cousin."

"Your cousin," Thora said. "The other Nightwalker?"

"I'm afraid so."

Thora shook her head. "If you don't mind my saying so, Mr. Rune, your family is messed up."

Once again, Rune had no counterargument. "You may be right, Mrs. Brackwater—Thora. It's not like I had a say in the matter."

Thora's dark brown eyes bore into Rune, and she pursed her lips. She turned to her children. "You two go check on the cooking. See if Hilly needs any help."

"But Momma!" they protested.

"You heard me," she said, quietly but firmly.

As soon as the workshop door shut behind them, she gave Rune her full attention. "How a person is raised is a big part of who they are, Mr. Rune. There's no denying that."

Rune slouched back on his cot.

"But that don't mean a body can't start fresh. Maybe even get some new raising."

Rune sighed. Getting some new raising sounded awfully nice.

"He's just got to want it," Thora added.

He locked eyes with her. He'd seen the fierce momma bear ever since he woke up yesterday, but now he saw something else, something deeper. She wiped a sleeve across her eyes.

He cleared his throat. "Let me get dressed. And then I'd be honored if you'd let me help with supper."

The whole Brackwater clan was busy in the kitchen, either cooking, washing pots and pans, or gathering place settings. Hilly noticed Rune come in and chimed a happy greeting.

"Good afternoon, Mr. Rune!"

Laurin appeared from the back storeroom with a vase of fresh autumn flowers to decorate the table.

The kitchen smelled like all the traditional Hallowfest dishes: turnips, lamb, fruit bread…and apples! Kettle sat at the table, nursing a large pot filled with applesauce. He stirred the mixture with his right hand. His left hand, faintly glowing, rested against the pot.

Duren and Ulfa hovered around him. There was only one person missing.

"Where's Brack?"

"Off on a job," Laurin said.

"A job? On Hallowfest Eve?" Rune puzzled.

"The Burntails' clock threw a gear," Laurin said. "There's a little automaton that hits the gong every hour. I guess the gong started hitting back."

"He said it's an easy fix," Thora added. "He should be back any time." She returned to stirring a small pot on the stove. "I just wish Brack could get a real day off," she said.

"Well, tomorrow's the start of a brand-new year," Laurin said.

"What do you think, Kettle?" Ulfa asked. "Is it ready?"

Kettle lifted the wooden spoon to his mouth and pondered for a second. "More ginger, I think."

The ingredients were lined up on the table: nutmeg, ginger, honey, and a small pitcher of milk. Ulfa reached for a bottle of crystallized ginger, emptied a single pellet into her hand, and tossed it into the pot.

Just then, the workshop door swung open and heavy boots clomped across the stone floor. Brack entered the open door to the living space with a twinkle in his eye. He gave the room a hearty sniff. "Is the wassail ready?"

"Almost, Papa," Duren said. "Right, Kettle?"

Kettle tasted the mixture again. He smiled and nodded.

Brack pulled several mugs down from the shelf and carried them to the table. Hilly came from the stove with a steaming pot of cider and a whisk. "Who's first?" she asked.

Ulfa and Duren scrambled for mugs and held them out as Kettle spooned dollops of the apple mixture into them. Then Hilly applied the cider, whisking until the drink developed a nice, foamy froth.

With the children served, Hilly replaced the cider with a somewhat larger pot of mulled ale. By the time she returned to the table, Kettle had filled mugs for the adults.

"Now I know it's Hallowfest," Brack said, licking his lips.

Rune gestured to him, but the dwarf insisted Rune take the first mug. The beverage was warm and tingly, not too sweet and not too spicy. It left a comfortable feeling in his stomach, something he couldn't quite put his finger on. Home, probably.

"Are you going to the mummers play, Mr. Rune?" Ulfa asked.

Rune tensed. He shared a wary look with Brack.

"I'd better stay here," he said.

"Good idea," Brack grunted. He lifted the mug to his lips and pulled it away with satisfaction. "Ahh!" He wiped the froth from his mustache and studied his mug, which was already mostly empty. "Be whole!" he shouted, and splashed the few remaining dribbles of wassail on Duren's and Ulfa's heads.

"Be whole!" they replied as the liquid ran down their noses. They giggled and tried to catch a taste of their father's drink.

Brack then blessed Kettle with the same greeting.

"Be whole!" Thora said. She splashed Laurin and Hilly, who then splashed each other, their faces beaming.

Thora took a tentative step toward Rune. Her deep brown eyes met his, and her cheeks reddened.

Rune bowed slightly and closed his eyes.

She splashed the last of her wassail over his head. "Be whole," she whispered.

Rune softly returned the greeting as the children started a rousing chorus of "Good Queen Joan."

As everyone sang, Brack took his seat at the head of the table. Everyone else followed his lead and found their own chairs. At the last note of the song, the room became still. Brack looked at each of them, smiling.

He cleared his throat and said, "Tonight the world changes." Hilly and Laurin held each other close and gazed into each other's eyes. Laurin silently moved his lips as his father repeated the traditional blessing. "One year comes to an end, and a new year dawns," Brack continued. "Tonight, the boundary between the worlds is at its thinnest."

And that, of course, was what interested the King of Shadows. He was up to something with Jericho, and Avice was helping him. Rune wondered if the King could really step through.

"Tonight is a night of deep magic," Brack said. And here he offered Rune a wistful glance. "The magic of transformation. The magic of ancestors." He paused and looked down at his rough, powerful hands. "We hallow this night," he said. "May it welcome a year of joy and good fortune."

Everyone rapped on the table in approval.

"Is everyone ready to go?" Brack asked.

"The cooking is mostly done," Thora said. "Hilly and I can make the potato pancakes once we get back, and Kettle can warm up the rest."

Brack smiled. "Good. I hear the mummers have been working extra hard this year. Should be a lot of fun."

29

Rune watched from Brack's workshop window as the people of Goblintown gathered at the square. All the interior lights were off, and he stayed in the shadows. He was safe in the dark, but curious about Brack's neighbors and how they celebrated the new year.

A wooden stage had been constructed in front of the well—Rune had slept through whatever hammering and sawing it took to put it up. The whole area was festooned with pumpkins and cornstalks and bright orange and yellow bunting. Torches and lanterns bathed the square in vibrant light. All of that, at least, was familiar.

There must have been forty or more people on the square: the whole neighborhood as far as Rune could tell, and likely some from the aboveground portions of Dunswale. There were humans, goblins, small folk, and even a few other dwarves. They milled about as they waited for the play to begin. To one side of the stage, a fiddler and a drummer played a sprightly tune.

Rune wondered what a goblin mummers play might be like. And the more he wondered, the more confined he felt. Most of the town didn't even know he was there. But Mote Crankshaw knew, and he would probably try something if he found Rune outside the protection of Brack's home.

But his mind was clear, and it had been nearly two full days since he'd used any magic to speak of.

It would only take a little bit of glamour.

He drew the airy chaos around him and faded from the view of any curious eyes. The gentle breeze that accompanied his magic felt warm on the back of his neck. Everyone was focused on the stage, which made it easy for Rune to slip out to the cobblestone street unobserved.

Thora was right: Gimp Hollart's bata made a serviceable walking stick. Rune eased around the back of the crowd, keeping plenty of distance between him and any residents of Goblintown.

The play began as these things usually did, with the star-crossed lovers pining for each other from a distance. A dwarven woman portrayed the Knight, decked out in a red velvet surcoat and a tin helmet, a wooden sword at her side. The Lady was a goblin with a scruffy red beard and an improbably ample bosom beneath his linen robe.

Rune skirted the circle of onlookers, keeping his distance. He had to dodge some children playing and a vendor with a tray of pies, but it was easy enough to find a dark alleyway from which to watch.

The characters introduced themselves with rhyming couplets, and the usual comic hijinks played out as the Dragon—a couple of youths almost concealed beneath a blue tablecloth and an elaborate papier-mâché mask—threatened to devour the Lady. The fiddler's tune took on a mock-epic aspect.

This much was predictable, one of the stock plots common in a mummers play. Before long, Rune wasn't even paying attention. People stood watching with their families as vendors weaved through the crowd with pies and greenbrew. Parents held their children's hands. Spouses and lovers stole kisses while they thought no one was looking.

Watching the people was more enthralling than any mummers. They were enjoying life. Enjoying each other.

Rune had felt the same way last night at supper. The normality of it all hit him like a charging thunder horse.

The dumbshow interlude featured a mock battle: two rival Gentrymen vying for supremacy. Of course, the Knight was wounded—he took a sword thrust straight to the empty space under his armpit.

Children scampered behind the crowd, playing out their own mock battle.

The Lady returned to the stage, which she now shared only with her wounded and dying Knight. The remainder of the play proceeded according to the standard plot. She fed the Knight her healing potion, and he sprang to life and confessed his undying love.

The play went on, but all Rune could think of was the danger he posed to everyone here. Avice was still looking for him. The longer he stayed, the more likely someone would get hurt. He had to leave. Now.

He stepped out of his corner and turned toward the narrow street that led from the square to the Brackwater house. Behind him, the fiddler and the drummer led the crowd in a jaunty tune.

His satchel must be in the bedroom where he'd first awakened. He'd reclaim his gear and escape while the townsfolk were still—

"Oops! Sorry, mister!" The goblin boy had come out of nowhere and bumped into Rune, breaking the spell of his glamour.

The boy stared up at him. Rune stared back at the boy. He was older than Ulfa, maybe the same age as Duren, with a tangle of flame-red hair on his head.

"You're him, ain't you? The one Duren talked about?"

Without thinking, Rune touched the boy's mind with a whiff of glamour. His eyes went blank before Rune realized what he was doing and broke the spell.

The boy wobbled. He shivered and caught himself while Rune slipped away. Pressure grew at his temples. A light was on in Brack's workshop. He stopped short, but only for a second before powering on.

He covered the remaining distance to the house at a fast walk. At the end, he hazarded a light jog. It left him out of breath, but his body, at least, didn't give out from the effort. He'd have to leave a thank-you note to Thora for healing him.

Inside the workshop, Brack was at his workbench. Their eyes met. Brack looked at least as surprised to see Rune as the other way around.

"You didn't stay for the singing," Brack said.

"You didn't either."

"I already sang once today. Besides, I had an inspiration." He turned his eyes to a box of tools and spare parts on his workbench. "Didn't want to forget." He set a huge magnifying glass on a wooden stand and then rummaged around for his tools.

"I…I have to go."

Brack stopped what he was doing. "Did Thora say you're healthy enough?"

"It doesn't matter. As long as I'm here, you're not safe." He gestured toward the open window, toward the singing crowd. "None of you are. You don't know Avice. You don't know what she can do."

Brack sighed. "Can't say I didn't expect it. Your pack is on the kitchen table. I hope you don't mind, but I cleaned and oiled your pistol this morning."

"Not at all. Thank you. For everything."

Brack waved it off. "Come by anytime. Thora loves to feed company. And I could always use a king's table opponent. Duren's learning but—"

"I'm not staying around." It was the first time he had said it out loud. It sounded wild and powerful on his lips. Liberating. "What I mean is, I'm moving on. You won't see me again."

Brack's face darkened. "And this business with the King of Shadows?"

Rune tapped his fingers against his thigh. His voice nearly broke as he said, "I can't stop him."

"You can't stop him." Brack sat stone-faced, his lips tight and emotionless underneath his black mustache.

Rune couldn't believe he had to explain this. "He's a Gentryman. He's been around since the Barrow Lords. Do you know how much magic it takes to live that long?"

"I'm sure he's all kinds of impressive."

"I've defied him once already—and will probably die for it in the end."

"Ah. You've defied him before. You survived that, did you?"

Rune sputtered. Was he really having this conversation? "Not personally, no! Avice and I are pretty evenly matched. I just got lucky. What am I supposed to do against the King himself? You saw the shape I was in two nights ago. If it hadn't been for you and your family—"

"Do you know why Thora and me settled in Goblintown?" Brack interrupted. "When I was a kid, my family moved around a lot." He went back to rummaging through his box until he pulled out a small leather pouch. "Papa was a metal-weaver, like me. You understand what that means, right?"

Rune took a breath. "I don't see what—"

"It means a lot of people look at you funny when you come to town. Especially when you come with a big iron forge and a whole mess of iron tools."

"Mr. Brackwater…Brack. I don't doubt that you have seen more than your share of prejudice."

"I ain't talking about prejudice," Brack said. "I provide a service most folks can't. And people pay me for it! They don't mind me using my tools; they just feel awkward being around 'em. Can't say I blame them. Somebody comes around with a bunch of stuff that'll snuff out my magic if I touch it, I'm gonna get the jeebies, too!"

"Then…what are we talking about?"

"My kids were all born in Goblintown." He used a set of tweezers to pick up something that looked like a tiny ball bearing. "This is home. Say what you want about goblins, but they'll find a place for you if you want it. If you're willing to work hard and look out for everybody else, you won't find anybody more loyal."

"Brack, I—"

"Now, I'll be honest, I probably tested the limits of that loyalty, bringing you in like I did. But it was the right thing to do. Mote Crankshaw'll cool off sooner or later and he'll figure that out, too. But you?"

He used the tiniest screwdriver Rune had ever seen to pop open the ball bearing's outer shell. "Go ahead and leave if you want. I'll be here fighting for my town. Whatever it takes. And maybe one of these days, you'll figure out what you're running from." He made some kind of adjustment and curled the device back into a ball. "'Cause I ain't sure it's the King of Shadows."

Brack finally looked up, and the two of them stared at each other for the longest time. Rune wanted to say something to defend himself. But he couldn't. Everything he thought of sounded rude or shallow or evasive. Avice had always said Rune was best at running and hiding. Brack was a little more polite, but he was saying the same thing.

Rune looked away. "I'll be going now."

He turned toward the kitchen but stopped in his tracks as he heard the growing, angry murmur of the crowd.

"What the…?" Brack said. The dwarf was hurrying toward the window, cursing under his breath. "Get in the kitchen. Now!"

30

The crowd was marching toward the Brackwater house with Mote Crankshaw and his flame-red hair in the lead. Brack locked his door and set the deadbolt.

He watched the streetlamps. One flared up on the square. It burned bright for a second, then waned away to its usual amber glow as another lamp, closer to home, surged to fiery life. *Kettle!* Brack's assistant was flame-faring, dashing home from one fire to the next.

The dwarf snatched a work rag and wrapped it around an unfinished axe handle as he watched the window. Another streetlamp flared. The makeshift torch lit easily from Kettle's fire box. Brack held it at arm's length in front of the window, knowing he needed a clear line of sight.

Brack's own streetlamp burst into radiant light, followed by the torch itself. Finally, the torch flame spit out a ball of orange and gold light that spread itself into the shape of a feathered reptile with leathery wings.

"Thora! The children!" Brack called.

"Safe," Kettle croaked as he shapeshifted into the form of a young boy. He glanced toward the nearing mob with a grave expression and reached for the torch. Brack handed it to him flame-first, and it extinguished in his hands. "Is Mote Crankshaw. His boy Jemmy saw Rune on square. Looks like boy got himself glamoured a little."

"The elf forgot to mention that part," Brack grumbled. He eyed the door to the living space. As he expected, it was cracked open. Rune had been watching and listening since the instant Brack had sent him from the workshop.

"Can't be helped now," he muttered.

"Should I get Frieda?"

"Not on your life!" Brack said. "I ain't shooting at my neighbors." The mob was almost to the house. He turned the crank to shutter the window.

"Listen, Kettle," he said, peering through a crack below the shutter to see the world beyond. "Get Rune. He's in the kitchen. Take him out the back door and get him home. With any luck, this'll all blow over before you get back."

"Heptifilius Brackwater!" Mote Crankshaw's gravelly voice echoed off Goblintown's cavernous walls. "Enough is enough! You bring the Nightwalker out here! All of us deserve a say in what happens to him!"

Brack looked over his shoulder. Kettle was gone, and the door was closed tight. He gritted his teeth and summoned the metallic chaos to himself, steeling his will, bracing for battle—though hopefully this would only be a war of words.

He stepped outside and shut the door behind him. "Mote, you gotta calm down."

"I gotta take care of my own," Mote said. At his side, his son Jemmy looked on with a dazed and frightened expression. Behind them, goblins and small folk murmured agreement.

"How d'you reckon to do that?"

"I'm gonna make you a deal," Mote said. "The same deal I offered you last night." Brack snickered. "But this time, I brought witnesses."

"Silver and gold, Mote, are you really going down this tunnel?"

"It's a good deal, Brack. It gets you what you want: we turn the Nightwalker over to the Merlady, and she owes us one. Then maybe she leaves us alone. We get to go back to the way things were before."

"For how long?" Brack clenched his fists.

"Longer than if we don't do nothing!" a voice called from the crowd. Tom Burntail. Others agreed.

"You're talking about a man's life, Mote."

"I'm talking about the life of this town!" Mote set his hands on his hips and threw his chest out. It would have been more intimidating if he weren't four feet tall. "I remember when you'd do whatever you could for this town, Brack. Are you gonna throw all that away for a stranger?"

Brack gazed into the eyes of his neighbors. "Looks like."

"He glamoured my boy!"

Jemmy looked shaken but unharmed.

"Could have done worse if he was serious." Brack turned to Jemmy. "You feeling all right, boy?"

"Y-yes, sir," the boy said. Mote glared at him.

"He'll be fine," Brack said.

Mote clicked his tongue. "Do you remember when you and Thora first came here? Do you remember who put in a good word for you when folks were antsy about you opening up your shop?"

"I remember," Brack said. "That doesn't change anything. He's still a guest in my house."

"You gotta look at the big picture, Brack!"

"That's what I'm doing. If you—if any of you—want to trash sacred hospitality and lay hands on my guest…well, there's only one of me, and there's—ten, twelve, about twenty of you." He took a step forward. "So go ahead and do what you think you gotta do."

"Brack!" Thora's voice cut through the crowd. Goblins and small folk parted as she plowed forward.

"It's fine, Thora."

Mote backed away, his eyes darting between wife and husband. He lowered himself into a defensive stance, ready to run away in a heartbeat. His arms fell loosely at his sides and he nodded. "Thora."

"Mote." She stepped closer to him. "If I knew you were coming for supper, I'd have cooked more."

Brack made eye contact with his wife. He asked about the children with an arched eyebrow. She got his message. A subtle smile and an even subtler nod assured him they were all right. A second later, he spied them at the back of the crowd: Laurin and Hilly with Duren and Ulfa huddled close under their arms.

Brack had one job: stall. He had to give Rune the best chance to get away safely. The Brackwater house was carved into the side of the cavern, but there was another way out, a narrow tunnel that opened onto the street twenty yards away in an open patch where children played. Now the children of Goblintown were home with their mothers or older siblings. Brack kept one eye focused on the spot between two wooden posts, waiting for the hidden door to open and Rune and Kettle to sneak into the street.

"How's your wife, Mote?" Thora asked. "Haven't seen her in a few days."

Brack forced himself not to grin. Thora could be a terror when she was mad, but when somebody threatened her family, she was a force of nature. Mote had no idea the volcano was about to blow.

"Well…erm…she's fine," the goblin mumbled. He kept his eyes on the ground. "If you'll excuse us…. That is…Thora, we was just discussing some business with Brack."

"Then you got business with both of us." She moved to Brack's side. "Brack never makes a business decision without me. Do you, sweet?"

Brack stifled a laugh. "Learned that lesson pretty early on."

Mote swayed nervously. "Then maybe you can talk some sense into your husband."

She wrapped her arm around Brack's, and his heart warmed. "Not even gonna try," she said. She looked into his eyes. "I learned *that* lesson pretty early on."

People tittered.

Mote canvassed the crowd. They were all still on his side. Tom Burntail nodded to him. "Get on with it, Mote."

"Yeah," the goblin said. "Well, Brack, be that as it may, the fact is, the Nightwalker's a danger to the whole town." The crowd murmured again. "He don't belong here. He ain't one of us."

"Now listen here, Mote—" Brack tensed his muscles and took a step forward.

Thora held him back. "No, Mote," she said. "No, he ain't one of us."

Her intervention let Brack take a breath. He moved to her side. Out of the corner of his eye, he saw a depression open as a portion of the rock wall slid in and over. Rune and Kettle emerged from the hidden door. Now he just had to buy a little more time. Let them get across town to the tunnels that led from Goblintown to the Mere and to the Fallow beyond.

"Well then," Mote said as Brack shifted his position, forcing the goblin to turn his back more directly to the secret door. "It's him or us, don't you see?"

"So why are you still out here?" Thora said.

Mote furrowed his brow. "I beg your pardon?"

"Well, you say he's a threat. To all of us!" Her eyes flashed. It wouldn't be long now before she let loose. "So? Why haven't you gone in and taken him?"

"Sweet," Brack whispered. "You don't want to give him any ideas."

"Well, Mote?"

"You know we can't do that!"

"Oh?" she said with mock ignorance. Her voice was calm, measured, hard. Momma Bear was sharpening her claws. "Why not?"

Mote sputtered. "Nobody wants to cross your threshold, Thora. Yours and Brack's."

"You want us to bring him out," Brack said. "Let us breach the Rule of Hospitality, is that it? Better us than you?"

"That ain't exactly—"

"Does that sound fair to you, Mote?" Thora asked. "Letting us take risks you won't take yourself?"

"Now, Thora. Brack…nobody—"

Brack looked over to the rest of his family as Mote's voice trailed off. At his nod, they hurried to his side.

"Nobody *what*, Mote?" Thora's words came out in a low, feral hiss. She stooped down and wagged a finger in his face. "Nobody wishes us any harm? Nobody wants to start a riot? Nobody wants to squat on sacred hospitality?"

Mote backed up. The crowd parted to give him space. "Well…no."

The earth subtly trembled. "Then stop all this," Thora said.

The goblin's eyes scanned the crowd before landing on Brack. He gulped. "B-brack?"

Brack crossed his arms. "If you haven't noticed, my wife and I usually see eye to eye on things." How long had it been? Just a few minutes, but maybe long enough. Surely Rune was well away by now.

"For what it's worth," Brack said, "our guest ain't even here no more."

Mote's eyes widened. "What?"

"Left before you got here." He smiled at Thora and then looked back toward Mote and the crowd. "Happy Hallowfest. Be whole."

The goblin looked flabbergasted. "Of all the…" Behind him, the dejected crowd slowly dispersed.

Only Mote remained. "You made your decision," he said. "What are we gonna do if this all blows up on you?"

"I figure we'll deal with it. You. Me."

Mote's face scrunched up like he'd swallowed something nasty. He glared at Brack, at Thora. Then he hung his head and trudged back toward his house.

Brack put his arm around Thora's waist and drew her close.

"Rune's really gone?" she whispered.

"Kettle took him out the back way."

"Good." She relaxed in his arms, and Brack expelled a long, slow breath. The children gathered around. Everybody hugged.

"It's getting on suppertime," Thora said. "Anybody hungry?"

"You know it," Brack said. He leaned in until his lips touched Thora's ear and whispered, "But maybe we oughta eat first."

31

Zoey couldn't count the number of sermons she'd heard her dad preach about the sin of idolatry. The golden calf. Ahab and Jezebel. Daniel in the lion's den. Almost always, his point was that idolatry wasn't really about graven images and weird sacrifices. It was about the state of your heart, what consumed you, what demanded and received your full attention.

So nothing prepared her to find herself in a cemetery in the middle of the night, standing in a circle with a bunch of college kids, watching a guy in a black and crimson robe getting ready to perform a magic ritual.

There weren't any graven images (thank God for small favors), but there was a table in the center of the torch-lit circle, also covered in crimson and black, on which Jericho had set candles, a chalice, and a dagger that gleamed in the moonlight.

I am so dead, she told herself. *Dad is going to kill me. And Mom is going to help.*

She pretended to go along, silently praying for a way out and miffed that she couldn't find one. But she'd come prepared. An Internet search confirmed that what happened in Jericho's study with her wrought-iron necklace wasn't a fluke. There were lots of old legends that said iron was protection against all kinds of super-natural nasties: witches and fairies and whatnot. One web page said jinn in the Middle East could be scared away just by someone shouting the word "iron."

She wasn't willing to try that one just yet.

But she had done what she could before meeting Caitlin. She'd raided her dad's toolbox for all the nuts and washers she could find, testing them with a magnet to find the ones made of iron or steel. It turned out that most were aluminum, but she stuffed her pockets with the ones that might help and even tied a string of washers on a length of yarn and wore it around her neck under her shirt.

Maybe it would be enough.

She hoped it would be enough.

Jericho's commanding voice gave her goosebumps. "Not everyone can handle the truth," he said. He gazed around the circle, smiling his winsome smile. Zoey stood with Caitlin to her left. Zack was on Caitlin's other side, and next to him was another girl from Jericho's party. Maybe her name was Cassie? Zoey had been too busy panicking to catch the introductions before they hopped a fence on the back side of Cave Hill Cemetery. Whatever her name was, the girl was way too perky for a trip to a graveyard on Halloween night. She had no respect at all for the vibe Jericho was creating. Finally, completing the circle of five young people was a sullen guy named Mike who was dressed, appropriately, all in black.

We've got to get out of here!

You should have thought of that before.

I know, I know.

"Most people prefer to live in ignorance," Jericho continued. "It's comforting to think that this world can be constrained by rules, by science and logic. But not you! You long for something more—I've heard it in our conversations. I can see it in your faces even now."

Eager eyes flickered with the torchlight. Zoey still hoped this whole thing was just for laughs. She knew Jericho was bad news, but the others were probably just here to do something spooky on Halloween. Right?

But something in Jericho's voice hummed with power. She remembered the way he had stared down Mike's friend Davanté at the party. Was he doing the same thing to them now, manipulating them somehow? She brushed her hand across her waist and felt the subtle pressure of Madam Samarra's charm against her skin. She fervently hoped it was working.

Mike licked his lips and leaned in as Jericho continued. He was eating the whole thing up, which didn't help Zoey's mood at all.

"The world is broken." Jericho moved casually back and forth, obviously at ease at the center of attention. He could have given Zoey's dad a run for his money in the public speaking department. "The great Hermetic philosophers told us as much. The world is less *real* than it should be. The shapes and shadows, the energies and forms that we see and feel and hear…these are mere reflections of what is *really* real."

Okay, dude, you're creeping me out.

He gazed around the circle. Something dark and melancholy shadowed his expression. "My parents worked hard their whole lives. They always tried to do what they thought was right." He clenched his fists and his eyes flashed anger. "For all they did, they got nothing but pain. People walked all over them. Took advantage of their kindness."

He moved casually from his place to get closer to Zoey and the others. "When I was about your age, I met a man who showed me a better way. Tonight I'm going to show you—if you can accept it."

Jericho set his hand gently on Mike's shoulder. Mike flinched, but only for a second. "What do you want out of life, hmm? Wealth? Fame? Sex?" People tittered at the last one. Caitlin blushed and studied her shoes.

Jericho moved away from Mike and turned his attention to Zoey. "Then why not have it? Why not take it? It's easy—or, I should say, reasonably easy—if you know how. Do you want to see the world? Let me show you worlds you could never imagine."

Been there, done that, Zoey thought. *I'll pass.*

"Tonight, the boundaries between the worlds grow thin—a dreadful prospect for our ancestors as they huddled together in the dark and mumbled their prayers to hold the shadows at bay. It was dreadful to them, but not to me." He spread his arms wide. "Why not get the most out of this fleeting world while we can?" He let the question linger in silence as he slowly, deliberately made eye contact with everyone in the circle. "My friends, I propose we do precisely that."

Avice watched from the shadows as the sorcerer made his speech. When he stepped away from his conjuring circle, the younglings behind him spoke to one another in whispered tones.

Phipps didn't seem interested in eavesdropping on his young charges. Neither was Avice; she could imagine what they were talking about. Some would be excited. She could almost taste their curiosity, their thrill at the thought of seeing a display of real power. Others would, of course, be skeptical. Jericho no doubt understood that—he was a realist, after all. Some people's eyes opened to her world more readily than others. So be it. They didn't need to believe. If Jericho had read them rightly, they had all had some spark of magic in them. They just had to be there and do their part when the ritual was complete.

The sorcerer walked several yards into the forest of gravestones, many as tall as a man if not taller. Avice silently bridged the distance between them, still concealing her presence.

Boggs waited in the darkness. He came out from behind a gravestone and stood, hands clasped in front of him, as Jericho came near. Avice drew on the airy chaos to enhance her senses and listen in.

"I was beginning to worry," Jericho said.

Boggs extended his hand to offer Jericho a worn felt bag. "Mummy wrappings are hard to come by in these parts, Master," the sorcerer's servant said.

Jericho opened the bag and peered inside. He furrowed his brow, then hefted the bag in his hand. It was nearly weightless.

"Will this be enough?"

"It's twenty-seven hundred years old, give or take," Boggs said. "And very well preserved. A little bit will go a long way."

Jericho quirked an eyebrow. "And how, precisely…?"

"I know people. Some of them can be very cooperative if there's something in it for them."

Jericho appraised the bag and slipped it into the pocket of his robe. "Well done, Boggs."

"All in a night's work." Boggs offered a weary smile. "Master."

"And what about the rest? Dancer spoke of a sacrifice."

"My understanding is that she's handling that detail."

Avice threw back the hood of her cloak and stepped forward, suddenly visible. "And so I shall." Jericho whipped about and fell into a half-crouch, hands out and ready to defend himself. When he recognized who it was, he straightened up…though he kept his hands out and his eyes trained on her.

Avice flashed a mirthless smile. It felt good to be respected. "No need to fear, Magister Jericho." She brushed a lock of coal-black hair out of her face. "There's no one here but us shadows."

"No," Jericho said, his jaw set. "I don't suppose there is."

She could read the man well enough. He was the sort who hated to show weakness of any kind. When she had bested him in his work room, it sent a signal: don't mess with me. Now Avice, predator that she was, could sense his fear even if he didn't show it. He might not want to give her an advantage, but it was too late for that.

Jericho took a breath, pulled himself up to his full height, and declared, "Don't you think it's about time, then? It'll soon be midnight. Or is this one of those situations where time works differently for…your kind?"

"Not on All Hallows' Eve," Avice said. She approached him with a slow, deliberate stride. Her cloak didn't so much blow in the breeze as undulate around her legs and feet, like the tentacles of an octopus gliding over the sea floor.

"Our worlds are in almost perfect alignment," she said. "And as for the sacrifice…" She held out a small copper disk, a compass she had repurposed to use as a tracking charm. With a flick of her wrist, the top flipped open to expose a dim, blood-red gleam. Inside was a sealed glass container. A bubble of air floated above the center, and around the edge writhed a glowing red blob of blood, formless yet distinct from the clear liquid around it. "It has only now become available."

Jericho peered at the device. "What do you mean, 'only now'? I'm aware of the astronomical and metaphysical peculiarities of this night." He sounded impatient, which was fine with Avice. Let him sweat a little.

"I've double-checked everything you told me," he said. "If I'm really going to touch the power you've spoken about, it has to be tonight. The clock is ticking, Dancer, or whatever the hell your name is." He clenched his fists. "Or are you reneging on our deal?"

Avice sucked in a breath and flashed a withering glare. She tucked her tracking charm into her doublet and poked at the sorcerer with a white, slender finger. "Are you challenging my honor, human?"

Jericho stood his ground. He swallowed a smile almost before it reached his mouth. "No need to get worked up," he said, his tone shifting from impatience to resolve. "Something tells me you're feeling the time pressure, too. Good."

She could only admire his insight. Yes, this scheme had to succeed. The King of Shadows expected her to provide him an entryway into the Fallow. Her father and mother were counting on her. And yes, it had to be tonight. After that, the worlds would diverge once more, and it would be months, possibly years, before things aligned this perfectly again.

"Tick. Tock," Jericho said.

She pursed her lips. "Then lend me your servant."

Bogg's body stiffened.

"I need him here," Jericho said.

"I won't keep him long. Only long enough to deliver a message."

Jericho kept his eyes on Avice as he addressed his servant. "Boggs, I give you leave to go with Dancer and deliver her message. But remember that the pact between us remains in effect until sunrise. Complete her errand and return to me at once."

Boggs gulped. "Y-yes, Master. It shall be done as you s-say." He stepped forward, tripping slightly on something Avice couldn't see.

"This would be easier if you were smaller," she said.

Boggs nodded, shrugged, and his body collapsed in upon itself until he had taken the form of a toad.

Avice knelt and extended her hand. Boggs croaked and hopped into her embrace.

"Thirty minutes," Jericho said.

"I doubt it will take that long," she said. She turned around and pulled her cloak back over her head, vanishing into the night.

She drew the airy chaos to herself, and the wind picked up. She leaped into the sky, cradling Boggs in one arm. Brown autumn leaves swirled into a tiny tornado and then just as suddenly fell back to the ground.

32

Rune worked to keep up with Kettle as the firedrake threaded the narrow passageways without hesitation. He'd simply told the Brackwaters' servant where he lived, and off the boy went, with a ball of golden fire hovering near his head to light the way.

"I never knew these tunnels went so far," Rune said.

"They don't," the firedrake said. "Not usually, anyway. You're lucky it's Hallowfest." He leaned back against the rough-hewn stone as Rune caught up to him. "They call this Undermere. It goes on for miles, but only at certain times of year. Come midnight, everything fades away. By morning, tunnels barely get you out of Butchertown."

"But you know where you're going?"

"Trick is to make tunnels go where *you* want."

"You can do that?" Rune was impressed.

"It takes practice," the firedrake said. "I've lived around here for while. You listen to Mere long enough, it's bound to tell you some of its secrets."

He stopped at a fork in the tunnels. "We're almost there, I think." He started off again without warning. Rune trotted to catch up.

Rune was grateful to have his bata for a walking stick. Kettle was naturally full of energy and eager to keep going. It wasn't often that Rune met his match in quickness. He assured himself he was only struggling to keep up because of his injuries.

They stopped at another fork. Kettle extended his hand, palm out, and closed his eyes. Seconds later, a tiny orb of fire appeared from down the rightward passage and drifted toward them.

With a flick of Kettle's wrist, the orb turned back the way it came. "This way," he announced, pressing forward. "Wanderlights always know."

The passage did seem to slope upward. After a few more twists and turns, the rough stone gave way to brickwork and then to plaster and drywall. At some point, Rune realized, they had left the Undermere and passed back into the Fallow.

They came to a wooden door, its faded paint chipped and gouged with waymarks and the initials of several decades' worth of Fallow folk adventurers. Kettle turned the tarnished doorknob and put his shoulder to it. It wouldn't budge. The firedrake moved away and gestured for Rune to give it a try.

He gritted his teeth and hobbled forward. The doorknob turned with a little effort. He leaned into the door, hoping his greater weight would be enough. When it wasn't, he stepped back and drove his shoulder into it.

Rusty hinges protested as the door creaked open.

Rune and Kettle stepped into a storage room full of musty wooden shelves, mostly empty and draped in cobwebs.

Kettle shut the door behind them. "Almost there," he said. He rubbed his hands together, took hold of the knob, and pulled the same door back open. Now, however, the door led not into the tunnels the way they'd come but out into a darkened alley.

"Stars above," Rune muttered.

"Like I said," Kettle explained, "you make it go where you want." He extended a hand. "After you."

Rune walked to the end of the alley. The moonlight overhead filled him with unexpected energy. It had been too long since he'd seen the stars and the sky, and he grinned in spite of himself.

When he reached the main road, he knew exactly where they were: no more than a block or two from his apartment. A gentle breeze kissed his face.

"I can make it from here," Rune said.

"Probably," Kettle agreed, "but I promised Brack I'd see you all way home." He gestured for Rune to lead the way.

The two walked in silence on the streets of Louisville. Rune didn't know what to say. He'd brought so much trouble to the Brackwaters' doorstep that he wanted to just disappear.

He stifled a rueful laugh at the thought that this was exactly what he had done. He'd stirred up a hornet's nest in Goblintown and disappeared, leaving it all for Brack to deal with. He didn't want to do the same thing again. Brack's comment about what Rune was really running from cut deep. He could run from the King of Shadows, but not from himself.

"I wish we could've gotten here couple of hours earlier," Kettle said. "Trick-or-treaters are all inside by now."

"Trick-or-treaters?"

"I forgot," the firedrake said. "This is your first Hallowfest in Fallow. You don't know their traditions yet."

"No."

"The children dress in costumes. Doing it for hundred years now. Mostly heroes and villains from their stories, but you'd be surprised how many could pass for Saynim folk."

"That's right," Rune said, remembering what Zoey had once told him. "A friend of mine said something about that. They go about begging for candy, right?"

"I give Fallowmen credit; they make fine sweets!" Kettle smiled. "I love watching little guys—and I don't even have to change my clothes!" He gestured to his linen tunic and feathered flat cap. Any other night of the year, he would look completely out of place in the Fallow.

They crossed the street. Rune was only a few minutes from home. He pulled his weathered bomber jacket close against the autumn breeze.

"I'm only going to the next corner," Rune announced. "You really don't have to…"

"What is matter?" Kettle said. But he was looking past Rune to something up ahead.

Rune followed Kettle's gaze. The lights were on at the Colemans' house. Zoey's parents weren't usually up this late.

"Ooh!" Kettle interrupted. "Here comes trick-or-treater after all!"

Sure enough, a short, stocky figure ambled into view. It was shabbily dressed with a jaundiced face and long, stringy hair.

"That's not a child," Rune said, picking up his pace. He gripped his bata tightly below its weighted knob.

Jericho's servant bowed curtly as he and Rune met on the sidewalk outside the Colemans' house.

"Boggs," Rune said. "I suppose it's too much to hope you're bringing me good news?"

"Not tonight, Nightwalker," he said. He pursed his lips and looked up at Rune with his watery eyes.

"Rune, who is this…person?" Kettle said.

"Bad news," Rune said. He glared at Boggs. "Well?"

"M-my master demands your p-presence," Boggs said, licking his lips. "He's at C-cave Hill Cemetery. You're needed for his ritual."

"I'm sure I am," Rune said. "And once he's through, I expect we'll shake hands and part company as friends?"

"I d-don't know about that," Boggs said. He gulped. He was visibly shaking. "I'm just supposed to tell you that's where you'll meet him."

"And—hypothetically, of course—what is he going to do if I don't come?"

Boggs eyes darted right and left. He gestured to the house. "You know the g-girl who lives here?"

Rune's heart pounded. "What about her?"

"I'm supposed to t-tell you, she's waiting for you…she's with Jericho."

"Stars above! You can't be serious!" He grabbed the little man by the lapels of his ill-fitting jacket.

Boggs yelped and tried to pull away. The knob of Rune's fighting stick pressed against his cheek. "Now d-don't blame me, Nightwalker! I'm just the m-messenger!"

Rune pushed Boggs away so hard that the servant stumbled backward and landed on his backside.

"C-cave Hill Cemetery!" Boggs said. "Y-you can get there faster than I can—and you damn well better! You d-don't want to know what'll happen if you d-don't show up!" The sorcerer's servant stumbled to his feet and shuffled away.

"Zoey," Rune said. "By my breath…"

"Blazes," Kettle agreed. "Rune, what can I—"

"You've already done enough," Rune said.

"What's going on out here!" a voice called from the Colemans' front door. Rev. Coleman stepped onto the porch, wrapping his dressing gown tight. Mrs. Coleman peered over her husband's shoulder.

"Rune? Is that you?"

Rune sighed and took a step onto the lawn. "It's me, Rev. Coleman." Pressure was building in his temples. Zoey was in trouble. He couldn't escape the memory of when the two of them were in Jericho's study, the look of insulted fury on Avice's face when her magic misfired against Zoey.

"We were hoping Zoey might be with you," Rev. Coleman said. He glanced at Kettle.

"She went out with friends," Mrs. Coleman added. "She hasn't gotten back, and it's almost midnight."

She had somehow crossed paths again with Jericho. Rune couldn't shake the feeling that Avice was behind it somehow.

"Are you sure there's nothing I can do?" Kettle asked.

The wind picked up as Rune began to summon the airy chaos. "No," he said through gritted teeth. "This is my problem to solve." The King of Shadows was coming, and Rune had led him here.

Rev. Coleman glanced between Rune and Kettle. "Do you know something about this? Do you know where Zoey is?"

"I'm afraid so, Rev. Coleman," Rune said. "I'll bring her back." At least, he was going to try.

"What is this all about?" Mrs. Coleman said. She braced herself against her husband as the wind grew stronger and stronger.

"Too much to explain," Rune said. He was tired of his problems spilling out onto others. He took a step toward the sidewalk. "If I'm not back by sunrise…" He didn't know how to finish the sentence, so he left it hanging.

A quick glance assured him nobody else was outside. No prying eyes, no danger of violating the ancient Rule of Secrecy. It was just him, Kettle, and two Fallow folk whose world was about to change forever.

But there was no helping it. He might already be too late. He checked his pistol and cartridge box, gripped his fighting stick with both hands, and hurled himself into the sky.

As he soared upward, he could barely make out the sound of Mrs. Coleman's bewildered shriek.

He set down on a rooftop half a mile away. His heart was pounding, and the half-healed muscles in his thigh and abdomen were already tightening up.

If it was just a matter of putting a Fallow wizard in his place, Rune wouldn't have given it a second thought, but Jericho wasn't the half of it. Avice would be there too—rested and ready for him.

And if this ritual of Jericho's worked, the King of Shadows himself would make an appearance.

Stars above!

Rune needed leverage, and he only had one more trick up his sleeve. Thinking about it tore him up inside, but it was the only chance he had. For Zoey's sake, he had to try.

"Tempest!" he cursed.

Gritting his teeth, he reached into his pocket and pulled out a smooth stone, cool to the touch and heavier than it should have been. Warmed by his hand, it began to glow in the darkness with a pale green light, almost as if it anticipated what was to come.

He took a deep breath and let it out slowly, his mouth forming the last name he would ever want on his lips.

"Mayatakaamhshi. Mayatakaamhshi. Mayatakaamshi."

Almost at once, Rune felt lightheaded. His whole body seemed ready to float away as a murky, blue-green haze enveloped him.

And then he was somewhere else, if only in his mind. Pearls and precious stones covered every surface of a vast underwater cavern. Brilliant anemones and long-bladed sea grasses graced the floor. Rune's brain fought against his body's impulse to hold its breath.

A figure came into focus before him: long and sleek, with a torso at least somewhat reminiscent of a woman's and a whiplike, serpentine tail where her legs ought to be.

The Merlady grinned at him with her impossibly sharp teeth. "Mr. Rune. What a pleasant surprise."

Rune's hand, clenched in a fist around the Merlady's seeing stone, nervously rapped against his thigh.

"Was there something you wanted to tell me?"

Rune swallowed. He met her voracious gaze, looked her in her slit-pupil eyes. He summoned his courage and spoke. "I want to make a deal."

Maya circled around him, her black, scaled body undulating in the water. Rune worked to keep his bearings. He wasn't really there…wherever "there" was. He was breathing normally, not drowning. The Merlady came around to his face, no more than six feet away. "There's only one thing I'm interested in, Mr. Rune. And that is you."

He blinked. "What?"

"You have skills. I appreciate that." She hovered in front of him, swishing her tail back and forth to maintain her position. With a long, clawed hand, she reached out and brushed a loose strand of hair from his face.

"When I first learned of your arrival in Louisville, I knew I wanted you on my team. Yes, I have eyes and ears among the… ah…immigrant community there. But you should know that. How else would I know to pass your name on to Gimp Hollart? Now, are you ready to reconsider my offer?"

"I gave you my answer," Rune said.

"And yet you called me. Something about a deal?"

"You're so interested in what's going on in the Fallow. You might want to know the King of Shadows is up to something."

"With Mr. Phipps. Yes, I'm aware."

The water got suddenly colder.

"Don't be surprised," the Merlady said. "Boggs tells me everything."

"Boggs!"

"Of course. Why do you think I sent him to Phipps in the first place?"

"Boggs is working…for you?" Rune's throat went dry—which made the sensation of floating underwater even stranger. "But he has a pact with Phipps."

"And it is perfectly legal and binding. At least for the next few hours. But he served Phipps because I told him to. I can't have a rogue sorcerer stomping about, you must understand that. Certainly not one who's in league with your former employer."

Rune's mind raced as he thought through his interactions with Boggs. The fat little man always seemed a bit dodgy, but people who did his sort of work often did. Then he remembered Boggs's pot and the intricate tunnels beyond its back door. There was no way a common servant could have enchanted anything like that.

"When the King of Shadows starts mucking about in your backyard, you want to know what he's up to," Maya said. "It's only prudent."

"But…then you know what's going on. You know he has designs on the Fallow."

The Merlady spread her arms. "We've been over that."

Rune's pulse raced. "So what are you going to do about it?"

"Do?" She smiled. "Why, I threw *you* at him, of course."

Rune forgot to breathe for a good five seconds. He stared at the Merlady as terror washed over him.

"Oh, don't act so surprised. It wasn't that hard." She counted off the steps on her fingers. "I sent Boggs to warn you about Phipps and made sure he mentioned the King of Shadows. Anyone could have predicted you'd want to know more. Then I got you involved with Mr. Hollart."

"He was in on this too?" Rune's mind reeled.

"Of course not. Simply a happy coincidence. The business with his daughter was touch and go, though, what with discerning Avice's plan, bribing Nooch to put Avice on Hollart's trail…"

"Who is Nooch?"

"Vex tells me he's my new laundryman." She swam backward until they were perhaps ten feet apart. "Anyway, that unpleasantness at the University was the only time I feared I had thought too highly of you. But you came through. Well done!"

Maya's words confirmed something Rune had suspected. "I might have died! The only reason I didn't was because you helped me." The wounds on Rune's leg and stomach throbbed in the cool water.

"Call it an advance on your salary." Her black, snaky tail flicked with excitement. "You are quite resourceful, Mr. Rune. Color me impressed."

"I don't work for you," Rune said. "I won't work for you."

Maya circled around him once more. She came up from beneath him, and they floated practically nose to nose. She bared her fangs and bore into him with murderous slitted eyes. "You were at the point of death when my people found you in that drainage ditch. You were in shock. You wouldn't have lasted another five minutes."

She swam back behind him and grabbed him by the arms, whispering into his ear. "You owe me your life for stabilizing you and delivering you to Goblintown. Shame on you. Most people would be grateful." She tickled his ear with a tongue he could only imagine was long and forked like a viper's. It sent shivers down his spine. "And yet now you have come to me for help. Again."

Rune shuddered. This was a bad idea. She was going to kill him; he knew it.

The Merlady slid around to look him in the eye. "All right. You want to make a deal. Let's hear it."

Rune took a breath. Or at least, he imagined he did. He kept reminding himself that he wasn't really submerged in water. He was on a rooftop back in Louisville, halfway to Cave Hill Cemetery.

"It's in both of our interests to stop the King of Shadows," he began.

"You're repeating yourself," Maya said. "And you're not going to accept my offer. So tell me." She drifted closer. "Is there nothing you're willing to give me in exchange for my help? Nothing at all?" Her snaky, slitted eyes should have been devoid of emotion, but they sparkled anyway. She was hungry and ready to pounce.

"Think hard," she said. "Surely you can think of something. As I understand it, Phipps is preparing his ritual as we speak."

"But there are humans involved!"

"When have you ever cared about humans? I daresay you never cared about them before. Or do Nightwalkers ordinarily drive the people they care about to madness? Afflict them with every form of pestilence? Kidnap their babies? Kill them in their sleep?"

"I care," Rune said. "No, not before. I admit that. But I do now."

"Is that so?" She clapped her hands to the sides of Rune's head and gazed into his eyes. "Then you won't mind if I see for myself."

Rune gasped and held the breath. Maya grasped him even tighter.

He could guess what was coming. Water-weavers could plumb the emotional depths of a person: what they feared, what they hated, what they loved. He had no defense as the Merlady's magic spilled over him, drawing him under like a riptide.

"No—"

"Yes, Rune. Open your heart. I need to see what's in it."

Everything went dark. Alternating waves of heat and cold pulsed across his body so forcefully that he feared his bones would shake loose. It wasn't a vision. Visions implied intellect, rational communication. This was far deeper. Maya touched Rune's core and churned up a lifetime of primal feelings.

His mother's disappointment that he wasn't born a girl.

Avice's scorn at his very existence.

Whisper's patronizing.

They were all a jumble, poking out from the dark recesses of his mind—or not his mind. Not entirely. They may have started as thoughts in his mind many years ago. Now they had taken up residence somewhere else, somewhere deeper.

Why had he stolen the coffer? What did he hope to accomplish? It was driving him away from the closest thing to a home he'd ever known.

Tendrils of dark emotion lashed out at him, taunting him.

The man on the bus who would never realize how close he'd come to dying.

The frustration of never knowing what was expected.

Never knowing the rules.

Never having a hope of fitting in, in this world or any other.

If only there were more Fallow folk like Zoey!

What if she was already dead?

Rune let out a wearied moan.

He opened his eyes. He was no longer in the bejeweled grotto. He was standing on solid ground, his clothes and hair perfectly dry. Maya stood in front of him in her two-legged form, her hands still on the sides of his head.

"So it's not 'humans' you care for." She leaned in, closed her eyes, and took a whiff of Rune's neck. "It's one human. At least, one more than the rest."

She let go, and Rune crumpled to an ornate rug. He was in a drawing room, spare and dark but for a writing desk, a set of chairs, wall-hung tapestries, and a couple of floor lamps whose glowing stones cast a subdued blue-green light. In the corner, Vex the troll stood by, scratching the neck of the Merlady's water panther.

"And so much fear," Maya continued. "Fear of death—no surprise there. And your fear of failure is quite…zesty." She smiled. "Oh, but the fear of living and dying alone?" She licked her lips. "Delicious."

Rune pulled himself up onto his hands and knees.

"You should have followed your first instinct and run."

He lurched to his feet, his heart racing. He bowed his head. "Please. Zoey needs…I need your help."

"Yes, you do," Maya said. "I'm gratified that you finally realize it." She glanced over her shoulder. "Vex."

"My lady?"

"Take Mr. Whiskers out and see that he's fed."

"Yes, my lady." The troll tugged on the creature's neck to guide it toward the door.

Rune's eyes met Maya's.

"Now, Mr. Phipps's ritual will be starting in…I'd say any minute now." She made her way to the writing desk and sat down. As she pulled a leaf of parchment from the drawer, she turned to face Rune.

"So tell me. What precisely are you willing to trade for my help?"

33

Cave Hill Cemetery was the largest burial ground in the city and one of the oldest. Over the past hundred and fifty years, it had become the final resting place of war heroes, corporate and political giants, a famous explorer, a professional boxer of some repute, and, as Morty had once assured Rune, a man who'd made a fortune selling fried chicken.

It was a three-hundred-acre garden, a green oasis for what was once a young but growing city, with a creek running through it and an abundance of open spaces bounded by shrubs and trees. In one of those trees, Rune perched on a high limb and considered his options.

Five younglings stood at equidistant points around an imaginary circle. At the center stood Jericho dressed in black and crimson robes, hands at his side. His serene expression was apparently unshakable.

The sorcerer dominated the clearing, regal in his vestments, with a fifteen-inch rod in his hand—not a "magic wand" as if he were a Fallow stage performer but a steel-tipped, hand-carved blasting rod worthy of the name. He stood before a table draped in black and red that displayed the tools of his craft: candles, a silver chalice, and a ceremonial dagger.

"Are you prepared to take charge of your own destiny?" he asked. "Or are you mere children? Nobody's going to give you anything in this world. You've got to take it."

He spoke with steely conviction. The younglings circled around him looked on with expressions ranging from jitters to wonder. They would be a problem. Whether they knew it or not, they were likely meant to be human shields, hostages whom Phipps would threaten if Rune tried to interrupt the ceremony.

And among them was Zoey.

The sliver of moonlight was plenty for Rune to pick her out of the circle as she stood next to her friend Caitlin. She shifted her weight from one foot to the other, agitated. She didn't want to be there, that much was obvious. Rune wished she wasn't.

But his biggest problem was the others. Zoey was in the know. She had witnessed Rune's magic. She had at least caught a glimpse of the unseen world around her. The Rule of Secrecy no longer applied to her. But the others?

Magic tended to go sideways if more than three uninitiated Fallowmen observed it. Saynim's most revered sages had proposed numerous contradicting theories as to why. Maybe it created a psychic shock wave that unsettled the engines of chaos. Maybe too many skeptical or unenlightened observers simply threw things out of balance. Whatever the case, Rune would risk serious knotting if he revealed himself openly.

The others watched with expectancy as Jericho continued to talk. He walked around them, gesturing with his rod.

The sorcerer wasn't bound by the Covenant. He could do as he pleased and live with the fallout unhindered by the rules of magic that governed Rune and his people. He was a wild card. Too many of those were piling up.

Rune studied the edges of the clearing: the gravestones, the greenery. He didn't perceive anyone else about. Boggs hadn't yet had time to return to his master. Maybe he wasn't as adept as Kettle in navigating the ephemeral tunnels that presently criss-crossed the city. Or maybe he preferred to keep his distance, to find a plausible excuse to be delayed before…

That's when the gravity of the situation hit him. If Boggs was right, Jericho had come to Cave Hill to strike a bargain with the King of Shadows. It was unlikely that His Majesty would nego-tiate in good faith with a mere human. That fact only raised the likelihood of something bad happening, with Rune and Zoey and the others in the middle of it.

But Rune had made a bargain of his own. If he didn't at least try to stop Jericho, it was all for nothing. And if he tried and failed, well, nothing mattered anyway.

Maybe there was another way, but Rune couldn't see it. And it was too late to second-guess himself.

He peered into the clearing. Following the sorcerer's lead, the younglings began to drone a low, constant note, like the hum of a swarm of bees.

If it comforted Rune that Boggs was absent, it worried him that there was no sign of Avice. He couldn't see her, but she had to be there. She was orchestrating the whole thing, probably letting Jericho think he was calling the shots and all the while manipulating him, feeding him whatever lies he wanted to hear. Power? Knowledge? Money? It didn't really matter. Avice would spin whatever tale would tickle the sorcerer's ear, whatever would stoke his ego and lower his defenses. She was out there somewhere—if for no other reason, then because Rune was there, too.

He dropped to the ground, silent as a cat. Veiling himself in a cloak of glamour, he stalked forward. Zoey stood on the far side of the circle. Rune saw the fear in her eyes.

"How long is this supposed to take?" a dour, black-haired young man finally asked. The others stopped humming too.

"Patience," Jericho said. "When the time is ripe, she'll be here."

"Who?" a girl asked. It was Caitlin, Zoey's friend.

Jericho shushed her with nothing but a look and a subtle smile. He took a deep breath. "Soon." He began to drone again and gestured for the others to take the note back up as well.

Rune held his fighting stick firmly and filled his lungs slowly and deliberately, gathering the airy chaos to himself. The first order of business was to overcast the night.

He expelled his breath as intentionally as he had taken it in. The fog rose subtly at first, an indistinct gossamer haze to blanket the clearing and everyone in it. As the air cooled, the mist thickened. It wasn't long before Jericho noticed, and after him, the others. The sorcerer scowled at no one in particular, but he scanned the near distance. He knew something was up.

That was fine. Right now, Rune was just creating some cover. He'd done it dozens of times before, inflicting nightmares upon one of His Majesty's enemies or snatching away a sleeping human baby and disappearing into the night.

He brushed his hand across the front of his bomber jacket. His pistol was snug in his shoulder holster. He had a clean shot, but shooting would cause a panic and maybe tie a knot in the weave. He didn't need that. Furthermore, it would tell Avice where he was. She might already be watching from the shadows, ready to take him out as soon as he showed himself. Instead of drawing his pistol, he gripped his fighting stick more tightly and crept forward.

The wind shifted. Unbidden, Rune's heart raced as he spun through all the sensory data coming at him. The next moment, a fierce shove to the back lurched him forward.

He should have taken the shot after all.

He rolled into his fall and came up in a crouch, fighting stick outstretched in his right hand.

Avice only glared at him, silent, jaw set. Her sword pointed toward his heart. Her umbersay cloak rippled and undulated with impatient pseudo-life.

A sidewise glance told him no one in the circle had noticed them. His glamour kept him shielded from the Fallowmen's eyes. Though she and Rune could see each other, they would still pass unseen until one of them made a sound or otherwise disturbed the illusion. The first parry, the first clash of metal against wood—or the first gasp of pain—would give them away.

Avice stepped in, probing Rune's defenses with her sword. He sidestepped and started to circle around to his left. Neither said a word. A Nightwalker doesn't draw attention unless it serves a purpose.

"It is the witching hour!" Jericho announced. "From the heart of the night, we await a new day!" He began to intone an ancient chant, an invocation to the gods of misrule. As Rune and Avice continued to circle each other, resuming the dance they'd left unfinished days before, he saw the sorcerer processing around his makeshift altar.

Avice's cloak pulled away from her sword arm as she took another swing. She barely missed Rune's thigh. He moved to tie up her sword with his bata. As he expected, her cloak wrapped itself around his wrist. He grabbed it with his free hand and yanked it over her head.

She didn't curse or make any other noise, but she backed off, tangled for a second in her own cloak. Rune saw his chance and rammed the knob of his bata into her ribcage. She let out a sharp breath as the cloak wrested itself loose. The scuffle was fierce, but as silent as two elven air-weavers could make it.

Jericho kept chanting. An eerie stillness descended upon the cemetery. Some in his audience fidgeted, either from the cold or from a growing dread that what was happening wasn't just a silly diversion for a Halloween night. It was real.

Suddenly the clearing was charged with mystic energy. The change in the atmosphere caught Avice's and Rune's attention for a second. But they had more important things to deal with. They refocused on each other.

"This is the end," Avice whispered. Her voice never rose above the volume of Jericho's chanting. "Give up while you can."

"And let you run me through? Not likely."

Avice scoffed. "I'm not going to run you through." Cold fire danced in her eyes. "You're the guest of honor, after all."

Rune quirked an eyebrow, and Avice grinned.

"It's not that I wouldn't kill you in a heartbeat, but there's still the matter of the coffer you stole."

She lunged, but Rune hurled himself upward on a burst of wind. He cleared the trees and landed on the other side of the clearing, hidden from Jericho and his ritual.

Avice landed half a second later, tumbling onto her cousin's back and wrapping him in the twisting folds of her living cloak. A tendril of umbersay wrapped around Rune's throat while Avice placed the tip of her sword against his navel.

"And, of course, the sorcerer needs you. The King of Shadows needs you. Or I should say, he needs your blood."

Rune gasped as the blade brushed his half-healed wound. The faintest trickle of warm blood pooled above his belt.

He chuffed a breath and twisted out of the cloak's octopus grip. But he remembered what his cousin had said the last time they'd fought. Avice had sent the werecrows after the Hollart child for a reason. Tara Hollart was the product of two worlds: Saynim and the Fallow. In the logic of arcane ritual, she was the perfect bridge between the two worlds. If Rune hadn't rescued her, she would have been the one at the center of the King's scheme to gain a toehold in the mundane realm.

But he *had* rescued her. And that might have scuttled the entire plan, except that he was also the product of two worlds, with his Fallowman father and his elven mother.

"You pissed away your oath," Avice said, "but don't tell me you've forgotten the words. 'I pledge my life to the King of Shadows. My blood is a gift to be spilled at his whim.'"

His blood would serve the ritual just as well as little Tara's. He had likely been Avice's preferred sacrifice all along. The King of Shadows would have his revenge for Rune's betrayal, and Avice would have the satisfaction of presenting Rune's head to her sovereign on a platter.

He drew his pistol; away from the younglings, there was no point in secrecy. But Avice was on him before he could pull back the hammer. She kicked the pistol away and fell on him, smothering him once more in her infernal cloak.

The cloth inched its way to his mouth, his nose. He struggled to break free, but every time he thought he was gaining the upper hand, either another silken tentacle wrapped itself around him or Avice slashed at him with her nails or kneed him in the gut. He didn't want to know what she was doing to Thora's stitches, but it wasn't good. His whole side was sore, from his belly to his wounded thigh. His head was getting woozy.

"I've had enough of you, auph," she hissed, and slashed him across the face with her fingernails. Blood blossomed on his cheek. "I've had enough of your 'potential' and your 'birthright' and every other sarding thing about you. Your whole life, people fawned over you." She clawed at his throat as she mocked him. "They whispered your name in hushed admiration. 'Good old human ingenuity,' they said. 'What'll he think of next?'"

Avice's cloak now covered his entire head, so her next words sounded muffled and distant. "They bent over backward to give you every advantage. And what did you do?" A knee to the groin crumpled him to the ground.

"You betrayed your oath. You betrayed everything!" She spit in his face.

She grabbed him by the collar and hauled him to his feet, pushing the airy chaos upon him to reduce his weight to something she could easily manage. He grimaced and tried to pull away, but her cloak held him fast, and her magic made him helpless.

At some point she had sheathed her sword. Now she ran a shorter, slimmer blade of bronze across his chest—one of his own daggers, splitting the fabric of his shirt. The dagger, cold as ice, probed his bare torso.

With her other hand, Avice jammed something metal against Rune's side just below his bandage. A quick slash, and a new wound opened beneath the old one, long and shallow. She could have killed him if she wanted, but for now she just wanted him to bleed.

Her eyes danced in the moonlight as she rammed the metal thing into his gut. A cup. Something to collect the blood as it washed over his belly and onto his trousers.

"They gave you everything. Everything! And why?" He tried to break away, but he was no match for the cloak. "Because your ditch-whore of a mother sarded the first Fallowman she could find."

Avice marched him through the trees. As she went, she made slashing gestures with her hand, dispelling the fog that Rune had conjured.

It was only a few seconds before they burst into the clearing. Several of the students gasped as Avice shoved Rune to the ground right outside the circle. He was just conscious enough to recognize Zoey yelping, "Oh God!"

"Magister Jericho," Avice announced as she lifted the cup. "Behold your sacrifice."

34

Zoey could barely believe her eyes. Caitlin let out a trembling "Oh!"

Avice had a cup in her left hand, a goblet or chalice, ornate and silver. With her right hand, she gestured toward Rune, who lay crumpled at her feet. She unclasped her cloak and tossed it over Rune's broken body. It curled around him like a living thing.

Zoey wanted to bolt from the circle, but her legs wouldn't let her. Some unseen force had pinned her feet in place, iron or no iron. Looking around the circle, she saw that some of the others were in the same boat. They looked like they wanted to move, to run away—she could see it in their faces—but they didn't. They couldn't.

She looked into Caitlin's eyes and saw fear along with something else. Her friend's eyes were distant, unfocused. Like she knew where she was and what was going on, and yet she was detached from it.

When people watch a scary movie, their bodies react to the horrors on the screen: their hearts race and their palms sweat. But it's all in their heads. They know it isn't real, no matter how good the special effects are. That's what Caitlin looked like. It's what all of them looked like as Zoey glanced around the circle. Something—the droning, the circle, the midnight hour—had gotten into their heads.

Whatever happened next, they had to watch it unfold, maybe shield their eyes against anything gory. They'd even jump back if they could. But Jericho's magic had convinced them that none of it mattered.

Zoey tried to tug her foot from the ground, but it refused to budge. She cursed, then blushed for cursing. Then she cursed again.

This is not *rated Z for Zoey!*

"I see," Jericho said. His voice pulled Zoey back to the present. Did she hear hesitation? She looked up. The sorcerer looked at the fallen Rune. If he was surprised, his face never showed it. His eyes rose to meet Avice's.

"You…you said the sacrifice was symbolic."

"It is," Avice said. Her face opened into a grin. "Do you really think I would kill someone to further *your* ambitions?"

Jericho looked back at Rune. He was breathing, but he didn't look good. He was pale—paler than normal. Zoey hoped that was just the silver of the moonlight.

"But—"

"I have no love for this one, Magister Jericho, but his life is not mine to take. My lord has business with him. You brought the wine?"

He gestured toward the table.

"Wonderful. You may begin. I'll add the final ingredient."

No one asked what final ingredient Avice held in her chalice, but Caitlin squeaked at the realization even in her befuddled state, and Zack whispered something blasphemous under his breath.

What did they think they were seeing? Did they think it was all a put-on orchestrated for their entertainment? A haunted house dialed up to eleven? Zoey forced down the sour taste in her mouth. All she could do was look on.

For his part, Jericho stood stoically as Avice passed within the circle and approached the ceremonial table.

The sorcerer straightened up and held out his hands in a gesture of receiving. Everyone somehow knew to continue droning as he began to chant. It wasn't English. It might have been Latin. Zoey didn't know and didn't care. But it was doing something, shifting their perception of reality, maybe shifting reality itself. Jericho had said something about looking for people with a spark of magic. Maybe he'd found them.

The wind picked up, and high, thin clouds gathered above the cemetery. The candles blazed brightly, and their flames took on an impossible greenish hue.

Jericho's voice got louder and more frenzied, but his body was stiff, his hands outstretched, his feet firmly planted.

Avice poured the contents of Jericho's chalice into her own and swirled it around, mingling the wine and the… No, she didn't want to know. Zoey glanced at Rune as he lay on the grass, wrapped in a cloak that twisted tighter and tighter around him.

The sorcerer strode forward. Avice lifted her chalice to the sky and joined Jericho in the climax of his incantation. She lowered the chalice and stretched it toward him. When he hesitated, she took another step, grasped the back of his neck, and guided his lips to the rim.

She tilted the chalice toward him, grinning.

Jericho shut his eyes and grimaced as the wine ran down his throat and down the front of his robes. Avice didn't let him loose until he had drained the last drop.

Thunder cracked.

The sorcerer jerked backward with a gasp. His eyes flew open. Only…

Zoey had long prided herself on how she could read people. Her mom said she took after her father that way. It's part of what made him a good pastor.

She would rather feed her hand to a malnourished crocodile than be the pastor of a church, but the observation held. She could read people, and something about Jericho had changed. It was as plain as day. He shook himself off and stood up to his full height before Avice, who took a half-step back and averted her gaze as he strode confidently toward her.

It was as if Jericho had shut his eyes as one person and reopened them as someone else. But that didn't make any sense.

And yet something was different. Jericho sensed it, too. Everyone did.

"You have done well, child," he said, his voice full and bold. Overhead, clouds rolled and thunder rumbled. He spoke with the slightest trace of an accent that Zoey couldn't quiet place. German, maybe.

Avice dropped to one knee, visibly trembling. She still hadn't looked Jericho in the eye.

"Arise," he said.

She took a breath and simply said, "Your Majesty."

Your Majesty? What's that supposed to mean?

The question had barely formed in Zoey's mind when Jericho let out a satisfied "Aaah." He walked in a small circle, stretching his limbs. He noticed his right hand and, with a bemused grin, clenched and unclenched his fist, spellbound at the sight. It was as if he'd never seen his own hand before.

"The host suits you, my king?" There was the slightest quaver in Avice's voice. She was nervous, frightened even. Zoey knew the type. She could tell Avice aimed to please and was afraid of messing up.

Jericho smiled and extended a hand. "You did well, child," he said again. Rune groaned, and Jericho whipped his head toward him. His smile grew even broader. "And you've brought me a present, I see."

He swaggered through the circle with Avice two steps behind him. Caitlin and Zack and the others stayed in their places—as if they could do anything else. They watched him pass with the same detached curiosity they'd shown ever since the ritual began.

Jericho planted his feet in front of Rune.

"Claeus, son of Herdis of the house of Claea, kneel before your king." The sorcerer's voice was calm, but it brooked no dissent. Rune took a weary, heaving breath.

Avice yanked him to a kneeling position, reclaiming her cloak in a single, fluid action. No, that wasn't quite right. Rather, the cloak itself, as if sensing her presence, leaped from around Rune, slithered up her arm, and fastened itself around her neck.

"You heard him," she snarled.

Rune had to work at first to maintain his balance, but he spread his knees a bit farther apart and managed to kneel with his body fully upright. He was beaten, but his eyes were bright with steely fury.

"The coffer," Jericho said, though Zoey had a strong suspicion that this was no longer Jericho at all.

Rune said nothing.

From where she was standing, still rooted to the spot, Zoey couldn't see the new Jericho's expression, but his body language screamed anger. His voice rumbled like a volcano, but he didn't yet erupt. "The coffer," he repeated. "Where is it?"

Rune sighed, half fatigued and half disdainful. "Safe."

Avice drew her blade and held it to Rune's throat. "You will address your king with deference!"

He studiously ignored the threat and looked Jericho—the King—in the eye. "It's in a safe place…Your Majesty. There it will stay."

Zoey winced. She could only imagine what was coming next, and she hated that she could do nothing to stop it.

But then King Jericho laughed.

Zoey's jaw dropped. Avice smiled, struggling to catch a joke she obviously wasn't getting.

"Of course it's in a safe place, dear Claeus. It's what I've come to expect of you." He moved about, boldly but not quite gracefully, not with the kind of winsome grace Zoey had seen so often in Rune. It was like he was getting used to a strange new set of limbs.

A hypothesis sprung unbidden to her mind, and she didn't like it at all.

I was right. There's more than just Jericho in there. And this other guy…

She grimaced. The other guy, the King, was bad news. He had a history with Rune, and it wasn't pleasant. Zoey looked to the sky for help, but none seemed coming.

"But now," the King said, "your little excursion is over. I'll take my property." He leaned over Rune. "Now."

Rune managed a weak grin. "Not today."

Give him what he wants, Zoey screamed inside her head.

You don't even know what it is!

Who cares? Rune's going to get himself killed!

"It seems you need encouragement," the King said. He turned askance and glared at Zoey and the others. Energy flowed past her, a shock wave she didn't feel with her body but with her mind. Her thoughts bucked against the pull of the King's magic as it needled into the depths of her soul.

The others gasped and gritted their teeth, and then their whole bodies went still. Those closest to the King, who had their backs to him as they faced the inside of the circle, slowly turned around. Mike and Cassie's eyes were blank, listless. Beside Cassie, Caitlin took a tentative step forward. Zack came up beside Caitlin.

Zoey stumbled forward…but of her own will. She smiled inwardly: it was something she chose to do, not something any magic compelled her to do. Maybe those iron washers were doing something after all. But how could that help her now?

Caitlin and the rest flanked the King, an honor guard of living zombies.

"I'm afraid your grasp of the situation is wanting, Claeus. I have every advantage here. Your life is in my hands, and you will turn over the coffer."

The King snapped his fingers, and Mike and Zack moved to either side of Rune. "Make him stand," he ordered. They each grabbed Rune under an arm and hauled him to his feet.

"I can't give it to you," Rune said. Was his voice stronger, or was that just Zoey's wishful thinking? "I'll die first."

"I'm sure you would," the King said. Now Zoey could see his face. He was still Jericho, only…not. There was something in his expression. Jericho had seemed confident and witty at his party Friday night. During his little pep talk this evening, he was much the same: cool, in control, in his element.

Now he was positively regal. His smile, his posture, the gleam in his eyes all bespoke a level of power that Zoey could barely understand. His movements suggested great physical might. Even his voice had changed. It was deeper and a bit more nasal, and he still had that weird accent.

This was not the man Zoey had met before. She wasn't sure that man was even in that body anymore.

"You'd gladly give your life to keep me from my prize," the King continued. "But I wonder, Claeus, if you would be so obliging of the lives of others."

He turned slowly toward Cassie, Caitlin, and Zoey.

"Please know that I don't want to kill you," he told them with a sadistic smile. He looked like he couldn't wait to kill them.

His eyes landed on Zoey, and she gulped.

"Of course," he said to Rune. "The one you were with at the party. Tell me where you've put the coffer, and this can be over this instant. Otherwise…" He lifted his hand and slowly formed it into a fist.

Zoey's stomach tied itself in knots.

35

Rune watched helplessly as the King of Shadows postured and threatened. If he hadn't been pulling the airy chaos for all he was worth, he'd have passed out from pain. But with his magic swirling around him, his head was clear and his senses sharp.

He weighed his options, and none of them were good. If he turned over the coffer, it would all be over. He'd be dead in a matter of seconds. Zoey and her friends might survive—but only until the King of Shadows launched the next phase of his plan, and then the world as they knew it would come crashing down.

Or he could fight, which meant he wouldn't die quite as fast as with the other option, and it might cause enough of a distraction that Zoey and the rest could get away…only to die in the apocalypse after a few hours or days or weeks.

"I'm waiting," the King said, his voice an almost feral purr. He leaned over Rune and lifted his hand in a fist. Magical energy crackled invisibly. Rune felt it lick at his face, his arms, his torso.

He thought of Maya and the deal he'd struck. Rune had regretted it a hundred times in the half-hour or so since he'd spoken to her. He wished he had never made the offer and that she had never accepted it.

But he had, and she had. And now it was the only way out. As soon as the King's attention had turned to Zoey, he knew that.

"Wait," he grunted.

But he was too late. Nobody heard him, and before he could get another word out, Zoey shouted and lunged toward the King.

She had pulled something out of her pocket, a nail at least four inches long. No one noticed it but Rune. Everyone else's eyes were trained on the King. She rammed the nail into his shoulder, just beneath the collarbone. He bellowed in shock and pain and fell to the ground.

Avice gasped. The two young men who held Rune let go and took a step back, as if fighting to wake up after sleeping too deeply.

He didn't understand, but he saw an opportunity, so he took it. He let the airy chaos flow. In a heartbeat he was at Zoey's side. He pointed her toward the nearest copse of trees and gave her a gentle shove. "Go!"

He spun to face Avice, who was already closing the distance between them. Jericho cursed in his own voice.

Iron, Rune thought. If Zoey's nail was made of iron, then stabbing Jericho with it might have broken the spell. It would have torn the King of Shadows from his elemental chaos, if only for a second. He would have to pull himself away from the sorcerer's body like someone jerking their hand from a hot stove.

Rune took a breath and pulled even more air as he scanned the ground for his fighting stick. It was only a few yards away.

The Blessing was falling over him, letting him see his situation with detachment. Feelings didn't figure into the moment at all. The only thing on his mind was stopping the King of Shadows for good.

With a grin, he spun about and dove to the ground. When he came up, he had his fighting stick. He held it in front of him in a defensive stance.

Time slowed as the airy chaos swirled around him. Zoey loped toward the trees while Jericho clutched at his shoulder where the nail went in through the slit in the front of his robes.

But everything happened at a crawl. Even the sound of shouting had dropped an octave. One of the young men slowly fell backward. The other one looked around, dazed, as if waiting for someone to give him an order. The young women in the circle wobbled as if drunk.

The scrape of metal against metal captured Rune's attention: a sword being drawn. Avice leaped ten feet into the air with a feral howl. She lunged as she landed, but Rune closed the distance and batted her sword arm with his fighting stick. They both hit the ground. Rune flung Avice free and scrambled to his feet.

Zoey had made two steps' progress toward the trees. The falling boy had finally reached the earth. The King was down—or was it now simply Jericho? Best to take the fight somewhere else, and there was only one choice.

Rune took flight with a violent *whoosh*! and soared out of the clearing.

A long, thin lake nearly bisected the cemetery from north to south. Forty feet in the air, Rune got his bearings and began his descent toward the water.

Avice slammed into him, still ascending. The two grappled in the air, spinning head over heels. Rune wrestled with both Avice and her cloak as they fought for his bata and tried to pin his arms to his sides.

With a rasping grunt, Rune tore himself free and plummeted toward the ground, pulling air to slow his fall. Despite the effort, he landed with a thud.

"Stars!" he gasped. Warm blood oozed through his bandages. His stitches were hardly more than good intentions now. He looked upward in time to see Avice's boots aimed at his body as she dove toward him, shrieking a savage war cry.

Rune rolled away, breathing hard. His side was on fire with pain. He looked up to see an elaborate monument: four white marble columns under a cornice, with the name of the deceased carved on the frieze. Underneath was a bronze bust of an old man with a goatee and a string tie. In front of the structure was the gravestone itself, flat on the ground, and all around were flowers and greenery.

The force of Avice's landing propelled her forward. "Give up the coffer!" She kept the point of her sword between her and Rune.

"We don't have to do this."

"You have no choice!" She bull-rushed him, and he barely sidestepped in time to avoid her blade, which instead whacked a couple of branches off a decorative shrubbery. But her umbersay cloak snagged Rune's leg and pulled it out from under him. He landed hard on his back. Avice spun about, and her cloak yanked Rune toward her.

36

Zoey stumbled to a stop. Over her shoulder, she saw Caitlin, Zack, and the others wobbling where they stood. Rune and Avice had vanished, but Jericho still lay on the ground, groaning and clutching at the grass.

Caitlin fell to her knees. Mike raised his hands to his temples before he joined her on the ground.

Caitlin needs help, Zoey thought.

Jericho is going to kill you!

But Caitlin needs help!

She pushed up her glasses and hurried back toward the summoning circle. "Caitlin!"

Caitlin muttered something. She and the other three—Zack, Mike, Cassie—were in a daze. Apparently the magical charm in Zoey's pocket protected her from the spell. She shook her head at the thought of it. An honest-to-goodness *sorcerer* had cast a spell on her and her friends. Only she had managed to shake it off.

She knelt and grabbed Caitlin by the shoulders. "We've got to get out of here!"

"What…?"

"Caitlin, you gotta snap out of it. It's time to go." Zoey breathed a silent prayer. Nobody looked ready to go anywhere. Zack was sprawled out with his face to the ground a few yards away.

Jericho let out a savage cry. He grimaced as he dug at his shoulder, finally pulling out the long iron nail that Zoey had planted there. The look on his face was a mixture of anger and despair.

"Gone!" he moaned as he pounded the grass.

Caitlin lurched back, pulling away from Zoey's grip. Zoey caught her eye, but she wasn't sure Caitlin even recognized her.

The wind picked up, and amid the rustling of leaves were other sounds: the snap of twigs, deep breathing, whispers and distorted voices that raised the hairs on Zoey's neck.

She looked around. The sky, rolling with thick blackness moments before, was clearing off just as quickly. Yet shadows flitted among the trees—or at least she thought they did. The world tried to tilt until she shut her eyes as hard as she could.

When she opened them, Jericho held up the nail in his bloodied fingers. He roared as he struggled to his knees.

Caitlin listed to one side. Zoey grabbed her by the chin. "Now, Caitlin! We've got to go!"

Caitlin gasped, but her eyes didn't focus.

Zoey had a thought—a desperate thought, but that's all she could manage. Beneath her waistband was the charm Madam Samarra had given her. Somehow, it blocked Jericho's magic. Maybe it could do something for Caitlin. She undid the velvet pouch with trembling fingers and stared at it in her hand.

Okay, now what?

"How is this thing supposed to work?" She waved the pouch in front of Caitlin. She placed it against her friend's forehead. She shook it in her fist like she was getting ready to roll a die. Nothing.

"This is stupid!"

Jericho slumped forward onto all fours. A mocking titter arose within the haunted-house noises that filled the cemetery.

"Hold on," Zoey said, lifting one finger to Caitlin as if she had any idea that Zoey was there. She jumped up and hurried to where Jericho staggered, breathing deeply.

This better not be a bad idea!

You won't know until you try.

"Hey," she said, her voice strong, more confident than she felt. "My friends are…I don't actually know what they are. They're in trouble. Can you help them?"

It took a second for Jericho to focus on the sound of Zoey's voice. His body froze but he didn't look up.

"I'm talking to you! You've gotta do something!"

He doesn't even know you're here!

He damn well better know I'm here!

"Jericho!"

He stared at the ground.

Zoey took a deep breath, willing herself to relax. As gently as she could, she said, "Come on, guy. You gotta get up. My friends need you."

Jericho opened his mouth, then closed it again. He lurched to his feet with a grunt.

"There you go," Zoey said. "Just walk this way."

"No," he said.

Zoey met Jericho's eyes. They were fierce and icy blue.

But didn't Jericho have brown eyes?

"I take no orders from you, child." The sorcerer's voice had changed again, back to that weird maybe-German accent.

Oh crap. The King is back.

Zoey felt her pockets. She'd only brought the one nail. She still had a bunch of washers, but King Jericho wasn't going to stand still while she hung them around his neck.

"Listen." She backed tentatively away with her hands outstretched in a defensive gesture. "I don't know what your deal is, but there are people in trouble here."

"Which is no concern of mine."

"Maybe not. But…I'd like to think Jericho sees it differently. He…You…wanted to help people. Okay, you didn't pick the best way to do it, but still—"

"No," the King said with Jericho's mouth. "I may yet have need of these thralls." He lifted his hand in a summoning gesture, and the other four young people rose to their feet.

"Wait a minute! Wait a minute!" Zoey took another step back. She would soon be surrounded by her friends, and they didn't look friendly. There was no feeling in their eyes, no hint of recognition.

"Iron!" she shouted in her best angry voice.

The King seemed unimpressed.

Figures. You can't believe everything you read on the Internet.

"Jericho, you've got to listen."

"Does he, now?"

Zoey had the sudden sense of the terrain shifting around her, as if a completely new reality was imposing itself upon her world. The cemetery, her friends, and Jericho's altar all competed with an image of someplace darker and more ominous, with stone walls, burning lanterns, and polished obsidian.

She gazed into Jericho's eyes, but the sorcerer flickered in and out of existence. In his place was…not quite a man. This someone was tall, muscular. Good looking in his own way, but with a heavy brow and a wolfish cast to his icy blue eyes. There was something fierce about him. Untamed. He lifted his right hand, and Zoey gasped. It wasn't a hand at all, but a monstrous, scaly claw ending in black eagle's talons.

A pulsating ball of golden light glimmered in the King's claw, slowly fading.

"Is that…?"

The King grinned. "Perhaps now you understand the futility of your situation."

She shook her head.

"Why are you unaffected by my spell, hmm? You must bear some kind of charm."

That's right, she did. And a necklace of iron washers. Zoey didn't know much about how things worked in Rune's old neighborhood, but she had to believe those items counted for something.

"This isn't real," she said. The new vista blinked, competing with the cemetery, and it was like the satellite was about to go out on the TV. When it came back a heartbeat later, the King's orb glowed slightly brighter.

"This isn't real!" Zoey scrunched her eyes shut. When she opened them, she was back in the cemetery. The King was still ten feet away, but now once more in Jericho's body.

She looked him in the eye. "Jericho, I'm pretty sure you can hear me. Are you going to let this guy kick you around?"

"The sorcerer is indisposed."

Zoey ignored him. "How about it? That's the one thing you hate, isn't it? When the big guys pick on people? Use them to get their way?" She softened her voice and dared take a step forward. "It's not right."

"Enough of this!" The King stared into her eyes, and her body was covered with spiders and centipedes, writhing over her, crawling up her pants legs and into her hair.

"This isn't real, either!" she shouted. She didn't know how she knew, but she did. She clutched at her chest, Madam Samarra's charm held tightly in her fist. The bugs vanished, but they left goosebumps up and down her arms.

"And I want to talk to Jericho!" She took a breath and settled her nerves. "I want to hear from him that he's okay with all this, because there are defenseless people in trouble out here, and I don't think he would like that."

She took another step forward. There was no way he didn't hear her heart pounding, but as calmly as she could, she said, "Am I right?"

The King swayed. He shut his eyes. When he opened them, they were brown.

"You said you wanted to use your power for others. Is that what this looks like to you?"

"Get away from me!" he yelled as he fell to his knees. He let loose a string of profanity, but Zoey couldn't tell if he was yelling at her or at whoever was invading his body.

She knelt to look at him on his level. "Listen, my friends need you. Do you understand?" It was all she could do to keep her voice from breaking. "You don't want to hurt them. You wanted to help them, remember? To help them unleash their potential."

The sorcerer groaned and fell back to all fours.

"That's going to be kind of hard if they're zombies."

"That is none…of my…ungh!"

"I don't know what you did to them earlier, but they need to get better so we can all get out of here." As if to drive home the point, another gust of wind blew through the clearing, carrying with it the sound of distant howling.

"So what do you say? Give a girl a hand here?"

Jericho shook. His breath was heavy and labored, like he had just finished running a marathon. He clutched at his side.

"Do you hear me? Jericho?" Zoey reached around her neck and pulled off the necklace of iron washers. As quickly as she could, she slipped it over the sorcerer's head.

He turned his face up to look at her. He seemed older than before. Or maybe he was just tired. His brown eyes were heavy with sleep. He shut them again and slumped forward.

"Oh no, you don't!" Zoey said. "You are getting up right now and you're going with me and we're going to help the others!"

The wind grew suddenly still, and that made the distant, unearthly sounds even more ominous.

"All I wanted…"

"You wanted power. I got the memo. But that doesn't look like an option right now."

The sorcerer's whole body shook.

"I understand," Zoey said. She reached out a tentative hand and set it on Jericho's shoulder. "You bet on the wrong horse, and that sucks. That king or whoever? The one who promised you all that power? Maybe you thought you were using him, but he was using you."

Jericho wrenched himself free from her touch. He stood up, snarling against the pain in his injured shoulder. He backed away. Something desperate gleamed in his eyes.

"You understand nothing!" he spat. "You can't… It was…" His eyes, barely focused, shifted to the left, then up and down in frantic succession.

Zoey gulped. "Just stay calm, okay?"

"He was *here*!" Jericho balled his fists. "His presence…and you ruined it! Your cold iron drove him away!"

"That was kind of the plan!" she protested. "Look, I don't know who was…inside your head, but he wasn't someone you really wanted there, okay?"

Jericho bent over, clutching the sides of his head.

"But you can think about your poor life choices another time. Right now, there are some people who need your help."

"Aaargh!" He spun in a circle.

"You said you only wanted to help people. Remember Friday night? You said everybody ought to use whatever power they have to help others."

The sorcerer straightened up and looked into the moonlit sky.

Something eerie and dissonant whistled on the wind. Goosebumps rose on Zoey's arms.

"Well," she said, "that's what you need to do. Right now."

Jericho breathed hard. His eyes bore into Zoey's, and the turmoil in his soul grumbled in her stomach. It was like he had reached his bloody hand inside her to twist her insides into knots.

"Don't do this," she said. Tears trickled down her face. "I need you. My friends need you."

He sucked in a harsh, gasping breath as he doubled over, grasping the sides of his head again.

Zoey took another step toward him. He mumbled something in a different language, some kind of chant or mantra that he repeated over and over.

She was close to him now. Should she reach out and touch him again? Would that help?

The sorcerer kept up his chant, gently rocking back and forth.

The sky took on an unsettling purple hue. Twigs snapped amid the trees. Something big slithered past and out of sight.

Jericho shouted, not in anguish but in triumph. He stumbled to his feet and looked about, taking stock of where the others were prone on the ground.

He stumbled to his altar table.

"Well?" Zoey said. "Are you going to help them?"

"That's what I'm doing."

He gave no further explanation but reached under the table for a plastic container filled with zip-top bags. He plucked out three and sprinkled their contents—herbs of some kind—into an empty dish. He swirled them around with the tip of his dagger, intoning an incantation.

"You should be going," he said.

"Not till everybody's all right."

"They'll be fine." He grabbed a white candle from his supply box and rubbed the herbal mixture into it until flecks of green and brown were embedded in the wax.

"If it's all the same to you, I'd rather see for myself. Caitlin and I have been friends forever."

Jericho nodded. His movements were curt and energetic. His demeanor was aggressive, like he didn't want Zoey to be there. Fine. All the more reason for her to hang around.

But something about him had changed. Before, he was full of confidence. Whatever had happened while the King was inside his head, it was something he had wanted. Only not anymore. Now he was working—angrily, impatiently—to fix what he had broken.

Sometimes you want something up until the moment you get it.

"What can I do?" she asked.

"Stay out of my way," Jericho growled. After lighting his candle from one of the others on the table, he went first to Caitlin, the nearest of his bewitched victims. He muttered a few more magic words under his breath while moving the candle in a circle around the girl's head.

She whimpered and shrugged her body as if waking up from a fitful sleep. Zoey hurried over and fell to her knees at Caitlin's side. "Can you hear me? Cait?"

Jericho moved on to Mike and repeated his spell. Zoey listened to his chant and gently patted Caitlin's cheek.

And then he stopped mid-syllable.

Zoey whipped around. The sorcerer had toppled over. He lay on the grass, still as a stone.

She hissed a curse and turned back to Caitlin. Her friend was working to wake up, but it was a battle.

The wind picked up again, and with it the weird howling that seemed to come from everywhere at once.

"Caitlin, we've really got to go now!"

Caitlin's eyes opened with an expression of fright. She drew in a breath and propped herself up.

Then, just as suddenly, her eyes rolled back in her head, and she flopped back down.

Zoey started to swoon. She hadn't noticed in the confusion, but there was a misty haze in the clearing, something barely visible but carrying the subtle scent of lavender.

She felt her eyelids grow heavy.

"NO!" she thundered. Her charm from Madam Samarra and her iron trinkets had kept her safe so far, but she was quickly running out of hardware. She jumped to her feet.

Everyone else was out cold. Even those Jericho hadn't gotten to were perfectly still, no longer moaning or twitching in fitful sleep.

Zoey's own limbs felt leaden. It wouldn't be long before she was in the same mess.

She rushed to the altar table. Jericho had left his ritual knife there. Grabbing it by the carved ivory hilt, she pointed it into the darkness toward nothing in particular.

"Don't come any closer!"

The howling in the trees resolved itself into a deep, throaty laugh. Zoey still couldn't tell where the sound was coming from or how close it was, but she was willing to bet it was closer than it used to be.

Her eyes darted about. *Just come out and get me if that's what you want!*

Five seconds passed. The wind became still, and the eerie laughter subsided.

She expelled a breath and flexed her fingers around the hilt of Jericho's blade.

And then the shadows emerged from the trees.

There were two of them, human-sized and wearing hooded cloaks that fell to their ankles. The hems whipped about despite the sudden stillness of the air.

The smaller shadow pulled the hood away. It was a woman with a youthful face that wouldn't have been out of place at Zoey's high school. Her expression was bemused, almost playful. With her upturned nose and arching eyebrows, she could have easily played the role of Tinker Bell—if Tinker Bell had neon pink hair and carried a sword the length of her arm.

The taller figure was male. He kept his hood in place because his hands were busy. In one he held a wooden bowl. With his other hand, he gestured over it.

The tiniest ember flew up from the bowl, a pinprick of reddish orange against the roiling blackness of his cloak. It was some kind of incense, and he was drawing the smoke upward and breathing it out over the clearing.

The scent of lavender tickled Zoey's nostrils.

She slashed at the figures with the dagger. "I said stay where you are!"

The tiny woman tittered. "There's no point to that, Zodiac," she said. "Looks like she's warded."

The man, Zodiac, shrugged and blew the last of his incense into the air. He slipped his bowl beneath his cloak and pulled back his hood. He was dark-haired and aquiline, with arching bushy eyebrows and eyes that gleamed like a cat's in the moonlight. His close-trimmed hair framed pointed ears, and his goatee highlighted the toothy grin he gave his partner.

He threw the hem of his cloak over his left shoulder, revealing a knobbed stick strapped to his belt. His hand slipped over the weapon's weighted end. "You want me to handle her the old-fashioned way?"

His malicious grin frightened Zoey more than anything else she'd seen that night. His eyes danced with the promise of unspeakable evil.

"I'll take care of her," the woman said. "You finish your job on the other Fallowmen."

"Your call, Saffron." His face darkened. Before he turned away, he looked Zoey in the eye and made a kissing noise.

Saffron stalked forward with an unwholesome gleam in her eye.

37

"I want to talk," Rune gasped.

"Time for talk is past." Avice set her foot on Rune's chest none too gently. His shoulder blades scraped against the marble slab atop the grave of the goateed gentleman in the string tie. His cousin lowered her sword almost to his chin. "You're going to tell me where the coffer is."

"And then you'll let me live?"

"And then I'll turn you over to the King of Shadows."

"I must say, your negotiating skills are lacking."

"No negotiations," she said. She leaned down. Rune could hardly breathe for her weight on his chest. "We're long past that. It's time for you to answer for your crime."

"Then I'm afraid I'll have to answer for one more," he said. He studied her smoldering blue eyes. "I don't know where it is."

Her mouth dropped open, but only for a second. "You're lying."

"Look at me, Avice. I'm spent. Do you think I would violate the Covenant now? Can you imagine the knot it would tie? But I'm not feeling it, am I? No scales. No bursting into flame. Nothing is happening to me. I swear by my breath, I don't know where the coffer is."

Avice knitted her brow, looking for a trick, a reason to doubt Rune. Over the course of several seconds, her face changed, darkened, as her angular features seethed with anger and confusion.

"I told you to give me the coffer! Where is it?"

He sighed. "I just said—"

Light brighter than the sun flashed across the cemetery. A momentous thundering crash shook every bone in Rune's body. For a second, his hair stood on end.

He rolled onto his belly on the slab. Avice lay prone on the grass, rubbing her eyes. "Tempest!" she snarled.

Rune leaped up. The light had blinded him, but he made out two approaching shapes, one stocky and broad-shouldered, the other small and slim. The stocky one carried a firearm.

"Stop where you are!" It was Brack's gravelly voice. The dwarf trudged to Rune and lifted him by the arm. His hair was pulled into a tangle on the back of his head, and he wore a tan long coat smudged with grease and smoke. "You all right?"

Rune's head swam. "What? How…?"

"Kettle told me you was in a fix," the dwarf said. "We'll talk about it later. Here." He shoved Rune's pistol into his hands. "Found it on the way."

Brack turned the crank on his musketoon, chambering a fresh round along with the correct measure of black powder. Avice stumbled toward them.

"Not so fast!" Kettle said. Flames sprung to life in both of his hands, and he braced himself as if to throw them at her. She stopped in place.

Rune's ears rang, and blazing white globs of light danced in his eyes. He struggled to piece things together. "That was a thunderstone!"

Brack grunted. "I missed her by an inch. She must have ducked. Sorry about that." He swung around, brought the musketoon to his shoulder, and trained it on Avice.

"We've got to go," Rune said. "That way."

"You sure?" Brack said.

"It's the only way out of this."

"What do you mean?"

"There's a lake in the middle of the cemetery. That's where I'm going."

Avice found her sword and lurched toward Kettle. His eyes flared, and the weapon started to glow. Avice threw it down with a curse and clutched her hand.

"If you say so," Brack said.

"Cover me," Rune said. "I think this would go faster if I…"

He trailed off as the sky erupted with the cries of a dozen or more birds. Above him, fluttering black wings blotted out the moon.

It was the werecrows from Saturday night, the ones who'd tried to steal Gimp Hollart's little girl. And it looked like they had brought friends.

"Fly," Rune finished, crestfallen.

Brack studied the sky, looked back at Kettle holding Avice at bay, and then sheepishly turned to Rune. "So maybe we just hoof it, then?"

"Good plan." Rune had lost his night vision with the flash of Brack's weapon, but at least the glowing sparks were subsiding. He *thought* he knew which way was west.

"Kettle, you want to give us a little cover?" the dwarf called.

"Radiant!" Kettle said with a gleeful expression. He flung his fireballs at Avice's feet, and she teetered away.

Kettle began to glow as his body folded in on itself, his limbs rearranging, sprouting clawed leathery wings of vibrant red and orange, vicious talons, and a feathered tail. His face morphed into something between a lizard and a predatory bird. He squawked and took flight, a trail of sparks in his wake.

"We ain't got much time," Brack said. The whiff of sulfur hung in the air.

"Follow me." Rune set off at a sprint, making for a patch of trees in the distance. The werecrows were on him almost at once, but Kettle wove among them, squawking like a murderous rooster and singeing their feathers as he passed. Brack fired once into the sky, and the werecrows scattered from his weapon's lightning bolt. One of them hit the ground as a charred, smoky lump.

Rune crossed a road and dove into the trees. Seconds later, Brack joined him, huffing and wheezing.

Right. Not everybody moves as fast as an air-weaver. Rune wondered if he should just leave the dwarf there and press on alone.

"Listen," he said. "No offense, but—" He coughed, and his belly reeled in an explosion of pain. Leaning against a tree, he pressed his hand to his side and felt the warm, squishy wetness of bloodied cloth and the tender flesh beneath.

"You don't look so good," Brack said as he reached into a pocket of his coat and pulled out a roll of bandages. He glanced around and then upward. The trees gave them cover, but the werecrows still circled above. "Undo your shirt."

Rune's shirt was already ripped open from when Avice had collected his blood for the ritual. He pulled out his shirttails to give Brack a clear view of his ruined bandages. The dwarf started cutting them away with a knife.

"No time," Rune said. "We can do it properly when we have a minute." But the bloody wrappings had already fallen loose.

"There's always time to do the job right," the dwarf grumbled. He tucked the knife in an inside pocket and rummaged until he found a tin of Thora's healing salve. He smeared it around Rune's stitches and started wrapping a fresh bandage around Rune's waist.

Somewhere above, a werecrow squawked in terror as the sky erupted in a fiery blast.

"How much farther?"

Rune winced as the dwarf pulled the cloth tight. "Half a mile, I think."

"Tree cover?"

He shook his head. "Only on the other end."

Brack looked over Rune's shoulder, scanning the terrain. "By the Seven," he grumbled as he jammed his hand back into yet another pocket. "Half a mile at let's say five miles an hour…"

"I can go ten, maybe faster."

Brack sized up the wounded, sweating elf from head to toe. "Five miles an hour, maybe less. So that works out to…" He produced a dull leaden box the size of a small book. It had a crank on its face and a plunger-like handle at the top. "Uh…" He gave the crank three turns, then threw a catch to hold it in place.

"Anyway, the point being: this thing only works for a few seconds, and I can't exactly rewind it on the run."

"Is that…?"

"An indifference engine. You heard of 'em?"

"Madam Samarra has one in her shop. She said you built it."

"This one, too." He nudged Rune onward. At the edge of the woods, they surveyed the naked, open space between them and the next cluster of trees.

The werecrows continued to circle overhead. Another insulted squawk rose above their angry calls, but this one sounded different. A glowing form fell to the earth a dozen yards away. Kettle landed roughly, his feathers smoking.

"You okay, old man?" Brack called. Kettle bobbed his beak as he stumbled under the cover of the trees.

The werecrows didn't seem to care about any of this. If Rune was right, their orders were to get him and him alone.

He turned to look at Brack and his little metal box. "Just a few seconds, then?"

"Maybe that'll be enough. Stay close to me till it runs down. After that…do what you gotta do."

"I can't thank you enough."

Brack grimaced and set his stance. "Three, two, one. Got it?"

They both gazed into the sky. The werecrows circled, but they hadn't found them yet. Then, in concert, the flock curved back, and for a fleeting instant the sky was clear.

"One!" Brack shouted as he slammed the heel of his hand against the handle on his device. Inside the mechanism, something tripped the catch and the crank started to rotate backward.

When moving under a veil of glamour, Rune was accustomed to the murky haze his magic cast over his senses. Like most effects of the airy chaos, it was subtle: a gauzy distortion on the edge of his peripheral vision, an almost imperceptible echo in his ear. With a moment's concentration, he could dismiss the sensation and use his fine elven senses to the fullest.

This was different. As soon as Brack activated his device, the cawing of Rune's flying pursuers was smothered to a dull hiss. All the colors of the cemetery, already washed out under the moonlight, vanished into a grainy vista of contrasting shades of gray.

"Let's go!" someone said as if from a hundred miles away. It was Brack, and he'd already taken a handful of steps out from the cover of the trees.

A second passed.

Rune sprinted forward. The werecrows reappeared but merely circled overhead as if they didn't have a care in the world. That was how an indifference engine worked. Anyone using it was simply of no interest or concern to any observers. Let the werecrows circle around the trees; Rune and Brack had ground to cover.

Another second passed. The indifference engine whined as if straining to soldier on. They had barely left the clearing, and their goal was still close to half a mile away.

Stars above! Rune kept running as he gathered the airy chaos to himself. He felt himself edging ahead of Brack and, with effort, managed to hold himself back.

Any time now.

Another second passed, and the whine of the indifference engine hiccupped to a halt. Suddenly the tableau regained its subtle colors, and the caws and shrieks of the werecrows assaulted Rune's ears as clear as a bell.

"Keep going," Brack huffed. "We might get…another sec…"

"Before they notice us," Rune finished. He grabbed the dwarf by the arm and hauled him along, though his own side burned from the strain.

They made it another twenty yards before the savage avian call went up and the werecrows dove toward them.

"Keep going!" Rune called to Brack. He spun about and lifted his arms, drawing to himself the full force of the chaos he had summoned. As he brought his hands together in front of him. The wind picked up.

Rune's arms trembled. It was like an isometric exercise, slow and controlled but bristling with power. He gritted his teeth and willed the airy chaos to take shape. The breeze became a dozen tendrils of magical force slithering into the minds of the werecrows, filling them with revulsion, making them wish they were anywhere but there.

They veered off left and right.

Rune allowed a sly grin to cross his face as the forces of creation surged through him, overtook him, giving form to his whims. He backed toward his goal, just a few hundred yards away. Brack was already halfway there.

Confusion and fear melted away. As the magic surged around him, he hid the pain from his wounds in some forgotten corner of his mind. It didn't matter. Not now.

Half the werecrows circled back to make another run. With the flick of his wrist, Rune bent his glamour in their direction. It might not harm them, but it could drive them off course.

With every passing second, he fell deeper into the Blessing. All his emotions began to slip away. Keeping the gathering storm of bird-creatures at a distance was just an intellectual exercise, a game of mental manipulation. When he got bored with it, he'd resume flight and take his chances.

"Rune!" Brack called as if from the bottom of a well.

He shook himself and sucked in a breath. He'd forgotten all about Brack. The dwarf had made it nearly to the woods but wouldn't go on until Rune caught up.

"Coming!" he called, now turning and sprinting toward the trees.

Brack raised his musketoon to his shoulder, pointed it at the sky, pulled the trigger…and nothing happened. The dwarf's eyes opened wide. "Silver and gold!" he yelled as he flung the weapon high into the air. "Of all the…"

The weapon exploded. Multiple rounds of thunderstone split the sky, and the last of the werecrows scattered. Rune bounded for the trees, now drawing in his chaos to propel him at unearthly speed.

He fell into Brack's arms at the edge of the wood. The dwarf spat a curse and dragged him under the cover of the branches.

"What was that all about?" Rune asked, his breath ragged.

"Blasted thing jammed on me. I might have known Frieda would go out fighting." He huffed and wheezed. "But by the Seven, what were you trying to do out there?"

Rune stumbled and decided it was easier to go all the way down than to try to stop his fall. He clutched his side. The run had pulled out at least one of Thora's stitches and maybe more.

He was winded.

The thought tickled him. When was the last time he of all people couldn't catch his breath? He must have thrown more into that glamour than he realized.

But he didn't have time, or the inclination, to worry about it now.

The first time he'd pushed his magic that hard was under Whisper's instruction when he was young. "Take stock of how you're feeling, Claeus," his uncle had said. "It's like you're watching yourself from the outside, right? Like you're eavesdropping on somebody else's life. That person can do whatever he wants, and it won't affect you in the least. You're just along for the ride."

Young Claeus—he hadn't yet taken the name Rune—could only nod stupidly.

"In this line of work, you need that kind of detachment," Whisper continued. "So learn to embrace it. Find strength in it. But be careful." He wagged a pale, slender finger at his nephew. "When the Blessing comes, you're not far from the brink. You lose yourself for good and…" He shrugged.

Rune was barely a youngling then. Years ago. Or decades, depending on how you counted. As he lay beneath a tree with Brack gently patting his cheeks, trying to get him to focus, he struggled to understand what his uncle had said. Why it mattered.

"We gotta move!" Brack hissed. When the dwarf was angry or upset, something in his voice sounded like metal scraping metal. Rune had never noticed that before.

"The werecrows—"

"Gone. For now." It sounded like there should be a *but* at the end of the sentence that Brack didn't voice.

"But?" Rune supplied.

"But I don't think we're alone," the dwarf whispered.

38

"There's always somebody making things harder than they need to be." The tiny Tinker Bell woman named Saffron stalked up to Zoey. She had a homicidal gleam in her eyes as she grabbed her by the arm.

"Let go!" Zoey said.

Jericho charged forward, fists clenched.

Saffron pulled Zoey closer and put a knife against her throat. Jericho skidded to a halt.

"Don't even try, sorcerer." She looked toward her goateed partner. "Zodiac?"

He finished his incantation. Still kneeling beside a sleeping Cassie, he said, "Done. They won't remember a thing."

"Good job," Saffron said.

Zodiac rose to his feet. "Once Dancer takes Rune, we're ready to go."

Zoey didn't dare struggle. Saffron's knife was cold and sharp.

The wind picked up. Saffron and Zodiac both looked to the skies. "I'm thinking that's going to take a bit longer than we'd like," Zodiac said.

Avice landed gracefully in the center of the conjuring circle. "Sard!" She glanced at Jericho, who flinched at the sight of her.

"You lost him?" Saffron said.

Avice stomped toward them. "The menseless, wind-wracked canker had help!"

"Tempest!" Zodiac spat. "What kind of help?"

"A dwarf and a firedrake." She gazed into the distant sky, where a black swarm of large birds circled about. "Zodiac, am I correct that His Majesty won't be joining us?"

She and Zodiac studied Jericho. He had pulled off his ceremonial robe, exposing a bloodied shirt beneath. "The connection was severed before we got here," he said. "The girl…"

"The girl has become a liability." Avice reached out her arms. Saffron shoved Zoey toward her, and Avice grabbed her, wrapping her arm around Zoey's and locking her hands behind her neck. She turned to Zodiac, yanking Zoey off balance. "You might as well work on the sorcerer's memory as well."

"As you say."

Zodiac took a step toward Jericho. "This won't hurt a bit," he said, then chuckled. "Who am I kidding? This is going to wreck you, you sarding plague sore, and it serves you right!" His cloak whipped and thrashed around him.

Jericho bowled into him with a desperate howl, but Zodiac threw up his hands to fend off the sorcerer's blows. Shifting his weight, he sidestepped the attack and sent Jericho to the ground.

"Get away from those kids," Jericho whispered.

"Make me," Zodiac said, circling about as the sorcerer regained his footing.

Jericho advanced again, more tentatively this time. Zoey's heart pounded.

"Boo!" Zodiac taunted. His eyes flashed with sinister anticipation.

The sorcerer spun into a roundhouse kick that sent Zodiac tumbling to the ground. He tucked into a roll and came up in half a second, barreling back toward Jericho.

He feinted, drawing Jericho in close enough that he could wrap his arm around him and apply pressure to his wounded shoulder.

Jericho cried out.

Zodiac's mouth opened in a gleeful smile. Standing behind Jericho, with both his arms locked around him, he pressed his hands against the sides of the sorcerer's head.

Jericho moaned even louder as his eyes rolled back into his head. He began to weep, and then he began to sob, gulping for every breath. Sweat poured off his forehead.

Zodiac's grin broke into a cackle of delight and finally an exultant whoop until he let go at last. Jericho crumpled like a dead man, and Zodiac stood over him, breathing heavy and laughing with satisfaction.

"That…was…awesome!"

Avice seemed impatient. "All I needed was for you to take his memories."

"Getting on it right now, Dancer, and…oh, stars above! It's been a lifetime since I let loose like that! Give me another one!" He turned his eyes on Zoey.

"Not yet," Avice said. She held up a hand to end the conversation as she closed her eyes. She mumbled something, or at least her mouth was moving.

"The werecrows tell me we have eyes on the traitor," she said. "That way, near the pond in the middle of the cemetery. Saffron?"

"Yes, Dancer."

"Follow the werecrows," she said. "They'll lead you to him. The rest of the team needs backup."

"We'll get him," Saffron said.

"Find him," Avice said, "but don't kill him. I claim that privilege for myself."

"Yes, Dancer." Saffron took three bounding leaps. The wind kicked up a flurry of dead leaves, and on the fourth leap she left the earth entirely and took flight.

Zoey's mind reeled.

Avice tightened her hold. "I should have known you'd cause trouble."

"You don't know the half of it," Zoey hissed.

"Such bravado for one so…helpless," Avice said.

"Let go of me! I'll show you helpless, you…hufter!"

Avice chuckled. "Claeus has been a bad influence on you. Maybe I'll take you home with me. You could be entertaining."

Zodiac chuckled. "I saw her first."

Zoey screamed and struggled, but Avice was too strong.

"Now settle down. Maybe you can still be of some use to me."

"No!"

"I can't seem to get through to Rune any other way. He just won't cooperate."

Zoey kept fighting, kept screaming.

"Maybe he needs you to convince him. To help him see reason."

"And maybe you can kiss my ass!"

"Now, now," Avice said. "Play nice and I'll let you live. Play your cards right, and I'll take you to a place where you can live a long, *long* life."

Zoey craned her neck to look for Jericho. He was still crumpled on the ground, with Zodiac exulting over him. He'd pulled out his bowl to work his memory spell again.

"The sorcerer is no longer of interest, unfortunately," Avice said. "I suppose you'll have to answer for that at some point. But first, it's time you and Claeus were reunited."

Zoey grunted and tried again to pull away. It didn't work any better than the last time.

"Come on. You'll want to see what happens next." Avice pulled Zoey around and pushed her forward. "You've got a front-row seat."

39

The dwarf yanked Rune up with one arm and held him steady until he got his footing. The pain in his side welled up. He wasn't going down just yet. If he was still hurting, he was still fighting.

"Which way now?" Brack asked.

Rune gestured, and the two stumbled forward together. He focused his senses and felt the gentle night breeze against his cheek, heard the rustle of the leaves, watched as subtle shadows danced in the occluded moonlight.

Brack was right. They weren't alone. Rune knew it in an instant, and if it weren't for the Blessing his heart would have fallen into his stomach.

The air was rich with the scent of dry leaves and gathering dew, but underneath, imperceptible if not for his magically enhanced senses, was the smoky whiff of umbersay.

He put a finger to his lips and held out his hand to stop Brack. With his night vision restored, he looked about, quickly but carefully, unwilling to miss the slightest detail.

Nightwalkers were on the move, and more than just Avice. The King of Shadows didn't believe in half measures. Avice would have demanded the right to take Rune in, but there would be a backup plan. There was always a backup plan.

Someone had been watching, studying the werecrows' movements, probably spying on them from some hidden copse or hillock.

They'd run straight into a trap.

The path was narrow, at least. That was good. Rune maneuvered Brack so he was standing with his back to a tree trunk. Rune took his own position opposite him. He slid his pistol out of its holster.

Brack reached into his long coat and pulled out another firearm, a pistol with a bell-shaped barrel like a blunderbuss. He raised it but, like Rune, had no idea which way to point it.

People were approaching from both directions, silently but not quite silently enough. Sometimes Nightwalkers let their quarry know they were there just to make them sweat.

It was time to get this over with.

"I don't have all night!" Rune called.

"You don't have another minute," a woman called back. To his right, back the way they'd come, a shadow slid across the path and resolved itself into a brooding, cloaked form. A tiny woman with an almost childlike face pushed the hood back on her umbersay cloak as she strode forward.

"Rune."

"Saffron."

"You two know each other?" Brack said.

"A friend from work."

"Not anymore." Saffron leveled her pistol on Rune and smiled. "Do you know how many quigs the King of Shadows is offering for your head?"

"You never struck me as the mercenary type." Rune faced Brack the whole time, looking toward Saffron but keeping his pistol pointed skyward and ready to shift to the left when the other Nightwalker decided to reveal himself. When he knew who it was, he'd know which of them was the greater threat.

"I suppose he's offering enough to share." He raised his voice. "Isn't that right?"

He glanced to the left. Another smoky figure stepped into view. Tall and dark. Even under his cloak, Rune could tell he was well-muscled.

He recognized this second Nightwalker immediately from his silhouette and the way he swayed when he walked. Rune hissed an exasperated breath and turned three-quarters of the way toward the newcomer.

The second Nightwalker pulled off his hood, loosing a shock of black hair and revealing arched eyebrows above a squared jaw.

This would not go well.

"Good evening, Rune." The newcomer took a step forward. The barrel of his pistol gave a fleeting reflection of the moon above.

Rune expelled a breath. "Good evening, Goodfellow."

The big elf took another step forward. Rune pivoted toward him. As he did, he caught Brack's eye, arched an eyebrow, and nodded subtly toward the woman.

Brack nodded and turned his body toward her, his pistol ready.

Rune took a step toward Goodfellow.

"Stay where you are." To both Rune and Brack, he said, "Put down your weapons."

Rune stopped. "We're not going to do that." He lowered his pistol but kept his finger on the trigger. Goodfellow returned the courtesy.

"You betrayed us!" Goodfellow blurted.

Saffron gritted her teeth and took half a step forward before Brack waved her back with his weapon. Her eyes smoldered, but he stood his ground.

"You were Whisper's favorite," Goodfellow said as he took another step toward Rune. "You just…threw it all away. And the errand! The errand failed—because of you!"

"You've got to understand," Rune said.

"There's nothing here we don't understand," Saffron spat. "You squatted on every one of us, even Goodfellow. Especially Goodfellow!"

"Mind your manners, you canker!" Brack growled.

Saffron drew back the hammer of her pistol. They glared at each other down the barrels of their weapons. A tense second passed.

"Just give me half a reason," she said.

"Not yet, Saffron," Goodfellow said.

"He rotting deserves it."

"I want answers first."

"Listen," Rune said. He didn't know what he was going to say next, but if Goodfellow was willing to talk, that at least was an opening he didn't have before.

He glanced at Brack, who kept Saffron in his sights while rocking from one foot to the other. The dwarf was nervous, though he'd never admit it. Rune hoped he wasn't also trigger-happy.

"We got out of Cruc Máw alive," Goodfellow said. "As if you care. We lost some of the shapeshifters in the tunnels. And Dollick the troll, remember him? He didn't make it either."

"I never meant to hurt anyone."

Goodfellow scoffed. "Is that why you shot Dancer?"

There was no denying that shooting Avice had felt good. There was only so much abuse a person could take. Elves were famously touchy about insults of any kind. Rune had lost count of how many of his cousin's jabs he'd bottled up over the years. Say what she might about his human ancestry, it was the only reason she was still alive.

"You know what the King of Shadows is like—"

"I know that I swore an oath!"

The werecrows were regathering, calling to one another in the darkness. The shiver of leaves and the rustle of branches told Rune that at least some of them had lit in the branches overhead.

"And if he gets the coffer?" Rune said.

"Let him have it!" Goodfellow's face flushed.

"What's he going to do with it?"

"That's not up to me. I'm not an oathbreaker."

"Tell him, Goodfellow!" Saffron said.

Brack pulled back the hammer on his pistol. "Stay out of this!"

"It's all right, Brack." Rune took a breath and turned back to Goodfellow. "No" he said, "you're not an oathbreaker." He took a tentative step forward. The big elf eyed him warily but didn't wave him back. Rune spoke slowly, deliberately. "You're anything but. And you are a good man—that's never just been your byname, as far as I'm concerned. It's what you always were. That's what I'm counting on now."

Goodfellow's face was a passionless mask.

"I'm serious," Rune said. "I remember how you stood up for me back at the Haw."

"Lot of good it did me."

Rune dared to draw the airy chaos, but subtly. If Goodfellow or Saffron sensed it, let them think he was sharpening his wits, preparing for their attack. They wouldn't be far wrong.

He pressed on. "All the name-calling. By Dancer especially, but the others, too. Auph. Half-breed. Son of an outswiver. You know what I mean. You defended me when it would have been easier to keep your head down." He forced a chuckle. "Remember the time you took on Breeze after he sprinkled fox piss on my lunch?"

"Kind of ended it between us," Goodfellow said. "He didn't understand why…"

"You did what was right," Rune said. "What else is there to understand?" Goodfellow's face still betrayed no emotion.

Was the situation settling down, or was it just Rune's imagination?

"You were my friend," Rune said.

Goodfellow sighed. His face showed hurt, but only for an instant, and then the mask was firmly back in place. "This is what you do to your friends?"

Rune winced. He was on thin ice. If he let Goodfellow go much further down this road, the situation might turn hot again.

"I'm sorry if… I hated hurting you," Rune offered. "At Cruc Máw. Or before that. And I know that I did." The chaos surging through him helped him keep his voice steady.

"I stood up for you," Goodfellow agreed.

"You did. And it cost you. And not just Breeze."

Goodfellow shrugged. He blinked tears out of his eyes. Rune couldn't imagine what it had cost the big elf to be his friend. "Let it flow downstream," Goodfellow finally said.

They stared at each other in awkward silence. "Except…?"

"Except here you are: a fugitive. An oathbreaker. And I'm supposed to bring you to Dancer as if…as if we were never friends. As if I never took your side. As if I never risked my own good name for you because you were different."

"That was a long time ago," Rune said. "And the fact remains that you are a good man. You're"—his voice caught—"you're still my closest friend."

Goodfellow scowled. "And what do I have to show for it?"

"Far less than you deserve. I'm sorry."

"You're sorry?" Goodfellow took a step forward. Rune stepped back and pivoted his body away from Brack, his pistol still trained on the elf he had once loved like a brother. "You're *sorry*?"

"Enough talk!" Saffron said. "You're coming with us. Dancer is expecting you."

Rune and Brack were side by side, each aiming a weapon at one of the Nightwalkers. The airy chaos sharpened Rune's senses, revealing the distance between him and Saffron and Goodfellow, the openings in the woods behind them, the positions of the werecrows in the trees overhead. He would have to see the opportunity when it came and move like lightning to seize it.

But he was ready.

"Do whatever you have to do. I'm not giving up the coffer."

Saffron shrugged. "Then you're of no use to His Majesty alive."

Brack couldn't decide which way to aim. The pink-haired woman to his left was tiny, but that meant nothing if she was strong in magic—and he had to believe she was.

The man to his right was bigger than any elf he'd ever seen. Muscular, square-jawed, with just a hint of animal ferocity in his eyes.

These were Rune's people. At least, they'd been his people once. Nightwalkers. Killers through and through.

He whispered a curse.

This is it, Brack thought. He had a clear shot at Saffron, but he needed to get Goodfellow closer. But Rune was in his line of sight, which meant they were going to have to improvise.

"Ahem," he grumbled under his breath. Rune cast him a sidewise look. Brack furrowed his brow in a way that he hoped conveyed he was ready for action.

Rune arched an elvish eyebrow, and Brack didn't like the sight. Something about Rune's expression was distant, impassive. But there was something else: excitement. The thrill of danger.

The dwarf gritted his teeth. Air-weavers took unnecessary chances when they pulled too much of their elemental chaos. He dreaded what might happen next.

"Your life is forfeit," Saffron continued. "Unfortunately for me, Dancer has given word that she alone has the right to take it from you."

"We mustn't disappoint Dancer," Rune said. His voice shook as if holding back laughter.

By the Seven, he's almost giddy! Brack thought.

Saffron pretended not to hear. "Lay down your weapons. Now."

Rune's hand was against Brack's chest in an instant, shoving him back into the trees. He wasn't expecting that! At least he kept from firing his weapon. A rush of wind raced over his bearded face. The report of pistols rang in his ears.

The dwarf gasped and struggled to maintain his balance as he scrambled back to the path. Only a couple of seconds had passed, but Rune was gone. The acrid stench of black powder tickled his nose.

Saffron and Goodfellow had managed to miss each other. Now they had converged in front of him, exactly where he and Rune had stood before. They looked up into the trees. The wind swirled.

There was no time left. Brack leveled his pistol and pulled the trigger.

The projectile left the barrel not with a bang but with a tremendous *thump*! It wasn't properly shot at all, but a dozen tiny clockworks, each no bigger than a pea. As each one hit one of the Nightwalkers, it unfolded eight tiny bronze legs and skittered across their body.

"Aah!" Goodfellow gasped, slapping at the clockwork spiders that had landed on his arm. They held firm and began to crawl over him.

Each one spun out a dainty gossamer thread, fine as a baby's hair. Saffron tried to shake Brack's creations off her, bumping into Goodfellow in the process. Soon the two were wrapped together in an ever-expanding web.

Brack grinned.

Saffron tried to snap the thread but cut her fingers on it instead. Grabbing it was like grabbing a cheese slicer.

"I'd be still if I were you," Brack said as he stepped back into full view. "That thread's pretty much unbreakable."

Goodfellow glared at him and flexed his muscles. The thread sliced into his cloak and the shirt underneath.

The Nightwalkers toppled over and lay on the ground, thoroughly wrapped up. They called the dwarf some unpleasant names, but he only shrugged and grinned.

"Come on!" Rune called from above. Brack looked up and saw him dropping to the ground. He landed a few yards ahead on the path with a werecrow in its half-avian form pecking at the sleeve of his leather jacket. He jammed his pistol into its sternum and fired. The werecrow shrieked and fell flopping to the ground.

"You could have given a guy some warning!" Brack griped.

"No time." Rune grunted and wobbled a bit, but he kept his footing. "Follow me!" He bolted into the next clearing. The lake was a quick sprint ahead of them, along with whatever it was Rune was so worked up about.

The next clearing was smaller than the last one, but the werecrows were already waiting in the trees. Now that they weren't sprinting across a clearing or facing down angry Nightwalkers, Brack took a few seconds to crank up his indifference engine, and it bought them just enough time to reach the next patch of trees.

With every exertion of magic, Rune fell deeper under the power of the Blessing. His emotions slipped into the background. The twinge of guilt that had overcome him while talking to Goodfellow was gone. Everything in him was subservient to the task at hand: to get to the lake alive.

At the end of their dash, they reached the wall of the cemetery's stately administration building. Brack doubled over with his hands on his knees. Rune leaned against the tan stone wall and grasped his thigh.

"How's the leg?" Brack asked as he shoved his indifference engine back in one of his many pockets.

"A little stiff. Are you all right?"

Brack puffed and nodded. "How much further?"

"Not far. Around this building and it's a straight shot to the lake."

The dwarf stretched his arms. "What's so all-fired important about this lake?"

"It's where this ends." Rune forced himself to move again, edging rightward against the wall.

Brack wheezed and followed a second later. "What's that supposed to mean?"

"I don't have time to explain. There are things you might not—" He stopped mid-thought. A twig snapped just a few yards away. He held out a hand. "Shh."

"What are you—?"

"Someone's out there." Rune scanned the moon-bathed tree line as he reloaded his pistol. He'd trained himself to do it blind, instinctively: load the paper cartridge, ram it tight, replace the ramrod in its ring along the barrel. Beside him, Brack was doing the same thing with his own weapon.

Rune kept still as his eyes darted back and forth. He drew in more of the airy chaos. He made a clicking sound with his tongue and listened for how the sound echoed around him.

Brack fumbled with his blunderbuss pistol. He obviously wasn't used to reloading under pressure. Rune bit back a caustic comment.

The wind picked up. Rune took a step back and leveled his pistol at the incoming Nightwalker as he fell from the sky in front of them, bronze daggers in both hands. He fired high as the Nightwalker landed in a crouch and charged forward.

"Silver and—" Brack stuttered, fumbling with his weapon.

Rune twisted his body away from the Nightwalker's daggers. He grabbed his opponent's arm and flipped him to the ground. But the Nightwalker's cloak grappled Rune's arm and yanked him to the ground.

The Nightwalker was on his feet again in a heartbeat. His cowl fell back, revealing a gaunt, swarthy face. He stepped back and pointed one dagger each at Rune and Brack.

"Sparrow," Rune said as he regained his feet.

"Rune. Been a while."

"We'll have to catch up later." Rune sheathed his empty pistol and drew his fighting stick.

Sparrow lunged toward him without warning, but Brack was closer. He made a grab for Sparrow's arm, and the Nightwalker rounded on him, slashing downward across his face.

The dwarf staggered backward with an anguished groan.

40

Rune rounded on Sparrow. He came in under his defenses and clubbed him in the ribs. Sparrow hissed and fell to his knees. Rune kicked him away and darted to Brack.

Blood poured from a slash that started in the middle of Brack's forehead, cut across his heavy brow, and ended above the corner of his left eye. Rune dispassionately noted the blood, the expression of pain and disorientation. Manageable.

He rummaged through Brack's pockets, looking for a medical kit. He had just found it when he sensed movement to his right. Sparrow was once again on his feet and diving toward him.

Rune swept Sparrow's legs with his fighting stick. He was on the Nightwalker as soon as he hit the ground, with his hand against Sparrow's nose and mouth. The airy chaos churned around them both as they struggled for dominance.

Rune tapped into the depths of his power and channeled it into a sphere around Sparrow's face, willing the breath to leave his opponent's body. The Nightwalker struggled for a few seconds, eyes bulging, before he passed out.

He kept pushing until Sparrow's face turned pale. A few minutes, and his opponent would be good and dead, but that would take too long.

And Brack might be dying. He'd almost forgotten.

Rune scrambled back to the dwarf. By now, Brack had managed to sit up with his back against the wall. Rune dabbed a finger's worth of healing salve on the dwarf's forehead. "He won't be out long," he said impatiently. "Can you move?"

Brack grunted. His eyes were vacant.

"Listen to me." Rune bandaged the wound and tied it off with an ugly knot. There was no time for anything else. "We have to get to the lake. Remember?"

The dwarf groaned.

"Come on." Rune hauled Brack to his feet. "We're almost there."

He scanned the area. It was all a mathematical problem. Dancer. Goodfellow. Saffron. Now Sparrow. The whole team from Cruc Máw. Only Zodiac was missing, but he was bound to be around somewhere.

A few yards away, Sparrow began to stir.

"Now, Brack!" Rune shoved the dwarf forward, and none too gently.

They rounded the building and turned right. A tree-decked lawn sloped downward to the left until it met the lake, gleaming with reflected moonlight. A light breeze made it look like something rippled beneath the surface.

To the right was a cave entrance, twice as tall as a man and wide enough for three or four people to walk comfortably side by side. The opening tapered to a narrow point at the top and was decked with clinging vines. A shallow stream snaked from the cave to the lake.

Rune stalked toward to the stream with Brack in tow.

He stilled himself, listening for the slightest sound, scanning for the most fleeting shadowy movement.

It wasn't long in coming.

"You still have something I want, auph. But now I have something that you want."

He spun around. Avice stood at the edge of the trees—with Zoey in her grip.

He watched them approach as if from outside his own body. He was an observer here, watching as the drama played out.

"R-rune?" Zoey whimpered.

Rune took it all in without comment.

"You can't win," Avice said. She raised her voice and said, "Zodiac, explain to Claeus why he can't win."

There was a shimmer of movement in Rune's peripheral vision. He pivoted as Zodiac dropped his glamour and appeared at the edge of the lake. "Because Dancer's got the girl," Zodiac said, brandishing his fighting stick. A malevolent grin split his bearded face. "If you don't play nice, maybe later the girl gets me."

There was more movement, this time from the administration building. Two shapes: one big and burly, the other petite. They had doffed their umbersay cloaks, no doubt sliced to ribbons by Brack's clockwork spiderwebs. Razor-thin streaks of red crisscrossed their hands and faces, and similar slashes tore into their clothes.

"And because I saw what you did to Goodfellow and Saffron," Zodiac continued. "It wasn't too hard to undo it, to be honest. Just took a little patience."

Brack fell to his knees with a moan.

"You're running out of sidekicks," Avice said. "And I've still got a full team."

Sparrow stumbled onto the lawn with his hand to his temple. He'd have a headache from oxygen deprivation, but he still managed to make it to the party. Even the werecrows had regathered in the trees and on the spire of the administration building—at least those that hadn't been electrocuted, blown away, or scorched by Kettle's trail of fire.

Rune bit his lip. If it was going to happen, it had to be now.

Avice stepped forward, dragging Zoey behind her.

"Let go of me!" Zoey stomped and fought, but it was hopeless.

Rune hadn't counted on Zoey as a variable. Things would have to move fast. He stifled a grin. He liked it when things moved fast.

"Isn't it about time we ended this stupid game?" Avice said.

More movement, this time at the entrance to the cave, was answered by more rippling in the water of the lake. Out of the shadows stepped a man, over seven feet tall and nearly as wide, dressed in drab colors but for a smart, royal blue vest. Water sloshed as he waded toward them in the stream.

"I couldn't agree more," he said.

Vex, Maya Tecumseh's right-hand man, strode forward with the kind of brash swagger that only a troll could pull off. He took his time, but he moved with barely restrained power. The air was suddenly colder as his command of the watery chaos permeated the little patch of woods. Vex held all the winning cards and he knew it.

Avice mouthed something, a brief telepathic command. Her Nightwalkers shifted positions, bracing for action. Her eyes bored into Rune as she braced her hands against the sides of Zoey's head. "Think carefully about your next move, Claeus."

Rune weighed his options, which quickly shrank to only one. There was no way to get to Zoey before Avice snapped her neck. Any one of the other Nightwalkers could shoot him from this range.

The calculation was almost too easy.

Rune turned and headed toward Vex.

Sparrow trained his pistol on him and fired. Rune didn't flinch, and the shot whistled behind his back.

The lake churned white as a huge, coppery shape darted out. It was Mr. Whiskers, the Merlady's water panther. It landed on Zodiac and chomped onto his abdomen. He didn't have time to shriek. In a second, both the beast and its prey had disappeared under the water.

"Zodiac!" Goodfellow cried. He took a step toward the lake, but Saffron held him back.

Just that quickly he was gone. Rune didn't feel inclined to mourn.

Avice moved behind him.

Vex locked eyes on her. "Not so fast, missy."

Rune glanced to see the pure terror in her eyes. An air-weaver could manipulate a person's mind with their magic; water-weavers could touch the emotions—the nightmares, the dark and forgotten corners of the psyche. An accomplished water-weaver, at least a vicious one, could unleash unimaginable horrors. Rune didn't want to guess what could frighten Avice so badly.

She let go of Zoey and crumpled to her knees. She glowered at the troll as she sucked in great gulps of air.

Zoey shrieked and scrambled away.

Vex stepped out of the stream and onto the grass. He raised his voice. "Now if the rest of you will kindly settle down."

Saffron and Goodfellow stood speechless, their eyes on the spot where Zodiac had vanished under the lake.

Sparrow kept his focus on Vex. The troll's magic had left him stunned. His pistol fell to the ground at his feet.

Brack sat up, rubbing his bandaged forehead.

The werecrows squawked from their various perches.

A jet of blazing light plunged from the sky, and Kettle landed next to Brack. He listed to one side. His wings and back were streaked with beak and talon marks. He shook embers from his feathers and took on his two-legged form. Though his clothing remained pristine, he had a nasty scratch on his left hand from his battle with the werecrows. He looked very much like an injured little boy.

"Brack! What happened?" Kettle said.

"Quiet!" Vex snarled. "The Caretaker and I have business."

Avice groaned. "What do you mean, 'Caretaker'?"

"Did I stutter? I said quiet!" His eyes flashed, and Avice flinched. She steeled herself and rose slowly to her feet. Rune watched as Zoey took a few steps away from her would-be captor. She headed toward the lake but then, seeing movement in the water, she circled around behind Avice instead.

"Zoey, this is Brack and Kettle," Rune told her. He faced Vex. "These three are leaving now."

Vex smirked. "Not till everything's official. They can be witnesses."

"Witnesses?" Goodfellow said. "What…?"

"Does *nobody* understand what 'quiet' means?" The thunder in his voice sent a wave of dread across the clearing, bringing everybody to a halt.

"A pact is invalid unless it's witnessed by…well…witnesses," Vex continued. Rune's pulse began to race as Vex strolled back toward him. "And it goes without saying that you can't complete the formalities through a telepathic vision. It can only be done in person."

The troll extended his right hand toward Rune.

Rune looked at the hand, then up into Vex's eyes.

"No," Brack mumbled from where he sat. Rune didn't look down, didn't look back. This was the only way out.

"You can't give her the coffer," the dwarf said. There was a little more strength in his voice, but only a little.

"The coffer!" Avice hissed. "You wouldn't dare…"

Rune glared at his cousin and fought back the urge to curse. He stuck out his hand and grabbed Vex by the wrist. The troll wrapped his much larger hand around Rune's wrist. A pulse of power surged across Rune's body, cold and dark and deep as the ocean.

"Sard!" Avice cursed.

The air grew deathly still.

Then the pulse erupted from Vex and Rune and bathed the whole area. Rune's body felt light but wobbly, as if he were walking in chest-deep water. Out of the corner of his eye, he saw Goodfellow lowering himself to kneel. Saffron followed suit. Rune guessed that the others were doing the same, but he didn't look around. He couldn't. His eyes were locked on Vex's.

That's when the shadows began to shift. It was subtle at first, hardly noticeable. Then a pair of baleful eyes peered out from the trees, and a man stepped forward—a soldier in a dress uniform decades out of style. He was joined by a woman with bobbed, curly hair.

It seemed the dead had also arrived to bear witness. Vex grinned, both surprised and pleased that they had deigned to join him.

Wherever they stood, the Nightwalkers stepped back, unsure where to train their weapons.

Zoey fell to her knees and shielded her eyes.

More of them appeared, wrapped in mist and mostly transparent outside a sphere encircling their heads and chests. A goateed man in glasses, a suit of pure white, and a narrow string tie. A boxer in a white satin robe. More military men, some in blue and some in gray. A robed, bald academic with a hawkish nose and a disapproving scowl.

They said nothing, but they formed a ring around the clearing and gazed at Rune and Vex as they conducted their business.

Vex cleared his throat. "I am the voice of Maya Tecumseh, she who is called the Merlady." His voice rumbled like a fast-approaching storm. "Let it be known that the Merlady recognizes Claeus, he who is called Rune, as the rightful Caretaker of the coffer of Corcc the Peacebringer, and pledges to defend that right against the King of Shadows or any other sarding Gentryman who would dare to challenge it."

"W-what?" Brack said. Behind his back, Rune heard a scuffle, Kettle trying to keep his boss steady.

"Sard!" Avice cursed again.

The dead said nothing, but the sound of inarticulate keening echoed amid the trees.

Vex smiled and nodded to Rune. His turn.

He took a breath and held it for a count of three.

It was over. Avice couldn't touch him now, not without inviting the wrath of the Merlady herself and likely starting a war. Not even Avice had stones like that.

He let out his breath. There was no turning back now. The Blessing nudged him on. There was nothing to fear. There was only the thrill of defying certain death.

"I am Claeus, he who is called Rune," he said, his eyes trained on Vex. "And I speak for myself."

"Rune, what—?" Goodfellow began.

Rune cut him off. "Let it be known that I hereby claim the title as the rightful Caretaker of the Peacebringer's coffer, and that I thank the Merlady for her endorsement of my claim. Let it be further known that, in exchange for her endorsement, I pledge to render her bounden service as per the agreement recently struck between us."

"You can't mean that!" Brack snarled.

Rune kept talking. "We agree that I shall remain fully, truly, and perpetually independent." He gritted his teeth and frowned at Vex before he continued.

"We further agree that I shall undertake such errands as the Merlady deems appropriate no more than twice per year, once on or after Hallowfest and once again on or after Brightfest, for as long as I remain the coffer's Caretaker."

"No," Brack moaned.

"Rune?" Zoey said.

Vex squeezed Rune's wrist so hard his hand went numb. The pulse of magic surged back through Rune's body, up his arm, and into Vex. The troll grinned.

The dead vanished without fanfare.

"Welcome to the team, Caretaker. You'll find the Merlady is a joy to work with."

"We're not on the same team," Rune said. "Or did you miss the part about my independence?"

The troll scoffed. "Semantics." He raised his voice to address Avice and the other Nightwalkers. "All right, everybody, the show's over. Thank you all for such a great turnout."

Avice took a step forward, her hand on her sword hilt. "You bald-assed son of a ditch-whore!"

Vex chuckled. "Language, Miss Dancer. Language."

"I wasn't talking to you."

Rune turned to find Brack still on the ground just a few feet away with Kettle re-dressing his wound. Zoey stood at a distance, as if she were frozen in place.

Avice stormed forward. Her sword was drawn, but she kept her eyes on Vex. The air was deathly still.

"There's nothing for you to do here, Dancer," Rune said. "Just go home."

"No," she spat. "You've done enough."

"Listen to your cousin, Dancer," Vex said.

Avice scowled. She breathed out another telepathic command, and Goodfellow, Saffron, and Sparrow retreated into the shadows.

"I'll be seeing you, *cousin*." She whipped her cloak around her and vanished in a puff of smoke.

"Well, I'm out of here," Vex said. "Nice doing business with you, kid. We'll talk."

"Not for six months," Rune said. "I'm calling this business with Jericho my first errand for the Merlady. I don't want to see you again until Brightfest."

Vex chuckled. "That's fair." He clapped his hands. "Come on, Mr. Whiskers!"

The lake rippled again. The water panther emerged and gave a tremendous yawn. It waded up the stream toward the cave entrance.

"Is your tummy full? Are you ready to go inside? That's a good kitty." The troll ruffled the enormous beast's shoulders, and the two waded into the cave and out of sight.

Zoey launched herself toward Rune and landed with her arms wrapped around him, sobbing. Rune tentatively hugged her back. Her body was warm with sweat and exertion.

"You're safe," he said.

"Oh, Rune!" She squeezed even tighter.

"Ribs," Rune said. "Ribs!"

She eased off but kept her hands on his waist. Her whole body shook. "I didn't know what to do. Caitlin called. I had to go. I had to…"

"It's all right."

"My parents are going to freak out!"

"Yes," Rune said. "We'll probably need to have a conversation."

Brack stirred, and Rune looked down at Kettle. "How is he doing?"

"Just kill me now," the dwarf said.

"With that thick dwarven skull?" Rune said. "You'll be up and about—"

"No." Brack wouldn't look at him. He kept his beady black eyes on the lake. "You made a deal with the Merlady."

Rune gently pulled Zoey's arms away. "I had to, Brack. It was the only way."

The dwarf wouldn't meet his eyes.

Kettle did look up at Rune, his expression half fear and half bewilderment.

Rune reached out a hand to Brack, but the dwarf flinched away.

"All I could do was buy some time. Six months. Six months to destroy the coffer, then all this goes away."

Everyone rested in the uneasy silence.

"Come on, Brack," Kettle said. "Let's go home." He helped his boss to his feet and led him toward the cave entrance. A flitting wanderlight showed the way.

Zoey fell back into Rune's arms. She couldn't stop shaking.

"You should go home, too," Rune said.

"My car's parked…around here somewhere."

"Good."

Rune nudged her gently and took a step forward. His whole body was stiff. The Blessing must have kept him from noticing, but he hadn't used any of his own magic for a while. The fog of disinterest was beginning to fade, replaced by restlessness.

"Your friend, the beardy guy," Zoey started.

"Brack."

"Brack. He was acting like…like maybe whatever just happened could mean trouble."

"Maybe. We'll see."

"But the world isn't ending?"

"Not tonight."

Zoey sighed. "Call it a win, then." He held tightly to Rune's arm as they walked side by side. The warmth of her presence comforted him somehow.

"I can drive us home," she said. "Or to a hospital."

"Are you hurt?"

She pulled away. "No, you are, you big goof! Let's go."

"I'm not sure that's wise. Fallow doctors are bound to ask questions."

"So fight me. Come on." She pulled Rune forward. With his arm wrapped in hers, they started south toward the clearing where the night's adventure began.

"I'm taking you to the hospital. End of story."

Rune's head buzzed. He didn't feel like putting up a fight.

41

The emergency room visit went better than Rune had hoped. A little bit of glamour convinced the doctor that Rune had merely suffered a freak lawnmower accident and that all he needed was a prescription for pain pills and some antibiotics.

The meeting with the Colemans took a little more finesse. Unlike the ER doctor, Rune had to deal with Zoey's parents long-term, so glamouring them was ill-advised. Thankfully, they were so happy to see their daughter safe at home that they were at least able to listen to the utter weirdness of what Zoey had to tell them.

They didn't ask a lot of questions about Rune's injuries and said nothing about his dealings with the Merlady. Thankfully, Zoey didn't grasp what had happened well enough to say much. Best of all, they didn't throw him out on the street.

An hour before dawn, everyone decided they had said and heard as much as they could. Mrs. Coleman called in sick at work and notified Zoey's school that she wasn't coming in, either.

Rune stumbled to his apartment and slept in his clothes.

Over the next two weeks, pumpkins and black cat decorations gave way to cardboard cutouts of pilly fowl, cornucopias, and humans in drab clothing except, inexplicably, for the buckles on their shoes and hats. The air turned brisk, though not yet truly cold.

Rune was warm enough. Rev. Coleman had found him a dark blue woolen pea coat in his church's crisis closet to replace his ruined bomber jacket. The sky above Louisville was gray as lead. It smelled like it might rain.

The Brown Hotel rested in stately majesty at the corner of Fourth and Broadway. Rune crossed the street, bypassed the main entrance, and swung around to the back.

Morty was waiting for him in tan trousers and a canvas jacket. "How ya doing, cohsh? Is the leg any better?" He glanced at the fighting stick Rune was still using as a cane.

"Fine," Rune said. "I don't really need this, but it's grown on me. And it's inconspicuous."

"Raises a lot less questions than a gun, I guess."

"Exactly. So, you're out of uniform?"

"It's my day off," Morty said. "But I can still get you in. You're gonna love my setup."

"Show me."

The ayleck turned the key and swung open the back door. He led Rune through a maze of service corridors deep into the guts of the hotel.

The bare spot of plaster Rune had noticed two weeks ago had been painted over. From the smell of it, not too long ago.

"I had to re-plaster that, obviously," Morty said. "Once you told me you didn't want to know where I put the...uh...thing, I opened the wall back up and took it home for a couple days."

"I appreciate that." Few places in this world would be as secure as an ayleck's home. And at any rate, the ploy allowed Rune to say truthfully that he didn't know where the Peacebringer's coffer was on Hallowfest Eve.

They came to a familiar service elevator. Morty pushed the button. While they waited, he flipped through his ring of keys and found the one he was looking for.

He gestured for Rune to get in first. He followed and turned a key underneath the floor buttons. The elevator jerked into motion and started to descend. "I didn't have time to paint the place, but he said he didn't mind."

"I don't suppose he would."

The elevator door opened onto a narrow corridor. Straight ahead were four rooms that Gamaufry set aside for guests who preferred to sleep underground. Two weeks ago, Gimp Hollart had inhabited one of those rooms while waiting for news about his wife and daughter.

To the left was a locked door. Morty flipped through his keys again, unlocked the door, and held it open for Rune to step through. It opened onto another corridor perhaps fifteen feet long. The walls were now cinder blocks painted an ugly shade of brown. The floor was dingy linoleum. A bare electric light lit the way to a single door at the far end.

Morty stopped at a metal panel to the right. He leaned into it and whispered, "Secretariat."

Somewhere behind the cinder blocks, gears turned and enchantments sighed into dormancy. Somebody had been busy! It gave Rune a glimmer of hope, though he couldn't help wondering how much all of this would cost him.

"We can make the password whatever you want," Morty said. "If I was you, I'd change it every now and then. Just to be safe, you know?"

They walked down the hallway. Morty's footsteps echoed on the bare floor and walls. At the end, Morty rapped on the door. Three knocks, then two, then one.

A peephole on the door went black as someone inside peered out. A deadbolt turned, then another. Finally, the door cracked open.

Kettle stood there in his human form, golden-haired and childlike. He looked away to someone inside the room. "It's them."

He swung open the door and let them in.

Brack was at a workbench, much smaller than the one in Goblintown but just as thick and sturdy. He had the cylindrical coffer in a clamp secured to one corner, and beside him was a wooden toolbox.

Weeks had passed since Rune was in the same room with the thing. Now every detail struck him as if for the first time: the bronze and silver facings, the ornate filigree, the dials and latches and sigils.

Everything else in the room was there because of the coffer. The bench, the security features, even the people. A few boxes were lined up neatly against the back wall, no doubt other things brought in from the dwarf's workshop.

Brack never looked up from his work. "Kettle, did we bring a tin augury?" he asked. "I need the tin one, not the gold one."

"Right here, boss." Kettle jumped to the boxes and fished out the implement Brack had asked for.

Rune took a second to steel himself. "How's it…uh…going?"

Brack scooted away from the bench and looked at Rune. The wound on his face was as Rune remembered it, though now cleaned and covered with scar tissue. It left a little bare notch in the dwarf's left eyebrow.

"It's gonna take some work," Brack said. "Looks like whoever made it used all seven alchemical metals one way or another. I might have to call in somebody to help with some of this."

"Well…do whatever you have to do. I trust you."

Brack scoffed.

Kettle set what looked like an oval hand mirror on the bench beside Brack. It was rimmed in silvery metal stamped with geometric sigils. Brack picked it up and held it in front of the coffer.

"So if this is right…," Brack mumbled to himself. He put down his device and jotted some notes on a leaf of parchment.

Rune tapped his fingers against his thigh. "Is Thora all right? The kids?"

"Thora's fine. Maybe a little furious at me for going off after you like I did, but she'll come around." Brack chuckled. "Duren thinks I'm three times a hero for saving your ass."

"I can't disagree."

Brack hunched back over the coffer. "I did what I had to do."

Rune sighed. "Listen, Brack, I…" The words caught in his throat. He wished he could have found a better way than making a deal with the Merlady, that he was sorry about the scar. Platitudes. They all sounded empty, so Rune swallowed them.

He stared silently at the dwarf until Morty tapped him on the shoulder. "Hey, d'you think maybe we should be going? The dwarf looks kind of busy."

"In a minute," Rune said. He looked at Brack. "I'll…uh…let you know about the password. Morty says I ought to change it now and then."

Brack grunted.

"If you need anything—"

"We don't move as fast as you," the dwarf said.

Rune arched an eyebrow.

"Metal-weavers, earth-weavers, we're more the 'slow and steady' types." Brack sat up straight and rested his hands on his thighs. "Air-weavers like you are all 'spur of the moment.' But sometimes things move fast. Somebody's got to make a decision in the moment. You can't always plan everything out first."

Rune hung his head. "Sometimes we move too fast and make mistakes."

Brack nodded. "Damn stupid ones."

"Well, I—"

"It can't be helped. You did what you thought was right. At least, you did what you thought was least bad. And you had a point." Brack patted the metal clamp that held the coffer in place.

"I've got six months to study this thing, find a way to destroy it without letting loose what's in it. I guess I can live with that."

"Are you sure?"

Brack shrugged. "You gonna be okay, hanging around? Last time we talked—really talked—it sounded like you had your heart set on leaving."

"I'm getting used to the idea," Rune admitted. "And I owe debts to some people around here. To you especially. I don't like the idea of leaving before all of this is settled."

"It ain't like you had any good choices," Brack said.

"No."

"But you had to make a decision."

Rune's thoughts turned to his time at the Haw, to Whisper. *Use your gifts*, his uncle would say. *Surprise me. I know you've got it in you. It's in your blood.*

"You're right," Rune said at last. "I had to choose."

"And live with the consequences?" Brack said.

Rune nodded. He took a breath. "I suppose that's what makes me human."